WHITE WATER NIGHTMARE

"HOLD on tight!" Henry Boise shouted to Harlan Henderson above the roar of rushing water.

The raft shot into the rapids, grating over the rocks with a terrible sound. It was thrown into the air, and crashed back down with a teeth-jarring thud.

For a moment, Nolan Fedderson forgot that there were over a dozen people on board, including his wife—and his young mistress. He was numb with the wonder of it all, gripped by a dreadful fascination. The raft was like an irresistible battering ram, thrashing down the narrow canyon.

Matt Monroe was thinking about his map, and the dire warning to avoid White Horse rapids. There would be no avoiding it now—they were already into its churning jaws.

The logs groaned and screeched in agony. The rawhide bindings grew loose from the wetness. The juggernaut was slowly ripping them apart.

Two outside logs broke away first. Nolan was not surprised or shocked. For many minutes he had known what was happening.

There could be no survivors. This raging white water was going to turn the raft into kindling wood—and every man, woman and child aboard was going to die. . . .

The Making of America Series

THE WILDERNESS SEEKERS
THE MOUNTAIN BREED
THE CONESTOGA PEOPLE
THE FORTY-NINERS
HEARTS DIVIDED
THE BUILDERS
THE LAND RUSHERS
THE WILD AND THE WAYWARD
THE TEXANS
THE ALASKANS
THE GOLDEN STATERS
THE RIVER PEOPLE
THE LANDGRABBERS
THE RANCHERS
THE HOMESTEADERS
THE FRONTIER HEALERS
THE BUFFALO PEOPLE
THE BORDER BREED
THE BOOMERS
THE WILDCATTERS
THE CAJUNS
THE DONNER PEOPLE
THE CREOLES
THE NIGHTRIDERS
THE SOONERS
THE EXPRESS RIDERS
THE VIGILANTES

THE YUKON BREED

Lee Davis Willoughby

A DELL/JAMES A. BRYANS BOOK

Published by
Dell Publishing Co., Inc.
1 Dag Hammarskjold Plaza
New York, New York 10027

ISBN: 0-440-09899-8

Printed in the United States of America

First printing—February 1983

1

Skookum Jim spat on the ground to express his contempt for his cousin's stupidity.

"Is this not the manner of rock he has been seeking?" asked Tagfish Charlie.

The barrel-bodied Indian shrugged. Rocks to him were most unimportant, white, black or brown. He thought only of the near wasted summer of sweat and toil for the husband of his uncle's daughter. They had paddled the squaw man up and down creeks that he would have spurned because they were just spawning grounds for the fish. The fish they would need for winter were still uncaught in the *Youcon*. They had hunted only for the needs of three. The bear, moose and deer, which he would need for the mouths of ten, still roamed on four legs. Had he suggested such a wasted summer, he would have been laughed out of the Tagfish tribe. But the squaw man, as a favorite son-in-law, could put all manner of foolish notions into the head of the chief. Did not his very name imply such foolishness? he thought sourly.

Before the days of George Carmack he was Skookum of the family Skookum of his father, as his mother remained a Tagfish of the family of the chief. The Chinook-speaking people had no trouble recognizing each other by face, but the squaw man needed names to tell them apart.

Then he chuckled to himself. In three days time they would put their canoes back upon the *Youcon* for the journey to their village. The squaw man had learned only one thing, in Skookum Jim's opinion. The *Youcon* was exactly as its name implied—"big river." They would return with nothing in their canoes and he could hardly wait to see how George Carmack would explain that to Tagfish Chief.

Tagfish Charlie had to look on the whole matter from a different view. The man was the husband of his sister and respected by his father for his wisdom. He had been charged by his father to protect the man and bring him back safely. It was very easy summer work, in his opinion. Others could catch the fish, hunt the forests and tend the reindeer herd. He felt he was fulfilling his obligation, although like Skookum Jim he didn't know what the rocks were all about either.

He found his brother-in-law sitting on an overturned and empty black powder cask close by the creek he called "Rabbit"—because that had been the only game they had found along its steep banks. It amused Tagfish Charlie that George Carmack had to put a name to almost everything he came across. The Chinook jargon was simple—fish were fish. But Carmack George, as the Tagfish family called him, had to call fish "trout," "salmon" or "pike."

George Carmack was not amused. Nearly three months, seven hundred miles in many directions and nothing! It all seemed so futile!

He was forty-seven years old—twenty-six of them spent in what he called the Yukon Territory. He had a son almost as old as he had been when he first came up with his father from San Francisco. Born during the "forty-niner" strike, his life had been one prospectors' camp after another. Too many of them for his mother, who had left them when he was ten.

There were no more than a half-dozen grizzled sourdough veterans who made it through the winter of 1870. George's father didn't. George wouldn't have if not befriended by the Tagfish. George had never had any form of family life. The Tagfish tribe was close-knit—a dozen families that never married outside the small tribe.

In George they found a jolly, devil-may-care young man—because he was happy for the first time in his life. Among themselves they commented on his zeal, his wisdom of a world they knew little or nothing about. He was content and stayed the winter and summer. After leaving the Tagfish he had come across a herd of reindeer the Russian Laplanders had imported and then left behind after they had raped the region of its pelt-bearing animals. The reindeer were tame and George herded them back to the village. He gave them as a present to Tagfish (the chief), and taught the women how to milk the cows, cook the meat of the bulls when they became too numerous for the herd and make clothing from the hides.

Such a gift demanded a gift of equal value in return—Tagfish (the daughter) as a bride. It pleased George Carmack. He immediately gave her the name Tagfish Kate. The next year came the first Carmack to the tribe—Carmack Henry. It was five years before they had another child, a daughter—Carmack Graphie Gracey. George was not quite sure where Kate had come up with the name, but he accepted it.

Those who hoped to insult him by calling him "squaw man" were disappointed. He was in love with his wife, his children and being an Indian. The Canadian traders in the area tried to insult him by calling him Siwash George—jargon which had a double meaning; "man who has flapping tongue" or "man who acts like Indian." Again George was not insulted. He came to enjoy telling tall tales just to make the first meaning stick and because he did like the Indians, and resented the way some men looked upon them in their own land. He made sure he acted like the people of his wife.

Then, in 1895, his past came back to start haunting him. Between the trading posts of Circle City, in American Alaska, and Forty Mile, across the Canadian border, over two thousand prospectors poured in determined to find gold. They found gold—over a million dollars in panned yellow metal. But divided among them it was not enough to make any of them truly rich.

But it stirred in George the lure of his youth. He was a prospector and son of a prospector. Why should *cheechakos*, newcomers, get the gold when it belonged to the Indians?

He thought long and hard about the area and where gold might be found—and no *cheechakos*. He thought about it all winter. When the Yukon began to give up its icy winter grip he put his plan before Tagfish Chief. Gold meant nothing to the old man, but he knew George to be a wise man—except for the river. Twenty-six years of travelling no more than fifty miles from the village had dimmed George's memory on how far he was from anywhere.

Now he wished for no place other than that village.

"Find." Tagfish Charlie thrust the sliver of quartz beneath Carmack's nose.

"Nice," George grumbled, although the quartz held no sign of gold. "Where?"

"Not far, maybe."

George did not want to disappoint his young brother-in-law. Quartz could mean gold or just quartz. This piece didn't really excite him.

"Let's make camp and eat."

"Good spot not far, maybe."

George shrugged. Of late he had been thinking much of the Klondike and Yukon Rivers and the rounded hills about. They were heavily forested. Perhaps the Tagfish people should become lumberjacks. From that point they could easily send the logs upriver to Forty Mile or Circle City.

"Damn," he muttered, when he saw the spot Tagfish Charlie thought was good. It was a little backwater off the creek, that had a grassy beach awash in wild flowers—but it was also awash with mosquitos.

"Get a fire started! Smoke them out!"

Skookum Jim smiled. They never seemed to bother him. But the fire would be needed to cook the fish he had caught, although he thought a stick would serve just as well as the skillet Carmack George made him use. Still, a fire would feel good for the night. Even though it was the seventeenth of August, the nights already suggested the approach of winter.

George ate the fish with little appetite. He had determined, while they ate, that they would start home at dawn. Had he been successful he had wanted to go back down to Fort Selkirk for presents, but he now had neither gold or furs to trade with.

Skookum Jim went to the creek bank and filled the skillet with sand. He scoured it around with his hand to loosen the fish skin that had stuck to the pan while frying. He dipped it into the water and swished it about, the loose sand floating away. In the base of the pan a few grains sparkled back at him. He had seen Carmack do this many times with his flat pan and was not aware what he was about. He scooped more sand in the skillet and emulated Carmack's actions. He grew more fascinated as more and more bright yellow flecks stuck to the bottom of the pan, with some a quarter of the size of salmon eggs.

More out of fascination than knowledge he took the skillet back and squatted down beside the squaw man.

"Look!"

George's hand began to tremble as he fingered over the remnants. The pan held gold worth at least three dollars. Never in his life had he seen a panning that would produce more than twenty cents to the pan.

"It's gold!" he gulped again.

"Important?"

"It may be the most important gold strike ever made, Skookum!"

Because he had left off the "Jim" the giant Indian beamed. He could respect a man who addressed him properly. He could also feel a surge of pride because a Skookum, which meant "big and strong" had found what the "squaw man" sought before "little" Tagfish Charlie. It would give him honor in the eyes of his uncle, the chief.

"How many hours of daylight left?" George almost shouted.

"Many, because of the season."

George jumped up and grabbed a hatchet. He ran to the spot where Skookum Jim had been scouring the pan and chopped a long slice out of a pine tree trunk. Then he took a lead stub from his pocket and began lettering in the white wood:

> *To whom it may concern. I do, this day, locate and claim, by right of discovery, five hundred running feet, running up stream from this notice. Located this 17th day of August, 1896. G. Carmack.*

Pacing up the stream he made a second claim for himself and one each for the Indians.

"It is certainly a bonanza!"

George Carmack started laughing. As he walked back downstream he added in under each claim the name *Bonanza Creek. Y.T.* It had not stayed Rabbit Creek for very long, he thought.

The skeptic turned enthusiast. Skookum Jim now sensed some of the value of the discovery and eagerly agreed to stay and guard the claims.

Three days later George Carmack and Tagfish Charlie pulled their canoe up onto the river bank of Forty Mile. The Alaska Commercial Company's trading store had been on the site since the days of Russian ownership. Now shacks leaned together about it to form a little miners' town.

A howl went up as George entered the store's saloon.

"Siwash! Where you been all summer? Off to tell the 'outsiders' how to solve their money mess?"

George resented these "outsiders" from the states considering themselves "insiders."

"Yah, Siwash, those politickers need someone like you to talk some sense to them."

"Perhaps I shall," he said, a little irritated, "for I shall soon be rich enough."

"Here comes another one," a miner roared. "How you going to get so rich?"

"I've made a strike," George said simply. "On a creek off the Thron-Diuck."

The laughter increased. Only one man, a miner standing off by himself, did not laugh. Robert Henderson was a quiet, unsmiling Scotsman, and a man who knew that the early fur traders had had trouble with the Tagfish pronunciation of Thron-Diuck and made it 'Klondike.' He was unsmiling because he had made a strike on a creek off the Klondike two weeks before and was there to file his claim and get supplies for the winter.

"A mon should be willing to prove such a claim," he said in a thick brogue.

For once George could back up his boast. He strolled up to Henderson and took out his cartridge case. He emptied the case out onto the bar.

The bearded, ragged Scotsman stared, speechless. Others crowded around. They were sourdoughs who could tell by the color of the dust in the nuggets whether gold had come from the fields of California, Colorado, Utah or the Black Hills. They had never seen anything like the nuggets and dust on the bar.

Robert Henderson had. "Interesting. Must have taken you some time to gain that much."

"Just a few scoops by me and the Indians," George gloated.

A man at the bar snorted. "Siwash, don't bluff us. That would come to three or four dollars a pan."

George shrugged. He didn't care if they believed him or not.

Henderson was both troubled and interested by Carmack's assertions. He had been elated that his own find had run about eighty cents to the pan. He judged that the two finds had to be very close. Up from where the Klondike and Yukon joined there were not many creeks. He was not willing to share his news and thought he could temper this man easily.

"You did say Indians, didn't you?" he asked Carmack.

"I did. What of it?"

Henderson shrugged. "It is my understanding that no natives can file claims."

"It is their land," Carmack said, fixing Henderson with a steely gaze.

Henderson smiled smugly. "Hardly, my friend. It is all the land of Her Majesty Queen Victoria. The Mounty will tell you the same, I am sure. Ah, my supplies are ready. Good hunting."

An old sourdough, who had been an acquaintance of Carmack's father approached him at the bar. "Say, Georgie, that's some tale. I shore hanker to make another strike before I die."

"Sure, Ludlow," George said, preoccupied with the worry the Scotsman had given him. "It's right up from the Yukon-Klondike branch. I've got to go file the claim."

Clarkson Ludlow then pondered. The Alaska Commercial Company didn't give grubstakes, but he knew a man in Circle City that he thought would take a tumble on something this promising.

Thoughts were rumbling in other minds, as well—especially in the minds of those who had overheard what George said to Ludlow. The nuggets were, after all, the largest they had ever seen.

After George and Tagfish Charlie left for the Mounty post the men filtered out of the saloon. The shanty sheds were quickly emptied of rolled tent, pick, shovel, pan and grub. At the riverfront they all had to sheepishly confront each other with the fact they all had the same idea. Then there was a mad scramble for every skin canoe and wooden boat.

Sergeant Morris Fletcher, Royal Canadian Mounted Police, listened to George carefully. He knew him to be a "squaw man" and a "teller of tall tales." He also knew that he had no trouble with the Tagfish tribe.

"Canadian mining laws are strict, Mr. Carmack. One claim to a miner and the approximate worth of the first pan recorded."

"I recall that from the first time I came here with my father. That's so the take can be taxed, correct?"

"Well, at least I don't have to explain that. Yanks seem to think they can ignore the tax. Now, can you give me an approximate location of the claim?"

"Claims."

Fletcher raised a single eyebrow. "One claim to a miner, Mr. Carmack."

George had been thinking over Henderson's words very carefully.

"I understand, Sergeant, but I had to leave the others behind to guard and start working the claim."

"And who are the others?" he asked coolly.

"Family." He handed him the cartridge case. "Here's the pannings from the four we staked out."

Fletcher started to question him further, but the contents caught his attention. He poured the nuggets and dust out onto his scale and adjusted it.

Now both of the sergeant's eyebrows raised. "Surely not just a pan sample from each, Mr. Carmack. This would be equivalent to nearly nine dollars American."

George whistled, not about to tell him that it was just a couple of scoops from one claim and not all four. "That would make it a little over two dollars a claim. That will make my sons happy."

"Oh, sons," Fletcher said expansively. At that point he

didn't care if he was a "squaw man" and they be "bastard" sons. It was a rich strike and the national treasury was desperate for money. Canada was in as deep or deeper economic trouble as was the United States. "Now, might I have the names for each claim."

"Mine, of course, shall be George Carmack. The sons are Henry, Jim and Charlie." He paused. "I named them all."

Fletcher wrote the information in his ledger book. He noted the entry made by Corporal Hardesty a couple of hours before. "Region must be better in your locale. There's another new claim ten miles north of you, though it only brought half your pay yield."

"Poor chap," George murmured and prayed it stayed that way for Henderson. He amazed himself that he remained so calm while the sergeant made out the papers proving his claims. Four would be quite ample for the whole village.

It took Clarkson Ludlow four days to get the two hundred miles downriver to Circle City.

In the 1860s, a man named LeRoy Napoleon McQuestan had wanted to be a voyageur for the Hudson's Bay Company, but his body was just too big for the bateaux canoes. In the 1870s he turned to prospecting and found just enough "color" to buy a Russian trading post.

When gold was found in several creeks draining into the Yukon near the trading post, McQuestan was the big money maker. But unlike the three Mizner brothers who owned the Alaska Commercial Company, McQuestan poured his money back into the building of a settlement.

The name at first was laughable, but by the late summer of 1896 Circle City had a school, a little library, and even a theater where miners performed the plays of William Shakespeare. McQuestan was a wealthy, contented man, and he was the man Clarkson sought for a grubstake.

"Clarkson, men around here are getting but twenty cents to the pan and are happy with it," the old sourdough said after he'd heard the story. "Are you sure Siwash George didn't salt his cartridge case?"

"Then why'd he give me directions? We both go back to the days of his pappy, you know, LeRoy."

McQuestan pondered, absent-mindedly running a hand through his long red beard. He hunched over the bar of his Emperor Saloon and pulled the grizzled miner close.

"Clarkson, I'll grubstake you for the winter, if you keep your mouth shut. I'll share my reasons, just to seal the bargain. I've got faith in both the Alaska and Canada sides of this river. I'd like me a trading post at Fort Yukon, Forty Mile, Sixty Mile, Fort Reliance and even the Indian town of Moosehide."

"They all got some form of trading post or other, LeRoy."

The Scotsman grinned, showing where some of his gold had gone. "But they are limited by their supply line, Clarkson. Canoes in the summer and dog sleds in the winter. I'm talking about offering the insiders anything an outsider would be able to buy down below. Remember how the rowers cursed me last spring for the heavy loads."

"I heard about it."

"What they brought in the canoes is down in that big shed by the river. It was all the parts for a steamboat engine, Clarkson. That old fella who always claimed to be a shipwright is a shipwright. It may take him and his Indian workers all winter to finish my *New Racket*, but come spring I can bring in enough supplies to give the Mizner boys a real run for their money. Snow is going to fly soon. Even if Siwash has a good strike it will be spring before the wild talk gets back here."

Digging his long shovel into the gravel, George Carmack could see the others from where he worked. They moved over the creek like a line of ants, each with their shovels and pans prodding endlessly through the sand and gravel, bending eagerly at the sight of a choice nugget or "color" in the sand.

It had taken him a week to get back with his family and supplies. A week in which the five-hundred-foot claims had started stretching up and down the creek from his own. A week in which the low hills had started to become denuded of their covering of white birch, cottonwood and spruce. Because the twenty-hour sunlit days of the short summer were now down to no more than ten hours, and still shortening, they had to take half of their time to construct a windowless cabin. Tents wouldn't make it through the winter, and they couldn't go back to the luxury of their shanty sheds in Forty Mile. A claim left unattended for sixty days was subject to re-staking and re-claiming.

Their main concern was to get as much done as they could before the crushing cold of winter and then wait for spring. This was much easier for the Carmack group. While the three older men worked the four claims, George's wife, son and daughter were free to make a 12′ by 12′ home for them. Kate had brought along two gunny sacks of old jars. In two walls of the cabin a square had been left open, and Kate brick-stacked the jars, with mud filler between, and had daylight within her home. Later on, when twilight and darkness would seem unending, she would take slabs of caribou and moose shot by Henry and stuff them into the mouths of the bottles. When needed, she could remove the frozen slabs and spit them over the open fire for thawing and cooking.

Satisfied, she and the children began to build a second cabin, a windowless structure, close by. Everyone took it as a dwelling for her brother and cousin, but they snickered when she and Graphie Gracey began carrying baskets of creek gravel and sand back to the cabin.

"Poor dumb squaw don't know she may be chinking and flooring that cabin with gold."

George paid no mind to the number of baskets they carted and that made the miners snicker all the more.

"Siwash has been around the Indians too damn long. Poor damn fool pays no attention to the size of the hole she's dug out of the bank. Must be plastering the walls for a permanent residence."

"Wish I had the sand she's wasting. Ain't getting but about a dime a pan out of my claim."

"Hell, that's ten cents more than I'm getting."

That was also the case for Clarkson Ludlow. By the time he arrived the claims were taken to almost the headwaters of the creek. Next to his claim was an old prospector he had known for twenty years. They had been this route before. They were too hardened to feel disappointment. It was all in the luck of a turn of a shovel, and each shovelful was becoming harder to get. The ground was beginning to freeze harder and harder each night.

Kate kept her eye on another trick George had taught her. Within each cabin she kept three vials, which she would set out at night. If the mercury vial solidified it was still hunting and working weather at an ear-splitting 38 degrees below zero. When the whiskey vial froze the temperature had dropped another twenty degrees and she would keep kettles of water boiling through the night to steam vapor the cabin. The steam would hit the log walls, moisturize and form icicle glaciers from ceiling to floor. Kate would break these off the next day and add them to the kettle for a constant water source. It was better than trying to make it to the creek for ice, because she knew that the third vial of kerosene would be solidified outside with another ten degree drop. As her people had always done at that time of year, she used fat-oil lamps. The miner's kerosene lanterns either sputtered or wouldn't work at all. While the Carmacks continued to have thawed fresh meat, they were back on beans, bacon and sourdough bread. Winter had come, but as yet little snow. It was too damned cold for snow.

Clarkson Ludlow had the provisions, Jackson Turner a lean-to. They "partnered up" until spring. At their end of the creek water was a problem. The creek was solid ice and the metal of an ax would be so brittle in the cold that it would shatter on impact with the ice surface.

"Might be easier to use the blunt side on the 'pup.' "

Ludlow agreed with a shrug and warmed his ax over the fire before cuddling it inside his macintosh. The "pup" was an unnamed stream that came into the Bonanza a short distance beyond their claims. It was in such a narrow gulch that no one gave it any thought, but its shallowness at its rocky edges would make ice chipping easy.

The underbrush was so brittle it snapped off as they walked through. It was so thick that only a small finger of white showed the course of the stream. They had to break away the underbrush to get clear a space to chip at the ice edge. They had brought along two wooden buckets.

"Best get enough for a few days," Clarkson said, putting the ax back into his coat. "Dump these buckets by the lean-to and come back."

"Why me?"

"My ax and my chipping power," Clarkson said sourly. There wasn't anything more to say.

It took Jackson Turner a little under a half-hour for the round trip. Nearing the spot he smelled smoke.

"Damn fool could have flapped his arms to keep warm."

Pushing through the underbrush he saw a fire, a stack of ice chunks and Clarkson a few feet away on his knees chopping at the gravel bank.

"What in hell are you doing?" he called with some irritation.

"Thawed me a space with one fire, and now I'm doing the same here."

"Damn fool waste of time, Clarkson Ludlow. Worse place in the whole world to look for color."

He filled the buckets with the ice as Clarkson scooped the inch or two of gravel into his pack. Then he stamped out the second brush bonfire and started chipping at the frozen ground again.

Jackson Turner had a rich vocabulary, but he couldn't even think of things nasty enough to express his opinion. He grabbed up the buckets and headed back to the lean-to. And he was damned if he would trudge back for more buckets. He dumped one in a kettle and set it on the fire to melt. He decided that no matter how long the winter might last, he would not speak to the old fool for the entire time.

He was speaking to him in less than an hour.

"What in the dang-blasted hell you doing with our water?"

"Using some of it to pan out what I brought back."

"Then you'll be walking alone, and in the cold, for more drinking and cooking water!"

The old man ignored him, squatting to sluice away the water and fine gravel onto the dirt floor. A few minutes later he stood up. His eyes gleamed but never left the bottom of the pan.

Curiosity got the best of Jackson Turner. He came and looked and then looked again. The pan held between five and six dollars' worth of gold.

They stared at each other in silence for a moment, then burst out laughing. They would stop, look into the pan, look at each other again and laugh even harder.

"Shall I walk back alone to stake my claim?"

Jackson looked sheepish. "You found it and chipped it."

"But you hauled the ice for the panning water."

They laughed again, then grew quietly serious, as though even the lean-to walls had ears.

"We've got to get it recorded at Forty Mile," Jackson said.

"You get it recorded and I'll stay and do the staking."

"We won't tell, will we?"

Clarkson mused. "McQuestan did my stake. Could claim one for him and make him split."

"Could do the same for Clarence Berry."

"Who the hell is he?"

"Young bartender chap that works for Edgar Mizner. He was here early and gave up quick. Said he could make more pushing whiskey. Left me what grub he had left and wouldn't need to get back. Owe him, I figure."

"For half?"

"For half."

"That gives us four. Fletcher will balk even at that."

"Berry will be there. He can sign his and vouch for mine. You can vouch for Leroy. Hell, Carmack was the only one who signed for his whole family."

"Settled," Clarkson sighed. "Canoe won't do me no good on the Yukon. I'll pack it on foot. We have about three or four more pans we can wash out. Might give me enough to get a sled to come back on."

"Don't hurry," Jackson said. "Ain't a damn thing going to be happening around here, and nobody knows about it but us."

"What'll we call it?"

"Damned if I know. Think about it on the way."

It warmed up enough that night to snow, as Ludlow left. He had figured a week on foot, but was wise enough to the country to take provisions for three weeks. The snows came thick and fast, slowing him down. It took him two and a half weeks to make the journey.

Clarence Berry was more than willing to sign for a half-claim. He would even further grubstake them and provide a team of dogs and sled. Come spring he even promised to come out with his wife and work, but doubly promised not to mention it to her until that time.

So, it was still a secret between the three. But they still could not decide upon a name.

Seregant Fletcher was greatly impressed with the pan report.

"George Carmack may have found himself a bonanza, but you boys surely got yourself Eldorado."

"What in the hell is that?" Berry asked.

Clarkson chuckled. Berry certainly wasn't any old prospector. "It's the name of a legendary city of gold and we just found our name. We'll keep it secret, too."

Neither took into consideration that it was now known by a fourth. Even though it remained a secret for a good month and a half after Ludlow returned.

Jackson Turner had been correct about nothing happening. The land was now a pure mantle of white. He had made sure that each time he went to stake a claim that he carried back buckets of ice. No one questioned that need. Snow water had a tendency to make you thirstier. And no one really questioned because each cabin was like a bear's den and every miner in a semi-state of hibernation.

Therefore no one questioned that smoke came each day from each of the Carmack cabins. Because they were Indians no one paid them much mind anyway.

They would have been amazed to learn that they all lived in one cabin by night, but spent many hours of each day in the other.

People of the Tagfish tribe did not hibernate in the winter. They planned their few summer months to give them indoor industry for the winter months. In the village they would be making new clothing, new utensils, new sleds for yet another winter or new traps. It was something Kate understood as a wife's obligation to plan for. This was a different life and would require a different winter activity to keep the men active.

In the second cabin snow could be melted for water, for it was used only for panning the mounds and mounds of sandy gravel she and her daughter had carted into the cabin. While others were forced to wait for spring, George Carmack was slowly becoming very rich. Kate filled every old tin can with nuggets and then buried them deep in the pile of sandy gravel that had already been panned. When she had time from her cooking duties she would sit and pan through that pile again for dust and minute nuggets. George laughingly called it "Kate's poke." Because the dust was so fine she cut up a black velvet shawl, the finest present George had ever brought her from Fort Selkirk, and lined a wooden box. Her 'poke' from the cabin mounds would total $87,000. She had only wanted enough to replace the velvet shawl.

In January, Morris Fletcher had to go with Inspector Cordine to Circle City to investigate a stabbing in the Emperor Saloon. He thought nothing of congratulating LeRoy McQuestan on his claim with Ludlow. It was overheard by others in the bar and Fletcher was questioned. Again he thought nothing about boasting of the largest strike in the territory.

In the deadly cold, with the temperature sixty below zero, men began to leave on dog sleds and snowshoes. As the rumor began to spread, more and more departed. They could do little until early spring, but if they waited they feared the claims would be all gone. In less than a week the population of Circle City had dwindled from a thousand to a mere handful.

At first McQuestan felt they would file their claims and return. No one returned in February and March. In April, Joseph Ladue and the Indians finished the *New Racket*. The Yukon, McQuestan knew, would still be frozen solid for at least another month.

"Joe, I've another project for you and the boys, if you've a mind."

"What you got in mind, LeRoy?"

"What I really have in mind is that we stand in a ghost town and the miners are soon to stand in a creek with nowhere close at hand to buy. I'm sure the thought will strike the Mizner brothers before long, so we'd best get cracking on it. We can break the machinery down from the sawmill and move it by sled. You take the boys and find a spot for a post. My family can help me pack up the goods here and get them on the steamboat. Soon as the river will allow I'll come down to set up shop."

Ladue had loved working with wood again, but was a little dubious.

"What if you don't like the spot, LeRoy?"

McQuestan roared with laughter. Ludlow had been generous with him, he could be generous in return.

"You're to be my partner in this, Joe. Pick a site that you know would be pleasing to us both."

Joseph Ladue had been born in Portsmouth, New Hampshire. His family had been shipwrights since the days of the Revolutionary War, when ship's timber had been brought from Europe. His father had built ships there for the war of 1812, when native American timber was used. He had been thirteen when a Portsmouth-built clipper was going to round the cape for a run to the California gold fields. For sea experience he had been signed on as a cabin boy. From the passengers he had come down with a bad case of gold fever and didn't return with the clipper. At sixty, his pockets were still empty of gold.

But experience of a sort he had. The timber was brought to the best spot for the shipwrights to build their vessels. The supplies for every gold field he had worked came to a logical point of delivery.

When the dog sleds reached the place where the frozen Yukon crashed into the frozen Klondike, he stopped. There was a flat, treeless stretch of ground along the two streams. Behind rose a high hill, with a tightly packed forest. For this kind of building any timber would serve his purpose. He was not sure how far up the Klondike were the creeks in question, but this seemed a logical place for a steamboat wharf and a trading post. The sawmill he could almost already see built at the base of the hill. If they did their logging now the trees could still be sent down the slope on the hard packed snow. He measured the area with his eyes and smiled. If he was going to be a partner with LeRoy McQuestan, then why not think like him. He wouldn't file just a post and lumberright claim—he would file a township claim.

But on the map he sent back to Forty Mile he never explained why he filed it under the name "Dawson City."

In early June, the *New Racket* pulled up to its new wharf. Against the hill stood a large warehouse and sawmill. A wide swath had been cut right up the hill, like a reaper had cut through a wheat field. For fifty feet on each side the forest stood as always, and new swaths were eating their way downward. Joseph Ladue knew the land. The snows were melting rapidly and there would be heavy summer rains. To denude the entire hillside would make it possible for mudslides to push all of his hard work right into the rivers.

Stakes with red flags rippled in the breeze like a field of poppies. Here and there among the stakes a few tents had been erected by enterprising miners who had been lucky enough to get an Eldorado claim. The gulch was too narrow and steep to build upon and so they bought a town lot from Ladue.

Joe had even gone so far as to stake out streets, and on what he thought would be a busy corner, he had erected a long, low, rambling log structure that would serve as trading post, saloon and McQuestan living quarters. He had wisely left room for expansion.

By the end of June there was no need for expansion. McQuestan had sold all the supplies that he had. The Mizner brothers had come down by canoe from Forty Mile with supplies, but Joseph Ladue would not let them sell unless they bought "commercial" town lots. They did, erected tents, and sold out.

It was three hundred miles on the Yukon to St. Michaels and the Pacific Ocean.

"And five hundred miles to our Canadian supply base," Edgar Mizner said sourly.

He was the oldest of the three and the most hardheaded. They had all known great wealth in San Francisco, but the youngest, Wilson, had nearly depleted the family fortune before they had become aware of his spendthrift ways. Addison had been a promising architect, but to recoup the family losses, the three brothers had determined they had to do it together. Forty Mile had barely made them a living.

"I have a feeling," Addison said, as though it would answer Edgar, "that we are—if you'll pardon the pun—sitting atop a gold mine. This Dawson City is going to boom. I say buy more town lots for me to build upon. Edgar, instead of the ten canoes to go down to the Canadian trading posts, hire a hundred. Even if McQuestan gets to St. Michaels and back with his little 'toot-toot', we can still outsupply him."

"And what am I supposed to be doing?" Wilson asked.

"Little or nothing at all, as usual," Edgar said, barely acknowledging the youngest Mizner. "I like it, Addison, but with refinement. I'll go downriver and hire a different tribe. McQuestan will then think we are using just our normal ten. Let the *New Racket* leave before you start building us a general store."

"Store?" Wilson asked.

"Ladies buy!" Edgar flared. "Berry and Lippy already have their wives here. Wives have always followed their husbands to gold finds, as I recall—among other types of women—and they do most of the buying. Wilson, why don't you try to think of ways to make money, instead of just spending it?"

By the time McQuestan was ready to sail for supplies others were thinking of spending money and not making it.

Joseph Ladue wanted to take the gold he had from lots and lumber and spend it on things that would make even more money for Dawson City. McQuestan agreed.

Tom and Salome Lippy had worked their claim side by side, day and night for two solid months. They had two suitcases so heavy with gold that they could hardly lift them. They were more homesick than greedy. They sold their claim to Charley Anderson for eight hundred dollars. Because they were such a close-mouthed couple, the other sourdoughs laughed at Charley for being a dupe.

"Charley, it ain't even right hot yet and they're getting out with nothing more than their suitcases and your eight hundred. You been had, sucker!"

Just as the claim had produced a million for the Lippys, it produced a million for the lucky Swede.

George and Kate Carmack were not leaving their claim; they had people who could stay behind to work it. George was happy with his claims, even though every claim on the Eldorado was producing more and quicker profits. Clarence Berry had found one nugget worth six hundred dollars.

But there were certain supplies that George wanted to buy for the tribe in Seattle, plus he had another cagey reason for wishing to purchase them that summer. The Mounted Police had not yet sent an inspector into the area. No one knew about the gold they had panned during the winter and he wanted to get it away before it could be taxed.

In all, ten other miners decided to leave, much the same as the Lippys. No one was really sure what they were taking away with them. Some of the wiser sourdoughs had left their claim as a "lay"—renting it out for a sum and a certain length of time. They had been rich men before in other fields, spent the fortune foolishly and ended up with nothing. This time they would not be foolish. They sensed that the tiny creek named Eldorado would come to be known as the richest little finger of water of its size in the whole world. But panning and digging would only scratch the surface of the true wealth. They wanted machinery, like they had used at Central City and Blackhawk, to get deep within the frozen ground.

Twelve lucky ones left for the Pacific and ships to take them to Seattle and San Francisco. Their Yukon luck was with them.

Steaming the sixty-five miles up the Pacific coast to St. Michaels from the mouth of the Yukon River, the *New Racket* was able to flag down the *Portland*, bound for Seattle. From the captain, McQuestan learned that the *Excelsior* was offloading for an immediate turn around to San Francisco. The country was near bankrupt and was pushing exporting, but didn't want a great deal of importing.

It was news the big Scotsman used to his advantage. The biggest St. Michaels importer was still a Russian used to bartering with furs and salted salmon.

"People can't even buy bread," the *Excelsior* captain roared, "let alone fur coats. Golden Gate Shipping says I get cash or I bring it all back."

The Russian didn't have cash. McQuestan and Ladue did. They bought the whole cargo at a bulk rate, bought out the Russian and hired him right back as an agent, and Joseph Ladue went on to San Francisco to open a steady supply line with Golden Gate Shipping.

The *New Racket* was able to make the round trip in twelve days. McQuestan was able to make two trips before Edgar Mizner was back from his first.

Addison Mizner was still dreaming of the structure he would build. His brother Edgar was forced not only to continue using the tent, but to lower his prices as well.

"All right, Wilson," he exploded, "you're going home to buy *us* a riverboat steamer!"

2

IT HAD not taken the captain of the *Portland* long to learn the truth from the boasting George Carmack. It had not taken the captain of the *Excelsior* long to figure out why McQuestan and Ladue had so much ready gold, why they wanted the whole cargo and why they wanted a steady supply line established.

Nor did it take the telegraph wires long to start humming after the ships had docked.

It was July 15, 1897. It had taken eleven months for the news to get out of the Yukon. By the next morning the strange name—Klondike—was being uttered all over the nation.

Gold was something that people had been hiding away in small piles of coins for four years. If they could afford the soaring prices of food, they spent "government" money and not their gold. That was about all they bought. Factories were closed because of lack of sales. Bank clerks stood idle because there were no depositors. Farmers let their land go fallow because they couldn't even get back the cost of the grain they would plant. Cattlemen left their herds out on the range because only those who still had some wealth were buying beef. With little to move, the train schedules were cut in half and engineers fought over who would get a run.

The army didn't want any more men. The burning, scalping and slaughter of the Indian wars was over. No one was pushing westward, because the west was just about as bad as the east.

"Mickey, I'm sorry. Mr. Ferguson just can't afford to keep two teachers employed come September. His brother might be able to use you in Seattle."

Charmichael Magraff was sorry, too. He had liked Pointer, Montana. He had especially liked Helen Ferguson. The schoolmaster's wife was a caricature rather than a copy of the schoolmasters' wives he had served before.

She had made a wry joke on the first day he had arrived in May. "In reading your file, Mr. Magraff, it would seem you have *taught* your way west."

Because she had smiled, he smiled back, his blue eyes laughing. "At six-month segments, so to speak."

"Would you care to speak to the reasons of such short stays?"

"Because of my looks," he said immodestly.

Helen Ferguson could understand that. At twenty-five he hardly looked old enough to shave, although the finely clipped mustache bespoke otherwise. He was not really tall—about five foot, ten inches, she judged—but his compact body in the stylish clothes exuded a certain male power. At first she thought his hair looked unkempt, but then she realized that the tight brunette curls would always look that way. If it had not been for his outstanding academic background she might never have passed him on for her husband's examination. She knew that every young ranch girl in attendance would be madly in love on first sight.

That had been Mickey's main problem since leaving Ohio five years earlier. Every school seemed to have its share of love-starved female students—mainly because they were not looked upon as worthy by the love-starved male students. There had been one room rural schools for his first three schools. He had been able to cope with the "puppy-love" class, but not those who took their day-dreams seriously. Their parents took their girls' wild talk as serious.

When he progressed to larger schools the wild talk followed him like a stalking ghost. The schoolmaster's wife was usually the first to hear and took to the gossip in two different ways: those who wished him fired at once; or those who wished to find out from personal experience if his reputation was deserved.

He usually got fired either way, because he never let those who really wanted to learn come anywhere near the truth. Thwarted, they added to the legend with further lies.

He began to feel like a rake, when in fact he had known only one woman in his life and that had been at age twenty. He had been in love, the girl in lust. When his friends had considered it their duty to disclose that she had performed a burlesque of virginity to snare him, he had felt ridiculed and hated them for the revelation. It had been his first teaching job, in his home town, and he felt he couldn't stay.

In five years he had developed a protective shell and a reputation as an "Irish brawler" when pushed too far over the gossip. That also accounted for some of his firings.

But this was something different. Fired for something other than gossip. It was almost laughable. He was sure that Helen Ferguson had heard the rumors, but had kept them to herself. He had thought that he had at last broken the jinx. He had even thought that he could fall in love with Helen, if David Ferguson hadn't been around.

He wondered if he would hate Henry Ferguson as much as he hated David. He shrugged off the thought. Seattle it would be. But what was farther west of Seattle if he failed there?

* * *

Nolan Fedderson, at twenty-five, had never known failure. He got up from the breakfast table and sauntered out toward the mill. His stomach was as tight as a drum from the mountain of buckwheat cakes and sausages he had eaten, all of it washed into his six-foot five-inch bulk by a whole pot of coffee. He whistled as he walked, content that it was a Sunday. A few of the lumberjacks would be at the mill to play pinochle. He always played best on Sunday because the other roughnecks from the logging company always had muddled heads from their Saturday night. He didn't drink. He saved his Saturday nights for Lolly.

The first three years of their marriage had all been Saturday nights. Then along came Kimberly Sue. He loved his daughter, but this first year of her life had made his life miserable. Saturday nights almost vanished until he let Lollaine Haskell Fedderson know who was the man of that family. She may have been only eighteen, but she had been a married woman for four years and shouldn't have to be reminded of her duties.

He whistled again. It had been a good Saturday night. He had only had to bash Lolly around three times before she gave in and gave him his due. It was an improvement. The week before he had almost had to break her arm before she collapsed in a crying heap, asking his demanded forgiveness.

The whistle dried on his lips. The mill gate was closed and his pinochle mates stood staring at a posted sign.

"What's up, McGinty?"

"You mean what's down," the burly lumberjack said firmly. "Whole company has gone belly up."

"Down? Up? Let me see."

He stood there for perhaps ten minutes, waiting for the words to change. They didn't and it didn't make sense. He had started at fifteen as a limber and de-barker, and he was now the best topper on the whole MacKenzie River. He got twenty-five cents for each tree he topped out for felling. He had to be sick unto death not to make two dollars a day, when the average man was doing well to make a dollar a day.

"They can't do this to me," he snarled. "I'll go down to Seattle and find out what those fat heads are thinking."

He was talking to himself. The other men had filtered away. It had been a worry on their minds for months. They could see what Nolan never took time to see. The bull-pens along the river had become fuller and fuller with logs the mill in Eugene could not saw or that the offices in Seattle could not sell. They had been expecting it, but had sighed each day when it didn't happen.

Now they would sigh each day waiting for the gates to open again.

Lolly Fedderson cringed when Nolan came back into the cabin. She quickly took Kimberly away from her breast and turned toward the crib. She prayed that Nolan had not seen her feeding the baby. She didn't want that fight to start all over again. His mother may have been nursing another by the time he was year old, but her mother had not. She had been her mother's only child. She wished that she could have had an older sister . . . anyone. Her mother had died a few days before her fourteenth birthday. It had been several days after that before Horace Haskell came out of his drunken stupor.

"What'll we do now, Paw?" she had asked, never so frightened in her life.

He had looked at her through his blurry eyes. Daughters weren't of much use to an old lumberjack. "Lolly, I think it time for us to find you a husband."

"Whatever you say, Paw."

She had been taught never to question anything her father said or did. Thus, she had not questioned his choice as the best man available. Best for Horace Haskell. He had no son. It was a foreman's right to train and elevate his son. He would do the same with a son-in-law.

Nolan, at twenty-one, was surprisingly single. He was a

brute of a young man but a bastard in the industry—that is, his father was not considered really in the lumberjack class, being a mere rafter of the logs down to the mills in Eugene.

To step up into a lumberjack family Nolan would have married Haskell's daughter even if she had been a beast. He couldn't even recall if he had ever seen the girl around the company town. He had lived in the bachelors' dormitory for six years and went downriver each weekend to see his family. He didn't go out of his way to learn who she was until Haskell had all the arrangements made.

He marched straight up to the preacher where Lolly stood. He put out his hand, and Lolly gave him hers timidly. But something—curiosity, perhaps—made him look down. She hardly came halfway up his chest, but had a comely shape for fourteen. Her flowing black hair made its own bridal veil. Then she lifted her head. Nolan had gasped. Her face was like a cameo brooch his mother owned, except her skin was a smooth pink and her eyes a warm brown. Her unsurpassed loveliness made him wonder at his luck.

He was in a state of trance for a week, then Horace began to train him as a treetopper and a husband. Women, to Horace, were to be kept naive and unknowing of their own worth. He had been cheated because his wife had given him only a daughter. Nolan was not to be cheated. He was to try and try until Lolly had given them a son and Horace a grandson.

The lessons were quickly terminated when Horace Haskell's life ended in a fall. But the worst damage had already been done. Nolan had believed every word uttered by his father-in-law.

"Pack!" he barked.

"Why?"

"Don't question when I tell you to do something, Lolly. Just pack."

"For how long?"

"How in the hell should I know? A week or so. It ain't as if we have a great selection to take to Seattle."

"I'm going?" she gasped. He didn't even take her to Eugene to see his mother.

He considered. He hadn't meant to say "we." Lolly would mean added expense. But the company had more than one cutting area. If they moved him it would be even more expensive having to come back for her.

"Pack everything," he said, as a way of an answer.

Lolly nodded. He had not started a fight over her feeding Kimberly, so she wouldn't start a fight by questioning what this was all about.

He had almost reached the edge of the lake when he knew he wasn't going to make it. He could see the men from where he lay, striking the field grass to see if he was hidden about. He lay there, trying to focus his thoughts; but he couldn't do that, either. He had done a lot of stupid things in thirty-one years, but this was the first time he had been shot for no good reason. Good cause, yes. A man didn't cross the entire continent eight times in fourteen years without running into trouble. Plenty of trouble.

Painfully, Matt Monroe turned over on his stomach and began to crawl. It took him an age, an infinity, to circle back toward the lights of the house. And all the strength he had left. He lay there staring at the three stories of gingerbread trim, with the wide porches strangely lit by colorful Japanese lanterns.

"Hell of a place to put a whorehouse," he mumbled.

He closed his hazel eyes and laid back on the wet grass. The wide-brimmed Mexican style hat fell from his head. The moonlight made him look like a thin-faced St. Nick. The shoulder length hair and flowing beard were bleached almost white from constant outdoor living. Amazingly, although his face was now pale from the gunshot wound to the calf, the sun had not weathered his fair complexion.

Beneath the almost invisible eyebrows and long lashes the skin was smooth and taut over the high cheekbones, strong nose and square jaw line. Had the beard been removed it would have revealed a deeply cleft chin. A facial feature he abhorred in a man, though he couldn't give a sound reason for his feeling on the matter.

And Matthew Buell Monroe was normally very positive about everything. He felt strongly that God had made a gross error in his birth by at least a century. Everything exciting, in his opinion, had already transpired prior to 1866. He spent seventeen miserable years in a South that had lost a war which it seemed unable to recover from. At one time the Buell and Monroe names had meant something in Alabama. To young Matt they meant only poverty . . . and the loss of the spirit of adventure.

Like a Don Quixote, that spirit became his personal windmill to tilt at and challenge. But everything of interest to him seemed to have happened in the past.

A dozen heartbeats later, it seemed to him—though, afterwards, when he came to think of it, he guessed that it was an hour or two later—he saw Clara standing on the veranda, peering over the field.

He called out to her. Not a muscle stirred in her large-bosomed frame, nor did her expression change. He realized then that no sound had escaped through his parched lips. He tried again.

"Clara!" he got out. It was a mere croak, but to his ears it sounded like a shout that would be heard over Queen Anne Hill and back down into Seattle.

She dropped her gaze to where he lay, whispered something into the shadows; and, at once, with no interval at all, in the dreamlike shortening of time that was a part of his fever, she was kneeling beside him, her face a mask of concern.

"Matt, you fool! I told you not to play poker with one of the sheriff's men."

"Had the drop on him when he cheated," he muttered.

"Then how the hell do you think he shot you under the table?"

"He cheated there, too."

"Naturally!" she said furiously; "He's allowed to cheat at anything he wants in my house, Matt! That's why I stay open and everyone else keeps getting closed down."

"You gonna help me?" he asked, "or you gonna just squat there batting your gums?"

"I should just let you die, you bastard! Every time your hunk of manliness starts acting like a bull in a spring pasture I know I'm in for trouble. Why didn't you just let me know you had a hankering for Susanella? You didn't have to challenge lard-ass to a game of stud-poker for her."

"Come on, Clara, and help me! You know you love me!"

She shook her head, laughing, and the little bells on her necklace tinkled.

"Matt, I would shoot myself if I thought I loved you. I took you on fourteen years ago in New Orleans because you were shantypoor white right out of the Alabama woods. First and last free one I've ever done. You've been a jinx to me ever since, lover-boy."

"Now, let's don't go into all of that, Clara . . ." He had tried to sit up and his head swam from the loss of blood. In his anger he had started to say "Clara the Cow!" But only her girls and some patrons called her that—and never to her face. Her girls had even given her a necklace with little silver bells on it so they could hear her coming when they had allowed an especially virile patron to overstay his limit. "I need a roof over me and some nursing," he ended lamely.

"I love the way you say *please*," she sneered.

"Damn, you are an unforgiving bitch!"

"Don't give me that crap! Everytime you come around here, dangling your pecker like it was some rare jewel, you con me one way or the other. Someday you're going to learn that women are not something you just use and discard."

He tried to laugh. It gave him cramps in the stomach. "That is priceless, Clara. Are you not in the business of letting your women be used by men who then discard them?"

"For profit, buster! Something you never seemed to grasp about my trade. You usually start by trying to sweet-talk me into my bed and somehow end up with one of my highest priced fillies."

"You always said for a farm boy I had mighty good taste. What's that noise?"

Clara listened, then rose, making the bells tinkle again. "It's only Bo bringing a carriage around. I told him to make sure all the hotheads were gone. Let me get you up."

"Carriage for what?"

She didn't answer. She put her arm under him. He lurched up with all his strength. Then he hung there, clinging to her. They were of a near equal stance, and under the full-sleeved gown her arm was like a bar of steel. He had once seen her knock Calamity Jane clear across a room in Central City with a single back-hand strike—before he had accidently burned down Clara's house there. His leg was near numb, and he grinned at her.

"I can't make it any further than the house."

"Carriage is closer. I can't afford to have lard-ass coming back and finding you here. He'd close me down flat. I don't need to remind you that you already helped bring that about in Boise."

"So," he murmured, like a little boy being punished, "I guess it's into town for me and a dump into the gutter."

"Oh, Matt," she sighed, "I don't know why I put up with you. Will you never grow up? Will you never find anything to settle you down? You can't go on forever just drifting from place to place, living from hand to mouth."

"Haaarrumph!" He made it sound as though she had

uttered something nasty and unbelievable. He never asked her why she had moved her house nine times in fourteen years. He wasn't responsible for every one of her moves.

"Bo," Clara said, "come here'n give me a hand. The deputy sheriff got him in the calf."

Bother Munson shook his midnight-black head. He had been with Clara Bennett since New Orleans. From that very first visit Matt Monroe had been one of his favorite people. He had been born before, lived through, and didn't understand the world after the war. He was a servant who enjoyed serving, but always wished he had Matt's youth and spirit to match what was supposed to be his new freedom.

The two of them got Matt aboard, and laid him down on the seat.

"Bo knows where to take you, Matt. The man owes me a couple of favors."

"But *I* don't know where Bo is taking me."

The woman stood there, staring at him with her enormous gazelle's eyes, of a shade between blue and green. And nothing, not even the overly bright clothes she wore, the smudges of paint on her face, the rings on every single finger, could hide the fact that she was still lovely at forty. She had hated herself for fourteen years for having fallen in love with a beautiful hunk of dumb male flesh right off the farm. The feeling had never gone away, no matter how hard she fought it. But he was a jinx and there was no place for love in her profession.

"His name is Foster Hall," she said gently, though she wanted to slap the sass right back down into his throat, "if you have to know everything. He has an old steam-schooner called the *Brisbane*, although it doesn't go much farther than Whidby Island and back. They will never think of looking for you there."

"I get seasick!" he croaked.

"He only makes about one run a month, Matt. The rest of the time he's out here trying to borrow money to fix up his rusty boiler. He was just here today, so you'll be walking about before he sails again."

"He won't mind having a hospital passenger?"

"Reckon not," Clara said, her great eyes fixed upon his face. "I figure I own about half of the old tub by now. He's a nasty old carp, but has a daughter who cooks for him and can help see to your needs." Then she quickly added, "*Medical* needs!"

He grinned, his pale hazel eyes devilish. "Do I detect a note of jealousy?"

She shook her head, with a sudden motion of pure disgust at herself, the long, pale golden curls, piled high on her head, flying down with the motion.

"Go! Before the pattyroller gets back here. Bo!"

"Lord God!" the old man muttered to himself, cracking the whip over the horse's head. "When am dat woman gonna 'mit she's got da love-misery fur dat stud?"

"Lord God!" Matt muttered to himself an hour later. "When is that woman going to stop doing things to me out of spite?"

Captain Foster Hall was not only nasty, he was uncaring in his roughness to probe for the bullet and clean out the wound. But Matt had gritted his teeth over that pain. The real pain he felt, and what he considered Clara had done to him out of spite, centered around Phoebe Hall.

She was as large and buxom as a whale. And nothing, not even the mountainous dress she wore, the hundreds of curls that covered her head like springs, the sweet little bow to her mouth, could make him think of her as a woman.

It was obvious, however, that she thought of him as pure male. As her father had worked, her little brown eyes, set in mounds of flesh, devoured him. Then, with indescribable grace she bound the wound and started to take off the rest of his trousers.

"What are you doing?" he gasped.

"Torn pant leg is bloody. Ain't going to have you messing up my clean berth sheets."

He clamped his hands over the belt buckle. "I can do it myself."

Her laugh reminded him of the braying of a mule. "Didn't those ole whores see your underdrawers?"

Matt started to explain something, but she pushed him flat back onto the cabin berth, holding him down with a firm hand on his chest. With the other hand she knocked his away, popped the buckle, undid the buttons and tugged the pants off his slim waist. He had thought Clara strong, but the pressure on his chest was like a cow had fallen on him while he was punching it for branding.

He let out his breath as she took her hand away, but the color in his face was not from holding his breath. Phoebe didn't even flinch over the fact that he was not wearing underdrawers.

"Shirt!" she snapped.

Before she could yank him up by the hair he sat and let her remove the shirt. He cursed the time of the year. Another month and he would have been properly covered by long-johns.

She sniffed. "I'll get hot water from the galley and give you a bath."

He looked at her wonderingly. "I think you have done quite enough for me already."

She smiled. He didn't know quite how to read it, but it made him nervous. "I'll decide when I've done enough for you, Mr. Monroe."

She was gone then, departing with that peculiar animal grace that was surprising for thighs that were as big around as his chest.

He pulled a blanket off the berth rack and cursed Clara. Over the years they may have pulled some rather odd practical jokes on each other, but this was plain sadistic.

To his relief, Phoebe's father brought the basin, cloth and towel.

"Bo didn't say. You get caught in the mob?"

"No, I was at Clara's on the lake. What mob?"

The barrel-chested old man scowled at him. "Bo don't tell me that, the sneaky nigger. I took you on as a friend of Miz Clar'—not as one of her heathen customers."

Matt laughed aloud. "What difference would it make?"

"Why, damn you!" the old man roared. "What's wrong with your brain, boy? I got me a virgin daughter aboard who don't know nothing about that seamy side of life. She thinks of Miz Clar' as a fine lady, an' I'll not have her learnin' otherwise."

"Fine with me," Matt said, "and I am a friend of Clara's. Known her and Bo for fourteen years."

"That sounds more civilized." Then he scowled again. "Then how'd you get shot?"

"One of her more uncivilized customers. Problem is, he's a deputy sheriff."

Hall grimaced. "Sounds like the ilk we have here in King County. Some of them been acting more like the mob than the ones supposed to keep order."

"What is this mob you keep talking about?"

"Don't no news get over the hill to the lake? Ship came in from St. Michael's wharf yesterday with a rumor of gold. Weren't proved out till some of the passengers had their stuff smelted and barred. One couple, with two suitcases, came out with over a million dollars. Town's gone mad. Battling each other to buy out the stores. Damndest thing I've ever seen."

"Where is this place?"

"Saint Mike? Old Russian cargo port on the Bering Sea. Been there many times when I was on a China clipper. Colder than a witch's tit, but that ain't where the gold is. Looked it up on my charts. Over a thousand miles due north, as the crow flies—if crows even fly into that frozen land. Even with the best damn horse in the world, it would take a man over four months to get over that rugged country."

"But they came out by boat."

"Makes no mind," the old man growled. "They had the same distance, about, to get out to the sea. I see'd 'em. Raggedest lot imaginable."

"Hmm . . ." Matt mused. "Should be an easy way to get there."

"Stuff'n nonsense! Said there ain't, didn't I? Here's your grub."

Matt was hardly aware that he ate, or that Phoebe sat and watched him eat. Always before, when things seemed to be going against him, something came up to move him along. Gold had never really interested him before. What he had seen in his travels had convinced him that the first on the scene got rich, but for the men who followed there was little waiting except for damn hard work. He wished he could find out more about this strike. He wondered if Clara knew anything about it. Clara always seemed to know everything from her customers. He considered sending Phoebe for Clara, then considered the odd hour and the storm the old man would raise.

Tomorrow would be quite soon enough.

3

GEORGE CARMACK was talking loudly to a reporter from the Seattle *Post-Intelligencer* in the plush dining room of the Northern Hotel. The reporter had been late because the driver of the horse-drawn trolley had stopped dead in front of Newcastle Hardware and joined the line to buy supplies.

The fashionable diners pretended to gaze out over Elliot Bay, but kept their ears glued to George's words. What they missed they were able to read in the paper the next morning. George, with a picture of himself and Kate, took up the whole front page. George bought a thousand copies to take back home. Hawkers on the street were getting a dollar a paper by mid-morning. George was considered an authority, which made him chuckle, for some of the tales he told were the tallest ever.

Still, his geography was accurate and opened up a whole new train of thought. It was the first people had heard of the *New Racket*, and it sounded as if a cruise on the Yukon would be little different than a trip on the Mississippi. But he also mentioned the little Indian fishing village of Skagway, and that approach to the Yukon and Klondike. That route was only 550 miles, except that

George failed to mention that it was an obstacle course designed by the devil himself.

Either way, the ship's captains and owners blessed George Carmack. The normal passenger fare to St. Michael doubled and then tripled.

And the population started to climb. The passenger trains were so overloaded that the railroads offered a special rate if miners—and prospective miners—would ride in freight cars. That didn't last long when outfitters demanded an equally special rate to bring in the supplies the men would need.

Cooper & Levy wired outfitters in Deadwood, Central City, and Leadville for stock that had been sitting on their shelves for years. Many times the supplies were purchased by passengers on the same train before it ever got to Seattle. Cooper & Levy would just rewire for more supplies. They didn't have to go to Alaska for gold. In the summer of 1897 they reaped a profit of $25 million.

The shipping industry could not keep up with the bulge the city was feeling. San Francisco couldn't help out with additional ships, nor could Los Angeles or San Diego. They were also bulging with people wanting sea transportation.

Matt fumed. For a month he laid in the berth watching ships depart through the porthole. He couldn't see that for every hundred who gained passage, a thousand new ones arrived. He cursed his unhealing leg. He cursed the unarriving Clara. Bo would pop in and out, but his time was also limited. The lake house was doing such a roaring business that Bo was kept busy carting customers back and forth from downtown.

He seldom saw Captain Hall. The man had to spend most of his waking days sitting at the gangway explaining to people that the *Brisbane* didn't go any farther than Whidby Island. Nor was it even going that far. The normal cargo it would carry had been sold to others for a higher profit. A $5 barrel of flour was bringing $25. A pair of two dollar leather boots sold for twenty. There were no more trolley cars running, for the horses had gone for $500 each. Residents who had no desire to leave put their winter clothing on racks outside their front doors. It never lasted longer than a half hour before they had realized as much as a thousand percent profit.

It was the same everywhere. A one-way passage to St. Michael or Skagway was up to $1,000 a person and $100 for each hundred weight of equipment.

Many were coming face to face with an old adage: "It takes money to make money."

"Damn my luck!" Matt growled. "If I was back on the *Delta Star* I'd make even that old riverboat taste salt—"

He stopped the thought short. The *Brisbane* wasn't that much larger or that much older than the *Delta Star* had been when Clara got him his first job ever. He hadn't known the first thing about a boat, other than the minute he stepped aboard his stomach went queasy. But he was strong and young and could heft the great lengths of chopped wood into the fire. When the paddle wheel would start turning he would heft the logs faster, to keep his mind off the movement beneath his feet. It was the first time he had ever had to work side by side with a black man. He had at first felt degraded, until he learned how much Moses knew about steam and boilers. Matt had absorbed that knowledge like a sponge, feeling his future might be as an engineer. But when he was still hefting logs a year later the desire faded. Clara had also faded from New Orleans and with her the desire to make it home port.

"Phoebe," he said slowly, when she brought his lunch, "how bad off is the *Brisbane*?"

"Bad?" she gasped. "She's the finest islander about."

"Don't give me that. If she was so fine that old horse thief father of yours would have been the first to leave for Alaska."

She began to quiver so that her bulk shook the deck beneath her feet. "Don't—you—never—call—my Pa such. I've—heard—Bo talk about you to Pa. You big—stud trash—bastard!"

"Then prove me wrong," he whispered. "Show me the engine room and boiler."

Phoebe hesitated. At first she had liked him because he was such a handsome gentleman. She didn't mind the things that she knew he had probably done at Clara's place. It actually excited her to think about it. Had she been slim and pretty she would have put Clara out of business by giving it away for nothing. But not to Matthew Monroe! She hadn't even been able to make a friend of the man. He ignored her and that hurt. She didn't know if she wanted to do anything for him or not.

Watching her, Matt smiled. To get his way he was going to have to turn on some charm, even with her.

"Where is your father?"

"Talking to a fat couple on the wharf."

He thought she had some nerve talking about other people being fat. "Our luck," he grinned. "We never can be alone here without the fear of him popping in. He won't even know that we've gone to the engine room—for whatever."

She gave him one of her gazelle stares. She had never imagined that her father might be the barrier between them. Why, it was so logical she wondered why she hadn't thought of it sooner.

"I'll go make sure Pa sees me on deck and won't come to trifle with us," she giggled.

Matt got painfully to his feet. He hung there a moment staring at the open cabin door. Well, he had gotten himself out of worse promises.

A few minutes later he wondered which was worse—the *Brisbane* or his promise.

Nine years of making only monthly runs had reduced her engines to a mass of rusted junk. They would have to be taken apart, piece by piece, soaked in oil and graphite, and the rust laboriously removed by hand. It would be less time-consuming to let his leg heal and book passage on another steamer.

Matt could hear footsteps coming onto the main deck, and couldn't believe his good luck.

"Your father!" he hissed. "I'll go this way and you take the inward passageway."

He limped off before she could protest.

He came on deck just as the captain was coming back along with a middle-aged couple, whom Matt would never have considered fat. Their dress was mid-western, bulky and coarse. He had seen many people like them in that part of the country. Tall and big-boned, his guess was that they were of Germanic stock.

"Ah, my other guest," Captain Hall called, with a jovial laugh. "Come and meet the Hendersons."

Matt was immediately on his guard. Foster Hall was never jovial.

"This is Matthew Monroe. He hurt his leg and is recuperating in one of my cabins. He can attest to the excellent meals prepared by my charming daughter. Matt, Mr. and Mrs. Harlan Henderson of St. Louis. They are presently at the Northern Hotel, but that establishment now has a new rule that a guest cannot occupy a room for more than a week."

"How do you do," Matt said politely, reaching out to shake Harlan Henderson's hand. The grip was firm, but the hand soft. He discounted farming as the man's trade. "A strange policy."

"Hardly," Harriet Henderson laughed. "Their rates change as quickly as the sheets on the bed—about once a week. When one now has to wait two to three months for passage, it is unaffordable. Luckily, we have just been able to talk dear Captain Hall into turning one of his cabins into a floating hotel for us."

Matt was silent as he pondered the Hendersons' situation. They hardly looked the type to be rushing off for Alaska, and the time they would have to wait for passage startled him. Then he wondered what Phoebe would say about the horse thief trying to turn this kind of dollar on the situation.

"Glad to have you aboard," he smiled. "Oh, Captain Hall, might I see you in my cabin when you have seen the Hendersons ashore?"

Foster Hall smiled and nodded, but wondered what it was about. Still, he was glad to see that Matt was finally up and about. The Hendersons had opened up quite a thought in his mind. The *Brisbane* had comfortable cabin space for about thirty—maybe a couple more if he crowded them in. If some had to wait that long for passage, he might as well make a profit—he certainly was making no profit whatsoever on Matt Monroe.

Matt had made his decision quickly. It would be easier to put up with Phoebe, talk Hall into breaking down the engine, and talking Clara out of a grub-stake than waiting like the Hendersons.

Harlan Henderson would not mind waiting—even if it was forever. He missed St. Louis, and he was already fretting over their dwindling cash supply. There had been no time to sell his small bakery in St. Louis. There had not been that much to sell; a few loaves of bread a day. He couldn't recall the last time he had baked and decorated a wedding cake—his specialty. Fate, he considered, had doomed him to failure ever since he started believing in William Jennings Bryant. Now they were both failures.

Nothing kept Harriet Henderson in the dumps for long.

"Tomorrow will be better, Harlan," she chirped, as they strode back to the hotel. "The money we save by moving to the ship will take care of the stable charges on the horses. I am also sure that we can talk Captain Hall into letting us move our equipment from the railway depot and save that storage charge. When I got up out of that lumpy bed this morning I just knew. . . ."

Harlan shut off the sound of her voice. After thirty years of childless marriage he had learned how to do it quite successfully, at any time. He knew, at fifty, that he was far too old to be starting over again. He was tired of starting over. He was tired of Harriet pushing him in every direction but loose, but one didn't buck Harriet. Where there would be a group of near womenless men, she figured, they would find hungry men. They had equipment. They had supplies that had not been turned into goods. They had horses to make deliveries—although she had no idea whether deliveries would be necessary, but Harriet always liked to be prepared. Her logic had been so simple. All it would cost them was passage, they had everything else.

Harriet tugged at his sleeve. He was not even aware that they had entered the hotel and were crossing the lobby.

"There's that couple, Harlan!"

"What couple?"

"The stylish ones from the train. There is a table free next to them in the dining room. Come on."

Harlan followed as Harriet swooped into the dining room like a *grande dame*. She was imposing enough to bring it off with a great flair. The other ladies were hatted and gloved. Hats gave Harriet a headache, because of her great mass of heavy dark brown hair. In some lights it was almost black, giving some cause to question a bit of secret tinting. But the manner in which it was always tightly braided and roped into a crown was more impressive than any hat she could have worn. Or was it the carriage of the head, on a slight angle away from the broad shoulders and the chin a slight, haughty angle? Or the face—eyes always dancing as though just having been amused, and a slight Mona Lisa touch to the lips?

Around her were gowns of velvet, silk, lace and brocade. She paused by her chair in her woolen travelling suit as if they were most impractical in their attire and she too much a lady to even notice.

Then, as Harlan began to pull out her chair for her, there was a polite little nod of her head, as though she had just that moment noticed the next couple.

Calvin Ramsey was forced to stand and nod back.

"Don't you dare speak," Amalida Ramsey hissed through clenched teeth.

Her thirty-year-old husband had no choice. Harriet was sweeping around her own table with hand outstretched.

"How charming to see you again, Mr. and Mrs. Ramsey. I do hope Mrs. Ramsey has recovered from her smoky train ride. I do declare that some of those cars seemed most pre-war."

Amalida accorded her the weakest of smiles.

Harriet had not expected more from the woman. From the moment of their meeting on the train she had sized up Amalida. At the time she had told Harlan that the woman was not "natural." As a man he had thought her pretty in her way—her way being a flair for creating beauty through her expensive clothing, outlandish hair styles, breast-lifters and corsets. The enormous picture hats shadowed a face that was really too small on the end of a long neck. A little black line was drawn at the outside corner of each eye to bring their nearness away from the small pugged nose. What the hats did not shadow the constant employment of an ivory handled fan did—mainly the extreme pointedness of a chin that seemed to have been given to the wrong face.

By contrast, Harriet had noted, Calvin Ramsey was almost too pretty to be a man on first sighting. This was soon softened by his suave, sophisticated gentlemanliness and rich baritone voice. Although he, too, employed a flair for most expensive clothing, Harriet felt he would have been charming even in buckskins.

"A few days' rest has helped, thank you, Mrs. Henderson. Do you depart soon?"

"From the hotel, yes. Mr. Henderson and I have been lucky enough to find other accommodations until we sail."

"I am most happy for you. We too shall have to submit to their policy and seek other lodgings."

"Perhaps where we will be staying?" Harriet said gaily. "I would be happy to inquire for you."

"Hardly necessary," Amalida snapped. "Calvin will just have to make these people understand that we will not tolerate being treated like the rest of the cattle."

The way Calvin turned on his wife was like the swoop of a cobra neck. His voice was vibrant with ferocity, rising from its usual baritone purr until it was almost shrill.

"It is very necessary, Amalida!" he spat. "When are you going to learn that your finger-snapping does not work with these people?"

Amalida only smiled at him, a little more strongly than the weak one given Harriet. Harriet had been troubled on the trip by the woman's apparent dislike of her husband. But now, through that smile, she saw that Amalida didn't dislike Calvin: she openly and actively hated him.

"I must declare, Calvin," Amalida said sweetly, "that Mrs. Henderson, being a woman, most likely agrees with me. It is hard for a woman to be uprooted from her home and lifelong friends. But it is insult added to injury to force us about from week to week. Do you not agree Mrs. . . ." She paused, and added a touch more smile. "I know I am most your junior, but as we have traveled together, might we enjoy a first name basis? I believe it was Harriet, wasn't it? I am Amalida."

Harriet smiled to herself. The little snip wanted something from her and was very shrewd. Such a husbandly outburst would have most wives reduced to a state of pouting or tears. Amalida seemed to accept it as part of the pleasure of her hating.

But there was an even more important thread that Harriet had picked up from Amalida's words. On the train Calvin had made a point of telling Harlan that travel was nothing new to them. Their home for two years had been Cairo, Illinois. Before that it had been several Illinois towns where Calvin was in banking. Lifelong friends?

"Oh, I don't blame you being upset about the uprooting," Harriet said slowly, to keep the point of her questioning curiosity alive, "and the greedy way in which they raised the room rates. It is understood by prospectors going to seek the gold, but hard for tradespeople like us to fathom. Captain Hall, who has offered us accommodations aboard his ship, paints quite a vivid picture of the hardships to be faced and why most wives are left safely at home."

"I've heard much the same," Amalida said. "But like you, Harriet, I can much better stand and endure the hardships of the journey rather than the anxieties of an absent husband."

"Except for enduring a move from this hotel," Calvin shrugged, his tone faintly mocking.

"I told them to raise their rates and be damned," Harriet said flatly.

Amalida opened her mouth to declare that money was of no concern to them and immediately did quite an about face.

"Harriet has just made a very valid point." She laughed lightly. It sounded almost like a giggle. "It has just come to me that they could raise the rates week by week by week. Perhaps, Harriet, Mr. Ramsey and Mr. Henderson could look into your kind suggestion after lunch."

Calvin stared at her, startled. After Harriet returned to her table he retook his seat and spread the linen napkin over his lap as though he had all day to accomplish the chore.

"What brought on the sudden change of mind?" he whispered.

Amalida reached over with great calm and patted his

hand. She smiled sweetly, but her eyes danced with cold ferocity.

"We are being watched," she whispered. "Don't turn around. He is now leaving the dining room and going out toward the desk."

"How do you know he was watching us?"

"He was looking over every couple about our age, but his eyes kept coming back to us and Mrs. Henderson." She began to tap her chin with the fan and suddenly that motion stopped. "He just showed the clerk something, and now he's looking through the guest register."

"He will find nothing," Calvin said, in a voice strangely high and quavering. "Rise as though we are quite finished with our lunch. We will stop by the Henderson table for you to say a polite good-bye to her, and I will make quick arrangements with him. If we get stopped in the lobby you let me do all the talking. Your voice slips back into being most New Orleans belle when you get nervous."

"Nervous?" she gulped. "Calvin, I'm scared pea-green."

He patted her hand tenderly. "My love, you have been perfect so far. Ann Forbes was a timid little sparrow, deathly afraid of her father and husband. They forced her into that marriage and made her a recluse. In contrast, you portray the part of a shrew very well. Even if Amos Stillman hired the best detectives in New Orleans they would have to go on his description of simple Ann and Raymond Forbes in his hand-me-down suits and steel-rimmed spectacles. Now, Mrs. Calvin Ramsey, rise."

After they left the next table, Harriet sat there beaming.

"There now," she chuckled. "You satisfied, Mr. Harlan Henderson?"

He nodded, his watery eyes twinkling. Solemnly he reached over and took her hand.

"You always look out for tomorrow, my dear," he said.

"Thank you," she laughed. "I figured it couldn't hurt to

have the man who will be the local banker owe us a wee favor. Still, you'd best hustle along to make sure Captain Hall saves them a cabin."

A man in a bowler hat and loud plaid suit approached the table.

"Pard'me, ma'am. I've a mind ah I know the couple ya'all were talkin' to from back home. Can't quite recall their names, though."

"Home?" Harriet asked, turning her beam on him. "Where might that be?"

"N'Orleans, ma'am."

Harriet rose from her chair, her meal not quite finished. She had done it on purpose. The man was rude. Not only did he continue to stand with his bowler on, but he had not jumped to help her from her chair.

"I'm afraid you have the wrong couple, sir. My niece and nephew are from upstate Illinois. Come, Harlan."

"Niece and nephew?" Harlan whispered to her as they left the dining room. "What was that all about?"

"Another little tidbit from Captain Hall, Harlan. He said not to appear to be prosperous or every down-and-outer would approach you for a grubstake. Obviously, that man was fishing for their name to make his first approach that much easier. Oh, there is Mr. Ramsey waiting for you by the front door. I'll do our packing."

Harriet bustled off, contented that Harlan had swallowed that explanation. She, too, had seen the man studying the Ramseys while she had been at their table. She had noticed Amalida's eyes darting toward him, and then how Amalida had made such a sudden change, a soft lilt creeping into her voice. When the man spoke, Harriet recognized the same lilt. Being the "mother to the world" she was never fully content until she knew every scrap of information that was to be known about her friends. For banking purposes she wanted the Ramseys as friends—even if Amalida was difficult to fathom. She knew, somehow, she had done right in keeping the man away from them.

Phoebe sensed the lift and surge of her father's mood. For now, at long last, he had many things to keep him occupied. In the morning, in work overalls, he would help Matt break down the engine and clean it. His opinion of Matthew Monroe had done a flip-flop. Now, when Matt expressed interest in a project, Captain Hall took it seriously. And there was nothing that Foster Hall loved more than an industrious man and a secret. Both men had agreed, at least for the time being, not to disclose the fact that they were overhauling the *Brisbane*. Seattle was becoming a strange and dangerous town. Men were murdered in their sleep for their equipment and to shorten the waiting list.

In the afternoon, Captain Hall would put on his best serge uniform and oversee his "hotel" business. Before, he had always been forced by the economy of the matter to accept any passenger and any cargo. Now he could sit on the wharf, chat to his heart's content, and pick and choose those he would have a cabin to rent to.

He took pity on the Feddersons. They were not gold seekers, but a young couple with a child who were caught in the middle of a bad situation. The company could give Nolan two days of work a week in Everett, but only bachelor quarters. With the business boom in Seattle, Nolan was sure it would affect the lumber industry. Because the company was giving him what work they could, he didn't want to get too far away from the men who made the decisions. He fretted over sending Lolly and the baby back to his mother, but in Seattle even a single room without water was more than he would make in the two days.

Finally, he decided to send them back, but as fate would have it he mistook the *Brisbane* for a steamer between Seattle and Portland. When he discovered that a cabin by the week would take only one day of his wages he decided to keep his family with him.

Mickey Magraff appealed to Captain Foster for two reasons. First, he was not a gold seeker, and, secondly, he was handsome enough that he might take Phoebe's mind off Matt Monroe. He liked an educated man who would trouble himself to pass his education on to youngsters. He would have educated Phoebe, had she been a boy.

Mickey shielded the turmoil in his brain. The Ferguson school was closed—Henry Ferguson being one of the first to leave his family behind and head for Alaska. Even though he pleaded to open the school in the man's stead, Mrs. Ferguson was reluctant. She was nothing like her sister-in-law. With each passing day Mickey wondered if he shouldn't put his name on a waiting list. He knew nothing about prospecting for gold, but then neither did the majority of those who were waiting to leave.

Lonsworth Crowley claimed to know something about everything, and had a story to back up every claim. The emptiness of his pockets told another story.

"I was looking for a ship that would let me work off my passage," he told Captain Hall. "The two ships that left this week said they wanted 'rounders' and no Indians."

"Are you really an in'jun?"

"The illegitimate son of that old Indian guide Broken Hand Fitzpatrick and a Crow maiden," he proudly boasted.

Foster Hall didn't know much about Indians and their history. He took the lad to be under twenty. The high cheekbones and lightly-bronzed skin of his face did suggest Indian blood, but his tall, muscular body, chestnut hair and pale blue eyes seemed ill-fitting for the Indian buckskins.

"What about room and board for work until you find a ship?"

"What work you got, Captain?"

"I'll show you."

One look and he claimed to know everything there was to know about rust chipping—and in the next breath was repeating to Matt the history of his father and mother.

"That's why everyone calls me Crow for short—because of my mother's tribe."

Matt smiled. He couldn't help but wonder if the nickname had not come about from the young man's *crowing*. He kept silent to the fact that he knew a bit about Indian myth and history. Broken Hand Fitzpatrick would have had to come back from the grave to produce such a young son. Still, a full day helper would be handy, especially since Foster Hall worked only half-days.

Therefore, when Matt learned that Lonsworth Crowley didn't know rust from metal, he said nothing of it to the captain.

"All right," Matt said gently. "Let me show you the way I like to have it done."

Wordlessly, Crow watched and absorbed. An hour later his tall tale had turned to truth. A day later he had memorized the names of every engine part. A week later he could even make intelligent suggestions on how unusable parts might be replaced.

Captain Hall took great pride in his wisdom for having tired the youth. Matt saw a lot of his former self in Lonsworth. A runaway from someplace, wishing to drift to another place and adapt to any given situation like a chameleon.

But, because Matt had been that way himself, he did not press for the real story behind Lonsworth Crowley.

Phoebe Hall didn't have time to press for anyone's story. On the Whidby Island runs they never had more than eight to ten passengers, and sandwich service because of the short trip. Now it was three meals a day—

with all of the shopping, preparation, cooking and serving on her shoulders.

Captain Hall stuck his head in the galley door. "Two more, my dear."

"Oh, no!" Phoebe wailed.

"Daughter," he said gently, "remember what we determined. This will get us out from under Clara's nagging for repayment."

Clara had never nagged Foster Hall for a cent, but the old man felt everyone worked better under a challenge.

"Y-y-yes . . . " she sobbed.

"Well, what you're doing for the cause pleases me a mighty heap. Thirty folks is no more than twenty-eight, now is it? But for my little girl, I'll go rustle up some galley help."

Foster Hall turned away and stopped. The passage was totally blocked by the bulk of a single man.

"Know how to handle wimmen nicely, Captain Hall."

"Sir," he answered coolly, "I don't think I have had the pleasure."

"Until now," the man beamed, extending a pudgy hand. "Henry Boise, sir. Our mutual friend, Father Durand, sent me to see you."

"Ah!" Captain Hall brightened, then as suddenly frowned. "I hope the good priest is not seeking passage to Whidby Island? My vessel is not quite ready to take him back and forth."

"No, no, no! Alex is most aware of your problem, captain. It would seem the Catholic Church is suffering most the same. His pews are filled nightly with those who come to pray, and somehow manage to sleep through the night. His heart is too generous to send them away. So generous, to be truthful, that the beds in the parish house are also filled. It is due to a rumor he has heard that he sent me along to see you."

Alex? Foster Hall mused. He couldn't count the number of times he had transported the priest back and forth to conduct mass for the few Catholic families on the island. In all that time he had never known the man's first name. Parish house? He had thought its beds only open to priests and nuns.

This man was clearly neither. His five-foot seven-inches of 220 pounds were tailored to perfection. In his cravat resided a most handsome diamond stick pin. The name and accent were very much French.

"You are not a gold seeker?"

Henry Boise rocked with jovial mirth. "Dear captain, I am a family man who has been seeing to the education of my daughter and now desires to return home. My reservations, it would seem, have become a tangled confusion in this hodge-podge of mass hysteria. What can one do but accept the fate of an entanglement?"

Foster Hall was impressed. A man of worth, as this man seemed to be, would have been ranting and raving and threatening to buy out the whole steamship line. Only a gentleman of quality would take such a matter in stride.

"Father!" Phoebe warned darkly from the galley door, reading his mind.

"Well, sir," Captain Hall said sternly, "it would—seem that—it would be to our advantage if you would turn and lead the way onto the deck. We are crowded almost to the limit—" His mind was racing. How could he juggle people about? This man had money, as had the Ramseys. And a daughter! Would that require one or two cabins? It didn't matter. Monroe, Crowley and Magraff were in individual cabins. All he was gaining from Matt and Crow was work, and Mickey Magraff had come along before he had a real price set in his mind. They would have to share a cabin or leave.

"My daughter, Captain Hall, Laura Lee Boise."

She sat on a pile of luggage as though it were a throne. Hall studied her critically. From Henry Boise he had fully expected something like Phoebe, but Laura Lee was a fetching creature, almond-eyed and sylph-like. Her clothing still smacked of school-uniform regimentation, but beneath the body was firm and womanly.

"My pleasure, Captain," she said, her voice soft and warm. She stood and curtseyed. "Your boat is nothing like Uncle Alex described. I expected something like the hustle and bustle of the New Orleans riverboats. It is most intimate."

Uncle Alex? Hustle and bustle? Intimate? Foster Hall's mind was fragmenting. He didn't have room for them. He did have room for them. Help for Phoebe! Two more! Total of thirty-two!

But she was so charming. Educated, didn't her father say? That was obvious. She was so polished. Nothing like Phoebe.

Phoebe stormed onto the deck, underscoring her father's thought, and stopped short.

"Father?" she said shyly.

"Yes, Phoebe?" Hall growled.

"Matt just said—did you know Clara was coming for dinner?" she whispered.

He had forgotten. How was he supposed to remember everything for everybody?

"My daughter," he said curtly. "Henry Boise and his daughter, Laura Lee, Phoebe. They will make two more. I must see them to their cabin—or is it cabins?"

"Two, if available."

"I will make it so. Phoebe, we will have to do some moving about and cleaning."

Laura Lee noted the harried expression that crossed Phoebe's eyes.

"Is there something I might be able to do to help?" she asked.

"You?" Hall mocked. "Why should you help as a paying guest?"

"Because she seems to need it," Laura Lee said, and her voice was so full of innocence that Hall felt ashamed. Then she laughed. "Besides, I'm a paying guest at the convent-school and the nuns still find plenty of chores to keep me occupied from dawn to dusk. Where might I be of help, Miss Phoebe?"

"In the galley," she said candidly, thinking that would back her off quickly.

"Splendid!" she chirped. "Father, see to our settlement. Miss Phoebe is about to learn that she made the worst possible assignment. I may look like a sparrow, but I eat like a bear coming out of hibernation."

"Really?" Phoebe said plaintively. "And you never get fat?"

"No. It's what you eat, I reckon. I am twenty now, but when my mother was the same—"

"Laura Lee!" Henry Boise's voice was like a thunderclap, his brow like the thundercloud. "We are keeping these people from their work," he said thickly. "Go help, if you must, but don't babble!"

Damn, he thought, I should have kept her away for another twenty years. But then he brightened. He had not seen his wife or eldest son for twenty years. Laura Lee should start remembering the past. Had she really remembered her mother, or was this just an outcropping of some story he had told along the way?

Twenty years? For most in the world that was half a lifetime. For the Reverend Father Henre Duboise it had been but a few grains of sand through the hour glass—a flick of a single page in his Catholic world. It took centuries to make a saint. He was therefore not fully amazed that it was taking nearly as long to transform a defrocked priest into a legitimate father and husband.

He didn't hate God. God had not created his problem. Nor did he hate the Holy See in Rome—only the little ants within its feudal system that made its wheels grind so exceedingly slow.

But, he reminded himself, that had nothing to do with Laura Lee. That was his fight with the Russian Orthodox Church and the Roman Catholic Church. He had promised Laura Lee's mother that he would return with her during her twentieth year—win or lose. He was, even though Father Alexander Durand had called him many other things, a man of his word.

"Oh, Father, how could you?" Phoebe cried. "You have only taken Mr. Boise and his daughter on board this afternoon!"

"And can gain at least a week's rental out of them. Wouldn't you say at least a week for engine trials, Matthew?"

"She's ready to go now," Matt said blandly. "All she requires is passengers and crew."

Foster Hall stared at him.

"Crew?" he said. "Phoebe and I are the only crew needed for the run—"

"But this is not a thirty mile run," Matt said brusquely. "It's nearly two thousand miles to St. Michaels."

"That far," he said plaintively, and not as a question.

"Not *that* far!" Matt growled. "We've turned her into a coal burner for you. It takes up the same storage space as the wood, but gives you three times the steam power. Come on! What have Crow and I been breaking our butts over? To get out of here. Phoebe is a fine, strong girl, but no one in their right mind would make her fire a furnace with coal! You've got to have an engineer and fireman!"

"And I still have to have galley help!"

Clara cleared her throat. "And you've got to give these people fair warning and determine a passenger fare."

This, Hall reflected, was all quite true. His emotions were mixed. He was enjoying his hotel business and yet elated to have the engines almost like new.

"Well," he said slowly, "the fare should be the same as the others are now getting—$1,000. However, I think it only right to give our guests first right of refusal."

Clara had to smile. She put her hand on his shoulder.

"That seems fair, Foster," she said. "But one more thing—I advanced you the money for the new engine parts and would like a piece of the action. If anybody wants to negotiate part of their claim for transportation and supplies, Clara Bennett wants first crack at them."

Matt breathed easier. Clara had just solved all of his problems, and it could be handled on a business basis.

For two days the *Brisbane* became as frantic as the wharf and bay front streets. The Hendersons were the first to quickly put up their money and make Hall see he had made one grave error in his announcement to his guests.

The Hendersons already had all of their supplies stored in the hold, except for their stabled horses. How could he now charge them a cargo fee? Before he could settle the matter in his mind, Calvin Ramsey was in his cabin to pay.

"Harlan Henderson and I have been spending our days out looking for livestock. His stableman has found me a horse and pack mule. When will we be able to bring them aboard?"

Captain Hall started to say the animals would require an extra charge, but the four thousand in gold pieces felt mighty good in his hand.

"Never carried more than twelve horses or cattle to Whidby, so I'd say you two better get your animals and feed aboard before everyone wants to take critters along."

The next time, he determined, he would not make this mistake. Then he smiled. It was the first time he had considered that there could be a next time.

An engineer, fireman and galley help puzzled him. He would need rounders, and not those with gold lust in their veins. Then he thought of Wong Soo. The old Chinaman had many sons.

But before he could go on that errand a line had formed outside his cabin.

It was not the port of call Henry Boise had wished, but from St. Michael he could find native transportation down to a Tlinget village.

The announcement of the departure had forced a decision on Mickey Magraff. From the toe of a knotted stocking he took every cent he had to his name, which came to only $400, but would serve as a deposit until he, Matt and Lonsworth Crowley could get out to the lake to see Clara.

To Foster Hall, Clampett Dunn had been "Cabins G to J." The sixty-year-old whisky-nosed Irishman was spokesman, overseer and payer for the four cabins that housed himself and eleven sons and sons-in-law. If asked, Foster would not have been able to tell anyone the first thing about them, except that they were clannish, quiet, and spoke to no one.

It took a little bit of time to count out $12,000 in gold pieces, with no coin larger than $50. Hall couldn't believe the size of the mound on his desk.

He was still in such a state of shock that for the rest in line he just accepted their money and added their names to his log: Fairchild—Freeman, Hazel, son David (14).

Calhoun, Jethro.

Lundgren—Lazlo, Mia, sons Michael (16), Lars (15).

That would give him thirty-two again when Mrs. Federson and her baby daughter left the ship. He figured he could squeeze four into that cabin, and he could easily find new passengers on the wharf.

Lolly stewed over the matter. Nolan would not be back until the next day—Saturday, of course. Her weekdays had been very peaceful. Little Kimberly was fawned over and loved by nearly everyone on the ship, especially Harriet Henderson. Lolly's weekends had been a little different from life in the lumber camp. The cabin walls were so thin that she had quietly submitted to Nolan. With the

Hendersons on one side and the Ramseys on the other, it embarrassed her to even think of what they did hear. But Nolan was not himself, either. He was quiet and brooding. The two days a week had sounded great at first, but then he had learned that they would only let him top four to six trees a day. That wasn't even covering Lolly's rent. Instead of breaking even, he was constantly digging into his dwindling supply of reserve cash.

"The world is upside down," he had mumbled the weekend before. "No work here and people just picking gold up off the ground up there. Wonder how they're getting lumber to build places to live? Sure as hell aren't getting it from here. Sawmill buzzes one day a week. Wonder if they got a sawmill up there?"

He had been speaking only to himself, as usual, but Lolly had heard.

Lolly considered Harriet Henderson a fine, smart woman—and perhaps the first real friend she had ever had. She had posed Nolan's questions as though they were her own.

"It's been a worry to Harlan and me, too, dear. We bought ourselves a big tent to start out in, but from what I hear of the weather it will be a problem. Dough has got to be kept warm to rise properly, you know. Well, if we're smart enough to go set up a bakery, I hope someone else is smart enough to cut some lumber."

But what if nobody had? Lolly kept wondering. Wouldn't they need experienced lumberjacks? But what of the passage money? For the two of them it was more than Nolan made in a whole year, and she didn't know if there would be a charge for Kimberly.

It was the longest Lolly had ever had to think on a subject in her whole life. She had never had to make a decision on anything. Nolan bought the provisions at the company store and told her what he wanted cooked. It had been the same with her father and mother and she wasn't one to question. When she needed a new dress, Nolan picked it out—and only when she desperately needed it.

About the only thing she ever had to determine was whether the baby needed a diaper change, and this was hardly in the same category. But she knew it was something she would have to do on her own, because Nolan would never put his name on a waiting list.

The captain's cabin was right down the passageway from her own. She had peeked out at the sound of so many voices.

"Marvelous luck!" Calvin Ramsey had enthused. "Best news I've ever had. Wait until Amalida wakes up. She just won't believe it."

Lolly hadn't believed it, either. The ship was going to sail. Those wishing passage could pay and the others would have to find other lodgings. Then Matt Monroe had made a curious announcement about a Clara Bennett. At the time she had only half listened. Then she had seen Matt Monroe coming down the passage after Mr. Henderson and Mr. Ramsey.

She made a quick decision and stepped out.

"M-m-ister Monroe," she stammered. "A moment, please."

Matt turned almost at once. He had wanted to meet her since she had come on board. She was material to dream about, even if she was always dressed like someone's poor country cousin. It was her skin that had caught his attention first. The color of anyone who lingered in the fresh air and sun of the woods—honey on top with dusk rose underneath. Lord God! He couldn't help but wonder if her whole body was the same.

Her hair was black, and plaited into braids like that of Indian maidens he had known; they hung loose, falling below her waist. And such a slim waist. He bet he could put both his hands around it and his fingers would meet. He knew she had to be under twenty. A horrible waste for her to be already married—and her brute husband gone except for the weekends. If she was Matt's woman, he would never let her out of his sight. He would never, ever let her out of his bed.

She stood there, staring back at him; then, very slowly, the full-lipped, wine-red mouth shaped itself into a smile.

"I've a favor," she said simply.

"Name it," he grinned.

"Clara Bennett?" she said.

"Clara?" he echoed. "What about her?"

"The loan matter. Was that for anyone?"

"Those who are going to make claims and are willing to pay her back a percentage."

Lolly frowned. "I don't understand none of that. My husband handles all the money matters."

"He thinking of going prospecting?"

"He might, but he has no money."

Matt pondered. Even though she was married, he sure would like to have her along. He had had his share of luck with married women, especially those left so much alone by their husbands. It was with a married woman that he had first learned that some women have stronger cravings than men.

"Well," he drawled, "tell you what, Mrs. Fedderson. You tell your old man, if he's interested, to take a hack over the hill to Clara's house. They all know where it is."

"Thank you," she murmured and started back in the cabin door. Then she tilted her head back. "Anybody ever tell you you're one mighty handsome man?"

Before he could even get his startled jaw to work with an answer she was inside and had the door closed.

Lolly stood trembling and cursing herself. "That was the damndest fool thing ever come from your mouth, Lolly Fedderson. Ain't you got no shame?"

She was so consumed with anger and embarrassment that she didn't hear herself start to giggle. And when she heard it she giggled all the more.

Well, she told herself, it were the truth. "Ain't ever seen so many handsome men, ever. Lumberjacks were like —well, like Nolan: three layers of clothes and bushy beards."

Eighteen years to see her first shaven man! At first they had struck her as most strange. Calvin Ramsey had been the first. In the dining room she had gawked at Amalida's clothing and then at Calvin's. Even the company men from Eugene and Seattle didn't come to the mill town dressed like this.

"Stop it!" Nolan had hissed. "Ain't fittin' to stare at her."

Lolly had lowered her eyes and snickered. Weren't fittin' either to tell him what she had really been staring at.

Then Matt Monroe had come into the dining room. She had to look at him through the veil of her lashes. The oddest surge jolted through her body. It was like when Nolan was finished with his Saturday night thing and she hadn't even started. Just looking at Matt Monroe made her feel like it could all happen in just a split second.

During the days when Nolan wasn't there she was asked to share a table with the Hendersons. Harriet made sure she met everyone. And Lolly made sure she looked to her heart's content.

Mickey Magraff, Lonsworth Crowley, the Dunn sons and sons-in-law, Matt, Calvin—even the sixteen-year-old Michael Lundgren.

It was like being in the company store without Nolan being there to do all the picking and choosing. Then Harriet Henderson said something that was almost like reading her mind.

"Harlan, it's a good thing I'm a married woman. With all this male handsomeness around, it would turn a girl's head having to pick and choose among them."

Pick and choose? Her father had picked for her the best that was available. Now the best didn't quite seem the highest quality that might have been available.

"Stop it!" she growled, cutting her giggle short. "You ain't being fair. Nolan is a fine-lookin' man and a good provider. I didn't see other women in the company town with as much as you, Lolly Fedderson! Shamed! That's what you should be? Pure downright shamed of yourself. When did you ever act like a wife? Like Mrs. Henderson, huh?"

There was a light rap at the door. It suddenly dawned on Lolly that she had been speaking aloud and now she was almost ashamed to answer the door. She had a horrible feeling it would be Matt Monroe, wishing to answer her question.

She opened it just a crack, lest she had to slam it quickly. She wouldn't know how to handle a man if he tried something funny.

"Dear, are you alone?" Harriet chirped. "Amalida has gone ashore to shop with her husband and I'm at loose ends."

"Alone," Lolly stammered and opened the door. Then the decision came quickly. "Mrs. Henderson, I, too, have an errand to run. Would you mind seeing after Kimberly for an hour?"

"Not at all. That will tie up my loose ends very nicely. I really should have had a dozen or two of my own. Not that we didn't try. The good Lord just has a strange way of sending down his storks, I assume. Now don't you just stop with one. When we come back from Alaska I want to look you up and find another one to cuddle. Here, baby, come to your Granny Harriet."

Lolly wasn't listening. She had to do this thing quickly or lose her nerve. She grabbed a shawl, pinched some color into her cheeks and waved a quick good-bye.

On deck she told Captain Hall the same errand story and then shyly asked if Matt were still on board. Hearing that he had left with Magraff and Crowley almost made her turn back. But when Captain Hall, who was finally going for help, offered to walk her along the wharf, her resolve returned.

Lolly had never had reason to leave the ship and the sights were astonishing. Supplies were stacked like barricades in front of the waterfront stores. Thousands of men milled around with nothing to do but wait. She didn't think there was enough gold in the whole world to give each one more than a pinch.

She mumbled something to Captain Hall when he left her and timidly approached a carriage.

Her eyes bugged and her jaw dropped. She had never seen a man with skin this black before.

"Sir—" she began.

"Ain't fur hire, miz."

Lolly fought for a bit of courage. "Can—can you tell me which might take me to a Clara Bennett, and how much it would be?"

Bo sat there, looking down at her and smiling.

She's sweet, he thought, real sweet—and maybe she would do for Clara, later on. Now he had to practically drive them off with sticks. Every train brought in a new load of old ones, used ones and unused ones that had their own dreams of gold. Clara could have had twenty houses going with what was available, but she was being picky and choosy with her customers and charging them more.

"It be a dollar by most hacks, miz, but ya'all won't do no good goin' thar. Miz Clar' done got all she can handle."

Lolly was deflated. She should have known that the woman couldn't loan money out forever. It didn't matter anyway. She didn't have the dollar to get there. Nolan had left her a quarter in case of an emergency. It was an emergency, but the quarter wasn't going to go very far.

She rounded behind the carriage to go back to the ship. At a nearby pier a two-stacked steamer was loading. More and more were leaving daily. The ships had cut their round-trip time to Skagway down to twelve days. Because it was twice that number of days through the Aleutian

Islands to St. Michael, most captains were now cancelling that trip. It was the first week of September and in that part of the country the Yukon was already starting to freeze along the banks.

"Mornin', Marse Calvin!"

Lolly heard the carriage creak as someone got in. Because of the high back she couldn't see the passenger.

"Good morning, Bo. My wife has found a woman who will wash and fix her hair. A lengthy process, I understand. I sent word by Matt Monroe for Clara to expect me."

"Yessuh," Bo chuckled. "Ah's been a waitin' yah."

The carriage rolled away and left Lolly standing there. It took her a moment to start fuming. Why should a man with all the money that Calvin Ramsey apparently had have need to borrow? It just wasn't fair. It just wasn't fair at all.

Without thinking, Lolly began to follow the carriage. Her pride would never have allowed her to call out and ask Calvin Ramsey to share the carriage with her. As she ran after the carriage, she thought of the things she would say to this Clara Bennett to convince her that she needed the money more desperately than the Ramseys.

"That needle-chinned pea-hen probably wears more than two thousand dollars worth of jewelry at a sitting. First diamond I ever see'd and she must have one for each finger. Ain't ever see'd her in the same dress twice, either. Mrs. Henderson says she's got a different pair of shoes for each of her dresses; and me with a single pair to my name. And didn't Mr. Henderson say that the man had paid the outlandish price of a thousand and forty dollars for a horse and mule?"

Her anger kept her feet churning as the carriage climbed Queen Anne Hill and then dropped down a deeply rutted lane that led to the lake.

On the downhill slope the carriage was able to get far ahead of her and then was lost to her sight behind the trees. She knew that if she stayed on the path she would find it sooner or later.

For Seattle, September was still a part of summer. The sun was almost directly overhead and Lolly had to take off her shawl. Her forehead dewed and tricklets of water tickled under her arm pits. She could hear water lapping on a beach, but the heavy underbrush hid the lake from view. Then she came out on a grassy field and the house sat before her. She had never seen anything so odd. Half of the three storey structure sat up on the beach and the other half sat on long stilts over the lake.

"Scare me to death to live on water like that," Lolly said to herself.

She didn't take into consideration that she *had* been living on water for nearly a month. Her mind was too preoccupied with the courage she had talked herself into during the walk. She marched right up on the wide porch and banged with the brass knocker.

"Oh, lawsy me," Bo moaned after he'd opened the door. "Didn't ah tell yah that—"

"I know what you told me," Lolly cut him short, pushing right on by him, "but if Calvin Ramsey from the *Brisbane* can see her to make a loan, then why can't I?"

Bo stood, his mouth working like a fish out of water, then he chuckled.

"Y'all walk out here, miz?"

"Every step of the way."

He shook his head. "Miz Clar' gotta see dis tah believe it. Let me hang dat shawl up fur yah and I'll take yah to her."

"I can wait for her to finish with Mr. Ramsey," she said quickly, starting to get a little frightened now that she was so close to her goal.

Bo chuckled again. "He ain't exactly wid her, miz . . . ah . . . what be da name?"

Their hands momentarily touched as he took away the shawl. It gave Lolly a surprise. "Fedderson . . ." she stammered, surprised that he felt just like any other human being. "Lolly . . . Mrs. Nolan Fedderson." She wasn't sure what would be the proper name to give.

Bo grinned. "Y'all just come along wid me, Miz Lolly. Ah just see'd Miz Clar's breakfast go in, so ah knows she be awake. Doz others gotta wait till she be dressed, anyhow. My name be Bo, miz. Can ah be fetchin' yah something to eat along wid Miz Clar'?"

"Frankly, I'm starved," Lolly said as if in a dream. For the first time she had been looking around the interior. She couldn't imagine what she saw.

She hadn't looked to the left before they started to climb the stairs to the second floor gallery. But those waiting in the music room had seen her.

"Was that. . . ?" Lonsworth gulped.

"I do believe it was," Matt chuckled, pretty sure why she was there.

"I'll be damned," Mickey intoned, half in and half out of his chair. "If she's here to apply for a position, the rates in this place will become the same as a passage fare."

Matt roared. "I didn't think you had even noticed her, Mickey."

"Noticed! I have to keep my hands off myself at night out of fear I'll have dreams about her. I wonder how in the hell she ever got mixed up with that husband of hers. Harriet Henderson says she's heard him beat her. I wish I could catch him at it. I'd let him know what Irish knuckles taste like. Oh, damn!"

"What's wrong now?"

"Her!" he wailed. "I've steeled my mind all morning not to think about coming here and what's upstairs. She's made it all come up again."

Crow burst into a fit of laughter. "She sure did make *it* come up. You're going to have to get a larger loan and then leave some of it behind."

Bo took Lolly along the gallery and then into the big hall on the second floor. Lolly hung back, staring. Her unaccustomed eyes were stricken with the splendor of the immense cutglass chandelier, tinkling like a stream over rocks, and the carpets into which her feet sank. The furniture held her breathless—richly sombre, polished to a high gloss. The curtains and drapes reminded her of Amalida Ramsey's dress fabrics.

"Y'all wait here a moment, Miz Lolly."

She was glad, for a new marvel had caught her eye. On the walls, row upon row, were paintings that made her feel she could walk right into them if she was small enough. Mill town houses didn't have paintings of any kind.

"I'm not believing this," she whispered to herself.

Bo pushed open the door to another room and waved her in.

The room was basked in sunlight. One wall was all French doors that looked out over the lake. Half were open and floated the sheer curtains inward like a dream. In front of those that were closed Clara sat at a glass and wrought iron breakfast set.

"Of course," Clara said, rising. "I remember you from having dinner on the *Brisbane,* Mrs. Fedderson. Come and sit down. Bo will bring you a bite here in a moment."

Recognition also lighted Lolly's face. The woman had sat with Captain Hall and Matt Monroe. At the time she had thought of how the woman made Amalida look overdressed. Now, in a chiffon and rabbit fur wrapper she looked like one of the angel pictures in the Bible.

"Bo tells me that you have come about a loan. I presume that it would be for your husband."

Lolly sat timidly, as though the cushioned wrought iron chair might break beneath her. "Except I don't know nothing about claims and percentages. I only heard those things from Mr. Monroe this morning."

"Then Matt sent you?"

"Oh, no! I came on my own. I walked."

"Walked?" she laughed. "You must have a very strong desire to get to the gold fields."

"Not for gold." Her voice was suddenly worried, as though it was going to be hard to explain. "My husband is a lumberjack. I figure they will need lumber and that should make him as worthy as those going for the gold. But he says I don't know my arse from a–"

Startlingly, the silver peal of Clara's laughter cut her short.

"You need not finish," she laughed. "I have yet to meet a man who would give a woman credit for having a brain. What you say is true, although it never dawned on me before. They will need lumber to build dwellings. I suppose we can work out something in lieu of a claim. Oh! I forgot . . . Lolly? May I call you Lolly? I am so used to calling my girls just by their first names."

"You have girls?"

"Yes, twelve of them."

"*Twelve*! You don't look old enough to have but one or two!"

Clara blinked. That would teach her to assume that Captain Hall would have made her profession well known to everyone on the ship. Then she basked under the genuine compliment. She knew it came from a very naive young woman, but that made it all the more special.

"Lolly, I was going to explain what a claim was, but let's just talk in terms of what you might need. How many are you?"

"Me, my husband Nolan, and our daughter. Kimberly is just over a year."

"That would be two thousand for passage. If Captain Hall tries to charge for the child I'll double the interest on what he owes me. Oh, there I go again, talking money and figures. Are you good at figures?"

"I ain't had no schoolin' at all."

"What about your husband?"

"Oh, Nolan," Lolly beamed. "He's smart. He can look at a standing tree and tell you how many board feet of lumber it will produce."

At that moment Bo returned and put a plate of scones in front of Lolly. They were still steaming hot and the melting butter oozed out of them.

"These be strawberry, Miz Lolly. I hope you like them."

Lolly took a big bite and the butter and strawberry jam dribbled down her chin. Bo politely unfolded her napkin and put it in her lap.

"My word," Lolly exalted. "These are the best biscuits and jam I've ever tasted."

Clara sat back with pure envy. How marvelous, she thought, to be able to bring everything back down to its simplest form. The crepes she was eating were, after all, just pancakes. This was one of the most refreshing encounters she had experienced in years. She tried to recall which of the men in the dining room might have been Lolly's husband. She had looked them all over from a professional point of view.

"I don't believe I met your husband."

"Oh, no, he works in Everett and only comes down on weekends. He don't know nothing about this yet. I don't even know if I'm doing the right thing, but it seemed right. I don't make much sense, do I?"

Clara stared at her. Then she shook her head at her own thought. Her whole life had been one of not knowing if she was doing the right thing, but doing it because it seemed the right thing.

"A woman has to go by her own instincts sometimes. Do you want to discuss it with your husband and then bring him back to discuss the loan?"

"No!" Lolly said firmly. "This is one time I'll just have to make him see that I did right."

"Well," Clara sighed, "it's your decision, though I would still like to have his signature on the papers before you depart."

"Oh, that's no problem. He'll be home tomorrow."

Clara shrugged. This was hardly the way she normally did business. "So, how much will you need other than the passage?"

"I reckon the same as the others," Lolly said.

Clara laughed. "The others are still downstairs waiting and I haven't heard their requests." Then she sobered. "But Lolly, I am a smart businesswoman. I have checked in town with people like Cooper & Levy to determine the costs and needs of an average prospector. Oh, some go first class, of course, but a good grubstake to get a man through the winter is running close to a thousand dollars. I would have to figure that it would run your husband near the same. See that metal box on the table by my bed? Bring it to me. I'll make out the papers later and bring them to the ship to explain to your husband and get his signature. Knowing Foster Hall, you'd best pay him quickly before he sells your cabin right out from underneath you."

When Clara finished counting from the box, she took an unused linen napkin and spread it on the breakfast table.

"Here is four thousand dollars in $100 pieces, Lolly. I am going to wrap twenty of them in this corner of the napkin. That is all you will give Captain Hall, and don't let him talk you into giving him more. Now, the other twenty I will knot in the other corner. You show those to your husband when you start to explain and I am sure it will make it go quite easy."

Lolly was still staring into the open box. She had never seen so much money.

"How'd you make all of that?" she asked innocently.

"Lolly, do you know what a prostitute is?"

"No, ma'am."

Clara had thought not. "Well, dear, it is the oldest profession in the world. Now, go down and tell Bo to take you back to the ship."

"Oh, I can walk back," Lolly said brightly. "I might even float back."

"And end up floating in the bay," Clara said sternly. "That town is filled with riff-raff that would hear those coins rubbing together a block away. Do as I say, and also tell Bo to send Matt right up."

Clara laughed to herselt as Lolly left. Making Matt Monroe the guardian angel over that little beauty was a bigger gamble than the money itself, but for once she would have to rely upon his being a gentleman.

Foster Hall had come back with three Chinese boys, as he thought he might, and a deposit from four miners for the Fedderson cabin. With such luck—and a mite of training for the Chinese, who had never seen anything more mechanical than a flat iron—he was sure they could leave by Sunday morning. He even considered asking Henry Boise to get Father Durand to come down and give them a blessing. Then he reconsidered. With the luck he had been having, who needed the holy water sprinkled around?

"You're out of your mind!"

He spun about. Phoebe was coming at him with a meat cleaver in one hand, dragging the Chinese boy along by his braided cue in the other. The Chinese boy shook as though he thought the cleaver was meant for him. In their wake Laura Lee Boise fluttered nervously.

"He doesn't speak English, father!" Phoebe stormed. "He doesn't even speak pidgin!"

Amalida Ramsey swept down on him from the other side.

"Captain!" she demanded shrilly, "Have you seen my husband? He is nowhere to be found on this vessel!"

Just then Lolly sprang out of the carriage and ran up the gangway merrily shouting, "Captain! Captain! I have our passage! I have the two thousand!"

Catastrophe! The word entered his mind unbidden. He turned damn near chalk white—as Laura Lee would later explain it to her father. He said nothing as Phoebe shouted; Amalida shouted; and Lolly shouted, plopping right down on the deck at his feet, undoing the knotted napkin and trying to force the coins up at him.

"Be still!" he bellowed.

They did so, and he poised, like a captain about to put down a dangerous mutiny.

"Didn't 'spec you to be staying," he said gruffly, handling the last problem presented first. "Taken a deposit on your cabin already."

"No!" Lolly croaked. Her voice was strangling.

There was a silence on the deck. It went on and on—broken by the improbable.

"Mrs. Fedderson," Amalida snapped, completely oblivious to the young woman's own problem, "did you see my husband while you were ashore?"

"Yes," she answered dully. "I saw him."

"Really!" Phoebe hissed, smouldering over the insensitivity of both her father and Mrs. Ramsey, the Chinese problem momentarily moved to the back burner.

But Amalida was not to be stopped. She bent over and poked her chin right at Lolly.

"Where did you see him? How long ago? Where was he going?"

Lolly had no reason to lie. "I saw him get into a carriage and I followed him. He went to borrow money from Clara Bennett, the same as me."

"*Borrrrrow*?" Amalida was incredulous. Then she laughed snidely. "He has no need to borrow. He must have been on a buying venture. What is Mrs. Bennett's sort of profession?"

Hall's chalk white face flushed pink. Phoebe rolled her eyes heavenward, having known that the question was going to be asked sooner or later—even though she wasn't supposed to know the answer.

Lolly shrugged. "I don't know, but she said it was the oldest profession in the world."

Amalida rose to a straight position as though a slow crane had pulled her torso backward. Her hat had gone askew in bending down, but she didn't notice. In New Orleans her father had tried to tell her of this little quirk of her husband's. She had not listened. Her father had lied too many times to her, and she refused to believe him. She had trusted her husband over her father. But at least all of that had been conducted in private. This was being aired in public, and it was quite humiliating. With a "*humph*" she rose stiffly and marched off.

Laura Lee started to giggle. The source of the giggle mortified her, but she couldn't help herself. One didn't live twenty years in New Orleans and not learn something about the "oldest profession." But her giggle was really over the reaction of the Chinese boy. He had come to life over the mention of Clara Bennett. He had been smirking and grinning ever since.

"You've understood every word said, haven't you?" she asked him.

"Understand Missy Clara," he grinned. "Work her three months."

"Why, you yellow heathen," Phoebe growled, threatening him with the cleaver for sure now. "Why couldn't you understand me earlier?"

"Understand," he shrugged. "No like ship. My brother like ship."

"Then why didn't your father send your brother?" Laura Lee asked curiously.

"Many brothers, and father old and confused. I no speak when he send me."

"My God!" Phoebe snorted, hitting her forehead with the flat of the cleaver. "Why didn't you just explain to your father in the first place?"

"Disrespectful to correct elder."

"Right! Right!" Foster Hall bubbled. "I will just take the lad along home and make the swap. Good-bye, now . . ."

"Wait just a minute," Phoebe warned darkly. "I'm not bound by any ancient credo that says I have to be respectful to my elder when he's being a greedy old fool. What are you going to do about the Feddersons?"

"Now, pet," he simpered. "I already have the gentlemen's deposit money on their cabin." He gulped. "There is no way I can wiggle out of–"

"Father," Phoebe said. That was all. Just that one word, flat, expressionless, soft-spoken. But it was like Moses warning his people not to worship the idol Baal.

"Lord God, Phoebe!" he spluttered. "You needn't take on so about it. Who would have thought they would want to go? Who would have thought Clara would lend them the money to go? I would give up my cabin . . . but my charts and desk and . . ."

"All right," Phoebe said wearily. There was no use to talk about it, her father would come up with a million excuses. It had always been that way. His excuses, her giving in and then the silence between them. A small silence that would become a gulf and then a chasm that the subject could never jump across again.

"Phoebe," Laura Lee said quietly. "My father and I each have separate cabins. I wouldn't mind sharing a cabin with you if it would help the situation."

"Remarkable suggestion!" Foster nearly screamed with glee. "I will even give your father a refund because of it. Come lad, let's see to your problem."

"Father," Phoebe said again. This time she did not hide the contempt in her voice.

"Well, what is it this time?" he said gruffly.

"Aren't you forgetting Mrs. Fedderson?"

"Must I do *everything*?" he flared. "You see to it and bear in mind that it is *three* passages!"

Lolly was still struggling to break through the mood that gripped her. She had heard only the last, but as she rose from the deck her face broke into a picture of malicious glee.

"No! Two passages! Clara Bennett said that if you tried to charge me for little Kimberly then she would double the interest on the money you owe her."

Foster Hall shook his head slowly. What was happen- to the world? What had happened to those good old days when women knew their place and stayed in it? He had even heard tell that they had let Wyoming into the union, even though they were going to let women vote.

"Take care of things, son," he said sadly and went down the gangplank.

"Who is he talking to?" Laura Lee asked, puzzled.

"Me," Phoebe scoffed. "Every time he starts feeling sorry for himself because I wasn't born a boy, he calls me that."

"Doesn't it bother you?"

"Hurt like hell when I was young. That's why I ate so much. If I was big enough, I thought, he couldn't help but see me and pay attention to me."

Laura Lee chuckled. "I was the opposite. I wanted to be small so the nuns couldn't see me and punish me. Now I don't care if I get fat."

"You'll care," Phoebe said dubiously, "when you start taking an interest in boys. Slim girls have a better chance to pick and choose than old fat hogs. Come on, Mrs. Fed-derson. I'll take you down to my father's cabin for your money."

Pick and choose? That was just the way Lolly's day had started. Now she just prayed she could pick and choose the right words to use when Nolan returned.

4

LOLLY LAY in her berth, bent double with pure weariness. She was ashamed that she could hear so much from the next cabin. Just as ashamed that the Ramseys might have heard an earful from her cabin. But this was different. When Nolan ranted and raved and beat her, she got quieter.

Calvin and Amalida seemed prone on topping each other with shrillness. The accusations were like none Lolly had ever heard before and a lot of the words she didn't fully understand. There were a lot of things she knew she should not be hearing and tried to put them out of her mind. Their words frightened her. Their threats frightened her even more. She prayed that someone would stop them before they killed each other. She tried to think who had the cabin on the other side of them, but couldn't recall.

Then it was deadly silent, and the stillness frightened her even more. She was sure that they had killed each other. The only dead person she was aware of having ever seen was her father in his coffin. They had dressed him in a suit. She had never seen him wear a suit. It didn't look natural.

The cabin door creaked open and she sat bolt upright with a stifled cry.

"Hush!" the voice was a hoarse whisper, edged with pain.

"Nolan?" she got out, tentatively.

"Who the hell else?" he moaned. "Where the hell is the damn lamp in this cabin?"

Lolly was off the bed at once. She got the lamp lit. He slumped into a chair beneath it and she gasped. She could see the crisscrossing knife wounds on his forehead and right cheek. She had seen him this way before, after brawls at the company tavern. After the first time she had learned not to ask questions about how it had happened.

"The bastards!" Nolan grated. "Said my trees were worthless and refused to pay me. I told 'em I'd take my pay outta their hide if I had to. There were three of them, Lolly. I think I killed one."

"I see," she whispered. "Let me get some water for your wounds."

"You *see*?" he said with a flash of tired mockery. "You don't see shit! I stole a horse to get away. I don't know if they followed to arrest me or not."

"I don't care!" she raged. "Just keep your voice down. These walls are paper thin."

"Don't you dare raise your voice to me, woman!" he snarled. "Get dressed! We've got to find a better place to hide."

"Please, hush," she said gently. "This is the best place . . . really. The boat is leaving . . . maybe even tomorrow."

"Lot of good that does us," he sneered.

Lolly took the napkin out from under the mattress and loosened the corner. She came and held it under his nose.

"Where'n the hell you get that?" he sputtered.

"Borrowed it from Clara Bennett."

"Who in the hell is she?"

"Lady friend of Captain Hall. She's loaning money to others to go with the ship. Oh, Nolan, she's got the most beautiful house I've ever laid my eyes on."

"Come on, Lolly," he frowned. "Ain't nobody just loan out money for nothing. What's the catch? What's her business?"

Lolly fought for the right words. It wasn't happening the way it was supposed to. She had planned on softening him up with a few loving kisses first before slowly explaining to Nolan about the money.

"Well, she's coming to the ship to explain and have you sign the papers . . . and . . . as for what she does, I don't know, except she said it was the oldest profession in the world. Amalida seemed shocked by it and Laura Lee thought it was funny."

Nolan leaned forward, a scowl on his battered face.

"You stupid little bitch!" he roared. "She's a whore! What did you have to do or promise to do?"

"Nothing," she whimpered.

"Don't give me that crap! *Jesus*! You are dumb! How much did you get?"

"Four thousand," Lolly sobbed.

"Goddamned old whore! It would take you a lifetime to put out that much poon-tang. Good damn thing she doesn't know how lousy you are at it. Well, we won't be around for her to find out. Four thousand will hide us out for quite awhile."

"Ain't got it all," she whispered, on a sob. "Paid two for our passage."

"God damn, you are dumb!" he roared. "Why didn't you wait for me to make a decision like that?"

There was a loud banging through the wall. "Shut up in there," came Amalida's muffled shout. "Can't you let a body sleep?"

Lolly had taken just about enough abuse from everybody. She jumped right to the wall and pounded back.

"You shut up in there, squint eyes! You ain't going to get anymore sleep now than you let me get earlier!"

All she heard was the muffled roar of Calvin's laughter.

"What was that all about?"

She turned. Nolan sat there, staring at her. When she spoke, her voice was very quiet.

"I'll tell you later. Decision? I ain't never had to make one before this, Nolan, and from what I see'd today, it seems to me I ain't missed much in not making any. Didn't fully 'spect you back till tomorrow and he was selling the cabin space today. I got the money and even then almost didn't get the cabin. I didn't know if you wanted to go, but I figured they needed lumber to build. She was grub . . . grubstaking prospectors and I talked her into the same. That's all."

Nolan's anger died. He had always had a real admiration for pure guts. And what Lolly had done had taken a whole heap of them.

"All right, little wife," he said. "You win. All I want to know is, what are we going to do?"

"Nothing," she said simply. "Talk to her about the papers and shop for our supplies. They ain't gonna be lookin' too hard for you around here, Nolan."

"How you figure that?"

"Every morning we hear tell of three or four who have been murdered during the night. Ain't heard tell of anyone being arrested for those yet."

"Sure is a lot different world than on the MacKenzie, ain't it, Lolly."

"Like the good and the bad have to walk side by side, whether they like it or not." She paused. "Nolan, answer me something."

"Sure."

"What is a whore?"

Nolan roared with mirth. "Come on, I'll tell you in bed!"

* * *

They stood out from Elliott Bay on the Sunday morning, with Captain Hall in an absolutely vile mood. The miners had at first refused to accept back their deposits and demanded a private cabin each. Foster then denied them passage whatsoever on his vessel, and the dock around the *Brisbane* was a near riot scene throughout Saturday.

Nolan benefitted from the confusion. He was able to slip off the boat early, purchase his supplies and have them delivered by a dory to the starboard side of the vessel.

When Clara came, Bo nearly capsized the rowboat several times before he had her safely alongside. To his amazement, Nolan was impressed with the woman. She had a good business head, and she was a beautiful woman as well. The only whores he had ever seen before were the "one-nighters" the bachelor lumberjacks would sneak into the mill town. Clara had made sure that he would be impressed with her business sense. She "borrowed" information from a lumber client to make sure the Fedderson contract was fair to both parties.

Because of the screaming and shouting from the pier everyone stayed well within their cabins and thus Amalida was not even aware that Clara had come aboard and departed.

They left port at two o'clock in the afternoon, so that Hall could establish the *Brisbane's* position by chronometer, escaping the adverse influence of the *Juan de Fuca* current upon his dead reckoning. They crawled along, the engineer unable to keep the engine steady, with Matt and Crow finally having to take over the training in that department.

Phoebe had near the same problem in the galley—the new Chinese boy spoke little more English than the last—and Laura Lee stayed to help. By Sunday supper they had few to cook for anyhow. The *Brisbane* was never intended for ocean use and the waves made it reel and pitch like a drunken sailor. Only Clampett Dunn escaped seasickness of his clan. Food was sent to the cabin of the hermit-like Jethro Calhoun, whom only Captain Hall had seen to date; he bodily tossed the Chinese boy, tray and all, back into the passageway.

Amalida's illness was not seasickness, but the humiliation she felt in her mind. Never again did she want to set eyes on Lolly Fedderson.

In their cabin, Kimberly and Nolan suffered the most. Lolly played nurse, just as Mia Lundgren had to do for her three men.

Henry Boise and the Hendersons never missed a meal.

Seven days later, they were still a long distance from Saint Michael, and ploughing into the teeth of a northern gale fiercer than any Captain Hall had seen in years. As a result, instead of a steady forward progress they were slowly being inched backward. Hall turned the wheel over to Phoebe and went to the engine room for a conference.

"Cap'n, this is foolish," Crow said frankly. "My vote is to get out of the storm and try it again when it blows over."

Hall looked at Monroe.

"Well, Matt?" he said.

"Nope," Matt drawled. "Boilers would still have to stay up for that and she's a coal burner. Best we do what the other ships are doing and head into Skagway. I'm only going by this map I bought in the supply store, but if those were the Queen Charlotte Islands we passed yesterday, then the Chatham Strait should be soon. It's inland waters then to Skagway and shouldn't be near as rough."

"Reckon that settles it," Hall said. "Matt, how long do you think the boilers would take it, if we tied down the safety valves to give us every pound of thrust?"

"Damned if I know how they've stood up this long.

They haven't been pounded this long or hard since they were new, I would venture."

"Well, forget it. It was only a thought."

Foster Hall had been having many thoughts—about all he had forgotten. Ploughing the same course back and forth in inland waters was a great deal different than challenging the open sea. His charts had not been updated in twenty years and they had no depth markings for either the straits or the 250-mile waterway to the Indian fishing village. He had not consulted other captains who had made the run because he wanted to keep his departure secret.

Arrogantly, he had not asked to see what manner of map Matt had purchased, and Matt never guessed that his charts were obsolete.

Correctly, Captain Hall entered the Chatham Strait between Baronof Island and the mainland. The gale did let up, but was replaced by an icy, driving rain that cut visibility to little more than the prow of the ship. He employed the fog horn to echo back from the island. When the echos kept coming back he mistook Chichagof Island to be a part of Baronof. He kept following the echo soundings without realizing it was taking him around the northern end of the island and back out into the Gulf of Alaska.

He heard the sickening sound of the horn blast drifting off into nothingness. They should have had land on either side in this 100-mile-long channel to Skagway. Keeping it to himself, Hall continued to move the horn on its turntable, degree by degree, and listened.

When the horn was back due starboard he got a faint returned echo. He held his silence. He refused to let Phoebe take over the wheel and stood the post throughout the night, tacking inward by degrees to increase the echo.

By morning the horn was needed to cut through real fog and not sleety rain. Again, wisdom that he had learned years before did not come back to aid him. They were back in the Japanese current.

His stomach began to crawl when he realized they had exceeded the 100 miles that should have brought them to Skagway. He looked aft and saw that the stacks were pouring out full heads of clouds. They were losing steam right along with the smoke.

Hall picked up the speaking tube.

"Half speed, Matt," he said. His voice, speaking, was very quiet, almost serene. He didn't have the foggiest notion where he was.

No one in the engine room thought to question him. If they had, they would have been astonished. They were quite proud that the old boilers had given them ten knots throughout the night and figured they were starting to slow down for the approach to Skagway. Matt, from talking with the crew members who had been there, knew that it was a shallow port and that the larger vessels had to anchor a good quarter to a half mile offshore.

Within an hour the fog began to burn off and a barren rocky shoreline peek through. Beyond a deep inlet, he saw fingers of smoke rising.

"Skagway," Hall said solemnly. "Phoebe, you are free to inform the passengers that they may prepare to debark."

He blew into the speaking tube. "Quarter speed, Matt."

"Cap'n, Sir," Matt wheezed back. "Is it Skagway?"

"Yep, it is," he said dryly.

He heard Lonsworth Crowley let out a spine-chilling war-whoop.

It didn't help his nerves, which were nearly shattered. It was a fair-sized village, he could now see. It would do. He just wanted these people off his vessel and a return home as quickly as possible. Only a damn fool would make this run and he wasn't going to be a damn fool ever again.

* * *

They were like children who had stayed home from school sick. As soon as the clock announced that school was over they were well enough to frolic and play. They didn't mind the tenth of a mile they had to row their supplies and equipment ashore. Those who had been strangers became friends. The Dunn clan, singing at the top of their rich voices, would row for anyone. The quicker they were all ashore, the quicker they could organize for the next leg of the journey.

In their excitement they didn't notice that the people of the village stood about their domed huts of interlaced twigs in a state of confused awe. They had too much to do to notice. The supplies grew into a stack that began to resemble a Seattle street. The horses and mules had to be hooded to get them into the boats and ashore.

"Strange," Amalida said while waiting for her turn to go ashore. "Where are all the men who preceded us?"

She had directed the question to no one in particular, but Henry Boise was the nearest at hand.

"I would venture they're all inland, Mrs. Ramsey. The Yukon, as I recall from hearing, is about fifty miles from Skagway."

"Venture?" she said, a little airily. "I was under the impression that this had once been your home."

"To be sure, ma'am," he chuckled, "but it is a vast home. I might as well still be in Seattle as Skagway. St. Michael's would have been a lot closer to home."

"Then I would suggest you return and start over."

"Hardly. As a young man I thought nothing of going a thousand miles by dog sled. However—"

He didn't finish the sentence. A man brushed by them with a heavy pack on his back and headed for the rope ladder. Amalida grasped Henry's arm in such a steel grip that it hurt.

"Who was that man?" she demanded.

Henry turned to look. He caught only a glimpse of the

man's face as he went over the side and down into the long boat.

"Ah, I do believe that is the silent Mr. Calhoun. For one who has been so ill he seems most fit."

"Will they take us soon? I must see my husband."

Henry gently removed her hand and looked ashore again. "I certainly hope that they do. I'm growing a little curious."

Amalida was sick with fright. Even in the stocking cap, and with new growth of beard and heavy winter clothing, she was sure this Mr. Calhoun was the same man who had been watching them in the hotel.

She had determined that morning to make Calvin treat her like a lady, even to carrying her ashore. It all went out the window. She climbed the rope ladder down to the long boat and equally waded ashore, regardless of her high button shoes and velvet skirt. As she pulled Calvin aside for a whispered conference, Henry waddled back toward the village, his face a mask of deep concern.

After checking through the mounds to make sure all the bakery equipment had been off-loaded, Harriet Henderson looked up and started.

"I do declare," she gushed, going to the man who was checking the name on almost each and every crate and oil-skin wrapped bundle. "Are you not the young man from New Orleans that we met at the hotel?"

Jethro Calhoun stared at her blankly. "Hail from Georgia, ma'am, and ain't ever been in a hotel in my life."

Harriet shrugged. No, the accent was too harsh and this man had a bright red beard. "I guess my eyesight ain't what it used to be," she said. "I'm Harriet Henderson."

"Jethro Calhoun, ma'am."

"Have you met the others?"

"Ain't a mixer, ma'am. First time from home and it's mighty strange."

"Well, if you need anything you just see Mr. Henderson and me."

"Thankey, ma'am. I'll be keeping that in mind."

Jethro Calhoun smiled to himself. He felt a lot better about his disguise than when she first thought she recognized him. He was now thankful that he'd bought the extra henna dye for the growing beard. Then he smiled at Harriet's retreating back. The woman certainly wasn't paying too much attention to her "niece and nephew"—and they seemed a little out of sorts at the moment.

On the ship, making sure that he had gotten the cabin next to them, he had almost come to the conclusion that they could not possibly be the Raymond and Ann Forbes that he had been trying to track down for over six months. This woman, Amalida Ramsey, was without a doubt the biggest bitch he had ever run across, but Ann Forbes was known to be quiet and shy. If Amalida had been his wife he would have drowned her back in Elliott Bay.

When the announcement was made that the *Brisbane* was going to sail, he was about ready to throw in the towel. The Ramseys just didn't fit the descriptions given him by the Algiers Commercial Trust Company.

Had he not been passing Captain Hall's door as Calvin Ramsey was paying his fare he would have departed. His hands grew damp in seeing what could have been Calvin's first mistake. He paid Hall with four $500 gold pieces.

His curiosity kindled again, Jethro then checked the hold for the Ramseys' supplies. Steamer trunks only and amazingly unlocked. But only clothing, no more gold—and no prospecting equipment or supplies.

His suspicious mind immediately gave that great import. After paying for his own passage, he had gone to add to his own disguise—supplies and proper clothing—and to await the next development.

He was stunned how little time he had to wait. The

fight upon Calvin's return from the brothel was ear-opening. As a man, he could not blame Calvin for seeking pleasure away from his impossible woman. As a bank detective he had to thank Amalida's—or Ann's—jealous mouth for opening the coffer dams, if not the flood gates.

It was evidence, but still not proof. These were only threads, but whole cloth could be woven from mere threads—a whole cloth worth $50,000 in gold.

He looked at their off-loaded steamer trunks again. They held no gold, at least not that he'd been able to find, but given the chance he would search them again. He looked over at the nervous couple again. Given the chance, he would love to have searched them.

Actually, if they were the couple he suspected, he thought them quite stupid and amateurish.

The suicide of Ann Forbes' father had rocked Algiers and New Orleans. He and Amos Stillman had been hailed as the commercial banking rock that would bring the river back after the War between the States.

Amos Stillman could not believe his old friend was capable of taking his own life. He was further shocked to learn that Ann had no money to bury her father. Amos knew that the son-in-law had no money, but it was impossible that. . . . The auditor's report brought forth the unbelievable truth and scandal. The man was not only a pauper, but had embezzled $50,000.

Ann Forbes had gone into seclusion, refusing to even attend her father's funeral. Heartlessly, Raymond Forbes was treated by the other bank employees as though he had been an accomplice with his father-in-law.

They might have weathered the storm, but Amos Stillman still could not believe. He had known his partner to be a spendthrift—Ann being a classic example of his never having spent money upon himself or his family. He had even made sure that Ann had married a man of the same ilk—colorless and bland. He also knew that Raymond Forbes would never amount to anything after the death of his father-in-law. The man didn't have an original idea in his head.

After three months of Ann refusing to see him, Amos Stillman began to worry. He made an unexpected call on the New Orleans house, when he was sure that Raymond would be across the river at the bank in Algiers, and found it empty and servantless. From the neighbors he learned that Ann Forbes had not been seen since the day she refused to go to her father's funeral.

Back in Algiers, Raymond Forbes broke down. It had all been just too much for his wife. She had broken down and he had quietly sent her to stay with an aunt in Mobile. The poor woman could not believe her father had squandered away such a fortune.

Amos Stillman was sly. He never once asked Raymond Forbes where he was staying with the house all closed down. He had him followed that night on the packet boat back to New Orleans and into the French Quarter.

In his hand-me-down suit Raymond Forbes dined elegantly, sipped on French champagne and was registered at the fashionable—and expensive—*Lyonais Place.*

Amos Stillman had never believed in the suicide, and now believed it had been murder—double murder. Personally, he spent the night going over the books again, and found that entry after entry had been made in a hand he was not familiar with. But the startling discovery was the manner in which his partner's personal account had been slowly transferred to another account—the very account that had been swindled for the majority of the missing money. A man did not swindle from himself and then commit suicide over it.

Here Amos Stillman made an error. He waited to confront Raymond Forbes with the facts the next day. The bank clerk never showed up.

That began Jethro Calhoun's six months search. At first just for Raymond Forbes, until he learned that, in fact,

Ann Forbes *had* spent time with an aunt in Mobile before leaving with her husband.

Had Ann Forbes attended her father's funeral and continued to see Amos Stillman, in the opinion of Jethro Calhoun, he never would have been on the case, because they never would have been suspected.

But then, he also considered, did one ever attend the funeral of one they had murdered?

"Stop him! Stop him!" Henry Boise screamed, waddling back as fast as his 220 pounds could carry him. "Fire off a gun! Turn him about! These people only speak a Yakutat tongue!"

"What difference does that make?" Clampett Dunn called back.

"Difference?" he roared, wheezing. "Great jumping balls o'fire! That's the Gulf of Alaska he is steaming back out into. These are fisherfolk with only kayaks and no dog sleds. He has left us with our face to water and our backs to that!" He turned and pointed with a shaking finger.

The ground fog had all burned away. In their excitement no one had really done much looking around. The distance was misleading. The lofty snow-capped peak seemed cone-shaped and near at hand. It was majestic in its white mantle. It hardly seemed to be over 18,000 feet above sea level, and they were not aware that the gentle-looking slope on its flank was a fifty-mile-long glacier that had been there since the beginning of time.

"It's impenetrable!" Calvin gasped.

Everyone started to jabber at once, although nothing was being said.

"Wait a minute!" Matt yelled.

They paid him no mind. Like any group of people anywhere, each had something to say, whether it was logical or not.

He jumped up on a mound of supplies, drew a pistol

from the holster he had strapped about his waist and fired it in the air. It echoed back through the ravines and deep canyons. Because they thought he was trying to signal the *Brisbane*, they turned toward the beach.

"He will not be turning back," Matt said, spacing the words out in deadly quiet. "We have got to turn to our own resources. If I read my map right, it's just a little over a hundred miles around that mountain and down into Skagway. I ain't excusing Captain Hall. He came in on the wrong side during the fog. There's no use screaming at him, he can't hear you. Boise, what's the story with these people?"

"Like I said, they're just fisherfolk with native canoes. Room for just one or two of the Yakutats and no cargo. So we can forget the canoes. I'll be frankly honest. They've not seen any of our race since the Russians stopped buying fish from them in '67. Ships bound for St. Michaels, which we all know have become rare indeed, would be on a course far out into the North Pacific at this point. Fishing trawlers might come close to shore, but not until spring."

"For God's sake," Freeman Fairchild exploded. "You ain't suggesting we stay here until spring, are you?"

"That wasn't his point," Matt said quickly. "He was just explaining our choices."

"Which are none!" Stacey Webb sneered. Quite a few people were startled to hear a member of the Clampett Dunn clan speak out.

The old man shot his son-in-law a wicked glare, his face purpling with fury.

"Mr. Monroe," he barked, through his rage. "I thankee for that point. Stacey speaks from youth, being the husband of my youngest gal. I think it is time we all spoke from our experiences."

"Sir?" Matt said, not quite understanding.

"As you say, it seems that to get back on track, we

must get around that mountain. It's the highest I have ever seen, I can tell you. But mountain treks I have made before. Anyone else?"

"Plenty of times," Crow boasted.

For the moment everyone else remained silent. Matt knew his various experiences would come off sounding like Crow, and felt Mickey felt near the same.

"I am a year here," Lazlo Lundgren said slowly, "but know snow travel in Sweden."

"You work snow as well as timber in logging," Nolan Fedderson added.

"Good," Dunn said, with a slight smile. "We have not said, but we are Mormon. Except for the younger ones, we have experienced snow in the crossing of the Rockies. We offer what we can."

As one they swung their gaze back up to Matt's face. Ht had been the first to speak. He had been the one who had repaired the engine. He was being elected leader by silent vote.

"I thank you, Mr. Dunn," Matt said. "Now, I suggest we pitch some tents and get some fires going for supper. Afterwards, I'd like to have a meeting to discuss our best course of action for tomorrow."

Activity proved to be a boon to forgetting, although preplanning proved to have been a hodge-podge arrangement. The past was too much in their lives. It was as though the majority had expected to arrive at a nice cozy bungalow, cook fire roaring in an iron range and a pantry well stocked.

Henry and Laura Lee Boise had thought to go right from the ship to the St. Michael hostel. Calvin and Amalida Ramsey just hadn't thought. Luckily, the Henderson's tent for their bakery was large enough to house extras.

But those selfsame people were not the only ones who had become so conditioned to Phoebe's cooking that they had not thought of food.

In the thousand pounds of supplies Nolan Fedderson had purchased he had only a sack of flour, a square of hard-salt, a quarter barrel of molasses, fifty pounds of pinto beans and a sack of corn meal.

In the wicker baskets of Mia Lundgren were the items she felt she would not be able to get in her new home: a hundred-pound sack of coffee beans, a ten-pound tin of tea, various spices, three kinds of sugar, dried fruits and nuts, and jars and jars of preserves wrapped in woven straw.

Hazel Fairchild had just automatically thought she could shop daily as she had done in Chicago.

Harriet and Harlan Henderson could bake up a storm and little more.

The Dunn clan was well prepared with two-man tents, cooking gear and basic pioneer staples.

After the tents had been put up, the men got together to take stock of the situation.

"Eight horses and four mules."

"What about Lundgren's dogs?"

"What good are dogs without a sled?"

"Thought I could buy one here. Besides, what good are eight saddle horses?"

Nothing had really been asked as a direct question, but kind of a rambling wonderment.

"Come on, let's get back to basics," Matt said. "Mr. Dunn and I asked each of you to look into these things before we met. Now, we are thirty-two—counting Nolan's child. Six women and twenty-five men and boys. Herschel Dunn figures we have close to 30,000 pounds of supplies on the beach. Does that include the iron parts for the Henderson bake oven, Herschel?"

"Yep!"

Matt waited for the forty-year-old eldest son of Clampett Dunn to go on. It was the only word he had been able to get out of him.

"How do you figure we can haul it?" Matt prompted.

"Can't take the saddles," Herschel said dryly, as though that were the full answer.

"Need 'em as pack animals," thirty-six-year-old Jerome Dunn took up for his brother. "Got packs for the four mules. Need packs for the horses."

"Made 'em 'fore," thirty-four-year-old Isaac took up as though it had been rehearsed.

"What about travois carriers?" Crow suggested.

Matt started to shush him and stopped. "Hey, that's a damn good idea. They could probably take double the load. What made you think of that, Crow?"

He hooted with laughter. "In case you haven't noticed lately, I'm an Indian."

"Might we please go on!"

Matt winked at Crow. They had been put in their place by no less than Elder Jeffrey Robb. The prune-faced man was not only an Elder of the church, but had married the eldest of Clampett's daughters and therefore felt he was the eldest spokesman for all the varied and sundry sons-in-law. He really was, in Matt's opinion, holier-than-thou. In lesser degrees, but still insufferable, according to the daughter they had married, came Frank Watson, Sam Daws, Guy Browning, Jim Mapps, and Stacey Webb.

Matt was learning to like the Dunn boys, including the devilish Cornell and sensitive Hampton. They were strange and quiet, yes, but good, solid men all. He was sorry Jeff Robb had ever opened his mouth. The man had been a pain in the butt ever since, with five echoes to everything he said.

"We can get on, Mr. Robb, if you have a backpack report for us."

"That is simple. We twelve have our own backpacks and have long ago conditioned ourselves to carrying the load we have brought along."

"Did you check on other backpacks?"

Jeff Robb stared at him, soberly, solemnly. "I didn't think it was my concern," he said.

"We're all in this together," Matt said.

Robb's face reddened. "Of course. I'll check on them."

"I've checked Lazlo's dogs," Henry said. "He's made a fine purchase. Made sleds as a young man up here. If we divide the dogs we can build two small sleds. I'm sure the Yakutats will help on that score."

"Why should a heathen people help you?" Frank Watson asked.

"Frank!" Clampett Dunn growled at the young clan member.

"It's quite all right, Mr. Dunn," Henry smiled. "The answer is quite simple. I shan't know until I ask them in a Christian way."

Six faces pruned as one, but Clampett Dunn's stern expression held them silent.

Then, to Matt's great surprise he noticed hidden smiles from the other Dunn men. It was a split clan. For the survival of everyone it might be to his advantage to learn how wide was the chasm.

Quickly he went into the materials they would need, how long it would take, and when they should leave.

It felt good. He was really taking command of the situation, and it really felt good.

It was four instead of two days before the line stretched out. Because they had made such an issue over their ability, Matt let Jeff Robb and his five take the lead to scout and break the trail.

Next came the sleds and yelping dogs. They were the pride and joy of Henry Boise, and a wonderment to the Yakutats. Until they climbed higher the ground was frozen but snowless. The sled idea was almost abandoned until Harriet had an inspiration. Packed in their equipment were the wheels for two tea carts that she had brought to use in her bakery. The cart axles were narrower than the sleds, so frames were built and the sleds placed upon them. Sleds gliding along without snow?

Even Henry Boise chuckled over it as he guided one team and taught Laura Lee how to handle the other. Lolly Fedderson trotted along beside the sleds, with Kimberly in a papoose carrier on one of them.

Then came Clampett Dunn and two of his sons, checking the terrain for the horses and mules.

Neither group of animals took well to their packs or to the long Indian travois poles dragging behind them. But the packs and the woven beds slung between the poles were so heavily laden with cargo that the animals had no choice but to move forward or fall in their tracks.

Behind them were the rest of the women and men, each with a pack loaded according to their sex, age and stamina.

The youngest three Dunn boys took up the rear of the column, to see that no one fell behind or strayed from the track.

Here, they knew, it was easy going. Higher up and onto the snow fields was where the difficulty would come. The name of the mountain didn't matter, they had been there before. Snow was snow, a mountain pass a mountain pass, and a blizzard nothing but peril.

They had studied Matt's map. They had stood below and studied Mt. Elias. They prayed that in ten or twelve day's time they would be safely arrived in Skagway.

5

Lolly blinked her eyes, but the light seared like acid and she shut them tight. Her head throbbed and her tongue was thick. She stood for a few seconds then slowly opened her eyes. She started. The sled was gone. It had been there but a moment before and now it was gone. All that was left in its place was whiteness. She turned back, her mind slowly tumbling toward panic. The second sled was also gone, and so were the horses and people.

She spun back around, knowing this just couldn't be. She hadn't strayed. She had only stopped for a moment. A moment in which she had looked up the massive flank of white to the tiny black dots of the advance party nearly to the horizon. She blinked again. The glacier was still there, all surrounding. The only world they had known for five days. A beautiful world in the daytime. The sky was the bluest blue imaginable. The sun so warm that it baked her arms and face like when she worked in her garden patch. She had never known that white could have so many shades and subtle changes.

At dawn, when they would still be in pitch blackness on the frozen ice field, the tip of Mt. Elias would start turning a vibrant pink. As though washed by a waterfall the color would spread, leaving the summit in blush tones as the lower regions became dusty rose and the shadowy crags reddish-purple.

It was a time when they prayed for the warmth of the sun. The full-mooned nights were eerie with their shades of silver, blue and black—and fiercely cold. At an altitude of over 10,000 feet the fires burned fitfully and it took forever for water to boil. The cold was a piercing thing, eating right into the bone marrow. Combined with the altitude it made breathing a painful chore. Each tiny little inhalation felt like taking splintery ice crystals right into the lungs.

At night, Matt and Clampett made them wrap extra clothing about their booted feet and sleep in groups. Their travelling feet were the most precious thing they possessed. Matt also worried about the hooves of the animals and paws of the dogs. These were not the snowdrifts he and Clampett had experienced before. Here, when they would have to stall for a snow-flurry, it was dry and powdery, the next wind whipping it right on down into the countless canyons and valley floors; leaving the surface like a plain of glass that could slice and cut. It was a world of deadly beauty.

But at that moment, for Lolly, there was no shading or beauty. Everything was white. White glacier. White Mt. Elias. White sky.

"Nolan!" she screamed, and wrapped her arms about her breasts.

She felt hands clutch her shoulders from the front. Her mind swam. There was no one there, only the whiteness. She was so frightened that her thick tongue would not allow another scream to escape. She felt a draught before her face, as though someone was fanning her. Then she heard footsteps pounding up. She could feel and hear, she thought logically; then why no sight for this nightmare?

Laura Lee had her by the shoulders and Henry was

waving his hand in front of her eyes. Nolan and Matt had come on the run. Even though it had been no more than thirty feet, they were panting and wheezing, unable yet to talk.

Henry took a deep breath. "Twenty years away makes you forget certain things about nature," he said earnestly. "I . . . I'm sorry—I didn't think of this."

"What's wrong with her?" Nolan asked, desperately.

"Snow blindness," Henry said quietly. "We will have to make room for her on a sled and wrap her eyes tightly, so that no light can reach them."

Nolan looked at his wife and his mouth fell open in shock. There was no trace of sympathy on his face. There was even a tinge of anger in his eyes.

"Will she be blind forever?"

Henry looked at the man blankly and forced himself to smile.

"No, her eyes just need a rest from the glare. Lolly, Laura Lee is beside you and will lead you to the sled. Sit quietly while we find something to bind about your eyes. Everything is going to be all right, little lady."

Lolly felt sick and ashamed of being so much trouble and angry all at once.

"Why me?" she wailed.

Henry dropped his eyes. "God has used you for a reminder, my dear."

"Then goddamn Him!" Nolan flared.

It was no time to call him down. The others were catching up and he wanted Nolan's mind busy.

"We will need the unburned wood we picked out of this morning's fire, Nolan," Henry said. "Break it out from the mule pack."

"What in the hell for?"

"Just do it!" Matt growled and then looked at Henry Boise for the reason.

"There's one thing I learned from the Russians, besides

patience. This land was really not new to them. They have their own frozen expanses. My first year among the Tlingits I suffered greatly from the constant whiteness. When the Russian seal hunters came to their village on Kotzebue Sound I thought they were trying to put on a fierce face to scare the Indians. Under each eye was a long black smudge. I soon learned it was for protection. In Siberia they would take charcoal from the fire and rub it under their eyes. Since ancient times they had learned that this kept the glare from bouncing into their eyes." Then he laughed. "They also learned to squint, like the Indian's eyes naturally do for them."

"Wish we could get that piece of news to Jeff," Clampett Dunn said.

Matt didn't comment. It had become almost a sore point. Each day the advance party got farther and farther ahead. At first they had feared calling out to them because the sound might start an avalanche. Then, as they got to know the glacier almost intimately they realized that there was, at least for the time being, no danger of avalanche.

But then their calls had gone unheeded. Jeff Robb was so far ahead that he and the men were really no help to the whole party. The route they took could only be guessed from day to day, obliterated as it was by the melting rays of the sun, and the force of the howling winds.

Matt could tell that the old man was about ready to suggest again that they send a couple of his boys ahead to slow the advance party down. He had talked him out of it the first time, and now had even sounder reasons for being against the idea. The glacier was not only wearing down the people, but it threatened to kill the animals. They had to be hand fed and hand watered, and if a man didn't stay with them each inch of the way they balked and refused to move. It was taking every able-bodied man they had to handle the animals and the women, and they just couldn't spare anyone.

Matt's train of thought was interrupted by a woman's shrill voice.

"I am not about to put that black stuff upon my face," Amalida Ramsey was protesting. "You know how sensitive it is, Calvin. I have used up almost all of my creams as it is."

Calvin's face was sullen. "It's for your own good." It was on the tip of his tongue to say that the creams didn't do her much good, but he decided to keep silent.

Amalida's face grew darker and she shrugged. "Okay, I'll wear the smudges on one condition," she said, turning and pointing to Lolly. "If *she* gets to ride, then so do I."

"She is riding only out of necessity, Mrs. Ramsey," Henry said.

"My legs are also a necessity," she snapped. "I should be riding, but my horse was taken out from under me without even my consent."

"Now, Amalida," Harriet tried to soothe. "We are all in the same fix."

Amalida's eyes were accusatory. "*We* didn't bring along eight hundred pounds of needless oven iron and equipment."

Harriet sighed. She saw that until Amalida somehow accepted that they were all in the situation together it was bound to be one outburst after another. The woman was acting like a spoiled brat. She wouldn't help with the cooking. She wouldn't help with the fires or tents, and her poor husband had to carry her pack the majority of the time. She seemed determined to make Calvin suffer for the wrong he had done her by taking her on this trip.

"Amalida Ramsey," Harriet said. "I am not carrying along needless extra weight, as you imply. You would do yourself a great favor if you divested yourself of a few pounds of those heavy corsets. I'm sure that fur coat of yours would more than cover any unsightly bulges."

Amalida flushed scarlet, and took a deep breath. Holding back her anger with effort, she said firmly, "I will thank you to mind your own business as to my apparel, Harriet Henderson."

Calvin was quick to step in, understandably anxious to change the direction of the conversation.

"My dear, I agree with you on the charcoal, upon reflection. Your hats afford you ample eye shade and you could wear the veils down. I'm sure that if you put your mind to it, you can make it from rest stop to rest stop."

Amalida nodded. She gave him a look which was suddenly rosy and amiable for having been so dour a moment before. She knew some of the other women had the vehement belief that Calvin coddled her by taking the pack from time to time. It was to save her strength, but for a reason that only they knew. Besides the heavy clothing, ankle length fur coat and heavy corsets, she was carrying a greater weight than any of the other women; sewn into the corset, in place of whalebone stays, were one hundred $500 gold pieces. On the *Brisbane*, at night, she could relieve herself of the burden, but on this trek it was too dangerous for her to part with the contraband.

Sometimes the forty extra pounds became so burdensome that she wanted to laugh at the irony of it all. Men were rushing by the thousands to the Klondike to find gold, not to bring it there. She didn't fully understand it, but then, she had never fully understood the banking business of her father and husband. She did know that one just didn't jump up and start a bank. One needed a certain amount of assets to convince others to leave their money in their banking care. Then, somehow, the money deposited made money for the banker.

Endlessly, her father had tried to pound that into her head, but he had finally become convinced that she was as stupid as her mother had been. Calvin, too, had tried to pound it into her head, and he was finally convinced that she was as stupid as he had always prayed she might be.

At sixteen, Raymond Forbes decided he was tired of being a hungry nobody. His mother had to fight the "nigger wimmen" in Mobile for laundry jobs. Only his agile mind at figures kept her from being cheated on "by the piece" ironing. One old widow woman *always* tried to cheat him. It became a game of who could be the sharpest. Raymond seldom lost.

One day the scrawny lad was introduced to the woman's brother-in-law. Pitted against the shrewd Randell Carter, Raymond lost—and yet he was the real winner, in the long run.

Stillman and Carter needed a young clerk, capable of blending into the woodwork. For four years he blended so well that he was almost overlooked when they moved to New Orleans.

He was quick to learn, but he never revealed just how much he really knew. Clerks were only supposed to think about the figures going in and out of the ledgers—they weren't supposed to have the brains to see that the ledgers were actually double and triple books on the same accounts.

Slowly, Raymond learned that Stillman and Carter were extremely clever crooks, though well respected in the community. When it became known that they were going to open another bank, in Algiers, Raymond quietly and effortlessly brought himself to the attention of Randell Carter. It was definitely a form of blackmail, but Raymond brought the book-keeping error to Carter's attention so innocently, that the man had no idea that the young man knew the real truth. He was indebted to Raymond for his discretion, for had the error surfaced, it would have ruined Stillman and Carter and caused a run on the Algiers Commercial Banking and Trust Company. As Raymond had suspected, Amos Stillman was not informed of the matter by his partner.

For two years after that, Raymond Forbes visited Randell Carter's home frequently. He innocently pretended that he did not know how he came to be so blessed, though he was elated that his plans were working so well. Then there had come Carleen Carter's affliction and death. Although a scatter-brained woman, Raymond had really liked her. Their daughter Ann, whom he had disliked from the first, had irrationally despised and avoided him. He had the suspicion that she envied the other young women for their gowns, their parties, their gaiety.

To Randell Carter, he espoused the feeling that such young women were spendthrift and foolish, and Carter's manner toward Raymond grew paternal and interested. Ann was heavily depressed after the death of her mother, and she was a burden to Randell. His wife had never questioned the mistress he indulged extravagantly, but Ann began to complain about his evenings away from home.

Raymond let Randell think he had to talk him into the marriage. Randell had married a woman he detested for her money, and Raymond planned to do the same. When Randell finally broached the subject, Raymond's acting was faultless. Along with a wife, he earned the position of personal accountant to Randell Carter, though Raymond knew that Carter kept his "real personal" books to himself.

For the next five years, Raymond Forbes rose no higher; his wife detested him as much as she did her father. His father-in-law was oddly withdrawn, and his own life very dull and mundane.

But Raymond didn't mind, in fact, he had needed the time to learn every little Carter trick and undermine what little regard Ann did have for her father. When he had to disclose what he had learned about Randell's mistress, he acted genuinely shocked and was convincing as a stalwart husband out to protect his wife from scandal. He became loving and attentive to her needs. It mattered not that her father was squandering the money left by her mother and his own money, Raymond would always be there to protect her and see to her needs—even if he did make such a niggardly salary.

Then, purposely, Raymond let Randell see him coming out of a New Orleans house of ill-repute. Randell went into a tirade and Raymond acted humble and chastised. Still, the tirade didn't carry over to Ann's ears, as Raymond had planned.

Randell had more immediate troubles, all baffling. Hell! The woman couldn't be costing him that much. But there were his own figures to prove it. The ledger of his former wife's account was devastatingly low. It had been willed to his daughter, which he had considered a stupid waste. He could make money with that money. But it was a losing account. He would just have to get rid of the woman and get his mind back on business.

As he was old-fashioned, he could not bring himself to discuss the matter with Amos Stillman. They were partners, but Amos didn't really know him or the number of times he had cheated him blind. Nor would Amos understand about this woman. Amos thought all such women of that ilk should be drowned in the Mississippi and left to float into the gulf.

He just had to tell the woman, but kept putting it off. His flush became brighter, his lips feverish. Only Raymond knew the problem and smiled to himself and was amused. He could hardly wait for Randell to see the woman again. He waited in desperate silence and then his plan grew to fruition.

He hid behind a screen in the parlor when his father-in-law stormed in. It was the most delightful scene he had ever listened in on. He had primed Ann's mind as though she were a play actress. She would not believe the lie about her husband being with a whore, when her father was only trying to cover up his own dirty linen. She knew all. Raymond knew all. Raymond had found the will. It was *her* mother's money being squandered on the hussy. Ann would not stand for it. She had sent Raymond to see the woman and let her know what was what. Now, he either made good on the money or she would go directly to Amos Stillman and a lawyer.

That was all that was supposed to happen, as Ann believed it. A frightening of Randell Carter to give Ann and Raymond their due.

But Raymond had been too clever with the books and they were too ominous for Randell to bear. His suicide was nearly as shocking to Ann and Raymond as it was to the rest of the community.

Raymond had to explain to Ann what he had done with the books. She didn't understand, except that they had somehow forced her father to kill himself. She was frightened, terribly frightened.

Her fright eroded Raymond's own feelings. He had to make Randell's death have a real reason. The money was still in the bank. He had only played with the books to make them look disastrous. Now he had to bring about the real disaster—and right under the noses of the auditors. He had learned well from Randell. Even as the auditors were beginning to question, even as Amos Stillman looked at the books, heartbroken, Raymond Forbes stood with a money belt about his waist.

The scandal, he felt, would give him time to figure out his next move. He never figured that Ann had a thought on the subject. There were many things she didn't understand, but one thing she fully understood: for twenty-five years she had been under the thumbnail of either her father or her husband.

She hated New Orleans and the mold of her life. Nothing would change if she stayed. If the real truth came out she might even end up with a husband in prison. No, she would be assertive for the first time ever.

It was her decision not to attend the funeral. It was her decision to sew the gold into a corset and visit with her aunt in Mobile for awhile. As she saw it, Raymond should stay for a short time and make her excuses. Then they could just vanish to a new life.

Raymond could buy the plan up to a point. The gold could not be spent as regular money. Five hundred dollar gold pieces were mint stamped with a number and she would be caught the moment she tried to cash one at a bank in Mobile.

Then he learned an amazing thing about the woman who had been his wife for five years. Ann and her mother had been "squirrels" right under Randell's nose. From her little nests throughout the house she produced $5, $10, $50 and $500 gold pieces until they amounted to nearly $20,000.

Instead of feeling elated, it had depressed him. He had schemed for five years when it hadn't been fully necessary. Now that Ann had all the money he would just have to start scheming again.

The breeze was at first refreshing through the veil. It had cut the glare, but forced her to pick her way carefully, cautiously, with her eyes forced constantly down. Then the breeze began to pick up and, for the first time, Amalida began to feel the heavy, insidious cold the others had complained about. It pierced right through the fur coat, velvet dress, petticoats, camisole, corsets and skin. Within seconds it was a continuous gale sweeping down the glacier and into their faces. It was brittle, and the sharp cold pulled her nostrils together and gave her the sense of suffocating. She pulled the veil aside and gasped for breath.

For a second she thought she was experiencing what Lolly Fedderson had been whimpering about for hours. She saw nothing but whiteness. But this whiteness stung her cheeks like a swarm of bees.

She heard the men shouting behind her and she turned. It was like a nightmare scene. Through the swirling, menacing vortex of flying ice crystals she saw the horses and mules swaying from side to side. The big Swede, Lundgren, took a mule and twisted its head until the braying beast and the travois carrier toppled onto their side.

"Get over here and huddle down next to the sled," Henry Boise screamed at her.

She was no more than five feet from the sled, but his voice, against the wind, sounded as though it had come from five miles away. She started to obey when a blast of wind struck with such force it nearly knocked her from her feet. It tore the breath from her mouth and left her gasping.

Then she was gasping out of fear. She would take a step against the constant wind thrust and it would move her feet to the side as though she were on skates. She tried to plant her feet firmly but was getting little or no traction. She thought if she could just get down on her knees she would be all right. But the stiff corset made it almost impossible to bend that far forward. Suddenly, another vicious blast swirled and roared about her. It dipped to the glacier surface and eddied up, ballooning out her coat, skirt and petticoats as though they were hooped. She jerked to gain her balance but was pivoting like a top. She stifled the sudden start of panic as she started to fall. The air under her skirt toppled her to the side and she began to roll.

She could hear herself screaming, the sound oddly mixed with a thunderous roar and other screaming being carried on the wind. Her scream seemed to last only a second. The other sounds seemed to echo on and on with each of her rolls.

Frantically, she clawed with her gloved hands until the pigskin was shredded; jabbed out with her feet until both boot heels snapped off. All she could think about was that long, long slope that seemed to go down forever to the jagged ice cliffs that towered over the gulf waters.

She felt herself falling. Her mind screamed against the

thought. It was too soon for her to be going over the cliff to her death. That was a thousand rolls away. But her arms and legs were flaying at nothingness. Her voice was screaming, but it was bouncing right back and deafening her own ears.

Then she hit the bottom of the small crevasse with such a force that it knocked the wind out of her. Her head spun and there was momentary blackness. Oddly enough, she found herself thinking it was better than whiteness.

Someone shouted and it came to her like a hollow chord. She relaxed. She was out of the wind and its bitter cold. Her clothing began to feel warm and comfortable again. Her face and eyelids still stung from a million little lacerations. She kept her eyes closed.

She didn't see the figure surge over the lip of the crevasse for a foot or two, slip awkwardly, recover itself on a thin ice ledge and then crawl the ten feet down, trembling and frightened.

From all indications it looked like he would be coming to rescue nothing but a corpse. His frantic dash down the icy slope, stumbling and falling, and nearly tumbling after her had been in vain.

Landing on the crevasse floor he turned. In all of his experiences he had never come upon a corpse before. It gave him an eerie feeling.

"Ann?" he said tentatively.

She heard, but had only enough strength to let out a little moan in response.

His sigh was enormous. He knelt beside her, gently questioning if she thought anything was broken. She was still dazed and could only shake her head back and forth.

He helped her to her feet and instructed her how to climb out of the crevasse. Amazingly, she found she could crawl up the ledged side. He followed behind her, ready to catch her if she lost her grip. But she was determined to survive, and struggled upward.

But once on the glacier surface, all of her reserve strength was exhausted. She began to teeter and he had to literally push her up the steep slope.

They were going into the face of the surging downward wind and he had to grasp her about the waist, stopping every two to three steps to get a better grip on her. It was a valiant effort on his part and each step was sheer torture. But with each step his spirit was lifted in hope.

Then figures were emerging from the vortex of the storm, and the burly Cornell Dunn was lifting Amalida into his arms as though she were weightless.

Calvin Ramsey had to shout to make himself heard over the shrieking of the wind.

"Mister, I can never thank you enough for going after her so quickly."

Jethro Calhoun nodded. Near exhausted himself, he allowed Calvin to help him scramble back up to the makeshift camp. The wind was now bringing snow instead of ice crystals. Even in the short time they had been down rescuing Amalida, the snow had almost drifted over their tracks and, as they approached, they could see it piling up against the horses they had gotten down onto their sides. The sleds had been brought back and put into a vee, with everyone huddling down together between them. But a foot beyond the sleds there were no runner marks or footprints.

It was a frightening sensation, as if the snow and wind, given the power to obliterate, also had the power to close off their links with the rest of the world.

But Jethro saw none of it. He could have been content in gaining nothing more than her answering to the name "Ann." But by accident he had gained so very much more. He had gained the way to the gold. He was impressed. He was greatly impressed. Never would he have thought the gold to be on her person, or so cleverly concealed within a corset. But it was information that would just have to wait for another time and place. It would be utter madness to confront them in such a place and during such a blizzard. He was smart enough to see that the madmen who had raced on ahead were of no help to the overall group, and they needed every available man—and woman. To reduce their number further—with him forced to guard the two day and night—would be insane. It would be best to wait. There was no hurry, as he was certain they didn't suspect him.

Despite the wind, some of the men had gotten the big bakery tent out of its pack and were throwing it over the sleds.

"Keep huddled," Henry advised. "The body produces more warmth than people realize. As soon as the snow piles a bit on the tent it will help keep the heat in. Farther north, in this land, the people even make their homes out of blocks of snow."

Few among them believed that myth.

But Henry had a reason for speaking, for distracting the others. He did not want them overhearing the guarded conversation between Matt Monroe and Clampett Dunn. He crawled over to where they were talking and sat down next them.

"Did anybody hear it?" Matt asked.

"I think not. If they did, they probably thought it was the wind."

"Does it still go on?"

Clampett nodded. "I heard it while I was getting out the tent."

"How far away?" Matt asked Henry.

Henry hunched his round shoulders. In the fur parka he had obtained from the Yakutats he looked like a chubby bear.

"Sound can travel on the wind for miles here," he said.

"But you're certain that's what it was?"

"Yes," he said sadly. "Deep under my feet I could feel it. It was like springtime on Kotzebue Sound. The ice can be breaking up miles away, but you can feel the shock waves under your feet. I'm sure that a new crevasse somewhere opened in the glacier."

"The advance group seemed almost ready to make the summit," Clampett said dully.

"I think not," Henry said. "Distances here can be as deceptive as sound. I have never taken them to be more than three to five miles ahead of us. Today, before the wind came, they seemed to be moving on a parallel with the horizon. That is the direction our search party should take."

"Who will go?" Clampett asked.

"I will, of course," Henry said at once. "And perhaps four or five others. We will need ropes, axes and lanterns."

"Ropes?"

"For two reasons. We will tie ourselves together, so we don't lose anyone in the storm. If they have fallen, then we will need the rope to get them out of the crevasse. Nolan Fedderson should go. He has proven his rope handling ability in topping the trees for the travois. Matt, I feel you are needed here, and the three who rescued Mrs. Ramsey have expended enough energy for the moment. Crow is a strong fine lad. I'll take him. And Clampett, I will need two of your boys."

"And myself!"

Henry knew better than to comment on Dunn's age. They were his family members out there, and he felt an obligation to be in the search party.

Quietly, the men assigned were told. Matt could tell the others later.

They crawled from under the tent, struggled to rise against the storm, and floundered to gather the supplies. At the last minute, Clampett had Herschel and Jerome each bring along a pup tent. Nolan belted the end of the rope about his waist, let out a three-foot length and belted the next man. One by one he did the same until they were a line of six. Henry was the last belted and smiled at the lumberjack. It had not been discussed, but

Nolan had automatically anticipated his role. He was the end man and the strength. At the first sign of a man ahead of him starting to slip, he was to brace himself and keep them all from tumbling down the glacier.

Henry started off, flinging the big *mukluk* boots outwards and forwards with the awkward rolling motion of the experienced snow walker. His angled feet bit into the soft snow and he braced himself, making sure it packed down hard and that he did not slip on the icy surface below. Each man behind him was to follow in his footsteps, and despite his short legs he strained for a stride that even the long-legged Nolan would have no trouble stepping into.

On a tent pole rammed into the surface next to the dog sleds they had left a burning lantern. It was their only return beacon. As they moved ahead, Henry had to lead by instinct. Herschel Dunn had raised a questioning eyebrow when he saw that the man was carrying his fancy walking cane. He soon saw it was not for show.

Before each step Henry would poke out with the cane to make sure there was no pot-hole or wind wave of ice. An even layer of snow on the surface hid many perils.

In the early going, Henry led them across the snow with remarkable speed. But sustaining that initial speed was something else entirely. To move quickly in such conditions was not only exhausting but dangerous. Suck too much of that frozen air into overworked lungs and one could get lung frost. At two miles above sea level it killed quickly and painfully. Henry kept his head well down in his parka, breathing into the space between the fur and his underclothing where his body heat warmed the air a little. By the time he had taken a hundred steps, his legs were trembling with the effort.

He rested for a silent count to fifty before going on. That would be the pace, he determined.

They trudged for hours with no sign and no sound but the wind. They did begin to find crevasses, most of which looked as if they might have been there for eons. Then they came upon a landscape that was like yet another world. Here was where the glacier had been ripped and torn, in a hundred different ways. Jagged ice walls jutted up and the crevasses ranged from an inch opening in the surface to yawning canyons. On the cliff-like sides was little snow.

"Halloooo!"

There was no returned answer. Henry tried to pierce the snow-swept darkness with narrowed eyes, but the storm lantern showed him a marble wall. He tapped his way along the edge of the largest crevasse, making sure it was solid and wouldn't break away beneath them. It was like walking along an eroded cliff, with deep gouges and smaller crevasses. After a half hour, the cane landed on a soft mound and sank deeper than it should have. Henry scraped away the drifted snow and found a backpack. He tugged the men forward, holding the lantern down.

"Jim Mapps' pack," Jerome said.

It was so close to the edge that it seemed odd. It could not have been torn from his back in this icy earthquake, because the front buckling strap was neatly rebuckled to the back.

Again Henry called down into the canyon crevasse and again there was no reply. They called together in unison. Only the wind answered.

"Hush! What was that?"

They strained. Then they looked at each other like they couldn't believe the sound they had heard. It had sounded just like a rasping snore a little ways ahead.

But they didn't rush. Each step had to be just as cautious as every one taken along the way.

The lamp revealed a mound of snow and a rope dangling down into the crevasse. Beneath the mound Jim Mapps' hands were still frozen about the rope. He could not have made the sound.

Again they yelled down into the endless blackness. Not even a snore returned.

Nolan cut the rope away from Mapps' hands and hauled it in. It was only a twenty-five footer. He square-knotted it to the twenty-five footer he had coiled around his neck and tied his lantern to one end. Cautiously, he lowered it over the side of the crevasse and began to play out the rope. Henry and Clampett went down on their bellies and stuck their heads over the crevasse lip. As a precaution, and without being told, Herschel and Jerome sat down behind them and grabbed hold of their feet.

"Lower," Henry called. "It's getting below the wind and starting to create an umbra."

"At least on this side. The other side is still pitch as hell."

Lonsworth took tapers out of his pack and started striking flint to steel. When he had one rag-wrapped stick blazing he ignited four others from it and stuck them in the drift behind to make a semi-circle of light.

"Up to the knot," Nolan advised.

"Keep going. No, wait. Walk it left. It looks like the start of a ledge. That's it. Now lower. It's getting wider and I think I see something on it. More to the left. Yes. Who is it?"

"Can't tell. Looks like a bundle of clothes."

"Don't call out," Henry warned. "He could start and roll right off into oblivion."

"Tie off the lantern line, Crow," Nolan said, handing him the rope. "The rest of you take off your rope belts. Herschel, you and your brother redo yours at the end. Once I'm over the edge you can play me down easy."

"You're going down?" Jerome asked incredulously.

Nolan laughed. "I guess it won't be much harder going down there than it is to come down a tree. And it's only about thirty feet."

"I'm much obliged to you," Clampett said.

Nolan shrugged. He wasn't used to kind words about his work.

As he started down, it took all five men holding the rope to keep him from going down too fast. It was a lot different from what Nolan was used to. In a tree, there were branches to bounce into to slow oneself. Here, the wall was like a vertical field of broken glass. Nolan had his ax, but the first time he swung it against the ice wall to slow himself, the metal splintered into two dozen tiny pieces and rattled down the crevasse wall.

"Well, I'll be a son of a bitch," he said.

The wonderment of it kept him from thinking how dangerous his task was. Finally, after what seemed an eternity, he reached the ledge. It was extremely narrow, and he didn't trust it to support his full weight. He called to the men above to keep a firm grip on the rope, as he moved carefully across the ledge to the inert human form.

By the light of the dangling lantern he could see it was Jeff Robb. The man was asleep, his senses lulled into a peaceful numbness by the cold. Nolan slapped him hard, then removed his mittens and pinched his cheeks cruelly. Robb stirred and opened his eyes. Nolan continued to slap him until his grey face was turning scarlet from the blows.

"His eyes are glazed, but he's alive," Nolan called up. "I'm going to tie the rope under his arm pits. Pull him up quick—I don't trust this damn ledge at all."

He liked it even less being left alone on the ledge with no supporting rope about his waist. It reminded him of the first time he had ever reached the top of a redwood. The branches had been so thick he had had to chop many away before he could get a protective rope looped around the trunk. He looked down and almost fell from the giant tree. It had been an indescribably frightening experience. After that, he made it a point never to look down, and never again did he experience such shattering fright.

But the feeling in the pit of his stomach right now was

much like that experience. He closed his eyes and waited. He didn't want to look down, nor did he want to look up, which would only cause him to agonize over the slowness of Jeff Robb's ascent to the top.

He began to breathe again when Henry said the rope was coming back down. He was never so glad to leave a place in his life.

By the time he had reached the top Robb was coughing and sputtering. They decided it would be best to stay there for the rest of the night. The wind had lessened and now the falling snow was soft and thick, not driving ice. The change made it seem almost balmy.

Herschel and Jerome put up the two tents, which now seemed too small. Then they recalled Jim Mapps' pack, and almost immediately started wondering about Jeff Robb's pack. To keep from wondering about things only Robb could answer they went for Mapps' pack and set up another tent.

Lonsworth had a straw-wrapped flask of cherry brandy that he thought might help warm up the unconscious Robb, but Henry advised against it.

"From the rasp, I'd say he has ice in his lungs. All we should do is try to keep him bundled up."

"And pray," Clampett Dunn added.

Henry nodded. The mental Rosary in his head had been in constant use since the start of the search.

"Herschel," Clampett said. "Jim ain't got no more use for his clothes and Jeff do."

"We just going to leave him nude?" Jerome asked.

"Good Lord saw him come into this world naked, so I don't think he'll be blushing none."

After the transfer of clothing had been performed, Henry and Clampett sat with Robb, while all but Nolan went to their tents. Crow had placed the tapers right in front of the tent where Jeff lay so he could benefit from what little warmth they put out. Nolan sat beside a taper and took a round tin from his pack. Inch by inch he rubbed goose grease into the hemp ropes to keep them from freezing solid from the moisture they had absorbed from the snow.

Henry smiled at the industry. He liked a man who kept his working equipment in proper order. He, too, kept his working equipment in proper order. Packed in his luggage, his vestments were as orderly as if he had used them daily for the past twenty years. But he smiled for another reason, too.

He had seen Nolan's face when he had come out of the crevasse. He saw the fright and he could sympathize. But when their eyes met, he knew they were both thinking the same thing. There were still four men missing. If Nolan had to go back down into that hell, he would go with his equipment in order.

A groan sent Henry back into the tent. Jeffrey Robb's mind was still dazed, but he had regained consciousness. They got the story only in snatches and over a length of time.

Apparently, the morning of their departure, Robb had determined that an angled course around the summit was less dangerous than a direct route over it. He had sent four of the men to chart that course, as the wind had started to rise, while he and Jim had started back for the whole group. They were below and to the right of the men when the glacier began to move beneath their feet. The wind was so loud that they didn't even hear the growling rumble. It was a scene right out of Faust.

Around the four men the glacier started cracking and yawning open in a hundred places, as Jeff and Jim looked on in horror. Jeff had seen Frank Watson's legs go wide as the glacier split beneath him. Then he was tossed into the air by a jutting mass of ice that thrust suddenly upward through the widening crack. There was a horrible grinding sound as Watson fell into the crevasse and the mountain of ice broke free and crumbled back down upon him.

Sam Daws and Guy Browning were clawing at each other to hold together. Suddenly, the ground upon which they had been standing was a gaping hole of nothingness. It's edges started to expand as tons of ice started to break away. Stacey Webb had started running from it, the ice crumpling behind him almost faster than he could run.

Jeff and Jim had started running for him, but he simply vanished, though they thought they could hear his screams above the howling wind.

Then, suddenly, it stopped. The glacier was completely still beneath their feet and the only sound was the wind and the deep, deep sound of ice crashing against ice.

Jim thought he had heard Stacey's feeble cries and took off his pack to crawl to the edge. Jeff was certain that the cries were further along the edge and a few moments later found himself falling. He landed on his back on the ledge, the backpack cushioning his fall somewhat, and keeping him from breaking anything. It was pitch dark, but by feeling around he found he was only inches from the edge. He had called for Jim to bring his rope, and slowly tried to get out of the backpack.

They couldn't see each other, but from the slap of the rope against the ice wall he figured it was a little short. He braced the pack against the wall and stepped up on it, trying to reach the rope. The pack began to slip from beneath him. Then it moved out from under his feet, skidding over the edge and down into the depths of the crevasse. Fortunately, he was able to plant his feet in a crusty sector of the ledge, barely escaping the fate of his backpack.

Jim was still at the top, sobbing and gasping, trying in vain to get the rope down to him. To his left, Jeff heard another rumble as a ledge gave loose, and Stacey's final scream echoed through the chasm. Jeff would never forget that sound as long as he lived.

He called up to Jim to get back to the camp for help. When there was no answer, he figured Jim had already left to do so. He sat there, trembling, his teeth chattering, and finally dropped off to sleep. That was all Jeff Robb remembered of his ordeal.

The storm blew away. Above, the sky was starry, with a moon that was three-quarters' full.

They waited. It was still a couple of hours before dawn.

Henry hadn't realized he had dozed off until Clampett spoke.

"I'll take him out and put him beside Jim."

Henry crawled from the tent to help Clampett pull Robb out. Then he rose. Nolan rose beside him, stiff from sitting hunched into his parka for so long. Several times he had started to rise to go to the protection of the tent, but the story had come in such spurts that he had not wanted to miss any of it. He had seen many new lumberjacks in his day who were like Jeff Robb. They knew everything and yet nothing.

"Damn fool brought it all upon himself," he mumbled.

"Son," Henry whispered, "don't think ill of a man in the hour of his death. God has a purpose for everything."

"It's because of men like him that I don't believe in God."

He stomped off to his tent on legs that were numb.

Henry didn't feel like arguing. He crawled back inside the tent. Clampett came in behind him and sat down. He couldn't sleep.

"I could not help but hear. Thank you for not arguing with the young man."

Henry grunted.

"I can understand his feelings. Jeff was a difficult man. He was twenty-five when Brigham Young died. He was a fire-ball who thought he should rise like cream. Ours is a simple religion. We are all equal, no one is better than any other. Jeff refused to believe that. Unfortunately, he convinced others to see his way of thinking. With the gold he came here for he planned to set up an opposition church."

"Why did you come along with him?"

Clampett chuckled. "Our church is close knit, and I believe it better to keep an eye on the devil, so he does not surprise you. Does that seem strange?"

Henry laughed, ruefully. "It sounds quite familiar. So did Nolan's words—about some men making him disbelieve in God. I have sometimes felt that way myself."

"When you were a Catholic?"

"How did you know that?"

The old man chuckled. "I was raised Catholic until I was twenty, Henry. I recognized the Latin you mumbled along the trail. Were you a priest?"

"Yes. And I still am in the eyes of God—if not Rome. I was sent up here as a young priest to do missionary work among the Eskimos. I was only eighteen years old. My youth didn't know the difference and I landed with a Tlingit tribe. It was still Russian land then, and the Russian Orthodox Church was most powerful. They didn't like me or my methods, and I, at that age, had not formed a very strong bond with celibacy. The Russian priests were old and bearded. I was young, clean shaven and French. My name then was Henre Duboise. I became involved with a young Tlingit maiden, and our liaison produced a child."

"Your charming daughter?"

"No, a son, Peter. Laura Lee came nine years later. Anyway, you would have thought I was another Martin Luther. I was defrocked so fast I felt a draught. I, a Jesuit, had brought the devil among the Tlingit. I fumed and ranted and fought them for twenty years—making them even angrier, because during those years I tutored to pay for the lawyers to provide a proper education for Laura Lee. I was financially successful, and they resented it. Of course, I lost my battle with them."

"And now you go back. Why?"

"Why not? I have a grown son I have not seen since he was a small boy, and these were people that I grew to love and admire. How arrogant are we sometimes as western-man. We came behind a golden cross and thought that made us intelligent—no, *superior*. A fallacy, to be sure. At one time the Tlingit domain encompassed the entire Alaskan Panhandle. Fish abounded in their waters and forests covered their lands. Their boats would go from the gulf to the Bering Sea and Kotzebue Sound for spring and summer fishing, then back to the gulf. Here they resided in striking gabled lodges that could house a dozen families. Where did they learn of gables? Nature taught them that it made the heavy snows slide off their homes. Their canoes could hold up to sixty men. Who taught them to build such craft? Necessity taught them to bring back the lengths of whale and walrus hulks. In front of their lodges sat 50-foot totem poles of magnificent carvings. Who taught them to thus depict their real and mythical history? Well, I still question that, Clampett. What did the Russians bring them? Liquor and disease, that's what. And they called *me* a devil among them because I dared to produce a child. Tht Russians turned the Tlingits' tangible wealth in nature into a mockery with the fur trade. Their wonderful, sophisticated native culture began to be ignored. Eventually, it was allowed to be forgotten, allowed to die. I do not mean to say that my own church is blameless—it has always hungered more for riches, than men's souls. But I talk too much."

Clampett laughed. "But you have much to say. When they found gold in Utah it brought many who changed the land. Do you not fear that here, also?"

"Certainly. Each incoming breed cannot help but change what was there before. Look at our little group. Mrs. Ramsey will probably demand a mansion no sooner than she arrives. Mrs. Fairchild is lost without a general store within a few steps. The Hendersons dream of baking bread for men who are probably used to pinching off a hunk of sourdough. Well, let them learn. From the Yakutats I gained information about my people. I will head for them once off the *Malaspina*."

"The what?"

"That's what the Yakutat call the glacier. It means 'the never melting.' "

6

Because they had been absorbed in the rescue mission they were not aware that two feet of snow had fallen on the camp. After their return to the main group, it took three days to move everyone through the thick drifts to a point near the new crevasses.

In the daylight, the main fissure was awesome. It stretched down the flank of the glacier for a full five miles. It was now really more an icy canyon than a crevasse, being nearly a half-mile across at the widest point. And even in the daylight they could not determine its depth that sank to blue-black shadows.

They assaulted the summit directly, a new feeling among them. Even though Jeff Robb had kept his advance party quite apart, they had really been a part of the whole. Death had touched them on the glacier and it was sobering.

Henry had been right about distance. One couldn't judge the summit by the horizon line. Each time they rose to a ledge, another loomed beyond—and another one beyond that.

Ribs began to show on the horses and a dog had to be shot because they feared it was rabid.

And once the backside of the glacier could be seen, it went on and on in a downward white slope.

It was twice as difficult to travel now. They had to take the glacier at traverse angles, working their way back and forth, in a slow, serpentine downward motion.

Lars Lundgren thought it was a great slide to play upon. It took him for a two-mile downhill tumble that ate away the seat of his pants, turning his buttocks to raw meat, and put his broken arm into a make-shift sling. Had it not been for his lack of fear, it would have killed him.

He had tried to talk David Fairchild into sliding with him. David did have fear—fear of his mother. He knew she would never allow him such sport. He had stood sniffling with a cold as everyone else screamed and yelled at Lars to brake himself. Their only answer was gleeful laughter from the daredevil.

That night David boasted to his parents that he had not gone along when invited. He was rewarded with a hunk of raw chocolate that Hazel Fairchild had been hoarding to someday bake with.

That night it snowed again. The storm had come down out of the Arctic Ocean and was moving westward. It moved over the 18,000 foot Mt. Elias in massive swirls. Two feet of snow had come down on the other side of the glacier, but here they had two feet of snow within the first two hours—and it was still snowing.

During the night David began to feel hot and feverish. He pushed the bed-roll blankets away to feel the coolness of the night. No one else in the big bake tent noticed.

By morning he was burning with fever. It was still snowing.

He had never been sick in his fourteen years, and Hazel Fairchild had no experience as a nurse. Harriet Henderson had to take over, and with Hazel talking herself into as feverish a state as her son, she had her hands full.

The Feddersons were in the same tent as the Fairchilds, and though Lolly's eyes were still sightless, she wanted to help Harriet nurse young David. Nolan didn't think she'd be of any help—why, Laura Lee had been taking care of little Kimberly because Lolly's condition had rendered her virtually helpless.

"Oh, Nolan," Lolly pleaded. "I don't have to be able to see to help nurse a sick boy. I can spell Harriet, at least."

"You don't have to be able to see to pleasure me, neither," he pouted, "but we ain't done anything intimate since the boat."

"Don't reckon anybody has."

Nolan wasn't too sure about that. The Ramseys had sure gotten mighty thick since Amalida fell down the glacier. They had even bought Jim Mapps' tent when they brought it back from the rescue. But perhaps it would do Lolly some good to feel useful, he thought.

"All right," he said. "I'll take you over there. Then I'll go check on Kimberly."

"Where is she?"

"Laura Lee said something about taking her to one of the other tents in case the kid had something catching."

That wasn't what Laura Lee had said, but Lolly accepted it. Nolan led Lolly to the other side of the tent, where the boy was bedded. Harriet gladly accepted the help, and was happy to have company.

The tent was smokey from the center fire. No one paid any attention to Nolan as he slipped out.

He stopped and held out his hand. He could hardly believe it. It was snowing so hard he couldn't even see his hand. It didn't matter. He had helped raise the tents, so he knew where he was going.

First came the tent shared by Matt Monroe, Lonsworth Crowley and Mickey Magraff, then the Ramsey's tent and the Dunn row. Except for Amalida and Calvin Ramsey, Nolan had seen everyone else inside the large tent at one time or another. After all, it was the only one with a fire.

He barged right into the first Dunn tent without announcing himself, almost knocking his head on the lantern hanging from the tent pole.

"How's Kim?" he asked, flopping down on a bedroll and stretching out.

Laura Lee started, the wash cloth just half way around one of her bare breasts.

She had not been able to stand one more day of the same clothing. She had decided to take a spit bath and change, but shivering in the cold she almost regretted having started.

"I–I–" she stammered, trying to make the little square of cloth cover her.

"They're nice," Nolan grinned, putting his chin into the hand of his crooked elbow. "Don't try to hide them. You got more there than Lolly–and she's had a baby."

Laura Lee did not know what to say. She frantically tried to think how the situation would have been handled by the heroine of one of the romantic little novels that were forbidden at the school–but which were smuggled in right under the noses of the nuns. Laura Lee had read a lot of them.

"The rest of you is nice, too," said Nolan. "Although I can't see much the way you're squatting down."

Laura Lee looked to where she had placed the fresh clothing. It was more than an arm's reach away. "May I have that garment?" she asked.

"Why? I think you are most fascinating this way." Then he added softly, "And desirable."

Laura Lee's breath became choked. He was beginning to sound too much like one of the novels.

"But–I'm cold."

"Really?" He moved over to her and touched her breast lightly. "I know many different ways to warm you up."

"Thank you, no," she replied in a voice that was fragile and shaking.

Nolan, who was no expert in seduction without force,

squeezed her breast roughly, and felt the girl's increased trembling. But she did not recoil, he noted.

Laura Lee's instincts caused her to wonder. She was twenty years old, but still treated like a child by her father and the nuns. All she knew was what she had read in the novels and they always seemed to stop short and leave a person wondering. Suddenly she wanted to be compromised. The fingers were tightening on her breast, urgently, pleadingly. Then Nolan put out his other hand, smiling up at her and touching her shoulder. She hesitated for a long moment, then let his hand pull her shoulder forward and down.

Her whole body was suddenly shaking, and this time not from cold. His lips were drawing closer and she wanted to taste of them.

Watching her very closely, he made sure the kiss was only a promise of better things to come. He felt the wild throbbing of her pulse and was amazed at himself. He was getting farther than he had hoped by being a gentle lover.

Now his own ready passion was obliterating caution. Someone could come crawling into the tent at any moment. He broke into a sweat in his urgency. Like an untried youth he fumbled clumsily with his trouser buttons.

When she felt the weight of his body roll her gently and come over her, she knew this would have to be the beginning of the rapture spoken of but never described.

The experience was one of intense and piercing pain. She opened her mouth to protest, but a quick hand moved to cover it. She pounded with her fists and thrashed with her legs. Her chaotic senses made her writhe and twist under him.

In the turbulence of this unfamiliar happening, Nolan was lifted to untold joy. With Lolly he had to fight her first and then release his passions into near lifelessness. This was strange, absorbing, alien yet again exciting.

And even when the pain was gone she did not stop fighting him. She did not know that their passions were building equally because of the struggle. Then, without warning, her body exploded with an unbearable ecstasy. It smothered her more than the hand on her mouth.

But the hand was no longer there. He was no longer there. He lay on his back next to her, his eyes shut and his teeth clenched.

His own reaction had startled him. From heaven to hell in a blinding second. This wasn't like him. He had taken on a few of the whores the lumberjacks had brought to the camp. But then, they had been sticks, too.

"You—you okay?" she whispered.

"I'm fine," he said curtly.

"I didn't know it could be like this. I simply didn't know."

Nolan was silent.

"I-I'm not . . . well, I thought I'd die of shame if I was to do such a terrible thing, but I'm not ashamed."

He rose, turning wordlessly away from her, and left the tent. It might have been all right if she hadn't talked about shame. Damn, he had never felt ashamed before. Why now? He felt cheap, and it dulled the joy she had given him. He hated the feeling, because he didn't understand it.

It became a maddening thing. The storm and his depression. Everything was just too confined. He couldn't turn without stumbling over Laura Lee. She was there to care for his daughter. She was there to care for Lolly. She was there to smile and cast her secret little glances his way. It was driving him insane because he didn't have the courage to cope with it. If only they could move on he knew he would feel better.

But day after day the storm raged. The wood supply dwindled. Packing crates were broken up for burning. On the fifth night of the storm no fire was lit. Everyone slept in the big tent to share body heat. Food became communal because the fire was now lit only three hours a day.

Oh, my God, thought Freeman Fairchild with genuine

alarm. Didn't these bastards want to protect his son? Or was that one of their schemes? Reduce the party of the ill to have food for the well. I should break their necks, thought Freeman, and maybe I will. What if his son died? That would break Hazel's heart. I know her; she has never liked these people. They should have waited for the boat that their other Chicago friends were scheduled to take. They were probably already in Skagway. Good God, what a mess. But what could he do? Nothing.

On the morning of the eighth day of the storm Lolly came and sat down beside Nolan. He wrapped a blanket around her shoulders and held her tight.

He watched her closely. "You don't have to sit with David?"

"He died a few minutes ago. I didn't want to be there when they woke Hazel to tell her."

His face changed subtly. "You got back here on your own."

"Been starting to see things through a fuzzy haze."

"Thank God for that!"

Lolly laughed lightly. "You thanking God? Thought you didn't believe in him?"

"I never said that."

She was too tired to argue. "Kim sleeping with Laura Lee?"

He nodded. "Glad you'll be able to look after her again." He didn't really mean it. It would be hard to spend time with Laura Lee now without raising eyebrows.

"She's such a sweet girl."

Nolan's face darkened, and he turned away quickly, afraid that Lolly might guess his secret.

"She did it because there was no one else who could," he said.

"Nolan!" she cried, outraged. "How can you say that? Look how she cared for me on the sled. You sound as if you don't like her."

"I don't."

Lolly regarded him with innocent astonishment. "Give me one good reason."

He grit his teeth. "I don't have to have a reason for not liking someone. I don't like most of these people, but ain't going to spout off why. I just hope we get out of this storm alive, and reach Skagway before all the gold is gone."

"Won't matter. We ain't going for the gold anyhow."

"Yeah, that's right."

He hated it; the lies, the half-truths, the pretense. How he put on a show of thanking God for the return of Lolly's sight when his daydreams had Laura Lee staying to help them forever. He had even convinced himself that Laura Lee had taken care of Lolly and Kimberly to be closer to him. He felt like he was the only man in the world who had ever married an almost total stranger just to advance himself in the world—only to find true love with another woman. A love that he couldn't share because there were so many damn people around. He had never felt guilty lying to Lolly before, because he never really told her anything of import. So why did he lie about the gold? From the moment he had first put his hands on Clara Bennett's money he knew he was just like all the rest of the men in Seattle. He wanted his share of the real gold and the equipment he had bought was mainly for that purpose. Laura Lee understood that about him. Laura Lee understood everything about him.

Two hours later, Henry Boise came and whispered to Nolan that he wanted to see him outside. Nolan thought Henry must have found out about him and Laura Lee, and that the whole incident was going to be brought out into the open.

The storm was starting to break up. Patches of leaden gray were visible. Henry ploughed to Matt's tent and ducked in. Nolan followed and stopped. The interior looked like a windstorm had struck.

"We have ourselves a problem, Nolan," Matt said. "Sit down."

Nolan sat, sensing immediately that he and Laura Lee were not the problem. He was relieved. He nodded at Crow and Mickey Magraff.

"We let Freeman and his wife go alone to bury their son in the snow. Freeman said he could handle the words said over David by himself. Mickey came out to our tent to get a supply of sugar and as he bent over his pack someone cold-cocked him from behind with a pistol butt. His own damn pistol, we have since learned."

"Fairchild?"

Matt nodded. "Let me go on. They went through this place like a whirlwind, for supplies and looking for something. The something, I have discovered, was my map. They also took a horse without a pack, and the tracks suggest that it was for Hazel to ride. Henry has Laura Lee getting the dogs hitched to the sleds. We want you to go along."

"Why me?" Nolan asked, though he really wanted to shout to the glacier top that he would go under *any* pretense as long as Laura Lee was going.

"It's not just to bring them back, Nolan, although they have to be brought back. They can't survive out there alone and we damn sure need the map back. But we also have needs. Before the storm broke we could see that we were all but about five miles off the glacier. There is wood and game down there. You could handle many of those things without our having to send several men."

Nolan shrugged, as though indifferent to it all. "Sure," he said after a pause. "I'll go."

But later, ploughing down the drifts, he felt cheated and put upon. Henry rode the back runners of the first sled and he was expected to do the same on the second. There was no Laura Lee to help him. He was on his own with the simple directions from Henry.

He had felt tongue-tied in not being able to ask why

Laura Lee was not coming along. Everyone was rushing him to wrap axes in blankets and Lundgren showing him how to use one of the new Winchester rifles he had brought from the east—as if he didn't already know everything there was to know about firearms. He didn't even have time to say good-bye to Laura Lee. It didn't dawn on him that he hadn't taken time to say good-bye to Lolly and Kimberly, either. If Henry hadn't been along he would have suspected that the whole mission had been created to keep him away from Laura Lee.

The Fairchilds had ploughed the horse straight down the bottom flank of the glacier. The sleds had to keep traversing back and forth across their plough path or they would have gained such momentum that they would have overrun the dogs.

The sky was breaking up and rays of sunlight streamed through. Far below they could see the moving black dots. Henry was amazed that Freeman was forcing the horse through the drifts at such a great speed. And it looked like the horse was being forced to carry both adults and their packs.

For a time he lost sight of them. The bottom section of the glacier had rolled itself into a series of foothills and gulleys. With the storm gone the constant winds of Mt. Elias started creeping down again. It caught the dry, powdered snow and swirled it about. The sleds moved in and out of miniature snowstorms. They also dipped in and out of the gulleys with so little warning that it took Nolan's breath away and nearly knocked his feet from the runners.

Then the land was suddenly flat. The horizon was a long black-green line. Nolan had almost forgotten what a forest could look like at a distance. The dot seemed three-quarters distance between them.

"Now we can catch them!" Henry called, letting the sleds come abreast. The dogs started yapping in delight, as though sensing they were going to be given their heads.

The sleds streaked over the snow the wind was beginning to freeze. The dogs panted and strained. Nolan gasped with the cold and pushed forward with his feet, as if trying to run with the huskies. Then he began to laugh, filled with the pure delight that the race was awakening in him. Now it wasn't just to get to the Fairchilds. It was to see which team of dogs could get there first.

As the wind whistled by his ears he could hear Henry return his laugh. Henry had forgotten the pleasure of the sport. His eyes glistened and he was no longer fifty. He could say good-bye to the *Malaspina*. He could say hello to home.

The dot grew in size as they sped closer. Then they realized why it was growing so fast. It wasn't moving. Nor did it move until they had reached it.

"Damn fools," Henry hissed, looking at the dead horse. "They won't get far on foot."

"And where did they go? The wind has already blown over their footprints. Damn, I wish it would stop. It's getting as cold as a bitch again."

"It's a good thing, Nolan. That snow on the glacier is loose, but the cold will freeze it to the surface and keep it from tumbling down on the camp. Well, it's a waste of time for both of us to look for them. You go on into the forest and I'll fan out and back from this point."

"How will we find each other?"

Henry grinned. "How do you find your way in your own forests, son? Blaze a trail on the trees that we can both follow."

Nolan felt foolish. Like a little boy who had to be taught by rote. But soon the feeling passed. He was back in his own world. It was immediately apparent to him that no man had ever cut here. He had never seen a forest as dense as this. Great trees pressed close upon him, thick and immensely tall, so that their interwoven branches had allowed only two to three feet of snow to cover the forest floor.

Nature had given him an overabundant supply of dead trees from which he could hack away massive branches, dragging them into a pile. He felt he could breathe again in the scent of resin and decay.

Twice Henry came back without having had any luck. Despite the urgency of his own task he could not help but chuckle at Nolan. The branch pile was already more than they could carry back up the glacier in ten trips. Nolan set to work chopping them into lengths that would fit on the sled.

When he heard Henry approach for the third time he didn't bother to stop work or turn around. When Henry remained silent he finally turned.

The moose stood inspecting him as though he were the oddity. The silence was absolute. Nolan had never seen a moose before, but the massive beast represented fresh meat. He let his eyes move to the sled and judge the distance. He would never get to the rifle and load it in time. The malamutes, seeing the moose, began to whimper. He wanted to hush them, but that might have driven the animal off faster than the whimpering. Turning his eyes back, he saw that the beast had turned its head to the sound of the dogs. The whole long neck was now exposed to Nolan. He slowly raised his ax arm. He tried to picture the neck as a tree stump. It was festival day. The stump had a target on it. The free-hand flung ax blade had to slice right through the center of the black X. Three years running he had been the champion, but the lumberjack just before him had come within a tenth of an inch of center. He would have to be dead center.

As though he had not even moved his muscular arm the ax went end over end through the air. The moose did not even have time to jerk its head back at the sound before the blade sank deep into the flesh and severed muscles, tendons and the jugular vein. The animal, without a sound, just scrunched down at the base of an ancient pine.

He would not even have to bleed the animal. The ax wound was taking care of that as well.

Nolan was so elated that this time he didn't hear Henry approach.

Henry screeched with delight. "You got him, boy! You got him with an ax!"

Nolan grinned, but couldn't think of anything to say.

Then Henry sobered. "Still no sign of them, but there's one bit of luck. Back down a ways is a clearing and then a dip down into a valley. It stretches southeast and looks passable. If we can get the moose and the wood to the clearing, it'll make a good camp site off the mountain."

Just minutes from the spot where Nolan had been working the trees began to thin out, and shafts of sunlight lanced through the boughs. The area was like a deep cove in the forest, with the open end giving a commanding view of the glacier flank and the lordly mountain.

They strung the moose up to a tree limb by its hind quarters. As Henry knifed away a front leg and thigh, Nolan took off his parka and unbuttoned the macintosh beneath.

"That's what has me worried," Henry said. "It's getting too warm and the wind is gone. Gotta get those people off the mountain quick, or at least lower. We made it here in three hours, but it'll take a lot longer with all those people and what's left of our supplies. Nolan, if I leave now, I might be able to at least get all the women down to the base by nightfall. I'll take some of this meat, some wood and both sleds. I want you to get a signal fire going right at the mouth of this glen. Keep it going all night so they can walk across the flat without getting lost. Keep up the good work with the wood, and keep an eye out for more game. After what we've all been through up there, I think it would be best to camp here for a few days and rebuild our strength before we try to leave."

"We giving up on the Fairchilds?"

Henry sighed. "Got twenty-one people up there who need us more than those two."

The work began to put a strain on Nolan after Henry left. Without the sled, the branches had to be lugged one at a time out to the edge of the glen. It was backbreaking work.

He lost track of time as he labored. He didn't see another living thing. Occasionally he would rest, and shield his eyes against the low hanging sun and try to spot Henry snaking the sleds back up the glacier flank. He had tried several times to spot the camp, but it was just a part of the overall whiteness. Once he thought he saw some black dots a quarter of the way up from the base, but when there were suddenly hundreds of them he realized they were just sun spots dancing upon his eyelids.

The winter sun dipped out of sight. Twilight still held the mountain and glacier in view. He was not aware that September had slipped into October.

The roar spun him around and he froze in place. The black bear came right out of the forest, waddling on its hind legs toward the hanging moose. It didn't seem to notice Nolan as it dropped to all fours and moved forward, sniffing at the footprints in the snow.

Nolan had kept his rifle with him at all times since the moose incident. Now he cautiously unslung it from his back, moving slowly and quietly.

The blood was pounding in his ears and his mouth was as dry as a bone. It seemed an eternity before the rifle butt was against his shoulder. He brought the barrel up, and got the bear in his sights. The huge animal was standing now, clawing at the carcass with his front paws, no more than thirty feet from where Nolan stood.

Then, suddenly, the rifle slammed hard. The noise echoed through the glen. The bear clawed at its throat, made a twisting turn and charged forward.

Nolan fired again. The soft-nosed bullets ripped into the

creature's flesh, and it roared again in its agony. But still it came on, refusing to die. Nolan looked into the jaws of death as the animal was upon him. He fired again, and the bear made a twisting leap and crashed to the ground.

The roaring and rumble wouldn't cease in his ears. He felt sick as he looked at the bear, blood oozing from the holes in its neck and side.

Weakly he sat down and put his hands over his ears. It reduced the sound but didn't make it go away. Then he realized it was coming from behind him and a long way off. He turned where he sat and it took him several moments to realize what he was looking at.

It looked like a snowstorm sweeping down from the top flank of the glacier. Like a fog bank rolling up the MacKenzie River. Boiling up, larger and larger.

Slowly he began to rise as the noise reached across the miles and grew steadily louder. In the twilight glow the front of the storm seemed like a rising cloud of gray smoke. Forest fire smoke. But there was nothing to burn up there.

A cry tore itself out of his throat. "Avalanche!"

He ran toward the edge of the glen and the bonfire. He ran even though he knew he hadn't a hope of doing anything about it.

Frantically, he scanned the lower glacier. Finally, he spotted the tiny sleds zigging and zagging their way back down. They were to the left of the steamrolling flurry of snow and ice. But the camp? Where in the hell would the camp be in the course of its expanding path? As he imagined the destruction of the camp, he suddenly remembered what Henry had told him—that sharp noises could set off an avalanche. *He* had done it! In killing the bear he'd been the cause of it all!

Nolan could not be aware that Lazlo Lundgren had taken it upon himself to take his two boys away from the camp for a bit of hunting themselves. In Sweden one could always find a rabbit or a pheasant in the snow. These type of snowdrifts were not new to them, although Lars had some difficulty with his cumbersome arm cast. They had left shortly after Henry and Nolan had set out after the Fairchilds, climbing back up the glacier at an angle to the camp. At about the time Henry and Nolan were standing over the dead horse, Lars was mistaking the sun shadows on ice ripples for a rock outcropping. A marvelous place for rabbits in their winter white coats. But distance was hard to judge on the glacier flank. By the time Lars thought he was getting close, the moose had been hung up and Henry was on his way back to the camp. And mirage delusions can be as deceptive on snow whiteness as desert expanses.

Both Lars and Michael saw the herd of white-tail deer leap and bound through the drifts. It took Lazlo a few moments to find the spot his sons excitedly pointed out. At first he thought it was just the setting sun moving the shadows about. But then he saw, too. Lars was just too exhausted to go on, and so his boys left him to rest while they tracked the herd. They would have venison. Mia did marvelous things with venison. They could almost taste the savory thick soup she made from venison, beans and rice.

A hundred yards after leaving Lars they saw the herd stop to graze, pawing through the snow to get to the tufts of grass. Together they took careful aim and fired again and again. Enough deer were falling to feed the entire camp.

As their bullets ate into the ice formations and snow, Nolan's bullets were ripping into the bear. Like Nolan, the Lundgrens heard a constant rumbling and roaring in their ears, but by the time they looked up it was too late to run. The wall of snow and ice was already seven feet high when it engulfed them. Seconds later it had doubled in force and speed when it rolled Lars into its smothering mass.

In the bake tent activity was at a fever pitch. Henry had come back with the moose and wood, but advised them to cook it when they got to a lower camp. He had Amalida Ramsey, Lolly and Kimberly climb aboard one of the dog sleds, and Laura Lee and Harriet Henderson on the other. Mia Lundgren refused to leave without her husband and sons.

Henry figured he could make two trips up and down the mountain before the twilight faded into total darkness. The horses and mules were to be packed lighter than usual, but the travois carriers were heavily loaded to flatten a trail through the deep drifts. The men could follow after the sleds. Not everything was to be taken. Later, after everyone had made it off the mountain, the sleds could be brought back up to pick up any necessary items.

Everyone was so busy that no one had asked Henry about the Fairchilds. He decided there was no reason to bring the subject up; he'd let them assume that the Fairchilds were down with Nolan.

Nolan was alone and struggling with strange emotions: helplessness and loneliness. He watched the sleds swerve in an arc, stop and almost immediately start back up at a sharp angle. His eyes travelled ahead of them on the angle and at last he spotted the camp, barely able to see the people through squinted eyes. Then he let his eyes go higher. The avalanche was like a locomotive bearing down on a station, its brakes pushing the steam release out to each side. It looked to Nolan as though the avalanche would brush the camp with its extreme left flank.

In the camp, before they became aware of the avalanche, everyone was hard at work. The smaller tents were already packed, and the bake tent was being taken down. Crow had the horses and mules packed and ready to go. Harlan Henderson had moved the crates of oven and bakery equipment to one side. They could come down later. Jethro Calhoun had been helpful. He knew exactly where Amalida was and was not worried. The Dunn men had their packs ready—they would be leaving nothing behind. Mickey Magraff had gone through what the Fairchilds had left behind to see if he could take anything that would make up for what they had stolen from him. Calvin Ramsey looked over the luggage and trunks he and Amalida had brought, and decided it could all wait except for the small wooden box containing his weight scale and weights. It was, in his opinion, as much a tool of his trade as the picks and shovels were for the miners.

Clampett Dunn was the first to hear the rumble and shout the warning. Twice before he had faced such an advancing wall and survived.

"Down!" he screamed. "Get down by anything that can shield you and form an air pocket about you! Let it roll over you and then . . ."

Mia Lundgren's scream drowned out the rest of his words. She raced away to warn her menfolk up on the glacier. Hampton Dunn ran after her to bring her back.

Matt and Mickey helped Crow untie the animals so they could run free.

Harlan crouched down by the bake tent, which he'd been trying to roll up for packing.

Nobody really had a chance to do anything. The wall of ice and snow was now nearly two hundred feet high and a mile and a half long. It crashed down the mountainside, moving at over seventy miles an hour. Even the outer fringe that touched the camp was devastating.

Nolan watched in awe and horror. It seemed to go on forever, leaving behind a powdery mist that seemed to take forever to settle in its wake. He lost his bearings on the sleds, which had disappeared, and had given up all hope for the camp. He listened as the rumble subsided, until the sound was as faint as an intaken breath.

Nolan needed something to do—anything to keep his mind off the destruction he had witnessed. He lit the bonfire. If anyone had managed to get off the sleds before they started back up they might have survived. They would need a beacon.

But no one came across the flat snowy plain. He waited, feeding the fire. Twice he went back into the forest to haul out more branches, even though his stack was ample. He knew he had to keep moving or go mad. He could not bear the thought of being left there completely alone—the sole survivor of a destructive force that he, himself, had unleashed.

He stood by the bonfire to warm himself, and peered through the darkness to see if anyone was coming. It had only been a few hours, but already he was starved for the sound of a human voice. Many times he had spent more than twelve hours alone in the forest topping trees, but that was different. He always knew that afterwards there would be a pint of beer with the others at the company tavern, and then there would be home and Lolly. Here, he didn't know if anyone else was alive.

The night was pitch-black. Before him was nothingness. No mountain, no glacier, no nothing. He walked away from the fire, out into the darkness.

As he walked, the Northern Lights began to send bands of green, red, blue and white arching across the black sky. He stood, his head tilted back, watching.

Something touched his arm and Nolan screamed.

"Sorry," Harriet Henderson croaked. "We're so weary. Been walking toward the light for hours."

He stood there, watching as the stocky woman moved toward the bonfire. As Amalida Ramsey passed by, clutching a bundle, she murmured something to him. He didn't hear her words, but from the way she tossed her hatted head he could tell she was angry about something. Then, through the darkness, he saw that someone else was coming. There was something familiar about the way she ambled along! His heart sang as he ran toward her. A minute later, she was in his arms.

He was crying and kissing her mouth. Her lips were salty with the taste of his own tears.

"I was so afraid," he whispered. "So afraid I had lost

you. The avalanche . . . and—you're safe. That's all that matters. Oh, Laura . . . Laura. . . . Laura Lee!"

Lolly pushed him away. "What did you call me?" she demanded.

Nolan stopped dead.

"What?" he groaned, and then got control of himself. "I called you Lolly, of course."

"No you didn't, Nolan Fedderson!"

"Oh, Lolly," he moaned. "I don't even know if I know my own name after being left here alone and seeing all that went on. I might have even kissed the hell out of old lady Henderson if she hadn't scared me so and sailed by so quickly. Where's Kimberly?"

"With Amalida Ramsey. Didn't she say? Probably not. She thinks her Calvin is the only one left up there. Henry and Laura Lee went back, but I don't think they're gonna find anyone alive. I don't even know if those two are still alive, because we lost sight of them. Laura Lee was foolish to go back. Henry said that she didn't have to go with him, but she insisted. I was wrong about her, Nolan. She didn't stay and help me when I needed her the most. And I think Amalida would have left us behind if Harriet had not protested. Nolan, I want you to take us away from this place . . ."

He looked at her in disbelief. He wanted to strike her, but controlled himself. No one wanted away from there more than he did—but he wouldn't leave without some word of Laura Lee.

Nolan was awake through the night. The Northern Lights had faded away, and the glow of dawn was touching the horizon as the first men struggled in.

Mickey Magraff and Lonsworth Crowley were badly cut and bruised, but shared the burden of Harlan Henderson between them. He was alive, but his pulse was weak and he was only semi-conscious. His bake tent was no more, and the horses and mules Matt, Mickey and Crow had tried to set free had perished. For the moment, they didn't even want to think about Matt Monroe. He had been with them one moment, but had vanished the next.

Near noon Jethro Calhoun arrived with Calvin Ramsey, whose shoulder was in severe pain. Then Herschel Dunn came in with his father. Clampett was in a state of shock. Hampton had disappeared with Mia Lundgren and Jerome and Cornell were still at the campsite digging around for Isaac. From the beginning, the journey had been tragic for the Dunn clan, and the deaths of his family members were finally getting to Clampett.

Dusk came early, and quickly turned to night. A new fire was lit and moose and bear meat was set to roast.

The Dunn boys dug a grateful Matt Monroe out from under the snow, but never found their brother Isaac. As the Northern Lights lit the sky both dog sleds arrived. One of the huskies had expired from the strenuous work, and they were now down to three dogs per sled. They had left six people and most of their supplies under the avalanche.

They were like a group of zombies. When some of their strength returned, Matt and Crow took the sleds back up the glacier to regain a piece of luggage here, a crate there, an uncovered backpack, an untouched barrel of flour, scattered picks and shovels, a hat box, a clothing trunk, and a few blocks of salt already melting into the glacier. Like a wandering band of gypsies they placed their last material things upon the sleds and headed down the valley to Skagway. They ate off the land and lost all track of time.

7

It was almost like leaving heaven for hell.

They had come through many valleys between the towering snowy peaks. They had skirted other glaciers with their craggy blue sides that dropped right off into the inland waterway. When they looked down into the waters of the Lynn Canal with the ships at anchor in the deep water, it was mid-October.

It had taken them thirty-two days from Yakutat. But even as they crawled down into the town that a short time before had been only a trading post, two more ships arrived. Over the rails and down into the long boats came boxes, bales, sleds, tools and supplies. Horses and dogs were pushed overboard into the icy water, and had to swim to shore.

Tents sprang up only long enough for the incoming supplies to be gathered, a rest taken, and then a start up the trail for White Pass.

Back from the beach, as though by magic, shacks had sprung up in those few months. Rough log cabins boasted of being stores, cafes and saloons. The Broadway Hotel, on a muddy street of the same name, was a crude structure made of rickety boards pried from packing boxes, and had all of four bunk beds.

One man, Captain Ebner Moore, had claim to all the land because of his trading post. He and the fishing Indians of the nearby village were ignored and overrun. People squatted where they wanted to squat and chased off others with shotguns. There was no law and order, or even much common sense for that matter.

In the crude store Harriet Henderson ran her hand over a potato as though it were a precious gem.

"Don't touch unless you're going to buy," shouted the clerk.

Nothing in the store was priced. "How much?" Harriet asked.

"A dollar."

The idea of buying enough food for everyone faded. She had paid a dollar a barrel for potatoes in Seattle.

But these problems seemed to amuse Jethro Calhoun exceedingly. It was forcing them to stay together for the moment and would equally force Calvin into digging out the gold. As wealthy as they were, he was sure they wouldn't continue living like they had been forced to for the past five weeks.

Henry Boise found them space to set up camp in the woods behind the Indian village. As they had been doing for days, they built pine bough shelters.

"The Chilkoots haven't kept an accurate count, but from what they say, I estimate a good 15,000 to 20,000 have already gone to White Pass and Chilkoot Pass. As many as four ships now arrive every day. They clog the passes, which are already snowbound, but the waters of the Yukon still run—although the river is becoming ice-choked."

"What are you really saying, Henry?" Matt asked.

"Under the circumstances I don't see how any of us can go forward or even survive alone. The Chilkoots have been packing for many. What canoes and small boats are available sell quicker than the dogs. Speaking of which,

I've been offered as much as $350 apiece for Lundgren's dogs."

"Perhaps some of us don't wish to go on," Harlan Henderson said wearily.

"Not go on!" exclaimed Harriet, with a good-humored laugh. "Bless my soul! We've been tested against the worst of odds. I don't care if 50,000 are ahead and 50,000 behind. They are going to have to learn what we already know."

"True, of course," Herschel Dunn grumbled, "but Harlan's point is well taken. My father has lost much on the journey, and it has been decided that I will take him home by ship. Jerome and Cornell will stay with you. We leave with them our supplies for the good of all."

"We are grateful," Henry said. "But food will be our biggest supply problem. You heard Harriet's report on the store prices. There will still be fifteen of us to feed."

Amalida looked around the group for a moment, and thoughtfully rubbed her hands against her shapely, corseted hips. "Some of you, I am sure, still have some cash left. I would suggest we make no purchase without consulting the others so that we have no unnecessary duplication."

Everyone was amazed but Calvin. She had stated it nearly as rehearsed. Like it or not, Amalida was going to have to show a cooperative face. There was safety in numbers and greater safety among people they had come to know.

"To add to my wife's suggestion," he said, "which I feel is excellent, my plan—as some of you know—is to continue banking in this country. My resources are limited, but if loans are needed, they are available."

That Calvin Ramsey was a prosperous man was of course clear to all who had travelled with him. The trunk found after the avalanche still afforded Calvin and Amalida a wide selection of clothing. But they had not lorded their wealth over anyone else, nor had they stayed apart from the others. In fact, Calvin had gone out of his way to help as much as any of the other men. Amalida had also held her tongue, for the most part. It was as though her near death on the glacier had done something to change each of them by a degree. Therefore, Calvin's offer was not seen as the plan of a greedy banker anxious to take advantage of desperate people, but as a sincere effort to help.

Only Jethro saw it as a fantastic opportunity. He had hardly believed that Amalida had openly patted the corset and then was dumbfounded that Calvin was ready to start loaning out the gold. The time was at hand for him to make sure the gold and the couple never left Skagway.

A chorus of good-intended suggestions greeted Calvin's own. The small tents, which they had not taken the time to pitch lately, could be lashed together into one. Mickey, Matt and Crow could combine what mining equipment they had left and eliminate the need to purchase more. With the Lundgrens gone they would consider the dogs and sleds as community property—under the care of Henry and Laura Lee Boise. The Hendersons had nearly been wiped out, but they had funds that they could add to the food supply needs. Henry felt they could do better if he did the trading for them in bulk through the Chilkoot people.

"And," Henry expanded, "we will be in finer fettle than the majority. We have our excellent lumberman with us. Nolan, you spoke once of helping your father build the rafts that helped float the logs down the MacKenzie. You still have your pack of logging tools and need but tell us what else you shall require when we get to the river."

Nolan nodded sullenly. Now he was going to be caught and couldn't lie his way out of it. He realized suddenly that he feared letting Lolly know about the mining equipment in the pack. She'd changed a lot since her eyesight had fully returned. Around him she was still timid, but around the women she seemed to have a strength she had never had before. The only part he didn't like about that was her closeness to Laura Lee. He knew that women had a tendency to share secrets. He feared he would become a shared secret between them.

"Nolan," Crow said, "when it comes to building rafts you can count on me. I've built hundreds of them."

It caused Mickey and Matt to laugh. Crow would never change.

The glacier had changed Matt. He still had nightmares of being buried alive under the snow. He had never really thought about life before, now he thought of nothing else. For days after his rescue he had been in a void. Lolly had cared for him and confiided in him about her own fears of being permanently blind. They were both seeing the world again through different eyes, and it was something they alone shared. There was also an undeniable physical attraction between them. In a blinding flash, Matt realized he was falling in love, but that he couldn't do a damn thing about it. He had come to admire Nolan Fedderson and his abilities, if not to actually like the man. With regrets, Matt decided that he would have to keep his thoughts about Fedderson's wife to himself.

"Mr. Ramsey," Nolan whispered, as Calvin and Amalida were starting to walk away. "May I see you for a moment—in private?"

"Certainly, Nolan. Amalida, I'll be with you in a moment."

As Amalida departed, Calvin turned back to Nolan. "My wife will never change," he said. "She is determined to see if that store has anything of worth and feels her face and clothing should be proper for shopping. Now, what can I do for you?"

Jethro had heard all he needed to know. He headed for his own pine bower and then circled back in the trees to come out behind where the Ramseys were to sleep. He would wait, catch Amalida with the goods and then present his evidence to Calvin when he arrived from his talk with Fedderson.

"Well," Calvin said thoughtfully, when Nolan had stammered out the truth, "I don't see where you have done anything different than thousands of others. Gold, after all, is what they are all seeking."

"But everyone thinks I have saws and axes and the like. Busted one ax in the crevasse and have chopped the other one down to dullness. I was so damn foolish I don't even have a hone to sharpen it. Cut most of the pines for the bowers with a hatchet."

"Are you seeking funds?"

"Got some left from the Clara Bennett loan." He hesitated. He had never had to make such a statement in his life and dreaded being laughed at. "I really need advice and help from someone smarter than me about money. When you buy in a company town you just write it down and they take it out of your pay. I ain't admitted to nobody, but I paid a hell of a lot different for my supplies in Seattle than some of the others—nearly double of what Matt paid for almost the same. Here, from the talk, it will be worse. I know what I need, but I don't want anyone knowing I need it . . . and I could use the help of someone like you to keep me from being cheated."

Calvin considered the idea. He had great respect for Nolan's knowledge and woodsmanship. In fact, he didn't think they would have survived without it. It gave him inner pride to have the man respect his ability and intelligence enough to ask for his help.

"Let me check on Mrs. Ramsey, Nolan, and then we will skip along and see what is available."

As they walked, Nolan thought to himself that Ramsey wasn't such a bad guy after all.

Amalida had changed skirts and was pawing through the trunk for a proper bodice when she heard Calvin flip back the blanket covering the front of the bower. She was about to scold him for exposing her to the whole outside world when she looked back. Then she whirled, grabbing the first thing at hand.

Jethro was bent over, peering under the blanket, shading his eyes with his hand. Amalida took a step forward, lifting the parasol, bringing it down across the man's back with all the force she could muster. It broke in half.

"Peeping Tom!" she snarled. "Trying to catch me in my camisole and corset!"

Jethro fell back, laughing.

"Only your corset, Mrs. Raymond Forbes!"

Amalida had enough presence of mind not to react to that, only his intrusion.

"Get," she said. "Get back out of here, you lecherous bastard!"

"Now, is that any way for a southern belle tah talk, Ann Forbes?"

"Are you blind or insane?" she snapped. "I am Amalida Ramsey!"

"The lie is over," Jethro said with cold fury. "You are Ann Forbes. I felt the gold in your corset when I brought you up the glacier. Now, take it off and hand it over."

"You're insane," she said sullenly. "I am not about to undress in front of you."

He took a knife from his waist. "If you won't take it off, then I'll just have to cut it off."

Amalida showed no fear. "I don't think you would dare with my husband standing behind you."

Jethro laughed. "Been expecting him." He quickly stepped to the side and pulled out a pistol with his other hand. "I am very good with either hand, Mr. Forbes. Step in, please."

"What is this?" Calvin gasped, as though greatly surprised.

"The end," Jethro mused. "The end of a very, very long chase from New Orleans, Mr. and Mrs. Raymond Forbes!"

"*Who*?"

"Oh, you are good, you two. Fixed yourself up a mite to make a change, but it is over. I know she has the gold in her corset, and I'm going to take you back."

"At gunpoint," Calvin growled, "it is hard to protest. I don't know your game, mister. Straggling and looking for a chance to steal, most likely. But there's nothing in her corset."

"Don't give me that! I felt the gold coins in her corset on the glacier. That was clever. When I couldn't find it among your things on the boat I was puzzled. The corset, please."

"You're welcome to it. Amalida, turn and I shall unlace you. Do not be embarrassed or afraid."

She turned and kept herself turned even after Calvin had taken off the corset and tossed it to Jethro.

"Do you mind if my wife covers herself?"

"Not at all. I can't take her down to the boat like that."

Calvin was unarmed so Jethro had no fear of sitting, putting aside his pistol and taking the knife to the corset. Section by section he sliced at the panels to expose the gold coins. The weight was wrong—something was changed about them. As he tore them out one by one a strange feeling tugged at his brain.

"What in the hell is this?"

"Exactly what you felt on the glacier, I would assume."

"These aren't gold," Jethro said tiredly. "They ain't nothing but the lead weights used on a banker's scale. Where is the gold?"

"I think it's time for you to leave, Mr. Calhoun," Calvin said, ignoring the question. "You have made enough of a fool of yourself for one day. I don't know who you are or what your game is, but I would advise you never to cross my path when we are both equally armed."

Jethro rose slowly, bringing the pistol up with him. He would not give up that easily. The gold had to be somewhere. He didn't even care now if he had to take these two back dead—as long as he had the gold.

"Take him," Calvin said quietly.

Nolan had come to see what was taking Calvin so long. With the blanket flapped back he saw Jethro rise and hold a gun on the couple. He had crept forward as quietly as possible. He had immediately thought it was robbery, because Calvin had announced he had money to loan.

Jethro did not struggle, but stood there as the big man pinioned his arms, knowing in his heart that it was now too late to struggle, even to try to make the lumberjack see the truth. It was too late to explain who he really was, and who they were. He had moved too fast, damn his folly and pride!

"What should I do with him?"

"Let him go. I don't think he'll try anything else."

"Don't count on it," Jethro sneered. "I shall leave you for the time being, but you're bound to make an error, Forbes, and I'll be around when you do."

He turned and stalked from the tent, cursing loudly. With Nolan having seen this he could not continue on with the group. He would just have to get ahead of them and wait for his next chance. He was just beginning to understand that Raymond Forbes was a master at trickery.

"Thank you, Nolan," Calvin said gravely. He turned to Amalida, who was shaking violently, her back to him. "I'm sorry, my dear, that you had to be frightened," he said. "Why don't you forget the shopping, and relax for awhile. I do have some pressing business to conduct, however. Nolan, would you please wait for me outside while I talk to my wife."

Nolan left without answering him. He had put himself in the man's favor and felt very good about it.

Amalida turned, still shaking. But it was not from fear. She had hardly been able to control her mirth while Jethro had torn through her corset.

"I wish I could have seen his face," she chuckled.

"I doubt if he would have shot you in the back," he said, not unkindly.

"You might give me credit for stalling him," she said icily.

"I give you credit, my dear, for smelling him out on the glacier. It was a good thing we moved the gold when we did, though frankly I have felt like an overstuffed pig coming away from a holiday feast ever since we sewed it into the lining of my vest. I don't know how you stood it for so long."

Amalida frowned. "Do you think Fedderson knows anything?"

"No, he's still in the dark. He has no idea what's going on. Anyway, we are about to seal his lips with gratitude. I will need two thousand dollars from your 'loaning' fund, my dear. Believe me, it will be the best investment we ever made."

"I hope so," she said. "That's half of what we have left."

"Five hundred miles, my dear," he said with a sigh. "Just five hundred miles more and we can put the vest money to use."

There were those who did not want to see them make their first mile—Jethro not withstanding. It wasn't anything personal; everyone wanted the advantage of the first forward step.

They were a large group, they were organized, and they were winter-hardened. Thus, they were resented.

The wagons that some still foolishly tried to bump along the first part of the trail out of Skagway, they passed in a steady single file. They were using the tea cart wheels on the sleds again because too many feet and wagons had made the trail marshy and muddy. It wasn't easy even with the wheels, but it was the only way.

When the trail turned into a path too narrow for the wagons, where there was still ice and snow, the wheels were removed, and the sleds moved along well on their runners.

Higher up, when Skagway and the fjord could no longer be seen, the path wound and twisted abrouptly around boulders in so crooked a fashion that it doubled back on itself a dozen times in a hundred feet. Grown men had to stop and catch their breath at every curve.

They were passed by the women, who would take a hundred steps, rest for a count of a hundred, and then go on. The would-be miners cussed and grumbled, resenting the easy mobility of the womenfolk.

They laughed when they saw Henry make everyone in his party remove their boots to ford the numerous streams and rivers on the way to White Pass. They didn't laugh that night, when the leather of their wet boots froze solid on their feet.

According to the hand-drawn map they'd purchased in Skagway, it was 45 miles to Lake Bennett and the interconnecting rivers and lakes to the Yukon. Like Matt's map, it was misleading. It was 45 miles of hell and then 500 miles of torture. Most of them thought they were in for just a few day's journey.

Then they saw the Scales. A path along thirty-five degree steep ledges that dropped off to the side for over 500 feet. One man froze in panic, unable to go forward, blocked from behind by the others and not daring to look down.

The scream was fierce as the man was toppled from the ledge.

"Lord God, man!" someone said to Jethro Calhoun.

"It was the only way to move him out of our way!" Jethro said. No one responded, but as they moved on many of the men burned Jethro's face into their minds.

Two days later, his former group passed the same spot. Roped together, they moved smoothly and expertly. Their packs were light, with most of the heavier items tied on the sleds that Henry and Laura Lee had taken the long way around by a Chilkoot trail the miner thought too long.

They didn't want to look down as they negotiated the Scales. The smell of death hung in the air. The miner Jethro had pushed over the edge had not been the first, nor would he be the last. Not only men, but also hundreds of horses and mules had taken that plunge. By the next spring the canyon would have claimed over two thousand animals, including many horses who, according to the miners, had committed suicide rather than cross the narrow ledges.

The Scales created another problem for the miners. It was only a half-mile long, but was so steep that it took six hours to climb. A city-bred man could only make it with about 50 pounds of his supplies at a time. Many had brought close to a ton of necessities that had to be taken up the Scales and then over the pass. The maps led them to believe that once over the Scales, from Lake Bennett on, boats could carry the burden. But even with Chilkoot packers—at forty cents a pound—it would take 35 to 40 trips to get their supplies up. That would take three months.

So men fought to get back down and then back up again. Many of them, on their way down, would force ascending groups back to a wide spot at gun-point. But how did one force back a roped party of twelve when the lead man carried a cocked and ready repeating Winchester rifle?

Ironically, because he was the point man, they became known up and down the trail as the "Fedderson group." The rumors that began to surround them would have made them laugh.

"Goddamn syndicate, I hear tell."

"Yep, smart-ass engineer types."

"See'd 'em before in Nor'Dakotee. Came in with all the latest tools, and put honest miners right out of business."

"That's why they travel so light. Heard tell they got a

whole fleet of steamboats loaded with heavy equipment going up the Yukon from that St. Michaels. Every damn claim will be owned by their big companies 'fore we can get there."

No one thought to question why the "engineer-types" would be taking this hazardous route when they might have been sailing with their heavy equipment. It was just that anyone who looked like they might be from a higher rung on the social ladder was resented and distrusted.

Above the Scales the real challenge loomed.

"I feel like I've been here before," Laura Lee Boise said, her voice quavering as she looked up at the pass. It was getting dark, and they were stopping for the night.

Nolan stared at her. It was the first time in a long while that they had been alone together, and he felt unsure of himself.

"Don't be frightened, Laura Lee. This is nothing compared to the glacier."

"It's about the same," she said dully. "When my father and I got here yesterday afternoon with the sleds, I thought it was thrilling to see over two hundred men in single file stairstepping up that white face. From here they looked like a line of ants. Then the rumble started, just like on the glacier, and the whole left side of that mountain just gave way and came tumbling down on them. It rolled and tumbled them away just like it did to our camp on the glacier. It was horrible."

"Don't think about it."

"What was really horrible was that no one went to help dig out the ones under the avalanche. Even before the rumble had stopped the line was just as full as before and moving upward. They are crazed animals, all. Father had to sit up all night or they would have stolen the dogs."

"Don't dwell on it," Nolan insisted. "Think about getting there. That's what I think about. That . . . and being there alone with you."

"We'll be moving right on," Laura Lee said, looking away from Nolan.

"You can't! What about us?"

"What *about* us?" she asked.

"Lord God, Laura Lee! I *love* you! *That's* what about us!"

"I have to go to my mother," she said flatly, "and forget all about you. You have your woman."

"I'll get rid of her," Nolan said at once. "That's what I'll do. I'll get rid of Lolly and then you and I can be together. You drive me crazy, Laura Lee—I have to be near you."

"Don't you think I feel the same?" she said scornfully. "I have had to force myself to stay away from you. I have never hated anyone in my entire life, but you've almost forced me to hate Lolly. I fight it and try to be nice to her, but can't escape the fact that she is your woman, your wife. You can't get rid of her. You're married."

"I can change that."

"You're married," she sobbed. "You can never change that."

"For God's sake, Laura Lee!" he burst out. "Haven't you ever heard of divorce?"

"I was raised Catholic," she said, her eyes blazing.

He stopped short, confusion in his eyes.

"I don't believe in any God!"

"Then I don't believe you're capable of loving."

"That's bullcrap," he roared, but his eyes were bleak and sombre.

"I'm sorry, Nolan. I hunger for you, but I have to say good-bye. It hurts me to say it, but I can't bring myself to hurt Lolly."

He faltered, his mouth open, the words trembling on his tongue.

"I'll find a way for us to be together," he said.

* * *

"Look at those bastards! They ain't playing fair!"

They had no intention of playing fair, only to play it safe. At dawn, after a freezing night, the sleds were discarded and little packs slung over the backs of each malamute and husky. Henry broke the trail with them, going far right of the long icy stairsteps. Here, where the sunlight would not reach them for hours, the surface remained crisp and hard, but more importantly less prone to avalanche danger. Again they roped themselves together, and formed a serpentine line around the overhanging cliffs of white. They were silent. They had seen what sound could do here.

Snow was falling in thick flakes that were as soft and dry as feathers. It was an element Henry had not counted on, but was thankful for. It was keeping the parallel line on the stairsteps greatly reduced. He was not in a race with them. He just didn't want two hundred-odd feet stomping in unison on the snow field, sending out dangerous vibrations.

He was growing quite fond of the group—proud of it, in fact. The degree of cooperation was remarkable. It hardly seemed possible that this was the same group that had off-loaded at Yakutat.

Even before they were halfway up, others were trying to emulate their route.

Excitement spread from man to man as they neared the summit, because once they made it over the pass and down to Lake Bennett they would finally be in the Yukon Territory of Canada.

But ahead of them were the men in the coats of frangipani scarlet, who had been rushed from Fort Constaine to slow, stop, or tax the great influx of men and women into their country.

"What is it?"

"Mounties. They have stopped the whole line and are turning some back."

"I don't like it," Jerome Dunn said.

"It is not a question of liking," Henry said. "We are in Canada now, not Alaska. We had best learn what rules they wish us to play by."

Jerome considered this point of view, not with the mocking derision still apparent upon his face, but seriously.

"I have a pack like most of the others, I'll go find out."

"Why you?" his brother sneered.

"Because I have brains," Jerome boasted. "Brains are mighty rare and mighty valuable, little brother."

Cornell, of course, didn't think his brother was particularly brainy, but he didn't bother to argue with him.

"They have a damned peculiar way of looking at things," Jerome said when he returned. "They say the waters are beginning to freeze, so no one can go on through to the lake unless they have a half year's supply of food, clothing and tools to see them through the winter. Oh, and five hundred dollars in cash. Ain't many getting through. Those that do are being sent to a camp down by the lake for the winter. Oh, another thing. Guess who I saw? Calhoun. Standing right by the Mounties as though looking for someone to come through. He didn't even recognize me. I wonder what he's doing with them."

"My love," Amalida said suddenly, taking her husband's arm, "since all we have of what's required is the money, I think we should turn back to Skagway."

"No one turns back," Henry said so low they had to strain to hear him. "We all lack one thing or another. One by one filter into the woods as though for a call of nature. Laura Lee and I will start back as though we're just Indian packers. Go about two miles and then head for the northwest corner of the lake."

As they slowly departed, one by one, Henry took Calvin to the side.

"Mr. Ramsey, I saw that man Calhoun leave your bower

in some great haste. If he is posing some sort of problem for our group I would appreciate knowing it."

"He is but a personal problem," Calvin said sadly.

"Perhaps at one time, yes. We have had a rough time as a group and that is now being used against us. I do not wish to pry into a personal matter. Mr. Ramsey, I was—and still am—a Catholic priest. I shall treat the matter as though in the confessional."

Strangely, Calvin found himself telling the whole story, omitting nothing, not even trying to conceal his guilt. When he was done, Henry stood there a long time in silence. The others had almost all vanished by now into the thick woods.

"I remember the stories from the New Orleans papers," he said at last. "I do not have an answer for someone who has basically stolen from himself—or from his father-in-law, so to speak. It is the rules you really broke, but rules that Carter was already breaking. I am not one who can rightly judge others for the breaking of rules. Thank you for your honesty. Now we have another set of eyes on the man. As you say, he is most determined."

Calvin had a sudden inspiration and whispered in Henry's ear. Laura Lee and Amalida heard the musical tinkle of Henry's laughter, and the glissando rush of his reply; but they could not make out what was said. Calvin's delighted roar, however, was clear enough.

"Stay with the dogs, Amalida," he called. "We have male matters to attend to."

"It's them . . ." Jethro Calhoun shouted breathlessly, even before the group were near to the guards.

"Which ones?" Sergeant Fontaine asked, roughly.

"With the dogs. The well dressed couple, and the fat man and girl in Indian parkas."

Fontaine shrugged and started back along the line. Calhoun's papers only gave him authority to the border.

That he had asked help from the border patrol had been taken by Inspector Pitkin as a sign of respect. He had but twelve men stationed at Chilkoot and White Pass, and another twelve out on patrol. He did want to keep criminal elements out of Canada, but this man Calhoun was beginning to make a pest of himself.

The sergeant snapped a salute at them cordially. Amalida looked at Calvin in wonder. There had been no time to explain the strange and sudden change in plans.

"Pardon me for this delay. I have with me a detective, Mr. Calhoun, who has papers for the arrest of one Raymond Forbes and his wife Ann. I shall require identification."

Henry stepped forward. Having judged the Mounty correctly he spoke in French.

"Calhoun is also known to us, sergeant," he said flatly. "He came with us on the *Brisbane* to Yakutat and then across the Malaspina Glacier and down into Skagway."

The French-Canadian sergeant frowned. The detective had related none of this to the inspector. "Did he make himself known or try to make an arrest, *monsieur*?" he asked in French.

Henry smiled, ever so slowly. "He held them at gun point and ripped at Mrs. Ramsey's corset, supposedly in search of gold. He found only banker's lead weights."

"What lies is he telling you?" Jethro growled. "I demand that they be searched for the gold and detained until it is found."

"Sergeant," Henry grinned, still speaking French, "if that is all he wishes, grant it. We have nothing to hide upon our persons or in the packs on the backs of our dogs. We have money, to be sure, for it is the regulation. We have food and equipment for the Ramseys in the Klondike, for it is the regulation. Beyond that, I have food enough to get the young lady back to her village of Tlingits."

"What the devil is he saying now?" Jethro demanded.

"That they do not mind being searched," Fontaine said curtly.

Henry threw back the hood of his parka and opened the front, grinning at the interpreter.

"I do not mind being inspected first," he said complacently.

"*Morbleu*!" said Fontaine, whose purple cheeks from the cold had suddenly become white with disbelief. He stared at the white collar and black vestments under the parka. "I did not know that you were a priest, Father!"

"More fakery," Calhoun hissed.

"You may search out that truth, too, sergeant."

Fontaine smiled at him, sheepishly.

"That will not be necessary. I am sorry about this whole incident."

"You are only doing your duty, sir," Calvin said quickly. "But the cloud remains. This man has made an accusation against me and my wife. I want it cleared up, once and for all. I insist upon a complete search to convince this man that we carry no stolen gold."

Fontaine shrugged. "Mr. Calhoun, I put the responsibility fully upon your shoulders."

Jethro studied Calvin a long time, and very carefully. He knew he was being tricked again. But how? One look at Amalida told him that she was no longer wearing a corset. Henry would not have agreed to the dogs being searched if they carried anything. It had to be on Calvin's person and he was gambling that he would not be searched.

Before Fontaine could protest, Calhoun was patting his hands all over Calvin's greatcoat, beneath the flaps to feel every inch of the suit coat, vest, and up and down each leg. Calvin stood stoically calm and poised.

"My wife, seregant," Calvin said, with equally measured calm, "has on her person our money belt . . . if *you* would care to inspect it."

"No more!" he growled. "Please be on your way."

Jethro Calhoun watched them go. If you're going to be a crook, he thought, that was the kind of crook to be. Unflappable!

But what next? It was obvious that the Royal Canadian Mounted Police wouldn't give him any more help and would probably prevent him from following them.

A mounted patrol came into view. Jethro saw that they had some captives. The young lieutenant commanding them raised his hand, and the column came to an abrupt halt.

"Caught them trying to steal boats and provisions, Sergeant Fontaine. Remember their faces, and be sure not to let them back in."

Jethro also studied their faces. They were of every species of villainy ever produced. He smiled. Perhaps a crook could catch a crook.

On the near shores of the lake a city of several thousand tents had sprung up. Here, too, the "Yellow-legs" patrolled, a nickname quickly given to the Mounties because of the stripe down their trouser legs.

Henry herded the dogs right through the center of the tents, boxes, bales and men. A mile back he had Laura Lee take the Ramseys into the woods and around the tent city. But he wanted to fill his eyes and ears with all the gossip and news.

He saw only two Mounties. One trying to keep the fights among the miners to a minimum and the other walking the shoreline from boat construction site to boat construction site. There were hundreds of them. Rafts, scows, dories—or so they tried to appear.

But each, Henry heard, were given the same precaution. No more boats would depart until spring. There was no time left to get all the way to Dawson.

Meeting up with Laura Lee he didn't mention all he had seen or heard. His mind was busy recalling the area. Twice in his nine years among the Tlingits he had come as far south as Lake Laberge. It wasn't even shown on the Skagway maps, but he figured it was a hundred to a hundred-and-fifty miles away. From the Chilkoots he had learned there was a Tlingit village on the northern shore of the lake. He was very doubtful that they would be the people of Laura Lee's mother, but he would go to see them anyway.

Matt Monroe had also considered the closeness of the tent city and the patrolling mounties. When they had regathered in the woods he kept them moving northwest, Nolan marking their path so Henry could find them. Ten miles along they decided upon a lake cove. Their fires would not be seen. The forest rose straight up behind the beach, making it easy to slide logs down. There was a natural cleft between two huge rocks that Nolan considered quite good for a saw-pit, and there was dead wood everywhere suitable for a fire. The waters of the lake still lapped, although an ice crust had begun to form about the edges of the cove.

By the time Henry and the others arrived with the dogs, Nolan was already in the forest cutting trees. Crow and Mickey had fashioned rope harnesses to go over their backs and were hauling down two freshly cut trees. Others were bringing in the firewood, and Harriet and Lolly had gathered stones for a fire-pit.

They were warmly greeted, but the work did not cease.

Jerome and Cornell took a log from Mickey and hoisted it up into the rock cleft lengthwise. Then, starting in the middle of one end, Jerome atop and Cornell beneath, they began to sever the log in two with Nolan's long two-man saw. It cut easily through the soft pine.

"Hey!" Cornell barked. "All I'm getting down here is a face full of sawdust!"

"Then keep your eyes closed," Jerome called back. "All you have to do is guide the damn thing. I'll do all the pulling and pushing from up here."

Harlan Henderson came to them excitedly, a Skagway map and stub of a pencil in his hands.

"This is the general plan Nolan asked me to trace out. Two rafts, with a longtiller and polers for each side."

Henry didn't want to tell him that the pencil lines looked fine for a craft on the Ohio or Mississippi, but that the lakes and Yukon demanded a different breed of boat. He held his silence. This was the man who had wanted to give it all up just a few days before. He was the only one Henry had really been worried about. They were of the same age, but the glacier had made Harlan seem far older than his fifty years.

"Oh, Ramsey," Henry said. "I believe that I am wearing something of yours."

Calvin grinned. "If my vest keeps you warm, Father, why don't you continue to wear it for awhile?"

Henry nodded and walked off to help Laura Lee see to the dogs.

Amalida stood for a moment, and then her smile flashed brilliantly under the inevitable veil.

"I can't believe it," she laughed. "I thought you had hidden it on one of the dogs."

Calvin stared at her with that icy contempt a master conspirator always has for a bumbling amateur, but then he smiled warmly.

"I am quite sure, my dear," he said, "that I haven't the faintest idea what you mean. I loaned a vest to the good padre, is all."

"He doesn't know?" she gasped.

"*You* shouldn't know," he said impulsively. "I doubt that we have seen the last of Stillman's detective friend. You were most brilliant in Skagway, I must say. But out of sight is out of mind. Well, I think I had best offer my services. Wood and I were not strangers as a youth."

Amalida pushed back the veil. For once she was glad not to know everything. Until she had stumbled down the glacier the gold had been the most important thing in her life. It had taken some time to get over the shakes and then slowly realize that Calhoun's hands had not been on her merely for rescue. Each day after that survival had grown to be more important than the gold. Coming off the glacier, with the avalanche rumbling down on the camp, she had been startled by a sudden realization. Calvin was still at the camp and wearing the vest that they had sewn the gold into. But the gold was meaningless. It was her husband who now faced death. She knew that Calvin could have gone on living if she had been killed. But she suddenly knew that she could not go on living if anything happened to Calvin. If he had still been Raymond Forbes she wouldn't have snapped her fingers over the matter. But he wasn't Raymond Forbes. He had been playing the role of Calvin Ramsey for so long that he had become Calvin Ramsey. She liked that. Still, she didn't fully like Amalida Ramsey.

Crow was true to form. He turned his lie into truth by having to be told a thing only once and then expertly going about it. Full logs were lashed together with rawhide, the cracks between them caulked with a mixture of lake mud and sawdust. Then, half logs were lashed together atop the base to make a somewhat flat deck. A hut was built on the stern for storage and protection from the river winds. Because of the lake's depth Henry talked them into fashioning paddles for the ends of the long poles. The tiller he did not comment on because Harlan Henderson had chiselled it out alone from a center plank sawed by Jerome and Cornell—this time with Jerome getting the sawdust in his face.

They were all justly proud that one whole raft was completed in four days, with half the "keel" laid and lashed for the next.

Above the cove, Nolan had carved the trees gently out of the forest, making two curves in the slide path so the logs wouldn't go down too quickly and right out into the lake. Even so, Crow and Mickey had to puff along to keep them on course and break them out of each turning.

"Ah, Nolan Fedderson," Crow kidded, "enough trees. We aren't building a schooner, you know."

He started to comment when something sang over his head, making a high-pitched whistling sound. It was only after it had bitten into the tree trunk a few inches from him, kicking out a great gash, that he heard the crack.

"Rifle shot!" he bellowed. "What the hell?"

It came again, this time exploding a puff of snow at Crow's feet. Nolan threw down the ax and reached for the Winchester.

"What in the hell you doing up there?" he roared.

"We like your raft!" a mocking voice floated down from the deep woods. "If you want to see it again, put down the pea-shooter."

Black rage mounted in Nolan's face. "Get down and warn the others," he hissed to Crow and Mickey. "I'll hold them off."

The minute the two started to run down the slide path a whole volley crashed down, and spurts of snow leaped up all around them. They dashed into the trees, their voices setting up an alarm.

Nolan tried to spot flashes in the forest shadows. Then he saw a smoke haze. Six rifle shots followed one another, right along the base of the haze. He heard a rifleman scream. Then he heard another heavy volley crashing down on the camp from a different angle and he threw himself down the hillside in the direction of that fire while the bullets sang around his pounding feet. Jethro Calhoun's gunmen were shooting to kill.

But the camp had their guns now, and they squatted behind the rocks and in the raft hut and in the saw-pit, well protected, sending a hail of shot pouring into the smoke cloud from the hill. The men on the hill fired back raggedly. They had been made deputies and smuggled across the border to catch these desperate crooks, who would shoot to kill if not taken by surprise.

They were beginning to believe and moved now to get better position.

As Nolan worked his way down, he could hear men pounding down after him. Then he saw them darting in and out of the trees to his left. He fired the rifle from his hip as he ran, then fell behind a rock to reload. There were more screams from the hill.

The camp guns fired another volley, and now there was a great scurrying on the mountain. Dark figures darted out from the rocks and trees and started running downhill, some of them whipping out pistols.

"Everyone onto the raft," Henry called to everyone. "This racket will bring a patrol on the double."

Henry and the men crouched there, waiting for more fire, but there was none. Calhoun was getting his men into position so that every shot would count.

"Push the raft into the lake," Matt called. "Henry and I will keep you covered."

This took little effort. They had already tested the finished raft and had it barely nosed on the beach. Harlan raced for his tiller post, while Crow and Mickey got two of the cumbersome oars into their waist-high Y shafts. Jerome went prone on the deck, after helping Harriet and Amalida aboard, his rifle pointed back at the hill. Cornell stood ankle-deep in the water and helped Laura Lee literally throw the yapping dogs onto the deck. Calvin pulled the heavy trunk to the edge of the water and with great effort lifted it up onto the deck. Then he jumped up behind it and redrew his Colt. Lolly made her last of three quick trips with the dog saddlebags. Suddenly she heard a piercing wail.

"Kimberly!" she cried. "Laura Lee—where did we leave her?"

"Asleep in the papoose carrier!"

Both women started to run back across the beach cove as the hill erupted with sound. Darting from outcroppings to the trees, they ascended the hill with a rush, giving vent to their frustrations by uttering fierce screams and curses.

"Damn brave women," Matt said admiringly, finding a target and firing. The shot caught the man in the knee. He turned back, limping, dropping his gun as he moved for cover.

Calhoun's men were falling in both directions, because they had forgotten about Nolan. He had found a perch where he could see them and the whole cove. He cursed when he saw Laura Lee and Lolly running back, without knowing what they were after. Down the slope behind them a big bearded man was charging, but the women kept blocking his shot.

They had almost reached the baby by the ledge when the man let out a bellow. Laura Lee spun, but Lolly kept running. Then Laura Lee saw the glint of sunlight on a rifle barrel higher up. It was moving, following the path of the man as he ran at them. She thought it was being aimed at her and looked for cover, but there was none. The rifleman raised, sighted, and she saw the spitting tongue of orange flame. But when the crack came she felt nothing. Around her, though, was sound and fury. Lolly was lifted high into the air and twisted back to the gravel beach. The man, twenty-five steps away, clawed at a hole in the center of his forehead. When he didn't fall, Matt came on the run, his pistol at the ready.

"Oh, God!" he cried. "I didn't mean to hit her. I thought I had perfect aim on him."

He would have used his pistol then, but the man crumpled right where he stood. Clumsily, Lolly got to her feet. There were no further shots. They ran to her.

"Thought you were hit for sure," Matt gasped.

"I think it must have been fright," Lolly quavered.

"You were hit. There's blood on the back of your coat."

"Didn't feel a thing," Lolly said, even as she started to faint.

Matt caught her as she fell and, lifting her into his arms, started on a run back to the boat.

Laura Lee looked to the hillside, where the shot must have come from, but saw no glint of sun on rifle barrel. Kimberly's cry brought her back to her senses and she ran for the child. Within moments she had her soothed into silence.

Her father was shouting for her to come and get on the raft. It was not safe for them to stay in the cove.

Nolan came bounding down the hill and ran for her.

"Bastards!" he growled. "That should teach them." Then he stopped and looked back up the hill. "Damn, I left a brand new ax up there. Well, let me have Kimberly."

He stretched out his hands but Laura Lee pulled the child close to her breast. She had followed the line of his eyes. They had gone right to the spot where she had seen the glint of the rifle. His horrible words echoed in her brain. She could not help but believe that he had tried to kill Lolly. She was terrified, even though she had no real evidence against him.

She ran quickly so that he couldn't touch her or speak to her.

The patrol found three badly wounded men on the hillside, as Calhoun had told them that they would. The man Matt had shot was dead. They sent the three wounded men back to the tent city and rode along the shoreline in pursuit of the raft. Calhoun had convinced this group of policemen that it was the wounded men who had had the raft stolen from them. Calhoun, riding a borrowed mounty horse, went along to identify the raft and the thieves.

As the day wore on, Harriet noticed that Lolly was losing more and more blood from the shoulder wound. Like so many others, the old woman had developed a real love for Lolly, and her expression grew more and more worried as the hours passed. She knew it was impossible to put in to shore. They had all heard the shouts and the warning pistol reports.

Now, with four at the oar locks they were straining to get out of rifle range and stay there. The wind rose against them, pounding the waves up onto the deck and soaking their feet with the icy water. The raft, designed for seven, rode precariously low in the water with fourteen aboard.

It was dusk when Henry and Matt announced a decision.

"The mounties will be expecting us to be sensible and put in for the night, so we have to stay on the water and out of range."

"What about Lolly? Sir, the wound is bluish and the bleeding hasn't stopped. She needs proper medical attention."

"She should never have been out in the middle of the gunfire," Nolan said hotly, immediately regretting his words. He had played shocked and numb coming onto the raft. In the confusion of departing he had left Lolly fully in Harriet's care. He wasn't quite sure he could look at Lolly without her seeing the truth in his eyes. It had been such a sudden thing. He had been aiming at the moving man when Lolly had come back into his sights again. He had pulled the trigger without thinking—or so he now wanted to believe.

"I—I am sorry," he stammered. "I'm just so worried that I don't know what I'm really saying."

They all understood—except for one. Laura Lee was miserable. His words had just underscored in her mind her worst fear. He had been looking down on them. He had fired the shot. She felt as responsible as if she had fired the bullet. She just had to make Lolly live.

"Father," she said quietly, "what about using some of the caulking on the wound?"

Henry blinked and grinned at his daughter.

"See to it, and don't let Mrs. Henderson give you any back talk."

And Harriet didn't, all through the time Laura Lee scooped lake water back on the caulking to loosen it and gather up a bowl of the mud and sawdust. Throughout the night, thin coats were applied and allowed to dry. When it became too soggy with blood, they would start all over again.

It was a fantastically beautiful night for the Northern Lights, but no one noticed. In one hour shifts, four men on and four men off—with Harlan never leaving his tiller—they rowed.

Laura Lee stayed constantly with Lolly, and even Amalida used her fingernails to claw the mud out from beneath the logs, until she couldn't reach back any farther under the split rail deck. Finally, the layers of mud began to dry without discoloring.

Whenever Matt took a break he would join the women, looking at Lolly with concern in his eyes.

"We've got a fire going on the deck, Mrs. H.," Matt said near dawn as he entered the hut. "I put some water on to boil in case you wanted to make her a broth."

"Aren't you worried about the smoke?"

"Spotted only one man riding on the shore. Henry seems certain that it's Calhoun."

"Him again?" Amalida scowled. "I bet he was behind those men shooting at us."

"Henry thinks the same, Mrs. Ramsey. He's told us some of the trouble you've been having with the man. Sorry we all didn't know sooner."

"Yes," Amalida mused, "sorry that you didn't."

"I've got to fix that broth," Harriet said.

"I'll help you," Amalida volunteered. She felt greatly cheered, now that Calhoun had become a problem for all of them.

Matt hesitated, and looked down at Lolly. "Guess I better go back." He paused again. "Is she going to be all right?"

"Yes, Matt. She'll be fine—and she'll be happy to know you kept looking in on her."

"She did the same for me after the avalanche."

He crushed his shapeless felt hat upon his head and left. Laura Lee sat there weakly, then took Lolly's inert hand and rubbed it gently along her teary cheek.

"You're lucky, Lolly," she mused. "The look in his eyes was something special. Now I know the look in a man's eyes when he is really in love—not just lusting after a woman."

She bent her head to Lolly's breast and wept.

8

THE ROAR and rumble was not unlike that which they had heard before. But this was not an avalanche. It was the sound of millions of gallons of water pouring into a canyon, rushing between its towering stone cliffs to form a giant, spinning whirlpool. The banks were littered with the debris of those who had tried to get through it before them.

"Portage!" Henry screamed over the roar. "The only way."

"You're insane!" Nolan bellowed. "We are not enough, nor strong enough, to lift this raft from the water and walk it over those cliffs."

"We'll have to leave the raft. We can build a new one on the other side."

"How many of these goddamn things am I supposed to fell trees for?"

"Look!" Crow called, pointing up the cliff. "Calhoun and two mounties!"

"Preposterous!" Henry fumed. "Harlan, raise the tiller and lash it down. It's either the whirlpool or that man of impossible determination!"

"What's beyond the whirlpool?"

"I wasn't privileged to be here during the first seven days of creation," Henry said sarcastically. "Quick now, everyone, lash yourselves down."

The incredible current caught their prow and immediately turned the raft around. A moment later they were turned right back around again. The cliff upon which Calhoun rode was to their right, then to their left, then to their right again. It was dizzying just trying to keep track.

Harlan Henderson had the greatest urge to put the tiller back down into the water and right their course until he saw Nolan attempt the same with one of the long oars. No sooner had it hit the water than it nearly took his arms out by the sockets, snapping the heavy oar in two as if it was a thin piece of kindling wood.

Lolly had the oddest sensation that she was having a relapse. She grew dizzier and dizzier, as though on the verge of fainting. With her good arm she held Kimberly close and began to giggle. Kimberly giggled back. The sound brought Laura Lee, on her hands and knees across the slanting hut-deck to see if they were all right. Their laughter was infectious. As she clung to them, each pirouette of the boat brought a new round of giggles and laughter.

At first Harriet and Amalida looked at them as though they had lost their minds. But when they looked at each other Harriet throated a dry chuckle and Amalida a nervous twitter. And then they couldn't stop, either.

Anyone hearing them, without knowing them, would have taken them for a bunch of drunken women. In fact, the laughter kept the fear from entering their minds.

"Oh, my holy mother—" Harlan stood frozen by the tiller.

Beneath the fierce cacophony of the whirlpool there came another sound—a low ominous rumbling steadily increasing in intensity. It came from downstream to his left. With a violent jerk the raft was spewed from the outer arc of the whirlpool and toward the bend. The shock wave of what he saw buffeted Harlan's mind and the sound almost burst his eardrums.

"Should have portaged," Nolan said in awe.

"It's a little too late for that now," Henry said. "Just make sure everything is lashed down good. These rapids will make the whirlpool seem like child's play."

He fought his way back to Harlan. The first group of rapids was a rushing torrent of water dashing madly over the rocks, throwing white spray high into the air. The spray was icy cold, yet when it drummed on his face and hands it stung like the touch of fire. He had to get his mouth right next to Harlan's ear, and even then he had to holler to be heard.

"Hold on tight. Don't try to steer away from the rocks, just let her go with the current."

The raft shot into the rapids. It grated over the rocks with a terrible sound. Had it been a hulled boat it would have been instantly bottomless. It shot up into the air and crashed back with a teeth-jarring thud. Henry crawled to the leashed dogs. They could not keep their footing and were being tossed about so that the leashes were becoming tangled around them, strangling the beasts. He knifed them loose, took the lead dog by the scruff of the neck and coaxed him to the blanket-draped hut opening. The others crawled along on their bellies after the lead dog. One by one Henry pushed them under the blanket and into the hut.

"Sorry I have to crowd you," he called, sticking his head in, "but it's a mite too rough out here for them."

No one answered. No one was laughing. Now they knew fear.

Nolan was numb with the wonder of it all, gripped by a dreadful fascination. It was an irresistible battering ram, thrashing down the narrow canyon, rumbling like a volcano.

Then, for a second, the raft bobbed and weaved into deeper, quieter water. But the sound before them grew even louder and stronger.

"More of them," Nolan exalted, as though looking forward to it.

Mickey Magraff moaned and looked downstream. All he saw were hundreds of white ponies leaping about.

Matt could only think of his original map, and the dire warning to avoid White Horse Rapids. There could be no avoiding, now. They were already into its churning jaws.

The logs groaned and screeched in agony. The rawhide bindings grew loose from the wetness. The underwashing took away the caulking as though in a tidal flood. The juggernaut was slowly ripping them apart.

Two outside logs broke away first. They caught on a rock and the water upended them. Nolan saw and it really didn't surprise or shock him. For many minutes he had known from the sounds beneath the split-log deck what was transpiring.

There would be no survivors. He knew it without fearing it. This rapid was a raging white water that was certain to turn the raft into kindling wood. Every man, woman and child aboard was going to die.

He heard Harlan's scream of warning and pulled himself around the hut and to the tiller.

The deck was beginning to split open in a yawning vee right to the back wall of the hut. Nolan leaned down and peered under the deck. Four of the center logs had simply vanished. To the left and right of the gap the other keel logs were wobbling themselves free. When they were gone it would drop the deck and the hut right into the rapids. For a moment Nolan felt beaten, helpless, but something stronger than exhaustion drove into his mind. He had to do something to protect Laura Lee inside the hut. No other person was considered.

"Ropes!" he screamed. "Tell them to bring back the ropes!"

He closed his eyes, pulled his lips flat against his teeth and heaved himself down into the water. Even though he was wet to the skin, the water was still a shock. It brought silver flashes in front of his eyes and his head rang. Holding onto the deck, he lurched his legs under the raft and tried to kick a log back into place. He missed the log entirely and it crashed against the side of his leg.

He put the pain out of his head and tried again. Matt yelled to Crow and Mickey, who sat down, trying to brace themselves on the slippery deck, and took hold of Nolan's arms. Jerome and Cornell Dunn went to each side of the raft and began to secure a rope around the outside deck logs. Calvin went to find the broken oar to use as a winding wench, while Henry and Harlan went to the hut to move the supplies and reduce the weight on the area that was splitting apart.

The women accepted the news in various degrees of anxiety, fear and worry. Laura Lee hated herself for the thought that came instantly to her mind: How could Nolan be hero and bastard at the same time?

A log crashed free on the far edge, ripping off a great chunk of bark from the next. Nolan threw out his legs and straddled it like a horse as it began to slip from underneath the raft. His quick movement and strange angle tore his left hand away from Crow. Mickey had to scoot along on his rump just to keep a grasp on his right hand.

The surging water pulled at Nolan's locked ankles, threatening to push him off the log. Only the combined strength of the two men's arms was momentarily keeping the log under the raft. Mickey had both of his hands around Nolan's arm. Crow kept straining for the other, but Nolan was waving it about wildly.

The front of the raft hit a rock outcropping with a shattering thud, twisting it to the side. It was as if a huge hand had ripped Nolan right out of Mickey's grasp and then propelled him into the water right after him.

Before anyone could react, the raft was hurtling around

the last bend in the rapids. The log flung itself out from beneath the raft and, just before it shattered against the rocks, Nolan jumped free and was swirled under.

Mickey was being tumbled along beneath the water surface in the terrible current. It pounded him repeatedly against the rocks as it swept him downstream.

With that log gone the others were quick to break free. With a rending like a crack of thunder the deck began to fully split in two. The rope wench could no longer hold the sections together and it suddenly snapped.

The freed logs rocketed past Nolan. He flung out his arms and caught one by the fingernails. The current was pulling the log away from him. He gripped with all his might, straining to pull himself to it. After a second, blood began to flow from his fingernails, but he was close enough to get an arm over, and then a leg. Another log came surging past and smashed the other leg between. He was so numb from the cold that he didn't feel it. He climbed onto the log and fell forward, locking his arms and legs securely around it.

A few feet away a body floated to the surface. The water flowing from Mickey toward the log was tinged with red. Out of the corner of his eye Nolan saw it, but he was too exhausted to move.

Everything seemed so strangely calm. The water was pushing the log along at an incredible rate of speed, but there was no tug on his legs trying to force him off it. And it was quiet. The roaring of the rapids was fading away, turning to a soothing murmur.

For once Crow had not had to boast or lie about his prowess. The moment Mickey had gone overboard he had begun preparing in frantic haste to go after him. Never taking his eyes off the white water, he had shed all but the doe-skin loincloth he always wore under the heavy western attire. The moment he saw the head bob out of the water he made a running dive off the raft.

Henry thought it was a futile effort, but couldn't stop him. He was having his own problems.

For a few moments they had not acted as a group, but as frantic individuals. The hut had stayed intact, but when the raft split it scraped half of the inside supplies, dogs and people right off into the water. For several seconds they could not be seen and only their screams could be heard. Most of the screams were coming from the women who had not been knocked overboard.

"Don't let the logs come back together!" Matt bellowed. "They'll be crushed."

Inside the hut he found mad confusion. The yapping dogs were trying to scramble back on board, but were getting in the way of the struggling people.

"Get those dogs out of here!" Matt bellowed at no one in particular. Amalida was the closest at hand and, disregarding their snarling and snapping, she kicked and shoved them out from underneath the blanket. With a sudden fury she yanked the blanket from the doorway, giving them more light within the hut. Laura Lee thrust a wet and wailing Kimberly into her hands, and Amalida quickly wrapped the child in the blanket before handing her to Harlan Henderson.

"My wife?" he stammered. "Is she all right?"

"She's fine," Amalida said before turning to start tossing supplies out of the splintering hut.

Harriet was down on her hands and knees at the back of the hut, trying to fish out supplies between the two halves.

"Forget the damn supplies," Matt growled. "Look for Lolly!"

"What in the hell do you think I'm doing?" she flared, in an unusual show of temper. "She was lying next to the supplies when they got raked in!"

Now all three pawed up the bales, boxes, backpacks and threw them back for Amalida to keep throwing out.

Lolly was jammed safely between two wooden crates, but her clothes had caught on the jagged split of the log and she had not been able to free herself. Matt grabbed her under the armpits and, trying to be careful of the wounded shoulder, dragged her up. Part of her dress was torn off in the process.

He drew her right up into his arms and headed out for the deck.

"Is Nolan okay?" was the first question that popped into her mind.

Matt took in a deep breath. He didn't have an answer for her.

Crow knifed through the water expertly, unaware that eyes were on him, marvelling at his swimming ability. The current was sweeping the log and unconscious body far to the right of the raft.

The force of the millions of gallons of water per minute being drained into Lake Laberge pushed the log into many currents. Like a magnet the shorelines would pull it in to each side and then force it back out. Crow followed it toward the eastern shore, while the split raft kept on a northwesterly course.

Crow reached Mickey and spun him over on his back in the water. There was a wicked gash that ran from the center of his skull to just behind the right ear. His clothing had been nearly ripped away by the jagged rocks and his chalk white limbs were bruised and lacerated. Putting his ear against the bare chest, Crow could hear a very faint heartbeat.

He took Mickey by the hair and dragged him to the log on which Nolan lay, unmoving, and heaved his body over it like a sack of flour. Nolan looked back but didn't comment. Crow took a firm grip around Mickey's body and the log and kicked his legs in slow measured strokes. It was a long way to the shoreline and he didn't want to fully exhaust himself after having accomplished this much.

He felt the thump and thought he had crashed into one of the other freed logs. At the second thump he looked up and froze. He was locked into the triangle of three huge canoes. Faces looked down at him almost savagely. No, he couldn't even call them faces. The whole picture was something out of a nightmare. Not even on the reservation had he seen Indians like this.

Above the wide forehead bands their hair was tangled and matted. The top half of each face was painted in the faintly greenish-white hue of a corpse, while the bottom half was charcoal black. From each nose dangled a large gold ring.

Crow was amazed that he felt intimidated. He called out a greeting in his own dialect and received blank stares. He then tried English and got no better response.

The harpoon-like spears pulled the log to the side of one canoe. Even as Nolan was being roughly hauled on board, the spears from the other canoe were tapping him on the shoulder. He turned in the water and guessed their intent. He released his grip on Mickey and they pulled the unconscious body up. Then they grabbed Crow and effortlessly hoisted him on board. Almost before his feet had landed a blanket was thrust into his hands and heads turned away.

He nearly laughed. The blanket, he knew at once, was not for warmth, but because he was somehow indecent in their eyes.

The canoe veered away and he almost toppled. Twelve Indians squatted on their knees, dipping paddles into the lake water. There was no sound or beat, but they moved in perfect unison as though connected by a piston rod. Not a drop of water splashed in to wet their leather breeches, or the colorfully beaded, smock-like tops that reached nearly to their knees.

They skimmed the water, with one canoe in pursuit and the other heading just as rapidly to the other end of the lake.

Crow surmised that they were heading for the raft and he prayed that Henry Boise would be able to speak with these savages as easily as he had been able to speak with the Yakutats and Chilkoots.

Even before the canoes reached the raft the Indian who had sat in the prow with his back to Crow rose and began to shout over the water.

When the returned shout was just as guttural and fierce, the rowers missed a beat and whispered among themselves.

Crow saw the tall Indian's muscular back go rigid under the frock cloth as he hissed them to silence. He, too, remained silent until the canoe was bumping against the raft. He stepped onto the deck and waved behind him. Crow took it as a signal for him to follow and quickly scrambled on board.

Henry walked forward and had to jump to the other side over a foot-wide gap in the raft. He studied the Indian's bead work. He was obviously an important man in the tribe, but not a chief or the son of a chief. Still, he greeted him with words of great respect. They were ignored.

"You break the law," the Indian said crisply. "The men of the scarlet coat tell us no more *cheechacos* to come."

"I am hardly a *cheechacos*," Henry laughed.

The man did not laugh back. "You will be taken to our village until the scarlet coats come to take you back."

"From which Tlingit village do you come?"

"That should not concern you!" He turned and began giving quick orders for lines to be attached to the raft for towing.

"But it does concern us," Laura Lee said shortly, breaking away from the huddled group, who stood in just as much amazement as Crow had felt. "It concerns us very much."

The man turned to face her, confusion in his eyes. For a white woman her command of his dialect was excellent—

nearly as good as was the short, heavy-set man's. The Indian looked back to Henry.

"Do you allow squaws to speak without permission?"

"Please forgive her," Henry said. "It has been a long, hard journey. I take her to the people of her mother. Kilria of the Tlingit people of Mallori."

The man stood there a long moment, looking from one to the other. A million emotions surged through his body. But, in reality, he had only a choice for one, and he knew it. He could not lie to them, although he hated looking upon them. They were as dead in his mind as they were in the mind of his mother.

"We are the people of Mallori the Lesser. Kilria is an old woman of this village."

"And her son?" Henry asked.

"Peter the Abandoned lives," he said, without further information.

Laura Lee stood there, staring at him, her eyes narrowing.

"And you are he?" she asked quietly.

He frowned, his mouth opened, a bitter retort on his tongue. Then he clamped his jaws down, hard.

"I take you to the village!"

He jumped to his canoe and refused to look back.

Henry found himself disbelieving. At twenty-nine years of age, his son was not what he had expected to find. He was too tall to be a product of Henry and Kilria, but was, perhaps, a kickback to a previous generation. That Laura Lee had gotten her beauty from the Duboise side of the family, Henry had always accepted and appreciated.

Seeing his son, he couldn't pinpoint him to either side of the family. Even smeared with the Indian paint he was an extraordinarily handsome man—lithe and muscular, with a pre-Raphaelite sort of face under a mass of soft-curling midnight hair. But his eyes seemed sombre, as if from some remembered grief. And that, Henry understood only too well. "Peter the Abandoned" he was called. Henry had a sudden, aching realization what life must have been like for his son. When he had left, Peter was a nine-year-old who was gentle, intelligent, and fine. But without a father to lead him and teach him, he would have had to learn to be strong and arrogant to survive. Without a father he would have had to teach himself, because his mother . . .

Henry stopped himself and his eyes darkened with disappointment that the thought had come to him. It had been his chief defense in his case against the church that he had never married the woman. At the time, marriage would have ruined his whole case. He could site case after case of Popes who had sired illegitimate children, some of whom even rose to the purple.

Laura Lee had been with him. It had never been important to let her know the full truth. It had never once crossed his mind how it would affect Peter among the Tlingit. Henry, a born scholar, had foolishly conditioned his mind to believe that Peter would still be a little boy upon his return.

The group was coolly received, for that was the way of the Tlingit. Once they had been a great people of many tribes who did not need to associate with other tribes and would not permit strangers in their villages. Marriages were arranged at birth between nobles of the Tlingit tribes, even down to second and third wives. If a girl child's husband-to-be had died or been killed prior to her coming of age, then she could only be considered as a second or third wife.

Kilria had been such a girl thirty years before, when Father Henry Duboise had persistently stayed around and finally won for himself a friendship with Mallori. But, on that rare occasion when a stranger was accepted as a friend, the nobles could not allow his lodge to go without a woman to care for it. Kilria had been the choice because the time had not yet come for her to become Mallori's third wife.

Still, with the birth of Peter she was not looked down upon. Henry was the friend of Mallori, and as Mallori did not discuss the matter, no one could. Gossip, amazingly, was unknown to the cultural Tlingit.

Laura Lee's birth was no problem either, until Henry felt he had to go and fight the verdict of the Church. His reasons were fully understood by Mallori and not discussed. However, Mallori's understanding died with him and was not passed on to Mallori the Lesser. In time, Kilria and Peter were abandoned in the eyes of the tribe. Peter could advance according to his own merits, but he could never reach the rank of a tribe noble. Kilria was in limbo; she could be the mother of the boy, but never the wife of another.

Henry thought he should at least be greeted by Mallori the Lesser. When he was shown to a gabled lodge and told that he would see him in good time, he took it savagely.

In the next moment, as though prearranged, a flap parted and Kilria stepped into the room. She was shorter than Henry, with enormous hands and feet, and the exaggerated heaviness of chin and jaw that bespoke older Tlingit women. Her hair had gone salt and pepper, and her little black eyes didn't focus very well. She kept blinking them in a convulsive, involuntary manner that was almost hypnotic to watch.

"Ah," she said, "my good Father Duboise! I trust that you are safe returned?"

"Just fine, Kilria," Henry said, smiling gently.

"And this is your daughter?" she asked, gesturing toward Laura Lee without looking at her.

"*Our* daughter," he corrected.

"If you say so, Father Duboise."

Laura Lee wanted to scream. They enjoy this play-acting ritual, she thought. Everyone in the village knew who she was. The minute they had hit the shoreline the rowers had scattered to spread the word of who had returned. But these two had to pretty it up. She just wanted to meet the woman she knew only through the words and memory of her father. She wanted to hug and kiss her, but this little comedy was devoid of all emotion. The woman might just as well be a New Orleans chambermaid passing the time of day.

"I hope you are well," Henry said with a smile.

"I am. Mallori the Lesser wishes you for *potlatche.*"

"I am honored."

"Father Duboise is remembered as a friend of Mallori the Greater," she said drily. "I must go now."

"But . . . but . . ." Laura Lee stammered as the woman turned back to the exit. Henry waved her to silence and let the woman depart.

Laura Lee was shaken. "What's the matter with her? She acted as though I wasn't even here."

"My darling, she has not seen you since you were ten months old. It has to be a shock for her to see you all grown up. And Laura Lee, I should tell you . . . I'm afraid she was . . . she didn't have . . . well, our relationship was not . . ." He just couldn't find the right words.

Laura Lee was growing increasingly suspicious. "Are you trying to say that your marriage to her was loveless?"

Henry closed his eyes. A tremor ran over his face and he dreaded this moment. After a second his lips moved. "My baby girl, you have given me so much joy and happiness and love—"

"That wasn't the question," she cut him short. "I am well aware of your feelings toward me and have always been aware of them. But her? Your wife and my mother! Am I being treated this way by her because of something between the two of you in the past that you never told me about?"

Henry slowly opened his eyes. There was anguish and desolation etched in his face. He was too honest a man to lie.

"Yes," he said, emptily. "She is your mother—but she was never my wife."

There was a sharp intake of breath. Then there was a horribly long pause. When she spoke there was no bitterness in her voice, only a kind of hollow finality.

"That wouldn't stop me from loving her!"

Then she turned and fled from the room.

Now that it was done, Henry was conscious of the enormity of the sin of silence. There was no doubt that his daughter loved him dearly. And Kil, by which affectionate diminutive he had once addressed her, had loved him better than if they had been married. And what of his beloved son? He had loved the boy with the passion of any father.

But had he told them? Had he ever once tried to communicate over a twenty-year span of silence? Oh, it was always his intent to tell them, but he had blundered by leaving it merely a good intention. His mind had been the servant of the will of the moment, and for the first time in fifty years he was unsure of himself. The Church had been his anchor, even when he was fighting it. Now he was adrift.

Laura Lee was lost the moment she charged away. The lodge was really one large room divided into family quarters by moose-hide partitions, with dark narrow passageways between. She wanted Lolly . . . or Harriet . . . or even Amalida. Just a woman to talk to, even though she might not say anything about all of this.

She stumbled through an opening and stopped. It was like a smokey cavern lit by oil-bowls with flickering cloth wicks. A shawled woman sat by a walled cradle. Another, with lantern bowl in hand, turned at her entrance. She nodded her head slowly, her hair, streaming loose, billowing about her small, angelic face.

"Please to enter. I am Fria."

"It does not please me!"

The bark came out of the shadows of the room like a

slap in the face. Laura Lee started, staring into the gloom, her lips pale and trembling in the flickering light.

"You—you don't wish to meet me?" she whispered. She had heard the guttural voice before and knew exactly whom she was addressing.

He stood up, the light of the bowl hurling a gigantic shadow of his frame over her. He stood there, looking at her, for a long time. When he finally spoke, his voice was bitter.

"Why did you come to see me after all these years?"

"I—I came when father said—"

"Father!" he snapped, cutting her off. "Do you speak of Father of the Church, or father of a few moments passion to produce us?"

Laura Lee reared back, her French temper surging. "No, I speak of the father who fed, clothed and schooled me for these nearly twenty-one years. Has our mother done the same for you?"

"Mothers are old women! Since fifteen I have had wives to feed and clothe me."

"Wives?" She paused, turning to the women. "I took Fria to be . . . what she is. A young girl."

"She is a second wife and a new mother. Iama sees to her son. Iama's three sons help with the *potlatche* for—" He stopped short.

Laura Lee couldn't help but laugh. "For *our* father?"

"He is well remembered by the older nobles," he said, his voice drowning in the bitter tides of despair, "and they do him honor."

"I—I don't understand," she said. "Honor? Forgive me, but I don't even know what *potlatche* is."

Peter chuckled at her ignorance. "It is a feast of opulent splendor. The finest dishes and the most lavish of gifts."

Laura Lee blinked. "Good! I am starved. Where and when is it?"

Peter blinked back, and then he roared with laughter. "You are a great portion of your father . . . but not enough. You are a woman and I am unnoble. We are among the uninvited."

"And what do the rest of us eat?" she demanded.

"What our womenfolk prepare," he told her flatly. "Do you wish to join us?"

"Do you really wish to invite me?"

Peter threw back his head and laughed again.

"No, but a few moments from now, according to my mother's instructions, I was to go for you one way or the other. She is preparing her own *potlatche*."

"Why?" Laura Lee got out. "Why didn't she invite me herself? Why wouldn't she even speak to me?"

Peter turned and looked at her. When he spoke at last, his voice was as icy as the lake water. "It is the way of our people," he said.

And this was Laura Lee's introduction to the Tlingit.

The others, because they were strangers, were given a different introduction. Families were moved out of an entire gabled lodge for them. Fires were lit, fresh boughs brought for beds, dry clothing provided and steaming hot food brought in. But all in total silence.

An old white-haired man came to examine Nolan and Mickey. Nolan's bashed leg produced a grunt and Mickey's head some sharp orders to two squat women of equal age. Still in silence, the leg was cleaned, and the broken bone set and put in a splint. Carefully, half of Mickey's head was shaven with a sharp fishing knife to expose the full wound.

Harriet Henderson hovered about, ready to do the man harm with her own hands if he dared use the knife for any other purpose.

"Lord a-mercy!" she cried aloud; and the old man, who, for some strange reason, had taken it upon himself to point out to her every step he intended to take, laughed aloud.

"Aye," he cackled, waving the dried fish jaws at her.

"Do you—do one of you—" She couldn't go on but

stared in fascination. The jaws were forced open as the man pinched an area of the wound together. Then he jutted the sharp teeth into the flesh and snapped the jaw closed. All along the wound he kept attaching fish jaw after fish jaw.

"Ain't that something," Crow marvelled. "I thought he'd go the rest of his life with half his brains hanging out."

"Waste of time," Nolan sneered from the next pallet. "Even if he lives, they're just going to kill us all, anyway."

"Hush that kind of talk!" Harriet insisted. "They haven't patched us up just to do away with us."

That was logical to all but Nolan. Actually, the others were very grateful for the rest in the snug, warm lodges. They were happy and content. Amalida got to sleep as long as she desired, a luxury she had almost forgotten about. Calvin sat and created ledger books in his head so that he would not grow rusty with figures. Harlan rested his weary bones, though he would not admit his aches and pains to anyone. The other men cleaned and sorted the equipment and supplies.

Laura Lee came daily to help Harriet with the nursing chores. Lolly was mending, but feared she would always have a stiff shoulder that would warn her of coming changes in the weather. Kimberly had a deep cough in her chest, but a chockcherry and pine resin syrup soon cleared that away. Mickey remained in critical condition, while Nolan continued to be impossible. As though he didn't care who knew his feelings, he was cross and critical of all his nurses except Laura Lee. She nursed him silently, but with a troubled heart.

Mallori the Lesser also had a troubled heart. For the moment Jethro Calhoun had backed off and left the entire matter in the hands of the Royal Canadian Mounted Police.

Chief Inspector Sam Steele had counted on the Tlingit to help, knowing they didn't want their country overrun, either. His main worry was the coming spring. Over 40,000 stampeders now waited in Skagway, Dyea and the tent camps. The boats they were constructing were nowhere near as sturdy as the raft had been, and look what had happened to it in the rapids. But his present worry were the "guests."

"Father Duboise, I am not questioning your word over that of Mr. Calhoun as to the attack on the lake, and the border incident with Mr. Calhoun will be investigated. I only question the law that you and these people have broken. People say that we Canadians have been making laws to fit the day and event of this surge of stampeders, and I admit that I'm making some now. Corporal Dixson will be in charge of this area, and he will not permit your raft to be repaired or removed from here until spring."

Henry accepted it with a shrug. He was home. Mallori the Lesser worried. He didn't like having so many outsiders around.

The *cheechacos* had considered it already winter. The Tlingit marvelled at the unusually long autumn. The days shortened, but into early November the storms had blanketed the mountain peaks with their winter mantle, driven the animal herds lower, but left the Lewes River and lower Yukon fairly passable. It was news, however, that Inspector Steele kept from reaching Skagway. All they knew was that the river was solid to Forty Mile. Their inadequate maps didn't show them that he spoke of the upper Yukon from St. Michaels to Forty Mile. No more strangers found their way to the village.

The news that they could not leave was received with mixed emotions. The only thing that kept those calm who wanted to press on immediately was the fact they would have a chance to get there first in the spring. Harriet Henderson had the strangest emotion of all. "Ain't fittin' to accept charity for a whole winter."

Laura Lee kept her emotions to herself.

* * *

Crow lifted himself up onto the large rock overlooking the lake, and waved to Laura Lee. Each afternoon for a week he had watched her come to this spot and gaze out over the lake, forest and mountains.

"Hello, Crow. It's beautiful country, isn't it?"

"A lot different than the Oklahoma reservation. There you can see for thousands of miles. Are you glad to be home?"

She turned and looked at the handsome Indian for a moment before speaking.

"Do you have problems, Crow, being the product of two worlds?"

"I just make myself the product of my own world."

"No, Crow, you've taken my question wrongly," she said seriously. "It is beautiful here. I hadn't seen snow since I was ten months old. I think I love it, but I don't really know. I don't really know anything. I just float from day to day."

"But you are back with your family."

"Am I?" she said mournfully. "My father is. He is having the time of his life with his old noble friends. I am accepted—at arm's length. Peter is busy with his own affairs. I like his wife Fria. She's fun and laughs a lot. Iama acts like I am stealing food out of the mouths of her sons. My father says that's because she sticks with the old-fashioned ways."

"So?" Crow said. "I see nothing wrong with that. I wish my people would have been allowed to stay with the old-fashioned ways."

"But," Laura Lee said, insistent upon getting back to her original point, "what if you are excluded from those old-fashioned ways? My mother talks, she prepares food, she cleans, but there is no love there for me or my father. It doesn't seem to matter to him, but it does to me."

"Peter took me hunting yesterday."

Laura Lee blinked. "What has that to do with it, unless it is a subtle change of topic?"

"Right on the point, really. We find we are quite alike. Abandoned. I tell some tall tales, but the truth of the matter is that I don't know who my father is—nor does my mother really know which of the pony soldiers on the reservation it might have been. Even though they are not married, at least you and Peter know each of your parents."

"He told you that?" She was incredulous.

"What's the secret? The whole village knows and has always known."

She had never considered that possibility. Then a worse thought came pounding on top of it. With her father again going about in his frock and vestments it would have to be a known fact within the whole group. She felt mortified.

Damn them! she thought; damn them all! One group holds me at arm's length and the others are probably snickering behind my back. For the first time she was homesick for New Orleans and the protective walls of the convent.

That night, Henry came into the lodge with a lantern in his hand. He held it up and bent over his daughter, asleep on her pallet, her face streaked with tears.

Poor child, he thought, my poor little girl.

She is not of this world, he was coming to realize. He had raised her too high in a different civilization. He would just have to take her back, but first he had made a promise to Mallori the Lesser.

Then he went back out of the lodge, stepped along the pounded snow path and entered another lodge. He knew at once that his message had been received. They sat silent and expectant.

And they were still silent after he had outlined the thoughts of the Tlingit chief.

Only Nolan Fedderson glared at him.

"If I ride flat in the canoe I can make it with this leg. I refuse to be left behind."

"We were thinking mainly of the welfare of you and Mickey."

"I will think of my own welfare. No reason I can't be seen to in the canoe as well as here."

"Lolly, are you up to it?"

"Lolly!" Nolan exploded. "Great jumping balls o'fire! She can hardly move that shoulder. Laura Lee will have to care for me—as she's been doing."

"Laura Lee is not going," Henry said gravely. "She will stay in the village and return to New Orleans in the spring."

Nolan started to protest, but a weird thought stopped him short. He could only think of one reason why Laura Lee had been so cool towards him of late, and why Lolly had been giving him strange looks whenever the girl was around. As the thought matured, he grew certain why it was planned for her to return to New Orleans. Oh, what stupid, absurd luck! he thought. Well, he would never admit that he was the father of her child!

The very next day the four canoes moved up the river through the dense and snow laden forest. The night had produced over a foot of snow. The river was mushy with slush. Henry saw that with a few nights well below zero the mush would start gathering together and slowly turn to a solid ice covering. But the current was with them, and the rowers powerful. In the old days he had seen these craft moving down such rivers with incredible speed. As a young man he had always been amused and confused that the river ran north and not south.

But that morning his amusement was not over the flow of the current. They had departed right under the watchful eye of Corporal Dixson. The young Mounty, recently transferred to the area because of the gold rush, had to accept the word of Mallori the Lesser that some of his people always went off at this time of the year for the last fishing of the season. His only orders had been concerning the raft, which still sat broken on the beach.

He had not checked the supplies that had been carried to the canoes and loaded. Fishing people would need supplies. He had not come close to watch the Tlingits board the canoes.

The chief had diverted his attention when Nolan had been carried down, shielded by some waddling women. That thought had been more on his mind than anything else since his arrival. Waddling women! He had heard tell of mounties, farther north, who actually slept with the Eskimo women. He thought the very idea most disgusting and sickening. Because he was new, the older men in the territory would add a word of warning about the necessity of delousing after such a night. He couldn't think about it or his skin would start crawling under his uniform.

He had therefore given a quick wave of his hand in farewell and not paid a great deal of attention to the departure.

Henry had not paid much attention either. He had come to feel he had a moral obligation to see these people through to Dawson. The sooner it was done, the sooner he could return.

There had been no sensual reawakening in him for Kilria after twenty years. In New Orleans he had been as celibate as though he had been a full priest. At fifty he did not have any strong desires to change that fact of life. But among the nobles he felt a kinship and a strong link with the past. He loved this land and these people. It was a life he never wanted to see changed or altered. His only regret was that he had kept Laura Lee away from it for so long. He prayed that this time she would be spending alone with her mother and sisters-in-law would open her eyes and heart to the beauty of her heritage.

The order of the canoes had been carefully worked out,

and everyone dressed in Tlingit clothing to board, knowing that Dixson would be watching. Henry and Crow would go in the first canoe with Peter. Calvin, Amalida and Harlan next. Matt and the Dunn brothers had started to get into their canoe when the fourth group arrived with Nolan.

In the confusion of getting Nolan down into the canoe without being seen, Harriet Henderson handed Kimberly to Matt. A second later she pulled Lolly from the group and quickly helped her in beside Matt. As the rowers were already pushing the canoe into the lake, there was no time for explanations.

Harriet had a momentary impulse to report the reason for the change but she thought better of it. No more quarrels from Nolan Fedderson, she told herself cheerfully. Time enough for that when they camped for the night.

A few minutes later, the rowers pushed that canoe into the lake and turned it toward the river. They were spaced at such a distance to prevent communications.

Matt didn't mind the change. He held Kimberly close and exalted over having Lolly so close, and more or less to himself.

Lolly had been thankful for the last minute switch. Lately, it was like the old days had returned, only worse than ever. She couldn't open her mouth without Nolan jumping right down her throat. He didn't even seem to care who heard—and in the shared lodge it was impossible not to hear him and every stupid little accusation he could dredge up out of the past. Most tried to pretend that they did not hear, which only increased her embarrassment. She cursed the sudden return of shyness that prevented her striking back with words of her own. She didn't want to cause embarrassment for the others. She could see it in their eyes, and it made her want to die of shame. They had become such a part of her, and Nolan was forcing them away. She didn't want to lose them. She was still naive enough to look into Matt Monroe's eyes and see only friendship there.

Harriet leaned back carefully on the stack of supplies, still wondering if she had done right or wrong. She stared down at Nolan, prone in the bottom of the canoe. "That brew really makes him sleep," she said. She paused, and her face colored slightly. "Laura Lee, I . . . I hope we didn't give him too much."

She peeked out from the heavy folds of the fur parka. "Even my father thought a potion from the medicine man was necessary to shush him," she said with a touch of scorn in her voice.

"Oh, dear," murmured Harriet, "I hope he thinks we did right."

Laura Lee stiffened, her slender throat tightening with a new convulsion. *Right*? Nothing had been *right* since before dawn. It was the first time she had ever fought with her father, and he had had far too much practice fighting with the church for her to think of winning against him. She wasn't even sure why she fought him—other than the fact that she didn't want to stay there alone. Surely it was just that . . . alone! At least with the group she had a few ties. They had become her breed.

Nolan had been more impossible than usual that morning. He had sworn shamefully and complained about everything as she dressed his leg for the journey. At first she didn't understand his frantic whispering. A woman had to do certain things—after what she had done. She still didn't understand, but his next question made her whole spirit writhe in violent denial. He asked her if she was carrying a baby—his child. He had taken her denial completely wrong and began to scream and rant so loudly at her that Henry had decided upon the sedative. He feared the man would give everything away.

Fria had gone with Laura Lee to the lodge of the old man. It had taken him time to grind the various tree barks and berries together. He, too, had ignored Laura Lee as though she were not there, but chatted away merrily with Fria.

"Were you ill?" she had asked Fria when they left his lodge.

"Not ill, but he had to take my baby out with a whalebone knife."

Laura Lee had shuddered and was freshly reminded of how little she really knew. She had denied a certain fact to Nolan and knew nothing about the fact she was denying.

"Fria," she had asked suddenly, before she lost the courage, "how did your baby get in you?"

Fria had looked at her, trying not to burst into giggling laughter. Every Tlingit girl learned that in childhood. She lifted her heavy hide skirt and pointed between her legs with a gesturing finger. Laura Lee had watched her, turning a shade paler than the snow banks they walked through.

But she had not arranged those facts in her mind or decided upon anything until they had Nolan fast asleep. Then she did feel all alone. Everyone was in a flurry of activity. The wives of Mallori the Lesser had brought clothing of all various sizes. She stared, fascinated, as her friends turned into Tlingit natives before her eyes. Mickey had been moved to the lodge of the chief for care. The people assigned to the first canoes were already dressed and leaving the lodge.

Laura Lee had felt slimy and cold. She stood there weaving. Harriet had put a hand on her shoulder with motherly concern and then hugged her closely.

"I shall miss you, child."

"I want to go," she had sobbed.

"Why in the world can't you? Mickey is being seen to."

It had poured out so suddenly and unexpectedly that it was like rushing to tell of a nightmare so it would not be so grotesque and ominous. But it had nothing to do with her and Nolan. It was just all of her pent-up frustration over her mother, her father and her brother.

"Shame," Harriet had soothed, hugging her even closer. "Thank God I'm Protestant. You just dress yourself in some of those duds and come along with Harriet. I'll figure out what to say to your father when the time comes."

The time did not come that day or night.

For the first four hours the canoes stayed a fairly equal distance apart. They traveled eastward, then back north through river connections that the Tlingit never questioned, but would hopelessly confuse thousands that were to follow. Then, for twenty-five miles, the river bends had them going nearly every direction of the compass, the rowers alternating to slice around the corners. After the last bend they were in the Lewes—a sixty mile stretch that gradually and steadily dropped down to the Yukon.

Here, the swiftness of the current brought the first two canoes abreast of each other. Rowers began to taunt rowers and laugh at the challenges cast back and forth.

Peter felt heady. Behind him sat a man he had come to admire and a man he wished to admire him. He rose, with evident enjoyment, and spread wide his large, powerful hands.

"I hope," he called back, mainly for the ears of Crow, "that you are not averse to a good race. The junction with the *Youcan*."

He had expected an immediate protest from his father before he dropped his arms. He looked back as he sat down, and saw that Henry's eyes were gleaming with excitement. He glanced anxiously at the other canoe and then measured his son's rowers. It was hard to tell who might have an advantage. His blood boiled as he counted the dips of one canoe against the other. Years floated away from him. These were the old times when such a race could mean much for the winner—and much more for the loser.

"Calvin," he shouted across, "shall we wager?"

"What have you in mind?"

"Not your beautiful vest," Henry roared in delight. "And I don't think you'd appreciate the traditional finish."

"And why not?" Calvin hollered back, laughing.

Henry chortled with mirth. "Because in the old days the losers were killed and used as rollers in beaching the winning canoe!"

"What makes you think that we shall be the losers, Henry?" Calvin yelled.

"Knowledge," he shouted, pointing to his brain.

"Well, then, shall we wager fifty dollars?" Calvin asked with a grin.

"Fifty it is!"

They broke all records, making the sixty miles by nightfall. It was a draw. It mattered not to either crew. They roared, they whooped, they guffawed; they pounded each other on the back, and talked about reaching Dawson the next day.

The second two boats camped no more than ten miles behind them, and it was like two warring camps from the beginning.

Nolan had come out of his stupor and he became alert at the sight of Laura Lee. He sat up on his elbow and looked closely at her, trying not to smile. But . . . why not smile? The wretched girl would chase him to the ends of the earth now that she carried his child. But he was a sly one, he was. By diverting their attention, he would see that no one learned the truth, and at the right time he would tell her how to get rid of the bastard.

If he had been impossible before, he was now intolerable. He made it sound as if he believed they had all purposely conspired against him to let the other canoes get to Dawson first. Didn't he have that right? Hadn't he done more than any of them to get them this far? They were all ungrateful bastards! He was sorry he had gathered wood for the bonfire to see them in off the glacier! Had anyone ever thanked him for his pine bough shelters? Where would they be without his raft?

Lolly wanted to stop him, her face flaming redder than a sunset with shame, but Matt held her back. He thought it best to let him rave himself into exhaustion and sleep. Everyone else agreed, except Laura Lee.

The others knew what he had been through and could accept, to a degree, his ravings. The Tlingit rowers did not know what he had been through, did not understand a single word of his ravings, and were growing nervous and frightened. Laura Lee was afraid that if he didn't quiet down they might all wake up in the morning to find themselves stranded on the river bank.

She thought she had a way to still him. She moved over to him, and sat down.

"You asked if I was carrying your child," she whispered. "How do I know for sure?"

He smiled with false solicitude. "You been sick in the morning lately?"

"Never been sick a day in my life," she said with a touch of pride.

"Don't lie," he hissed with vindictiveness.

"I don't have any reason to lie."

He dissolved into helpless laughter, which made the rest of the campfire wonder at the rapid change she had brought about.

"That's great!" he hooted. "You ain't carrying my kid!"

He sat up suddenly, forcing her downward; he found her mouth, kissing her savagely until her eyes flew open, flaming into his, then her hands began to beat on his back. He released her and hooted again.

The laughter died. Nolan was aware of a heavy hand upon his shoulder. He whirled where he sat, looking into Matt Monroe's unsmiling face.

"Excuse me, Nolan," he said ceremoniously, "but I believe you already have a wife—in case you've forgotten."

Then his fist crashed into Nolan's jaw. Nolan's head spun dizzily as he started to fall back. But even as the blackness came, it was a million shattered images of Matt's face. He knew he would never forget that.

"Matt," Laura Lee flared, "you shouldn't have done that!"

"I venture to suggest," Matt said blandly, "that you helped bring it about, in the first place."

Lolly squatted down by Nolan, who was semi-conscious and moaning. "He is my husband, after all," she said coldly as she saw the eyes of all upon her.

It was a very quiet night. It was a very quiet voyage the next day to Dawson.

9

The midnight sun that would shine twenty-two out of every twenty-four hours was still a month away. But the city Jack Ladue had mysteriously named after George Mercer Dawson, chief of the Geological Survey of Canada, was no longer a swampy river bank.

That mid-November you could hardly see his original sawmill warehouse for the three-hundred structures that had risen before it. His city lots had brought about Front Street, with Broadway and Wall Streets near by.

McQuestan Enterprises was a rambling barn—so rambling that most of its shelves were dusty from lack of use. LeRoy Napoleon McQuestan was having better luck caring for those who got stranded in Circle City during the freeze-up.

Mizner signs were here and there. Mizner Mercantile, which was run by Edgar, who could still chill the coldest day with his personality, had two locations—each with equally bare shelves. The Addison Mizner Construction Company had designed many, but built few buildings outside the family. Mizner Freight did own a steamboat, but both the ship and brother Wilson were stuck on a frozen sandbar outside of Circle City.

From a distance down the river it looked like a miracle city had arisen. But drawing closer, Henry could only hear running through his mind a doleful Orleans Negro spiritual:

> *O Lord, remember the rich and remember the poor,*
> *Remember the bond an' the free;*
> *And when you done rememberin' all 'round,*
> *Then, O Lord, remember me!*

Front Street along the river was lined with just as many men trying desperately to get out of Dawson as it seemed were waiting in the tent cities to get in! And behind them, and behind the slatboard buildings that suggested that some had struck it rich, Jack Ladue's "indians" had not followed his plan. The sawmills had denuded the hillside and moved on. Twelve sawmills now worked around the clock and knew they would never catch up with their orders before it was too cold for their steam-engines to operate.

A wild cheer went up for the incoming canoes. The sourdoughs saw it as a rescue from starvation. Times had changed. Now not even McQuestan would give out a grubstake to see a man through the winter. They talked in time as though it had been years, when it had been but a single one.

But the Lord had remembered the rich—and they had not, in turn, remembered the poor.

A tall, scrawny priest came bounding out of the crowd as soon as the canoe touched the new wharf, his pack in hand.

"Father, bless you," he gasped, taking Henry's hand. "I feared my replacement would not get here from Ottawa in time."

Henry was not quite sure if the man was pulling him out of the canoe so he could enter, or if it was a shake of the hand.

"Replacement?"

The owl-eyed priest went on as though he hadn't heard. "They should really leave it to the devil, for he is in full control already. If someone does not stop these people they will push God right out of this country. What is this?"

"What is what?" Henry asked.

"These people with you—" he said aghast. "They're *Indians*!"

"They rowed me here."

"You mean I am supposed to go back with *them*?" he paled.

"I suppose so, if you intend to go back. How did you get here, anyhow?"

"Steamboat from St. Michaels. Oh, this is just horrible! I have never been among the savages, although I did once come near to being sent to a mission in Africa. Same thing. Thievery, murder, adultery, witchcraft. However did you stand the journey?"

Henry heard Crow chuckle at his elbow, and saw Peter out of the corner of his eye.

"Well, Father," he said hesitatingly, "there're a good many things the Church can do to safeguard such a journey." He wheeled and pointed to Peter. "That is the son of a powerful man. I sprinkled Holy Water on his children to protect me. The very idea of *water* is foreign to their minds . . ."

"Minds!" the priest snorted. "Never met a heathen yet who had anything you could call a mind . . ."

"Ah—" Henry winked at Peter, "there you are wrong, my brother of the cloth. Some of them are extremely intelligent. They can read and write, and are good mathematicians. And they respect a man of God. Why, this man plans to charge these miners $50 to take them back to Lake Laberge, but he is only going to charge you twenty-five."

"But I thought," he stammered, "the Church . . ."

"The Church! The Church!" Henry said with loving grace. "Why, I bet they still have gold and silver in their vaults from the days of Pope Leo. Now, just step to the back of the canoe and get your coins ready."

"What the devil are you doing?" Peter hissed.

"Making you a small bundle," Crow chuckled.

"First, Peter," Henry said slowly, "I don't like what the man said, be he of the cloth or not. Secondly, Crow is right. If the weather holds you can make quite a handsome profit getting a few of these men down and dumping them in Corporal Dixson's lap."

"And if I choose not to—"

"That's enough! Why in the name of green sea witches do you think I am staying? To replace that ignorant bastard who can confuse an African with a Tlingit? I don't like the smell of things here. There are people on these canoes whom I admire and respect. If men want out of this place because they are starving, or fear they will starve, what manner of people would we be to just dump off our canoe loads and row back?"

"You have abandoned the needy before," Peter said quietly, but meanly.

"Impertinent pup, aren't you?" Henry laughed, refusing to lose his edge in the argument. But then he softened. "Will you come back for us if things don't work out here?"

"Is it an order?" Peter asked crisply.

"Hardly. A mere request."

"Here come the other canoes," Peter said, and turned away.

Crow touched Henry's arm. "Thank you for staying for us, sir."

Regrettably, Henry realized he was staying for himself. He could not stand to see the area left without some Church foundation. Would he ever learn to stop being a Father, and start trying to be a father?

* * *

Dawson, after three months of brutal struggle, was nothing like any town they had seen before—and it had a tendency to change from week to week.

The first "outsiders" had quickly established themselves as the "insiders" and were determined to keep all others as "outsiders" forever—unless they had some ability or talent that was needed.

Calvin Ramsey sat with George Carmack in an almost complete Victorian parlor, high above Dawson. Here, all of the muddy frozen streets and all night saloons were of a different world. George was magnificent in white silk shirt, Italian slippers, and the smartest English tweeds that money could buy. The enormous house was nothing short of an English maze nightmare. The exterior came out of George's memory of an San Francisco mansion.

There was no clear architectural plan, and when the basic structure had been completed, something had to be done about the cavernous interior. Kate decided it would have three floors, with doors tall enough so she would never have to stoop to enter again. But as to the number of rooms and their places, she wasn't quite sure. Whenever she would think of one she wished, she would tell the carpenters. When Carmack Henry thought of those he desired, he told the carpenters. Graphie Gracey wanted a suite of rooms like the ones her mother had delighted over in the Seattle Hotel. Although they were rich enough to have homes of their own, Skookum Jim and Tagfish Charlie suggested rooms for themselves on the third floor.

The back of the first floor, behind the massive kitchen and dining room, was the private sanctuary of George Carmack. Except for one area, the floors had been left dirt. The sanctuary was what had brought Calvin and Amalida to meet the man. The secret of all George brought back from Seattle for the house, was no secret at the Klondike Hotel.

But George and Kate had misunderstood the reason for

the visit. Kate immediately whisked Amalida off to show her the house. George did likewise with Calvin, showing him those things in which he thought a man would be interested in a house he might wish to rent.

Thus Calvin got to see the rocked-in furnace and smelter of the sanctuary and the one completed area in the far corner—George's private Victorian parlor.

"Well, Mr. Carmack," Calvin said, "how does it feel to be the man who found all of this?"

"It doesn't feel like anything," George drawled slowly. "I don't sleep good on a mattress—and I can't get the coldness of last winter out of my bones. Besides, this gold business is plain bothersome. Mounties scared pissless half the time. Check me all the time for taxes and nary a word to Big Alex."

"Big Alex?"

"Alexander McDonald. Makes his poke by 'laying' out his claims. Mounties can't figure out what is his and what is taken by the 'lay lease.' "

"I'm afraid what you are saying makes no sense to me," Calvin said dryly.

"It better make sense to you damn quick," George chided him, smiling. "The company up here is fast and rough. I don't mean to poke my nose in on what you have to invest in this here banking business, but some of these old sourdoughs walk about with $20,000 to $30,000 in a drawstring bag—just for drinking and gambling money."

"It isn't minted into coin?"

George roared in delight. "You saw my smelter and press. Fired it up once and Sergeant O'Toole was here the moment he saw the black smoke billow out the chimney. You would have thought I robbed the Bank of Canada. Despite that, I saw there was going to be little profit in it."

"For a miner, yes," Calvin smiled, "but for a banker even a small profit adds up nicely."

"Then you might be wanting to lease my smelter?"

"Might," Calvin said slowly. "This whole area has business possibilities. That outside door would keep customers from having to track through the kitchen."

"That's the reason it's there," George preened proudly. "Ain't a sourdough come or went that ain't knocked at that door for a loan or for a way to cheat the Mounties. Well, ain't exactly *cheating*."

Calvin, who had made a fortune for Stillman and Carter on his ability to read men, understood the quick disclaimer.

"Then you think I would have plenty of customers?"

"Well, it's not a bad idea . . . having a banker here. Mizner boys do a mite of loaning, but only to businesses they want to control. Got me a safe, case you didn't see. First thing I might like to see a bank do for me, which would make it legal in O'Toole's eyes, is to mint me my own coins. Got everything to do it with but the knowhow. Bankers should know that. How about $500 a month rental?"

"*Five hundred!*" Calvin gasped. "That's an awful lot for just . . . just . . ."

"Holy Hannah! They charged me that much to smelt my gold in Seattle. I'm giving you the whole house—kit and kaboodle."

"The whole house?"

"Kate won't stay another winter. She ain't got no friends here. We've got our claims out with Big Alex. I was going to close the house down today and take the dog-sleds home. Now I'd like to see that safe turned into coin. Give me your hand and $500 to seal the bargain."

Calvin took the outstretched hand; but he kept the joy from his face at the suddenness of it all. He had come merely to ascertain the possibility of smeltering down his own $50,000. He had known that there were risks involved, if the man was smart enough to know about the stamped numbering system. But the risk had to be taken.

Their double bedroom at the Klondike Hotel was $10 a night. The restaurant had charged him a dollar for a bowl of soup, a dollar twenty-five cents for a baked potato, two dollars for a plate of canned tomatoes and four dollars for a piece of venison roast that he could hardly cut. Twelve dollars and fifty cents just so he and Amalida could have dinner! A fine meal at the Northern in Seattle had cost him only two dollars and ten cents for both of them.

"Oh, damn!" George roared, seeing a figure pass the window and head for the parlor door. "It's McDonald." Then he brightened. "Son, just keep your mouth shut and I may have you your first customer. Don't take Big Alex wrong. He's just so damn stubborn that he has to fight with his tongue to make it wag."

Calvin was fascinated. It was like Amos Stillman walking through the outside door, but fully bearded and in heavy winter attire.

The man was not huge, he was gigantic, ham-fisted and, as George had warned, so taciturn that a nod of the head or a shake of the sandy-red beard could be a simple answer or a full statement.

"Alex, I know it will soon be Christmas, but what in the world do you need $150,000 for?"

"Lay," he grunted.

"Whose?"

"Brutceth. Panned $61,000 in a day."

"He offered it to me for $50,000 so he could go winter in Circle City."

"Didn't say just one lay."

"How many have you now, Alex? Mr. Ramsey, as a banker, will have to know such things before he can loan out to a total stranger."

Calvin's mind was reeling. He was in over his head with his first customer. In New Orleans a loan of $1,000 to $5,000 was considered quite sizeable. His $50,000 was no more than poker money here.

"Carmack," he gruffed, "I don't know. Hell, for such a short-term loan I could just go dig out $150,000."

"You well could, Alex," George chuckled. "Or you might bring in that bowl you keep on your sideboard and let Mr. Ramsey smelt it down for you. What you got in it?"

His massive shoulders shrugged. "About forty-five pounds."

Calvin gasped. "That's about a third of it right there."

"Mr. Ramsey," George corrected him softly, "you are thinking in terms of brick weight and not nugget weight. Still, you have a good point. Alex, you will appreciate this, too. Our trade here, Mr. Ramsey, is mainly in dust and nuggets. Ain't that many scales around and it's mainly guess as guess can. Some cheat and some don't, as in everything. But when a man wants to buy a claim, or lease a claim, to lease back out to another miner for a percentage of the results, he likes to do it in coin to get the full value. That's why my Seattle coin has been so ripe for loaning. Ladue did most the same with his coin."

"Excuse me," Calvin said slowly, "but on this basis how does a man know that he is getting his fair percentage out of this 'lay' system?"

"Damn smart question," Alex boomed. "Mister, we don't always know. I've got pieces of about 65 claims for this winter. Can't be at all of them."

"And you, Mr. Carmack?" Calvin asked.

"Leased them to Alex and he's leased them back out." George said with a chuckle. "That's got O'Toole running his banty legs off."

"If I might suggest something," Calvin said even slower, almost matching the slow drawl of Alex McDonald, "now that I am to establish a bank, everything taken from your claims could be brought in here for weighing, smelting, coinage—and then the man can be paid his share from that, with your percentage put on account for you."

George chuckled. "Sounds fine, except you'd have O'Toole moving a desk right in here."

"Not in my bank," Calvin said snidely. "Only authorized personnel in the smelter room. The books, of course, would be open for his examination at any time."

And Calvin knew how to handle books.

"I like it," Alex snorted. "Now, back to the loan."

Calvin was no better off than before and let George Carmack take over again.

"How do you need it?"

"In twenties and a thirty. Got Brutceth for twenty tomorrow. Harkness for a twenty on Tuesday. The rest by sometime next week."

It was hardly banking language, but Calvin was still fascinated.

"Well, let's start with Brutceth's twenty. One a day for thirty, as usual."

McDonald nodded.

"Kate and I wanted to leave with the children today, but we're going to wait till tomorrow. Ramsey is going to rent the house and this will be his office. He and I got some business to do first, so you come tomorrow afternoon and I think he'll be ready for you."

Calvin prayed that he might. He could take care of the loan tomorrow and on Tuesday. But what of next week? Then his mind boggled as a truth came to him. "One a day for thirty." That was one percent a day for thirty days. That was 365 percent per annum! His $50,000 would make him as much in a month as he made in five years of salary in New Orleans.

Now, if he could just make it all work.

In the next two weeks, Nolan Fedderson very nearly lost his mind. His leg was bad enough, but this—this was not to be tolerated.

It was bad enough that the cabin Lolly had found them was a hovel. The logs had been thrown together, improperly caulked, with split rails laid for an uneven floor. The roof leaked, and the stove was made from two old cod barrels wedged one into the other, set upon a pile of rocks, with a leaky chimney jammed into a crudely cut hole at the top. The constructing miner hadn't worried much about a stove door, as the jagged cut-out at the bottom which Lolly kept cutting herself on attested to. With the stove lit, the tin gave off a constant aroma of dried cod.

The furniture he had scoffed at—although three muddy lots away Matt, Crow and the Dunn boys didn't even have a stove. Here, at least, he had a rough-hewn table, two benches, a rocker that didn't rock and a log stump for his broken leg to rest upon as a footstool.

Lolly felt that they were fortunate to find the cabin. She and the others had spent their first three days covering every inch of Dawson. Places were available, if one had a fortune to spend. The cheapest business location Harriet could find for the bakery would cost $40,000, so she and Harlan kept looking. They couldn't afford the hotel for very long.

The others couldn't afford their tent area for long, either. Ladue agents came nightly to collect $5 a tent space—and no outhouse available.

It didn't take them long to learn a great deal about Dawson City. You almost had to be rich to live there through that winter, for those who had built it had forgotten the meaning of charity. They couldn't afford charity. Kerosene was $40 a gallon and hay $1,000 a ton.

Next, they learned that if you were an Indian—any type of Indian—you could not enter a saloon, eat in a restaurant, or stay in a lodging house or hotel. You could not own a claim, lease a claim, or work a claim unless it was as a pick and shovel man for the owner—which paid a dollar a day. That wasn't enough to buy a bowl of soup.

Because Matt couldn't take Crow along, and the Dunn boys were a little shy of such places, he spent a great deal of time the first two nights making himself known in all ten saloons. He had gone mainly for information and advice. He gained the former mainly from overheard conversation and the latter directly—"ain't no room left."

There had been only about four thousand good claim sites to begin with, and they had all been taken that first winter and summer. Now, if you didn't have a claim, didn't have the money to buy, lease or "lay" a claim, or have the provisions to last the sixty days a man might be off his claim to "jump" it, then you'd better head back or hole up for the winter in Lousetown.

Matt had purposely kept the name of the town from everyone. It sat across the Klondike from Dawson City on the Yukon mud banks. The Mizner brothers had claimed the riverfront for their steamboat quay, but had shrugged their shoulders at the quagmire behind. The miners and others didn't shrug. A shack and crate town sprang up without the formal lot plotting of Ladue and Dawson. Streets were curving mud paths for all but the winter months. Then they were frozen mud paths. But they possessed one element that was not to be found in Dawson City. If you could find a vacant cabin, you could move in for free. If you had a gun, your squatter's rights were assured.

There were some shacks in Lousetown that were for sale, but Matt kept that fact from Lolly.

It was the only straight street in Lousetown, and had shacks packed in a solid double row for a full city block. Because McQuestan, Ladue and the Mizners owned much of Dawson City, they would not allow these occupants to buy on the Dawson side of the river. They were the girls who primarily danced and pushed the drinks in the saloons—for $100 a night. Their real source of income, which was not allowed in Dawson City, was indicated by the red kerosene lanterns they hung outside their shacks at the end of a saloon shift.

But that wasn't what had Nolan roaring like a wounded lion, either.

"But why?" Lolly whispered. "Calvin said you could work on crutches until the leg was healed."

"You're so damn stupid!" Nolan howled. "He's just trying to protect his damn loan by putting me to work!"

"What loan? I thought we only owed Clara Bennett."

"What loan? What loan?" he sneered. "It's none of your damn business. All you've gotten out of this whole trip is a long pokey nose."

"Nolan? Is it her? Are you crazy mad because she hasn't been to see us since we got here?"

"Come here?" he roared. "Who in the hell would want to come to this pig-sty?"

The question uppermost in her mind was out before she could stop it. "Do you love her?"

"I don't love her!" Nolan howled. "I don't give a shit if she never comes to dress my leg! Damn squaw! Never touched a damn Indian in my life and damn sure don't intend to touch one now."

"You have, from what I've heard," she said miserably.

"Oh Christ!" he grated. "Get out of here if you believe that damn lie! Get out before I kick your stupid ass out!"

Lolly fled. Nolan sat in the thick darkness. His all-too-vivid imagination kept conjuring up a portrait of Laura Lee, creamy and naked, wrapped in his strong arms. It made him feel sick. He had never known a woman like her; he hadn't the faintest idea why she had followed him and then refused to come to see him—unless it was Lolly. Was Lolly keeping her away? Damn, why hadn't he aimed better?

"I heard you coming," Crow said affably, ushering Lolly into the shack. "Welcome to our mansion of glad tidings. The brothers Dunn, for an amount they will not mention, have secured a lease from an Alexander McDonald. As said lease has an equally charming ediface on the digging site, they are packing to reduce these to dual bachelor quarters. I hardly know what Matt and I will do with all the extra room."

"Oh, Jerome," Lolly giggled, running to hug him. "And Cornell. I am so happy. The very best of luck."

For them, to receive a good luck wish from her was a little embarrassing. They knew her plight, and knew that their luck was only based on the secret fund their father had sworn them to silence over at Skagway. Without that $20,000 they never would have been able to make contact with Alex McDonald. The quicker they got away the fewer questions they would have to answer.

"Where is Matt?" she asked Crow when the Dunn boys had left.

"Up seeing Father Henry. Laura Lee came for him. Something about the church starting to slide down the mountain. Can you imagine that other idiot building the church almost a mile upsteam?"

"Laura Lee was here?"

Crow knew he had made a mistake. "She was in and they were out."

"About like Calvin."

"What? You mean he came down off his mountain and walked across the water to us?"

"Don't be snide," she said. "He came to offer work."

"Oh?" He instantly knew that Nolan had turned it down or she wouldn't be there.

"I don't know what it is, exactly. Honestly, Nolan turned him down flat. Calvin then asked if I would have you and Matt come to see him."

"In that order?" he asked wryly. Then he softened. "I'm sorry. My Indian skin isn't as tough as I thought it was. I thought life on a reservation was bad, but these people make the soldiers look like angels. I had a man spit in my face the other day. Matt had to hold me back from killing him. No one treated me like that on the trip, Lolly."

"Of course not. For one thing, we all had to depend too much upon each other. Well, I hope things work out for you here. I want to go check on Harriet, now. But Crow . . . you will go to see Calvin Ramsey about that job, won't you?"

"Damn right! I'd rather be Calvin's Indian than a dead man."

In his first days at St. John's Father Henry tried to ignore the fact that Laura Lee had stowed away for the trip. He had turned his attention, instead, to the sins of Dawson City. He was told frankly to mind his own damn business. Then he turned for an audience with the other minister with a church in town. But that strait-laced, pious, devil-chasing New England Quaker blasted and damned Henry from his door as a papist without giving him a chance to speak. Thereafter, he tried to shame the miners into attending the cabin church.

He had one celebrant for his first mass—Laura Lee.

He had refused then to service her with communion because she had not attended confessional, and he feared she had much to confess. The silence yawned between them like the crevasse on the glacier.

As a priest he had always gone directly to God. But now he needed a man to bounce his thoughts off of.

"I don't know the good Father's reason," he said flatly, crawling under the structure, "but to put this church on pilings, on a mountainside, was idiotic. Back here they are slipping badly. Bring the lantern along, Matt. The building has kept the ground quite dry here, except for seepage." He lowered his voice, squatted and pulled his frocked knees right up to his chin. "Matt, what am I going to do? I love that child dearly, and don't want her hurt."

"No bad structure?"

"That can wait. This is more important. On the trail we could talk and share things. I need that kind of sharing."

Matt paused. Here was one man he could be truthful with. "I think I'm the wrong one, Henry. I find myself with a personal interest in the matter."

Henry grinned. "Exactly why you are the right man to talk to. I want to hear your palaver on the matter."

Matt sighed. "Might as well say right out that I'm very fond of Lolly Fedderson, though she only looks on me as a friend," he said flatly. "Nolan? I've summered and wintered with bastards like him, and many probably consider me near the same. He's going to get it any way that he can. Leg keeps him down right now, but watch out for him when he gets well. The question is, how does your daughter feel about him?"

"I wish I knew. I can't bring myself to talk to her about it."

"Travelled with a preacher man once, Henry. He didn't have no church so he would go right into a saloon and have a beer with the boys. Soon they were talking and then next thing you knew he'd have them all out in the field for a prayer meeting. I asked him once how in the hell he did it and his answer was so simple. He was a listener. He'd stand in the barroom and listen to everyone's woes for hours, and then, finally, they'd listen to his. If I were you, I'd start by listening to Laura Lee's woes."

"You know, Matt, I feel like I've out-aged both this preacher business and this father business, but I'll try. The real problem, to be blunt, is that I never loved her mother. I was too much in love with the Church—which I believe kept me from knowing human love. I was never able to teach Laura Lee what love was. I've got to educate myself, don't I, before I can teach? Oh, and here is another problem . . ."

Matt looked at the loose piling that had broken away from the quartz rock and gravel. He scooped some up in his hand and let it sift slowly through his fingers.

"Are you aware of what this is, Henry?"

The two men looked at each other soberly. Henry nodded.

"Most aware, Matthew. Now you know the trust and

faith that I place in you. No one but us knows of this find. It seems quite rich, does it not?"

Matt gasped. "But it's right under the church!"

"Strange, isn't it," Henry smirked. "The very crossroads I stood at in coming to check the slippage. Was this for Henre Duboise or the vaults in Rome? I have, over the years, presented myself as a man comfortable in life. Everything, frankly, went to make Laura Lee comfortable in school and in life. This trip has greatly levelled my accounts. That was how I planned it. We would be home, and have no need for great wealth. But when I looked at this raw gold I thought of Laura Lee. It could take her back and make her a princess—without Monsieur Fedderson. Then, naturally, the Pope's coffers loomed again. What can I do, my friend?"

"Oh, Henry," Matt moaned. "The temptation is great, but . . . but of all the things I have done, I have never stolen from a church before."

"I am glad to hear it," Henry chuckled, "but I knew it all along. Matthew, we will be stealing from no one. My predecessor, being a true product of the Church, just took the plot of land and arrogantly built St. John's as though the church owned the world. There is no claim on it—yet. But I advise caution. You must go quietly to Forty Mile and register the claim in our names."

"Our names? But it's your find."

"Granted. But a priest cannot stand in the pulpit one moment and crawl down a mine shaft the next. Yes, I said shaft, Matthew. I have some knowledge of geology, and I would say that this vein is a deep one—and therefore we must be that much quieter. Oh, don't get me wrong. I shall find a new location for St. John's. Are we agreed?"

It was all hard to believe, but Matt was in full agreement.

10

CHRISTMAS CAME and went.

January brought with it the long days of darkness and the sub-zero temperatures. As with the winter before, miners holed up by their claims, subsisting on little more than flapjacks and beans. Some, as far away as fifty miles, wouldn't come back into town until spring.

Dawson glowed day and night. New Year's Eve lasted for two weeks, with champagne going for $40 a bottle. Big Alex spent $1,700 just buying the girls in the Monte Carlo a glassful to toast the new year.

Out on Eldorado Creek, Jerome and Cornell Dunn settled down for the winter. They had already carted enough ore to Calvin Ramsey to cover their initial investment.

Henry and Matt also waited for spring. In digging a hole to put in a temporary piling brace, six shovels of dirt yielded $800 for each of them.

Suggesting that they were "contributions" to the church, Father Henre Duboise was able to play upon the heart strings of Joseph Ladue. A town lot was secured for a new church *and* a hospital. Jack Ladue was so enthused about the hospital that he agreed to donate the lumber if Father Henry would supply the labor and nails. Henry saw reason in this until he found out that Edgar Mizner had the only nails in town and they were going for $8 a pound.

Recalling Matt's words, he went into the saloons and listened. He convinced the people that *they* needed the hospital. He got his nails and more—Wilson Mizner would design it, if Henry could supply a building foreman.

Henry worried over Matt's suggestion on that point. He had thought that Laura Lee might take an interest in running the hospital, but to employ Nolan as foreman might be throwing them together again. As a father, he had still not been able to bring himself to talk with her about it. Matt had been staying with them since Crow took a room at Calvin Ramsey's mansion, and Henry had a secret yearning for Laura Lee to fall in love with Matt. Still, his regard for Nolan as a lumberman and builder had not lessened. Now that the man was back on his feet he would just have to take a chance. Miners could not mine because of the frozen ground, but builders could still build above it.

Harriet and Harlan didn't want to build.

"Everything?" Calvin waved an elegant hand. "Everything?"

"Practically." Harlan's smile was dour.

"Not quite," Harriet took over, "though there are possibilities. I let the man think I was looking for a home, and it does have ample living quarters."

Calvin said nothing to that, and his stare became more piercing. "What possibilities?" he asked.

Harriet looked down the table at Amalida, thinking it best to put it in a woman's point of view. "Well, I must confess that the kitchen is not as large as yours, although the man did think it would become a restaurant. It has three big ranges, with plenty of oven space. Harlan was impressed. I became a snoop as the men talked. In a back storeroom are barrels of flour, sugar, shortening—all the basic things for a restaurant or bakery."

"Why is it closed?"

Harriet involuntarily glanced again at Amalida, who kept her face without expression. "The man, as I got the story, ran up quite a bill having Mr. McQuestan ship all his supplies and equipment from St. Michael. Then, when he found out he could only get his supplies from McQuestan or Mizner, he balked and refused to pay the freight bill or the building charges. Mr. Ladue, the man who showed it to us, locked him out and hasn't seen him since. We—we think it is a good investment . . . but are a trifle short."

Calvin took up his glass of wine and drank it swiftly. He became aware that everyone was watching him now and that the dinner party was turning to business.

"When you say 'trifle,' how much do you mean?"

"You know what we have been through." Harriet laughed. "We brought a whole bakery with us and left almost all of it on the glacier."

"That will hardly cut mustard with Joseph Ladue or McQuestan. They do not take anyone's past into consideration when making a sale. How much are they asking?"

"Nearly sixty thousand," Harriet whispered.

"Lord!" said Amalida in a quelling tone; her eyes were glazed the way they often were lately, especially after too much wine with dinner.

"I'm amazed," Calvin said, but he wasn't. Such figures were becoming commonplace in his mind. Crow could smelt and coin twice that amount in a day. "How would you ever hope to pay it all back?"

"With hard work and honesty," Harriet said. Her tone was heavy. "We would not be vicious like Mizner, who charges five dollars a pound for flour and ten for sugar. There is already a savings of $15,000 from the flour and sugar in the storeroom—to say nothing of the other supplies. That brings it down to near the price of just a front street lot—and this building is new. The equipment is new. It just needs Harlan to start baking."

"It's too much money!" cried Amalida, her intoxication making her voice too loud, almost fierce.

"Amalida," Calvin said, "this is business talk."

She glowered at him. "That's all you ever talk! That's all *anyone* talks in this horrible place. Its *awful.* Harriet is the first woman to sit at my table and it turns to dull business talk. Dull, dull, dull!" She hit the table with a clenched fist. "I want a different subject."

"Amalida," he said again, and this time his tone was formidable. She looked at him in semi-drunken stupefaction, then turned to Crow as if to get him to side with her. But he kept his face averted, thoughtful. Every meal seemed to come down to this. He and Calvin had plenty to keep them busy throughout the day. Amalida had little to do. To really underscore that he was a banker of worth, Calvin had hired an Athabascan Indian woman as a cook, her ten-year-old daughter as a maid and her two teenage boys to cut the firewood for Crow's furnace. But the Athabascan women never had to cook for more than just the three of them. Except for a handful of miner's wives and a very few businessmen's wives, the women of Dawson were all "working girls." There was no society, as yet, for Amalida to attach herself to.

Harriet was watching, her mouth curled in a Mona Lisa smile. She knew that Amalida had just helped secure the loan. Calvin would have to help keep them "respectable" or Amalida to have at least one woman friend.

Crow thought it time for him to disappear. Another glass of wine and he would have to help carry Amalida up to her bed again. He was lately learning too much from her drunken ravings, things he really didn't want to know.

"I have to check the furnace. It helps if we keep it stoked throughout the night. Goodnight to you all."

Amalida suddenly turned eager and girlish. "Lonsworth, not more work. We have not yet finished the wine."

"He's a marvel!" Calvin exclaimed quickly, clapping his hands. "Just one showing and he took right over the mint. Sergeant O'Toole was so impressed he thought I had brought in an expert. Well, he has become one. Goodnight, Crow."

Crow showed all his white teeth. "Goodnight," he said again, and quickly got out before Amalida could protest again.

George Carmack's sanctuary had become the domain of Lonsworth Crowley, with many changes.

George's parlor remained, but had been expanded all around with a "U" construction of rooms to keep eyes from seeing into the mint. Calvin now had a private office, a bookkeeping office, the parlor as an entry area and a general area for the checking in and weighing of the ore.

Crow's domain was still cavernous, although a wooden walkway now stretched from the kitchen door to the back door of the office area partition. The north wall, on either side of George's safe, had been shelved and lined with wooden crates. Each crate bore a name, a number and a replica of the coins the crate stored. Only Calvin's ledgers knew how much each crate held, or what had been loaned out of it.

In the eight weeks since the smelter started boiling daily, the Dawson Commercial Savings Bank had accumulated assets of three-quarters of a million dollars. In a town of six thousand that represented very few miners or business houses. One saloon, taking in no less than $2,000 a week, did start having their own coins minted. It was a small account.

To enhance his reputation, Calvin had not been greedy, charging only one percent on any smelting and coinage order. He had also made a fast friend in Sergeant O'Toole. The taxes were taken out and "bricked" so they couldn't be used for barter.

His real money was being made on the loan interest charges. Nearly $2,500 a day.

Lonsworth Crowley's real money came from being smart. From the first day, Calvin had carefully instructed him on the scraping of the crude bullion from the furnace lip, hod carriers, coin molds and table. The cooled flakes and goblets Calvin considered part of the profit.

But nothing had ever been said about the floor in front of the furnace, the hod path to the mold table, or what splattered onto the floor in the pouring.

So, nightly, after he had taken the slag out of the top of the furnace to cool on the frigid dirt floor, Crow would stoke the furnace for banking and methodically rake the floor with a stiff broom. He would sift his little piles through a screen, carefully picking out even the smallest particle that had dropped onto the dirt. These he would put in a testing cup, used to determine when the furnace was hot enough to separate the gold precipitate from the impurities. When the cup was half full, he would shove the long-handled metal cup back into the furnace. Because this gold was 99.99 percent pure it melted quickly. This time he made sure there was no spilling on the way to the mold table. Laid out neatly were lead mold bottoms and tops, already sprinkled with a mixture of talc and corn starch. Into each hand-carved indenture the molten bullion was poured to a mark level. Five round indentures in each mold, each equivalent to a twenty dollar gold piece. Then the top mold, with its concave design marking was fitted in place and weighted for cooling.

On any given night Crow usually filled the two molds he had designed for himself—a crow sitting on a tree limb on one side and the Roman numeral twenty on the other.

His own little bank had amassed nearly $8,000 just from keeping the floor tidy.

"I told you all the man needed was work to calm him down," Matt said when he and Henry started back to the old church, which they were converting into a most comfortable house. "I also told you he is exactly what we needed. The hospital wing just flew up, and so will the church wing."

"Well, they don't seem to be a problem, do they?"

Matt laughed. "You can't get into trouble with silence. She seems to resist being anywhere near his working area."

"Are you sure about that?"

Matt reflected. "Pretty sure. Every time his name comes up she changes the subject. I would call it embarrassment."

"She used to tell me everything," said Henry, hurt.

Matt roared in laughter. "The simple things. Did you discuss the complex things with your parents when you were becoming a man?"

"No, because I thought I was smarter than they were." Then he said, with a frown, "Do you think we were wise leaving her there to work?"

"Very wise. She's taken an interest, hasn't she? Besides, I'll come back down for her before supper time."

Henry pounded his arms across his barrel chest. "Whisky freezing temperature. Sure glad Belinda Mulrooney sent up that pot-bellied stove from her roadhouse."

"Even though she cussed you like a horse-trader for asking?"

"Matthew, my dear boy, I learned many a moon ago that an Irishwoman might think she is taking herself out of the Church, but you can't ever take the Church out of that Irishwoman!"

Belinda Mulrooney and her Magnet roadhouse had also donated six beds for the hospital ward, even though the springs were so rusty that Laura Lee was nearly breaking through the coils trying to clean them.

"Mind if I warm myself?" Nolan asked, coming right to the pot-bellied stove that glowed pinkish-red. "It's so damn cold that the last six nails popped their heads as I hit them. I told the others to shag on over to the Monte Carlo and warm their innards."

Laura Lee was on her feet now, backing away from the cleaning of a bed spring. But Nolan could not see her face, or the anguish in her eyes.

"Don't go," he muttered, "I want to talk to you . . . I want to know what's wrong."

"You should know," she whispered. "You have a wife, remember?"

"I know," Nolan said sadly. "But I love you, Laura Lee. I can't stop that, anymore than I can stop living. Lolly is a wall between us—and I'm ashamed I can't love her."

Laura Lee's hands flew over her ears.

"I don't hear you! I don't want to hear you!"

But she did want to hear. Each day as the wing went up he was like a cancer eating at her slowly. She ignored him, but hung on every word he said to the other workers. She knew his faults and what they had almost done to Lolly. She tried to keep that thought uppermost in her mind, but other things got in the way. The sight of his muscular frame hoisting a rafter into place. His chuckle over a miner trying to volunteer his time as a carpenter. He wasn't all bad. He just wasn't! But he *was* married.

"Then hear this," he said grimly. "What about having some fun? How about laughing, Laura Lee? Haven't we a right to laugh, to be happy and have fun, you and I?"

Laura Lee looked at him, her almond eyes soft and tender, her mouth smiling a little; but Nolan did not like that smile. It was questioning his meaning of fun.

"I can read your mind," he said fiercely. "All fun doesn't have to mean *that*, you know!"

Laura Lee turned and warmed her hands before the stove. "Can you prove that?" she whispered.

Nolan stood there and looked down at her—tiny, fragile, proud. He wanted to run his hands over her small body, and hold her close. His Saturday nights with Lolly had become forced again, and were without fulfillment. He blamed their surroundings. The desolate cabin grated on his nerves. Each night, since he had gone back to work, he had stalled in returning to it. At first it had been just a quick stop to have one drink with the other workers. He was fascinated by the gambling tables, but didn't have that type of poke to play. He recognized some of the dancing girls as nearby "neighbors", but didn't have the money for their after-hour pleasures either. He was taken to other places by the workers, but just didn't have the money to really enjoy—

Suddenly, he had his answer.

"You want laughter and fun? Where are your wraps? I have the perfect thing to show you!"

"What is it? Where are we going?"

"Oh, no! That would ruin the surprise and the fun!"

Laura Lee looked at him, her eyes star-bright. Yes, she needed surprise and fun. She feared that every time her father opened his mouth it was going to be the beginning of the lecture that she dreaded hearing. She could enjoy Matt, but she couldn't really have fun with him.

She walked back in the mid-afternoon darkness in wonderment. It had been fun and exciting—even though a little barbaric. At first the ice pit, ringed by torches and half-drunk miners had frightened her. Quietly, Nolan had explained the matching of the dogs, the points awarded and how the gambling took place. The first fight she thought outrageously tasteless. Then she saw that the sled dogs were too valuable to be allowed to be maimed or killed. It was a show of strength and brute force. She had begun to pick her favorites and root them on. It made Nolan laugh and nestle close, his arm about her shoulder. She didn't mind. It gave her warmth and security, being the only woman present at the pit. When her choices kept winning, she became a favorite of the cheering crowd. She had added a little spice to their enjoyment as well.

Upon their return Nolan tried nothing improper, and it was not mentioned when Matt came for her.

Two days later, Nolan mysteriously came up with borrowed ice skates. Neither of them had ever skated on ice before and it was high comedy as they attempted to be graceful.

January slipped away and the walls rose to make St. John's and the hospital a single building. The six-bed ward gleamed with freshly painted beds and no patients. Laura Lee continued to find improvements she could make, and Henry was glad for her interest. Nolan began to fashion pews and an altar, and Henry was grateful for his industry.

Slowly, as Nolan had planned it, the hospital beds came to be used for other than their intended purpose.

"I have never seen or heard anything so horrible in all my life," Lolly sobbed, mixing melted snow water into the flour.

"You're young and unknowing," Nolan said. "You'll learn someday that they don't pay until the end of a job."

"But that's not fair. At home you still got weekly rations from the company store. I'm sick of flour pancakes and beans. I've even had to borrow a pinch of salt occasionally, we've been so broke."

"Who do you borrow it from?"

"One of the girls on the block."

Usually such a statement would rile him and he would fear that it was a saloon girl who could have seen him and might say something to Lolly about his drinking. But of late he did not feel one twinge of fear or concern. He no longer entered the saloons. He hadn't been drinking much. He seldom ate more than one of Lolly's flapjacks rolled around a spoon of beans. When Henry and Matt were off and busy, he and Laura Lee would sneak away for a restaurant lunch, or she would bring a basket down from the house.

It was quite easy. Matt was fully engrossed in building a home that would disguise a mine shaft and Henry had purchased a sled and dogs to visit the miners at Bonanza and Eldorado Creeks and bring them news of the town.

But Dawson City, even under the northern lights, didn't have many dark spots for a rendezvous.

"Excellent rolls, my dear. Aren't they, Lonsworth? Where did you get them, Amalida?"

"In town, of course. At the bakery after lunch."

Calvin could tell she was drunk, but tried to ignore it. He called it "mere nerves". No lady got drunk on a small glass of sherry before dinner and a little wine with dinner itself.

"Oh, you ate lunch in town?"

"Arcade. Harriet's choice. Bad choice. The love birds were holding hands at a back table. Harriet was aghast, but I laughed. That big brute didn't lie about them."

"Amalida," Calvin said in an incredulous voice, with no intent to be tactful. "Is . . . is that drink talking?"

"Drink?" she said, wiping her dripping eyes. She was horrified by his words.

There was a sharp silence. Her wet eyes blinked. She was speechless for a moment before trying to strike back at the insult. "I saw what I saw. The same as you with that hussy in Seattle, I presume. They would have been atop each other had it not been a public place. Oh, you men are all monsters!"

She flew from the dinner table, banging into the empty chairs at the far end. Her screaming voice trailed up the stairs in rattling echoes. "I don't drink. I know what I saw. Lonsworth, help me to bed!"

Crow didn't move. She had become like a toothache that wouldn't go away. He was tired of her drunken hands trying to clutch him intimately. He was a man, but he wasn't desperate. But there had been verity in her voice. She was a poor liar; she lacked imagination. But this jolted him. Matt had made him a party to the secret so they could have coins minted to keep operating. This, he feared, might make Calvin start questioning how Nolan got funds to eat in restaurants.

"I had best see to her," Calvin said, reluctantly.

"And I will see to the furnace."

But Crow's coins could wait that night.

Laura Lee rested her small face against the pillow of her bed.

"I've expected this talk for months, Father."

"I tried to hold my silence over things in the past that I did not want to believe. But now, being seen in public with a married man! Acting like a common harlot!"

"Oh, of all the damnable tomfoolery . . ."

He glared down at her, his face dark and angry.

"Is that how you see it? Have you no shame?"

"Did my mother have shame when she fornicated with you?"

"I was not a married man!"

"Oh no—you were married to the Church!" she hissed.

His own sins were being slapped in his face to make hers acceptable. That was miserable. But he answered by Church rote and not from a father's heart.

"I have sought my peace on that score, but you stand in the way of hellfire and damnation!"

"Then so be it!" she scoffed. "I no longer believe in being good because of fear of punishment. I laugh and it makes him laugh. I am warm inside because it makes him warm inside. With me he is gentle and good. Lolly doesn't warm him or help him. I am good for him and she is not. Does the Church have an answer for that? Hell no! Their sacrament laws order men and women to remain tormented by hatred and misery. I will not be tormented or miserable, even if I can be no more than his mistress!"

She saw him stiffen, his whole body become suddenly rigid, and when she looked up at his face it was blank with sorrow.

"Never!" he growled. "That I will not allow!"

Slowly, she shook her head.

"It is far, far too late to disallow. I have been his, even as recently as this afternoon . . . and probably will be again as soon as tomorrow afternoon. Who knows?"

"I guess only you do," Henry said without hesitation; but the moment he had said it, he regretted it. This was the time for words of wisdom, and he had none. He was failing as a father, and as a priest. That night he prayed that he could do better when he tried to talk some sense in Nolan's head.

"You been with her?" Lolly muttered.

Nolan ran his big hands through his hair, giving it a shaggy and unkept look. He kept his face averted.

"Nollie," Lolly began again, "you been—"

"Shut up!" he snarled. "What gives you such stupid ideas?"

"Being Saturday night," she said flatly.

"How in the hell can you tell the difference with day and night being almost the same?"

"Gertie. She works a double shift on Saturday. Comes home to put her diamond between her big teeth on a Saturday night."

"You and that—that—"

"Woman," Lolly supplied. "That wasn't what you were going to call her. I've learned what they are, living so close. At least they are honest in what they do. Is Laura Lee honest in what she is doing?"

"Those whores have given you a dirty mind. I don't see them doing it for love."

"Do you do it with her out of love?"

"Damn right!" he spat. "You never heard me say 'I love you' while going through the motions, have you?"

Tears sprang to her eyes. Miserably, she shook her head.

"Now don't start bawling, or I'll beat the crap out of you!"

"Might as well," she wept. "It's Saturday night."

"Hell, I don't ever want you again!" he said angrily and stormed out.

It was very still. Outside, a February storm was beginning to unleash its fury. Lolly was hungry—for food and affection. She had no one. Once she had taken Kimberly to see the new bakery, but Harriet and Harlan were too busy to hardly spare a minute. She had not felt right going back again. The bread had been selling briskly at two dollars a loaf. She had felt remiss in not even being able to buy a loaf from them.

I just can't keep this up, she thought. But she didn't have an answer as to what she might do about it.

11

HENRY STOOD listening, yet not hearing a word. The music blared around him, but he didn't hear that either. By midnight he was drunk. He had never been drunk before. He had always prided himself on his great capacity for alcohol, but this time he'd really overdone it. But he didn't care. He had roamed from saloon to saloon, not keeping track of what the barkeep put in front of him. He just didn't want to think about anything.

She is so mistaken, he pondered drunkenly. She thinks this is no different from my relationship with her mother, but it isn't. He just had to make Nolan see that. Just had to.

He stood up suddenly, tossed a coin on the bar and marched out. There was only a slight wobble to his walk. Outside, the snow was falling heavily, the wind fierce and howling. He had left his hat at one of the saloons, and the flakes clung to his hair, turning him into a white-haired little old man. He stumbled, then straightened up, swearing. He wouldn't wait until tomorrow, he would have this out with Nolan tonight.

The doors of the Monte Carlo burst open. Six men

hustled a brutish figure out and tossed him down into the snow.

"And stay out!" the barkeep barked. "Ain't no man allowed to treat one of my girls like that!"

"Crap!" Nolan snarled. "Then you tell that Diamond Tooth Gertie to stay out of my life! No damn cunt tells me how to treat my wife!"

Henry stumbled up and peered down. "Saints be praised. The Lord has delivered you so I don't have to tread across the water."

"God damn, you're drunk!" Nolan growled, starting to rise.

"Don't damn God for it. I did it all on my own. False courage they call it. The courage I need to tell you never to see my daughter again."

Nolan roared with laughter, dusting the snow off his clothes. "That's up to Laura Lee, old man. We'll see each other whenever we damn well please."

"And what of Lolly?"

"I have had it," Nolan screeched, "with everyone putting an oar into my life." For all his bulk, he moved like a cat. Without warning, his knee came up, catching Henry squarely in the groin.

Henry bent double with a grunt, trying to get his hands out of his pockets. Nolan thought he was going for a weapon. He chopped him behind an ear, using the edge of his open palm like the blade of an ax. As Henry went down, Nolan pulled a knife and fell on him.

The commotion had brought the barkeep back out to see if Nolan was causing more trouble. Others crowded around him, including Gertrude Selander.

"Hey," she called, "that's the preacher man he knocked down."

"Fedderson," the barkeep warned, "get your arse on home and don't come back here."

Nolan spun, brandishing the knife. "Are any of you big

enough to make me go home? I'm coming back in for another drink."

"No you're not!" A voice came out of the snowstorm. It was so very quiet, but so deep that they could all feel it.

Matt came into the light cast by the Monte Carlo's lanterned front. He had been going from saloon to saloon, worried about Henry. In one he had found his fur Tlingit hat. He had then headed directly for the Monte Carlo, cutting through the opera house being constructed by Addison Mizner a few doors down.

"Stay out of my way, Monroe!" Nolan snarled.

"Help Henry up," Matt ordered sharply. "We'll go settle this family matter in private."

"Family matter, my ass!" Nolan flung the knife directly at Matt. Matt spun away.

"He's going for a gun!" Diamond Tooth Gertie screamed.

As Matt whirled back he snatched an owl's-eye pistol from his belt, drawing both hammers back even before he had Nolan in focus.

This had not been his purpose in carrying the weapon. Dawson City was crime-free, except for saloon brawls. But one never knew what manner of hungry wolf or bear one might meet on the mile walk into town.

"I've got the drop on you, bastard!" Nolan hissed.

Matt started forward, step by step toward the muzzle of Nolan's pistol.

"Come on, you stupid sucker, give me a perfect shot," Nolan said. "You ain't boss of the trail anymore, so butt out. This ain't nobody's business. Suppose that damn wife of mine came running for you? Hell, ain't her business either. All she has time to do is flap her stupid mouth to whores and the likes of you. I don't give a shit! I'll do whatever the hell I feel like doing, and right now I feel like plugging you!"

He brought the pistol level, his finger clutching the trigger, squeezing. At that instant, Diamond Tooth Gertie hurled herself at him, falling on his arm with her bulky weight, so that the shot was deflected downward.

But Matt had also been primed. Just as Nolan had started to pull the trigger, he had begun to squeeze off his own shot. The shots were fired at the same instant. Nolan's plowed harmlessly into the snow, but Matt's bullet struck Nolan full in the chest. Gertie was still hanging over his arm, and felt Nolan's knees going rubbery, bending under him, the whole of him bending forward. She had to jump back to keep his large frame from falling on her.

After that, everything seemed to move in slow motion. Two miners came to help Father Henry to his feet and into the Monte Carlo. As though he were suddenly in charge, Matt silently handed his pistol to the barkeep, then went to see after Henry.

Gertie, unmindful of the skimpy dance costume and plumes in her bleached hair, ran through the snow toward the rickety footbridge over to Lousetown. She didn't know why she felt she had an obligation to tell Lolly. She just did.

Within moments, the body of Nolan Fedderson was covered with snow. He would lie that way until morning, when Sergeant Fletcher Morris and Sergeant Mark O'Toole would come to wrap him in gunny-sacking.

He would be taken to a log cabin warehouse down by the ice covered river. There, he would be placed with Horace Van de Coop, who had died trying to cross the street, and Fred Esterly, who had accidentally shot himself while cleaning his muzzle-loading musket.

If they couldn't dig gold till spring, they couldn't bury a man until spring either.

Gertie took Lolly to her shack, fed Kimberly and put her to bed. Here it was warm and a stew bubbled on the stove. She ate because she was hungry, but her mind was off on oblique, idiotic memories. She had no suit for Nolan such as they got for her Paw. How could she let Nolan's mother know? Her grief would be unbearable. But she felt nothing. There were no tears in her eyes. She felt guilty that she wasn't grief-stricken. She knew she should feel hatred toward Matt for killing her husband. She felt fear and helplessness, but not hatred.

As for Laura Lee, who Gertie insisted was the real cause of it all, Lolly didn't know how she felt. She knew she could never feel tenderness and friendship for Laura Lee again, only pity that they had to share in this sorrow and loss.

Laura Lee was bitter and full of hatred. They had stolen him away from her—Lolly, Matt and her father. She felt unbearably and incurably betrayed, as though they had purposely plotted against her. And she was so horribly lonely. She had no one she could confide in, who could console her, or share her grief. They had killed the only man she had ever loved.

Laura Lee put on her scarf and parka and gloves, and went out into the snow. Then she walked into town and to the hospital. It would be her home. She never wanted to see those three again. If her father came into the hospital she would treat him in a businesslike manner as Father Duboise. All through her life she had put up with nuns and priests she had detested. This would be little different.

The news spread, but little could be done about it. Three days of steady snow blanketed Dawson under eight feet. Tunnels were dug to the front doors of the saloons, for the brave and foolish ones who were determined to reach them.

Harlan started to tunnel out from the bakery. It was slow, tedious work, the snow wet and heavy. At first he thought it just the cold that made his right arm tingle and his breath come short. He stopped when the pain began to move through him like fire. His whole right side was numb by the time he got back inside. Because he could hardly move his mouth it was barely a croak he got out to call Harriet from the kitchen. She found him in a heap and struggled to get him upstairs and into bed.

She had planned to go see Lolly if possible, but now she had big troubles of her own.

"Oh, for God's sake! We should do something for the poor child!"

Amalida became angrily animated. "I don't see what we can do, or why. Her husband still owed us money when he was killed."

"Perhaps she could work it off here—as a servant."

He did not know that his usually impassive face was glowing like a youth's. He could well recall the Saturday night bouts from the next cabin. With Nolan dead, Lolly might need the comfort of a lover. He knew he certainly did. Since Amalida had begun to crawl into the bottle, he had not been able to crawl into her bed.

"For you or for me?" she snickered.

He turned away. "I will at least send Crow to check on her," he said, and left the room.

Amalida fell back on her cushions. He was not the same man as he had been on the trail. He had gone back to being the business-like, stuffy Raymond Forbes. She couldn't seem to recapture Calvin Ramsey. She had tried. She had tried to make him see the love she had developed for him, but he had been too busy with making money. And now Lolly. She couldn't feel anything for Nolan Fedderson. She detested a man who openly cheated on his wife. It was bad enough when they would sneak off to a whore, but Nolan had been brazen. That enraged her. She got to her feet, went to her locked dressing table, and took out a bottle of whiskey. Wine was no longer strong enough. She did not wait to get a glass. She lifted the bottle to her lips and drank avidly.

"He won't bring that tart into this house!" she said

aloud, and drank again. "He should hate her for snitching on him!"

She thought of that incident, and smiled vindictively. The drink made her see it all quite differently. He had never gotten angry at Lolly, because he had known that she was at Clara Bennett's all along. Yes, and he was always so sweet to her on the trail. Because she thought he frustrated and denied her, the whiskey made her start building it into whole cloth. The loan hadn't been made to Nolan out of gratitude, it would have been made anyway because of Miss Lolly-chops. Well, he would just have to get over his infatuation for Lolly.

"I'll damn well see to that!" she snorted, and triumphantly raised the bottle like a toast to the fact.

Crow found the shack empty and deserted. He did not know about Gertie and went to search out Matt.

Matt was so drunk he never thought to tell Crow about Gertie. Crow's report just put him in a deeper depression. He shook his head slowly from side to side, still disbelieving.

Women, he thought suddenly. He had used and exploited them his whole life through. And without pity. He had wanted either the illusion of them, or their money. This was the first time he had ever really wanted the woman herself, and now he had made that utterly impossible.

Ironically, he had brought about a change in Dawson. All hand guns were confiscated by Sergeant Fletcher and rifles had to be checked at the saloon door before entering.

Father Henre Duboise had a thick skin to pull about himself—the cloak of the church. He fasted, he prayed, he sought answers from God that he couldn't give himself as a mortal man. He was above hatred and bitterness. He prayed that time would heal the wound Laura Lee had helped inflict upon herself, and dampen the fire of her rebellion.

But time was something Lolly had little of—and no money to buy time.

"Chickee," Gertie said, almost gently, "I am going to give you some good advice. But first I want to ask you a question. You ever think about going into my profession?"

Lolly stared at her open-mouthed. "I ain't ever been able to do it right, even for Nolan." Her voice fell to a whisper. "And anyway, I ain't pretty anymore. And I'm getting old. Coming on twenty next year."

Gertie roared. "That really is getting to be an old bag. Well, for the advice. Some of the girls, as you know, got a kid or two. Errors from the past, you might say. Still, they gotta be seen to when we're workin' our tails off for J.T. That's why wherever we go we drag Flannel Sally along. We call her Flannel, because that's what she wraps the brats in and makes 'em sleep all the time. Me, Dog-faced Kitty, Nellie the Pig and Bray-mouth Hazel chip in to pay her seein' to our five. The girls have agreed to let you leave Kimberly with her until you can afford to chip in. Hope you don't mind, but I told J.T. I'd like to bring you along tonight for him to have a look see."

Lolly came back to the present with a start. "I'll . . . I won't be . . ." She gulped. Thinking about handsome men was one thing, but doing something with them was quite another. "Besides," she said lamely, "I ain't got nothing pretty to wear."

"Your present dress is fine. It's only an interview." Gertie smiled. "And you're very pretty, Chickee. And young. Let's take Kimberly to Flannel Sally and go get you a job."

Entering the Monte Carlo she turned a ghastly white, and her eyes seemed to fill her face. This was hardly Clara Bennett's.

It was long and narrow, smoky with tobacco and kerosene haze. Against one wall ran a bar from end to end, right up to the stage across the back. Right now the curtain was open and the stage seemed an endless black pit.

Only a few men sat at the many gaming tables crowded into the back third of the building, and no one was at the show tables that filled the rest.

Six bartenders cleaned glasses and prepared for the night. Gertie greeted them all gaily and pulled Lolly along to the end of the bar.

"Now, Chickee, J.T. owns the place, but Ned Bailey manages it for him. J.T. was one of the first to make a big strike on the Eldorado with Clarkson Ludlow. He's a lovable old coot, so don't let his bark fool you none. If he likes you, then Ned has to hire you, so you be real nice to him. You get my meaning?"

"You don't mean I have to . . ."

Lolly was ready to faint. Jackson Turner had put none of his million from gold on his back. He was still as grizzled and scruffy looking as ever.

Lolly was being introduced before Gertie could answer her.

"Yah sing?"

Lolly gulped. "To my daughter," she barely whispered.

"Dance?"

"Ain't ever."

Jackson Turner began to grin. He put a finger under her chin and lifted her small face.

"What they be callin' yah, honey?"

"We are going to call her Chickee here, J.T."

"Chickee?" he chuckled. "Cute little mite." Then he frowned. "Heard about your trouble, gal. Sorry. Now, I gotta be askin' a right personal question."

"No need to ask, J.T.," Gertie got in quick. "She ain't ever."

"Lord a gumption," he beamed. "That's just the gal this ole fossil's been prayin' fur!"

Oh, Jesus, Jesus! Lolly thought. What am I going to do? She wrung her hands.

"Yah ain't lying to me?"

Lolly was shivering. "Oh, no, no!"

"Then ring the bell for Ned."

Ned Bailey came from the back room, moving as quick as a snake. He looked quickly from the owner to Lolly, then back to J.T.

"I have a new girl for you, Ned."

"*This*?" He sounded incredulous.

"Just what I've been looking for. She don't sing, dance or fool around. Now, I ain't sayin' nothin' against your gals. They push the drinks good, warble and wiggle their fannies. But they all fight like shit over who is the best and never take one damn glass back to the bar. I told you I wanted this like a nice place. Chickee here can keep the glasses off the tables and the saw dust on the floor lookin' like more'n a stampede of cows went through."

Ned leaned toward Lolly, implacable. "I don't like the way she looks."

"Then find her some kind of a uniform. Simple, but nice. I don't like hanky-panky with the regular girls, and double don't like it for this one."

Ned nodded, as if he approved. "Good. Ten dollars a night."

Gertie leaned across the bar like a vicious cat, snarling. "You are just too, too generous, viper! She gets fifty or I'm quitting, and right now!"

Ned leaned back and seized the woman's flabby arm and pulled her right to his sallow face. "No, you won't. Because I've been wanting to fire your ass for a long time."

Lolly looked at them with horror. She was costing Gertie her job. Why didn't the owner speak up? Then she saw him wink.

"You man enough to throw me out on the street?" Gertie simpered.

Bailey turned an ugly scarlet. "Fifty it is! Go get her a uniform."

J.T. pretended impatience. "Do it! Do it! I gotta go have my dinner."

He stomped out of the saloon and Bailey slithered back through the back door.

"What made him change his mind so fast?" Lolly gasped.

Gertie chuckled. "I hit his sore point. He doesn't have any girl friends, only boys."

"I don't understand."

Gertie nodded solemnly. "It just means, Chickee, that you don't have to worry about him making a pass at you. Oh, speaking of passes, this is my regular night for Big Alex. After we close, take your time cleaning the sawdust. I don't want you barging in while I'm making a house payment."

She stared at her, blank-faced, as they went behind the stage to the dressing rooms. "Gertie, I don't understand any of this."

"Well, let's start from the beginning. Alexander McDonald owns Lousetown Row, in which we are living. He lets the girls from all the saloons buy them for a thousand—a hundred a payment. The big brute took a liking to me and I work off my payments. Well, here's the costume rack. Hmmm! Oh, there's a vacant one two doors down from me. I'll talk to Alex about it for you and Kimberly."

"But . . . but . . ." Things were moving so fast.

"Chickee, you can easily make a hundred a week payment out of sawdust money. Murton will explain that to you. He's our piano player. Hey, what about this outfit? The Grizzly Bear wore it for a number when she was trying to look like that chick who said 'Can't you speak for yourself, somebody-or-tother.' Real little Pilgrim maid."

Lolly inclined her head, satisfied that it would do. "It's all so strange."

Gertie spread her eloquent hands. "Chickee, it's a whole different world here."

* * *

Those words seemed even more portentous as the days went on. It wasn't only a different world, but it was a very tiring one as well.

Seven nights a week, from 5 PM to 1 AM, an average of six hundred customers a shift passed through—which meant glasses, glasses, glasses.

But it was the "closing hour" she had at first hated. The "better" saloons closed down for one hour out of twenty-four for cleaning, restocking and a change of crew.

It was a frantic madhouse. The girls were supposed to help clear the tables, but always quickly disappeared to the dressing rooms. They had a big 2 AM show to do to draw the customers right back in and bitched about needing their rest. Many took their hour rest back in their shacks turning a quick trick.

Likewise, the bartenders were supposed to help Old Charley get all of the glasses washed and back on the shelves. Naturally, they couldn't help until each had cleaned each of his long fingernails in his poke box. When payments were made in gold dust, a worthy little profit could be gathered under a nail in a course of a shift. And a long fingernail could run down the crack in a bar and dig out even more dust and tiny nuggets.

Besides the glasses, Lolly was to help Murton with the sawdust. The first night he had her rake away the cigar, cigarette butts and debris. When he came right behind her, screening and sifting the sawdust, she thought she had not done the job right.

"You just keep movin', lass. Can't get the whole floor every night with the screen."

She didn't understand, but then Murton was a puzzlement to begin with. At the piano he looked like the sections of three different bodies put together by a mad puppeteer. His shaggy white mane waved above a head far too large for his scrawny neck, vanishing shoulders and spidery arms. Although easily six foot tall, his legs were no more than two of it. He wore special little stilts to reach the piano pedals. During the show his head and arms were a picture of motion. When playing between shows only his long fingers moved on the keys.

No one knew his age or where he came from. Everyone considered him "tetched" in the head, but he was the best "ivory tickler" in Dawson.

"Here's the droppings for tonight, lass. We keep it in this box and divide it up each week."

"Gold?" Lolly guessed. "Oh, Murton, what a pretty sight!"

"Suppose. Drunker they get the more careless they get, lass. Gold gets so it don't mean much, the more you got."

"What does it mean to you, Murton?"

"My stars," he said, embarrassed. "It's my own little secret."

Lolly soon came to learn that many things were little secrets with the man. It was easy for him to keep them, because she was the only one who ever seemed to talk with him—unless one of the girls wanted him to play a special number for her.

But most of the numbers were the same, night after night. The customers the same, night after night. At least, they appeared to Lolly to be the same jolly, noisy, and profane men over and over.

She began to work things into a habit pattern. She cut the noise and profanity out of her mind and told the time by Murton's playing. For the first four hours it was lazy and slow. Each of the three shows, until midnight, got louder and louder.

Lolly could always tell when the midnight show was over. Gertie had the last number. Lolly had never seen anyone perform on a stage before, and had felt thrilled that first night when Diamond Tooth Gertie was announced.

Then she didn't know how she should feel. She didn't have anything else to judge by, but she knew she didn't like it. Gertie's singing voice was like a braying ass and Lolly had to turn away as more and more of her clothing came off and the men got dirtier and dirtier with their demands. Lolly didn't know that they didn't give a hoot about her singing voice, but just wanted to see how far she would tease and taunt them that night.

But she did notice two things after Gertie finished and left the stage: Murton's music got wilder during the next hour, and the tables nearest the stage vacated as the men moved back to the gaming tables.

Thereafter she started clearing the tables from the front back while keeping time to Murton's music.

J.T. sat, fascinated, and watched her for a few nights.

"Ned, I think we need her here on Saturday nights till four."

"I fully agree. Old Charley hasn't bitched about the glasses getting to him late since she came on."

Lolly didn't mind. Saturday nights had always been rough on her. Besides, that gave her one evening a week she could stay home to have dinner with Kimberly. It seemed that all she ever did was sleep and work.

"Mama, Mama, Mama," Kimberly screamed. She threw herself into Lolly's arms and kissed her, but kept pointing back into Flannel Sally's shack.

She had been expecting Alex McDonald to make the final arrangements on her shack. But it was not Big Alex. Instead, Calvin Ramsey stood there, smiling at her, his face flushed.

"Hello, Lolly," he said timidly, almost apologetically, "we are all so sorry about Nolan. I came to see what I could do."

"Oh, Calvin, I'm so glad to see you! Come to my shack! It's only two doors down. Come on, sweetheart, Mama has your supper all ready for you."

Lolly walked ahead of Calvin, leaving the door open behind her. She seated Kimberly at the table and dished her up a bowl of soup.

Calvin hesitated, brushed the snowflakes off his great fur coat and entered the dingy little room.

"So, this is what Big Alex sells," he said, looking around.

"You know him?"

"He's a good customer of the bank. That's how I found you. Crow came down at once, but you had vanished."

"I wasn't far," she said sadly. "Haven't really seen anyone."

"The storm and all," he said, as though it were an excuse. "And Harriet has problems of her own. Harlan has had a stroke and is bedridden. She thinks he'll be back on his feet again before long."

"I hope so," Lolly said fervently. She noticed that he was still standing, awkwardly holding a cossack hat in his hand.

"Sit down, won't you?" she said. "I can offer you a bowl of soup—I'm afraid there isn't any coffee."

"Hardly any in town, I hear. But no thank you on the soup, but don't let me stop you from eating."

"I already had a bowl while I was dressing for work. I was just going to sit and jabber with Kimberly while she ate."

"That's one reason I came," he declared. "Also, from Alex, I learned of your work."

She was too quick to judge his reason for being there.

"This is just my first week," she rushed. "As soon as I had some figures worked out, I was going to come see you. I—I didn't even know till late that Nolan had borrowed from you. I'm afraid I don't know how much."

"Don't worry yourself. I'm sure we can work something out—especially with your work being what it is, and all."

Lolly was too naive to get his meaning. Calvin had read too much into Alex selling her a shack, and her place of employment.

"I still need to know how much."

"Two thousand."

Lolly nearly dropped the second bowl of soup she was serving to Kimberly. "As much as that?"

"Things were most dear in Skagway," he shrugged, glossing over the real truth. Nolan didn't spend all of the two thousand on his equipment. The rawhide and other supplies had come out of that money, but he wanted to shock her into submission quickly. He couldn't stay away from the house for too long without Amalida getting suspicious.

"I—I'll just do the best I can to pay it back."

"I could make that very easy for you," he said softly.

"How?" she asked directly.

"How? That shouldn't be a poser, should it? You are working at the Monte Carlo, right? You are living here on Lousetown Row, right? Come, let's sit down on your bed and work out a payment arrangement."

"No," Lolly said.

"No?" Calvin's face was filled with astonishment. "I'm prepared to make you a most generous offer, Lolly. Say, two hundred each time. What are you getting from the others—ten . . . twenty?"

Lolly stared at him soberly, solemnly.

"There are no others," she said flatly.

"Excellent! Then I will have no fear of disease. Come now, I haven't much time."

As he started to rise she slapped him stingingly across the face.

"Why you—" Calvin roared and lunged around the little table.

Lolly stepped back, her face cold and still.

"Don't know where you got such a notion," she hissed, "but I am not one of the girls."

Calvin stood there, his face whitening. Then, suddenly, he stiffened. A slow smile lighted his eyes. The memory of all the noise from the next door boat cabin came swiftly back. If that was the only way to make her submit, so be it.

Then, to Lolly's great surprise, she was borne backward by the fury of his sudden attack. She was driven back to the edge of the bed by his whipping, slashing, slapping hands. So great was the ferocity of his stinging blows that she didn't have a chance to get out a gasp or a scream.

"Please, Lolly," Calvin almost wept, "I don't want to hurt you."

Perhaps, Lolly reflected, if I'm nice to him, he won't be like Nolan.

"Calvin," she whispered, "as a gentleman, can't you tell I've never been with anyone but my husband?"

"And I heard the way he treated you through the cabin wall. That's the way you like it, isn't it?"

Lolly gasped. She had always feared that they had been heard. But then she had a sudden inspiration.

"You didn't hear anything more through those cabin walls than I heard when you came back from Clara Bennett's place."

Calvin was stunned. The accusations that had flown back and forth that night were damaging. More damaging than anything he had told Father Henry in a "confessional" manner. So the little imbecile does have a few brains tucked away, he thought with alarm. Now, more than ever, he would have to be master of the situation to cower any blackmail attempt.

It was then that Lolly knew that she had been dreadfully wrong in making the statement. He thrust her down on the bed quickly, smothering her with his weight, his head dropping to her breasts, trying to tear the cloth away with his teeth.

She got her arms untangled and reached for his face, but he twisted his head away, and her nails dug bloodless furrows down his neck. He grabbed her hands and held them together in one claw of steel above her head.

For several seconds he lay immobile, as though totally unsure of what to do next. He had trained Amalida to be nude and waiting for him. It was the same order he had given every madam before paying for a whore.

He took his free hand and worked to raise her skirt and unleash himself. Suddenly, he was aware that she was no longer fighting him. He was able to accomplish his tasks swiftly and bring his weight fully back upon her. He felt he had fought her into submission.

He had nothing to do with it. Her reaction was not a new one. As with Nolan, she blocked the thought of what was about to happen from her mind and replaced it with another. No one could hurt her, if she didn't think about being hurt. She would just relax and it would be over quickly—just as it had always happened with Nolan.

She was aware of her legs being forced apart, and of his squirming over her to get himself inside. She started to lock her thought onto something else as the first thrust began, but she felt him instantly quake and shiver. He had hardly entered, but she felt herself drenched inside by hot, sticky fluid. He had hardly begun, but she knew he was already finished.

Calvin was taken aback and in that second he rolled from the bed as though she were something disgusting. Trembling, he repaired himself and put on the fur coat and hat. At the doorway, he turned toward her.

"I think you had best find another profession," he said.

He went out and closed the door silently. Lolly got up from the floor and dragged herself to the wash stand. Every part of her ached, but her pain was nothing compared with that which Nolan had always inflicted. At least there would be no bruises on her face this time.

As she turned from the wash stand, she remembered suddenly, blindingly, what had kept her from going to work early that evening.

Kimberly sat at the table wide-eyed and silent.

Nolan had always waited for Kimberly to go to sleep before he attacked Lolly.

"More soup?" she asked, shocked at how her voice came out and praying the scene would mean nothing to her young mind.

To her vast astonishment, Kimberly jumped right down from the table and raced for the door.

"Go back to play now?"

"Yes, darling, run along to Flannel Sally. Mama will see you tomorrow."

She breathed a sigh of relief that there had been no questions asked. She never once guessed that Kimberly had seen Nolan and Laura Lee in the tent on the glacier. But it opened a great worry in her mind.

She could accept the girls for what they were, but she didn't want Kimberly being raised with them and their children. She just had to find a way to better herself—and pay off Nolan's loans.

12

In late April, Jack Ladue's worst fears started coming true. It started as mere trickles under the melting snowbanks and then became rivulets of muddy water washing down the hillsides and into the Dawson streets until they were quagmires deeper than a wagon axle.

If a person wanted to keep their trade they built a wooden sidewalk in front of their establishment. Because the entry doors were of various heights, the sidewalk became up and down platforms all along the street.

Murton sat tinkling the keys and chortling to himself.

"You've got a damned peculiar way of looking at things, Murton," Lolly said. "Those muddy boots make the sawdust hard as hell to clean."

"Then rest yourself, lass, and let it dry a spell. Those muddy boots bring in with them all manner of dust and little nuggets. Didn't we do well last week?"

Lolly nodded and slumped down with her back against the piano. She was so weary. For awhile she had gotten so she liked the later Saturday nights. It always gave them two hours to clean up and Ned Bailey always supplied supper for his bartenders, which they would share with Lolly, Murton and Old Charley.

But with the snows melting the miners were able to start working their claims again and Saturday nights were getting busier and busier.

The only thing it helped raise was the cleaning poke. She could now count on enough each week to pay Big Alex. But gold dust still confused her. Gertie had given her a moosehide pouch to keep her poke and pay in. It took her a long time to think in terms of ounces, and $16 to the ounce on dust.

Gertie tried to teach her how to feel the worth of a pinch in paying Flannel Sally, paying for groceries at the store, or paying Big Alex. It was hard to get the hang of it.

The only time she knew she wasn't being cheated was the three times she had walked up the hill to the bank. Calvin had hidden in his office and Crow had weighed out her payment. Many was the time she wished she had all of that six hundred dollars back, but she wanted Calvin off her mind.

Calvin also wanted her off his mind. It had been near impossible to explain the neck scratches to Amalida. He was so determined to keep her away from the bank, and the possibility of running into Amalida, that he grandly told Crow to reduce her obligation to a thousand dollars. Crow had smiled to himself. He surmised that the neck scratches meant that Calvin hadn't gotten too far with Lolly.

"You got a misery?" Murton asked, letting the music grow soft and floating.

"Just dead tired."

"Been looking mighty pale of late."

Lolly shrugged. "Don't get to see the sun much, now that it's out. What's that you're playing?"

"Just something that came into my head. Don't know if it's a tune I played years ago on the steamboats or something out of the blue."

Lolly sat back and hummed along, as she often did

whole working. It was soothing. She didn't like the words to the songs the other girls sang. They were too saucy and suggestive. They made the men scream and howl too much, which gave her a headache.

Everything seemed to give her a headache or a queasy stomach of late. She put it down to nerves and overwork—and doubt.

Every time she tried to stretch the moonsehide pouch a little farther she cursed herself for never having learned her figures better. $50 a night had sounded like an enormous amount. She had to count on her fingers that that made $350 each week. Then, finger by finger, she would take them away. One finger a week to Flannel Sally for Kimberly's care. Two fingers a week for Big Alex, because she couldn't count on the poke money. Three fingers a week for just enough food to scrape by on. That left one finger to put away against the loan payment.

The first week the poke money went for a new pair of shoes to work in. The Pilgrim maid costume was perfect, but the material was old and shredding. It took two weeks of poke money to pay Mizner for new material. Then Kimberly needed some things . . . and . . . Her fingers always ended up in a clenched fist and an empty pouch. She would just never get out of Lousetown Row.

"Got words," Murton mumbled.

"What does?"

"What you're humming."

His voice was a high, soft tenor—as plaintive as the words he sang.

Strange place to be, here in the wild.
A mother alone with a child.
A hundred men there are here,
a hundred with no cheer.
They dream of Eldorado,
Rant with gusty bravado.

But they, like me, find it strange to be;
Here in the wild.
A mother alone with a child.

His voice and the music trailed off. Lolly rose, tears in her eyes. She gave him a big hug.

"Thank you, Murton. That was beautiful."

It was comforting to know that someone saw into her soul.

A week later things weren't so comforting.

The ice of the Yukon began to crack and break. It groaned and split with a recurring roar from Circle City down to Lake Laberge and then back toward St. Michaels.

It was the cause of shouting and toasting in every saloon. Summer was right around the corner.

The ice would break, move and then jam up. The Indians had not seen such a pileup in twenty years. But their concern went unheeded. The days were getting warmer, but weren't the nights still dropping well below zero?

Then one night they didn't drop. Both ends of the jam lifted at the same time, and the hollow booming shook the hills. Then a second later the middle of the jam poured big cakes of ice into the streets of Dawson. The empty warehouses on Front Street buckled with majestic slowness.

It pushed against the Klondike ice floe and the Klondike pushed back. It bent in the center and moved in the only direction left to it—Lousetown.

Lolly came awake with a start. It sounded as though someone were ripping the shack apart, a dozen rusty nails at a time. She quickly lit the kerosene lamp. The walls were tilted at a crazy angle and moving. Kimberly began to wail.

She stepped from bed and found herself ankle deep in icy, muddy water.

"The ice jam has broke!" she heard Nellie the Pig screech from next door.

Lolly had overheard Inspector Cordine talking with J.T. the night before. The mounty feared that when it broke it would bring disastrous flooding with it.

"Baby," she said calmly, "ain't nothing to fear. Mama is going to get her clothes on and then we'll get out of here. You be a big girl and help by putting on your stockings."

"Where we going?"

Lolly said the first logical thing that came to her mind. "To visit Granny Harriet. Won't that be fun?"

"Is that where Daddy is?"

"Honey," Lolly said, trying to hurry to dress, "I told you Daddy is on a long trip. Granny Harriet is only over in Dawson."

"Is that where Laur'Lee is?"

Lolly certainly hoped not. "Honey, put your socks on and stop chattering."

The row of shacks shifted, popping Lolly's roof right off. Before Kimberly could start wailing again she just wrapped her in a blanket and got out of the shack.

In the after-midnight darkness everything seemed to be river. Lolly waded among the ice floes to the foot bridge. She was not alone. Lousetown was being deserted en masse.

They found things little different in Dawson. Lolly felt she had been there before, catching perilous handholds on the ice cakes, moving inch by slow inch until it was only rising water that confronted her.

The Lousetown girls headed for the saloons like magnets. Most of them were one storey structures, and would not give refuge for long. Soon the muddy water had risen to calf depth.

At least the Monte Carlo had a second floor. Ned and J.T. already had the bartender and night girls moving tables and chairs up out of the water. Ploughing through the murky water was no better than being in the streets.

"Chickee," Ned barked, "go help Old Charley pack the glasses."

"I have to see to my child."

"Dump her anywhere. This is more important!"

"Hell, no!" She ploughed back into the street, Bailey screeching curses after her.

"Chickee do this! Chickee do that!" she mumbled. "Damn, I hate that name and that place. Just wait, that bastard will want me to shovel out all the mud when this is over."

Then she stopped, grinning.

"Well, Kimberly Sue, I guess your mother didn't lie to you after all."

It took her twenty minutes to reach the bakery. The streets were now flooded with people as well, evacuating to higher ground. The water on that street was only ankle deep, but on the rise.

With the front door standing ajar, Lolly began to fear that they had left. Kimberly wasn't dressed for spending the night on the mountain side.

In the kitchen, Harriet's face was a study in near-apoplexy. Since the booming of the jam she had been trying to pull things out of the storage floor area.

"Heavens to Betsy! You're a prayer answered. Can you be taking the tyke up to Harlan and then be giving me a hand?"

"Where is he?"

"First bedroom on the right at the top of the stairs."

Lolly was speechless when she saw the man. He had withered away to sagging flesh on his big bones. There was recognition in his eyes as she tuckered Kimberly in beside him. She nearly wept, seeing his jaw try to work out a greeting amid the forest of his muttonchop whiskers.

Downstairs his condition was not mentioned, nor the death of Nolan. The women had far too much to do for chit chat. By the time the storeroom was clear it was calf high in seeping water.

"I've seen floods like this on the Mississippi," Harriet said sadly. "It's going to last for days and get deeper. Perhaps you should consider taking Kimberly to higher ground."

"First let's worry about getting these goods up to the second floor." Lolly knew that Harlan couldn't be moved and that Harriet would never leave him. And anyway, she felt safer there with them than on the mountain alone.

By dawn they had moved everything worth saving, at least those things they had been able to lift and lug. From the second floor windows Dawson was a strange sight. A ghost town with rivers for streets. Across the Klondike, Lousetown was a jumble of logs and timber.

On the pot-bellied stove in the upstairs parlor Harriet made coffee and heated up three-day-old rolls from the bakery.

"Ain't much. Harlan has a bowl of soup now and then, poor dear. I don't cook much. Ain't no fun eating alone. Besides, I've got to be baking constantly just to scrape together the six hundred in interest money each month. Just our bad luck following us right along again. You doing all right, dear?"

Lolly wasn't at the moment. The coffee and roll weren't setting well. She should have known better than to eat. Usually she could force herself to sleep through the morning nausea and the all-too-frequent vomiting.

The nausea mounted. She clapped her hand over her mouth and ran from the parlor. Harriet's round pink face wrinkled with concern. She gave Lolly a few moments and then followed.

She found her vomiting helplessly in one of the spare bedrooms, kneeling on the floor and clutching the sides of a johnny-pot.

Harriet sat down on the bed. "How long, child?"

Lolly gulped. She was white and trembling. She wiped her mouth and looked up at the worried face.

"Harriet, I was never sick with Kimberly. Oh, I saw other women in the mill town who were sick, so I know about it. I guess that's why I kept trying to tell myself this was something else. I can't kid myself anymore."

"Fine kettle of fish," said Harriet, hitting the bed with her clenched fish. "Damn bastard getting you in this fix."

Oh, my God, thought Lolly with genuine alarm. She knows. Then she stopped to think. Harriet couldn't know. She had to be talking about Nolan. That was almost laughable. The timing was all off.

Harriet suddenly felt guilty for her angry outburst. Lolly was a picture of despair. She crawled off the bed and sat on the floor, gently putting her arm around Lolly's shoulders.

"Forgive an old fool, dear," she said. "Here I haven't even seen you since the . . . accident . . . and I put my big foot in my mouth. I once told you and Nolan to have lots of babies for me to cuddle. The Lord must have willed it."

Lolly looked up. If Harriet could believe that it was Nolan's child, then others would believe. Then, very slowly, she came erect.

"Sure comes at a bad time," she whispered.

"Ain't ever a good time. How soon?"

"About mid-November. I figure I can work on through the summer."

"No," Harriet said sternly, "you will not. I will see to you here."

"I must work, Harriet," she said with gentle dignity. "I have one payment left on my shack—if there's anything left to it—and only two hundred I still owe to . . . the bank. In four months I can have enough put aside for the birth and to hold me until I'm strong enough to go back to work again."

Harriet wished she could say the same. Alone, she could bake just enough to make the interest payments and get a few supplies. Each day, she too kidded herself, believing that it would be the day that Harlan got up out of his bed and returned to his ovens.

Each day the people of Dawson kidded themselves in thinking that it would be the one that they could return home. It looked like the Yukon and Klondike would never fall. It was a city of canals, for those still staying on second floors.

It was a strangely sober town, except for those crammed into the second floor of the Monte Carlo.

Some it did not affect, except in a strange way. George Carmack's mansion was high and dry, but the sanctuary devoid of customers. Amalida drank away the flood. Crow was kept busy with the Indian woodchoppers, keeping the dirt floor seepage off the hill from undermining the structure. Calvin sat in his office with a scheme he had been secretly developing since early April. Too many had been complaining about walking up the hill to do their banking. His new structure downtown would solve that problem.

Structure and seepage were also a problem for Matt. The spring runoff and seepage were doing his surface mining for him, but it took constant effort to keep shoring up the house and to shovel away the tons of pay load dirt.

Henry was of no help. He had gone directly to the church when the ice broke and the flooding started. His help was needed more in the hospital, anyway.

Laura Lee was already busy with many who had been hurt in the collapse of Lousetown's shacks and cabins, even though she had to work in ankle-deep icy water.

Without communicating, Henry began to move the beds and supplies up to the attic loft that they had planned for expansion. When the six beds were reset they were quickly filled, and soon after the floor was, too. Throughout the flood Henry and Laura Lee worked as priest-doctor and nurse—never as father and daughter.

A week later, Dawson was in a more reasonable frame of mind. They could come home and start digging out the mud and silt. In Lousetown it was a question of complete rebuilding. As though the place hadn't been bad enough before, they rebuilt with what they could pull and dig out of the mud and mire. Because summer was coming, the Row shacks were temporarily righted and braced up by poles. Askew roofs were set back on like lids, not even nailed down. There were no nails until fresh supplies came in. Addison Mizner had confiscated every last available barrel of nails for his opera house and the three storey bank and living quarters for Calvin Ramsey. It was his first building for someone outside the family and he figured to make a profit of $250,000. Already he had people approaching him who wanted to buy the opera house and the other building.

Lolly had been right. She did have to help shovel the mud out of the Monte Carlo. Bailey was furious that she had deserted him in his hour of need. Lolly gritted her teeth and shovelled right along with Murton. She had already lost a week of work and poke money. Then came the most crushing blow of all: Because the saloon could not serve customers and make money, there would be no pay until it was cleaned out and open again for business.

No one complained, because they couldn't afford to lose their jobs, and J.T. wasn't around to over-ride Ned Bailey. The second day of the flood he had taken a canoe up the Klondike to check on his Eldorado claim and help Clarkson Ludlow in case they were having any trouble up there.

"I'll never complain about carrying glasses again."

Murton frowned. "You'll complain over what Bailey has

in mind. He had carpenters in to measure and put down a wood floor. There goes your poke money."

"And yours."

"Won't be here for it anyway. I'm moving on."

Lolly looked at him speechlessly. He had become such a dear friend, and she hated the idea of losing him. She opened her mouth and closed it. She had learned that with Murton a direct question brought no response at all. Then, suddenly, there was no time to ask him anything anyway.

"Leave it! Leave it!" Ned Bailey screeched, running in from the street. "They will just have to tramp about in mud. Murton, get upstairs and wake up some bartenders. Chickee, get back to Lousetown and tell Gertie I need all the girls for them."

"Them? Who?" Murton demanded.

"The *cheechacos*! They're coming! The river is full of them!"

Murton and Lolly looked at each other and shrugged. If Ned Bailey said so, then they had to believe it.

On her way back to Lousetown Lolly began to believe it fully. Dodging ice cakes and shouting like banshee Indians, it seemed like every craft they had seen being built on Lake Bennett was now nearly upon Dawson.

Lolly had little trouble getting the girls stirred up. It meant fresh business.

Lolly couldn't stir herself to the same excitement. She didn't see how it could change her life, except make the work that much harder.

Then, crossing the *beanpole* walk bridge back to Dawson, a sight caught her eyes that made her stop and shield them against the sun. Her eyes widened at the sight until her cheeks were dominated by them. She stepped quickly off the bridge. Now the miners were racing for the wharf to greet the newcomers. At first she was being pushed along with the mass. Then she was running faster than the rest, her arms outstretched.

But when she was almost to the Tlingit canoes, she stopped abruptly, and the joy drained visibly from her face. She went forward once more, being pushed about, awkwardly; and when she was next to the knot of people she put out her hand.

"Hello, Mickey," she said.

Mickey did not answer her. He stood there, staring down at her hand. Then he put out his slender hand and covered hers, holding it lightly for a long time before he pulled her into his shaking arms.

"Oh, Lolly," he cried, "you're the first old friend I see and all you can say is 'hello.' Fine thing! Where is everyone? How are you?"

Lolly rested her small face against his Tlingit-clad chest.

"The most important question is, how are you?" she whispered.

"Never better," he laughed. "Although the old man wouldn't tell me all, Peter was blunt. I don't think I'll be hauling any more logs for Nolan. Where is he?"

"He got washed away in the flood," she said, as though it had been his final fate and not just what had happened to his frozen body.

"Lolly, I am sorry—"

"Why so many canoes?" she cut him short.

Mickey glanced at her strangely, then understood. It was not the proper place to discuss such a thing.

"In the first few days about one hundred fifty craft wrecked in the rapids and more than a dozen people drowned. The Mounties started making the women and children walk the five miles around and only a craft at a time was allowed through. It really backed them up. Dixson said there are about seven thousand craft ready to come up river—or downriver, as it were. Many making it through the rapids are sinking in Lake LaBerge. So Peter is taking his father's advice and starting a ferry business."

"Looking behind you it doesn't seem like there would be many to carry."

"See that skinny man getting off that ten man scow? That's Judson M. Walsh, the new Commissioner of the Yukon. He says there are over twenty thousand on their way. Those scows coming in next to his have all the equipment to set up two government banks, right down to the presses to make printed money."

"Calvin Ramsey will certainly love that," she said wryly. "Oh, Mickey, I must get back to work. I—I don't know where to find Matt, but Henry has a church and hospital just two blocks that way. You can't miss it."

"Where can I find you later?"

"Harriet is taking care of Kimberly at the bakery," she said evasively, not wanting to mention the Monte Carlo. "You can see us there."

She got away quickly. For the life of her she didn't know why she felt guilty telling Mickey about her place of work. Perhaps it was because he's such a good friend of Matt's, she tried to tell herself. But Crow was also a good friend of Matt's, and he knew, although it was never mentioned when she saw him at the bank.

"If you were honest," she mumbled to herself, ploughing through the mud, "you would admit you have been dying by slow inches without your old friends—especially Matt."

"Hey lady! Do you know the way to the gold creeks and how long it will take me to make, say $20,000?"

The young man was no older than herself, his face a mixture of frenzied excitement and fear.

She wanted to be truthful and say a lifetime, but she pointed up the Klondike. Everyone was going to have to learn for themselves.

"Depends upon the man," she said.

Because of the number of boats and people on the river, it was taking two weeks for most to make the trip.

In those first two weeks the ceaseless stream of vessels was dumping so many men into Dawson that it was becoming a nightmare.

Upon their return from the Tagfish village, the Carmack canoes could not even make shore because boats of all shapes were tied together far out into the river. Kate barked a single order, which George immediately agreed with. They would go directly to their cabins at the claim site and not even enter that circus.

Because the midnight sun now shone 22 hours of every day, the saloons were packed wall to wall for every twenty-four. There was no longer time to stop for floor cleaning. It didn't matter. Ned Bailey never got his wood floor in, the thrown buckets of sawdust just got trampled down to near concrete, and the real miners fearfully stayed at their diggings. The "outsiders" paid with coin and paper money, and most were so frugal with their cash that they would nurse a drink for an hour.

Poke boxes dried up for the barkeeps and the girls' "trick" prices fell to $5 and $10. Lolly found herself working 12 to 18 hour days for the same pay as she used to get for an eight hour shift. Days would go by when she didn't have time to get to the bakery to pick up Kimberly and take her back to the rebuilt shack.

When she did get by the bakery it was as wild and confusing as the Monte Carlo.

In those first two weeks every lodging house and hotel was immediately jammed to the rafters. Everyone who had a spare bed or an inch of floor space was begged to rent it.

It didn't take much begging to convince Harriet. She had an attic that would sleep twenty men in their own bedrolls and five extra bedrooms that would accommodate four men each. For $5 a night she even supplied coffee and rolls for breakfast. In time, when she could get the supplies, she laid plans to offer room, coffee and rolls, and a supper meal for $10. With Harlan still bedridden, she was so busy that the bakery business was forgotten for the time being.

J.M. Walsh, however, had plans for Harriet Henderson, without knowing her by name. He had left Ottawa with his own ambitions of becoming a millionaire—and also to help selected friends and the Canadian government do the same. He could do this with an easy mind, because he had left the Canadian capitol with full power of authority. And, best of all, he had lured tough, hard-driving Chief Inspector Malcolm McBridge to be his police voice and take charge of all Mounty operations in the whole territory. It had not been hard to lure him—McBridge was his brother-in-law.

Upon his arrival at Dawson, he went first to see Edgar Mizner.

"Ah, dear Edgar, good to see you again. You don't look like you fared too well this winter."

Mizner motioned him to a seat with a palsied hand. He was thin and bent, his cheeks hollow, great dark rings around his eyes.

"It's McQuestan and Ladue," he explained. "Damn near ruined me this winter. But that's not the main reason I fought Ottawa to get you here. I've got many things in mind for you, Judson."

"Now that you and your brothers are Canadian citizens," he said wryly.

"All right," Edgar snapped, "I'll give you credit for that idea. But how in the hell will it stop McQuestan? Wilson tells me that the wharf at St. Michaels is loaded with his goods and so are the docks at Circle City. My steamboat has to run all the way to Seattle or San Francisco and back."

"Edgar," he grinned, "don't fret. The McQuestan supplies will be coming from Alaska into Canada. I will just make them subject to import duty when they dock here in Dawson."

Edgar looked at him wonderingly.

"But my boat will be coming in by the same route."

Walsh smiled wickedly. "Now, Edgar, would I impose a tax on a Canadian businessman doing business in Canada?"

Edgar smiled back. It was about the first time he had smiled all winter. Everything had been a drain on him. Wilson had been ordered to leave the small steamboat in charge of the captain at Circle City and return to the states for another ship and supplies. Addison had drained him of nearly all hardware supplies for his opera house—and all on credit.

"What other little tricks have you up your sleeve?" he asked with a chuckle.

"A few. I have brought men and equipment to establish two banks. If Ladue doesn't want to sell us proper locations, at a fair price, then we'll confiscate the land for government use. This small banker you have . . . ah . . . Ramsey. For the present we shall let him operate, under our rules, until our size forces him out."

"What rules?" Mizner chortled, rubbing his bony hands together in glee.

Walsh shrugged, as though they were minor. "Weekly audits to make sure we are getting our tax share. No minting of coin except under the supervision of one of my inspectors. In a month's time I want only Canadian paper money floating around that they will have to purchase at our banks. If Mr. Ramsey wants to keep his customers, he will have to purchase the paper money from us, as well."

"He really doesn't have that many customers. The miners mostly keep their own poke."

"And that too shall change. Inspector McBridge is bringing in twelve Mounties of his personal selection—shall we say because of past difficulties they have had with the force. They will stay in the field and make sure that every claim deposits weekly and gets paper money in exchange. Failure to do so will close the claim for sixty days and leave it open for restaking."

Mizner whistled with pleasure. "That sews everything up nicely."

"On that score," Walsh said thinly, as though Mizner couldn't see the forest for the real trees of worth. "There are a few areas that are making a killing, as I see it. I tend to think we should be in on it. I will impose a per-drink, per-bed and per-meal tax. After all, someone has to pay the salaries of my staff and McBridge's men."

"Won't they be paid by the government?"

"I am the government," Walsh said simply. "And Edgar, keep in mind that we will have to pay McBridge's men extra to keep their mouths shut!"

"Won't that eat up all the profit?"

"Of course it won't!" Walsh exploded. "I am not in this for chicken-feed, Edgar. I have made arrangements for Jefferson Randolph Smith to come up from Skagway with some of his men. Because of some of his schemes he's known as "Soapy". As soon as he has the lay of the land I will give him authority to impose rules for us to make money from gambling and prostitution. They will go on, with or without us, so it might as well be with us." He chuckled dryly, but really over his next thought.

"The good people will scream, of course, but we will soothe them with some touches of home. There are two steamships coming up from Victoria. On board are some business associates of mine, with special equipment. By the end of summer, Edgar, Dawson will have electricity and telephones. Of course, we shall set the fee for wiring and connection. And, make it mandatory that every building be connected."

"I'll be damned and double damned," Mizner roared with mirth. "We sure got everything sewed up tight."

Judson Walsh smiled weakly. Only for the moment did he need Edgar Mizner to establish himself. He didn't plan on the "we" lasting very long.

13

Everyone was used to men like Fletcher, Cordine and O'Toole. They were Englishmen, younger sons of well-to-do families, who believed so firmly in law that they usually had no trouble in maintaining it with a quiet voice and reasoning.

Then they were gone, quietly removed before McBridge's men could be seen by them. It was for good cause. Every one of them had been drummed out of the service at one time or another. They wore mounty uniforms, because Walsh had full authority to hire men to handle the desperate situation that everyone feared the influx would bring about.

The local taxes were accepted with a shrug by most; everyone had more customers than they could handle, anyway. They just added the tax onto the bill.

McQuestan screamed and tore at his red whiskers, but he paid; then added it on the cost of his goods at the trading post.

He was solidly in the black now; his warehouses were bulging and a new steamboat was on the way that was four times the size of the *New Racket*. And, mysteriously, the Mizner steamboat had trouble getting off the sandbar until the *New Racket* had made two runs. Night after night Indians dug at the sandbar, with just as much sand there the next day, and the Indians started receiving gifts of hard liquor that left them totally incapable of work.

Walsh didn't want to hear about Edgar's "petty problems" and so went back to his old supply lines for awhile. But this time he employed Peter and his canoes to bring up supplies from Whitehorse.

"The work is good," Peter told Crow. "The money is good. But each trip I am spending time getting new rowers. The men like to see their families. I, too, would like to see mine."

"Then move them here."

Peter looked at Dawson and cackled. "Men roam from saloon to saloon because they have no place to put down their heads. How many are here now?"

"They say 28,000."

"And crazy wild beasts all."

"Then don't live among them," Crow said. "Find a spot downriver that is not too far and build your own village for the families of your rowers."

Peter leaned forward, his eyes bright and eager. It would solve many problems. He would then be the head of his people, and not have to answer to Mallori the Lesser, who was not in favor of any of this disruption and intrusion.

"But I don't have the time to seek out such a site and build. What of you?"

At that moment Crow had all the time in the world. Calvin was moving into his new bank and the present rules had him scared to death of using the smelter. Every time it was fired up, McBridge had a man right there who was more eagle-eyed than O'Toole. And once the move was completed Crow would be without a job and a place to stay. George Carmack, coming down from his claim, had been more pleased than disappointed at Calvin's quiet decision to move. Through a McQuestan contact in

Seattle, he had found a buyer who would pay a very good price for the mansion.

"I have time," Crow said, "and used to find camp sites for my people."

Peter laughed, having become accustomed to Crow's tales, but he was a man he had come to love as a brother.

Such was still not the case in his own family. He had found his father and sister greatly changed. Especially Laura Lee.

Around Mickey she had been quiet and civil. Alone, when Henry told him about Nolan Fedderson, she was snide and rude. When she learned that Mickey had learned about it from Matt, she went into a holy tirade against them all. Peter could not help but think that she was getting away with things that would not have been tolerated in any other Tlingit woman.

There was one thing he noted with great satisfaction. The quiet reserve of his father. He could not bring effective charges against Henry being the priest that he had always been. There was not a single pew seat available for any of his masses. He had tangled with Judson Walsh right from the first, and used his pulpit to speak out against what he thought was wrong. Since he had God on his side of the law, it seemed likely in Peter's mind that Henry would win.

And inside Peter had an even stranger private feeling. He had tried to make his father admire him, and was coming to admire his father instead.

For two years now, men had been calling Ludlow and Jackson millionaires. By that June they were each well over it, and George Carmack was ready to top his second million.

But they were angry. Damn angry.

"Forty percent!" J.T. spluttered. "The government now claims forty percent of every claim."

Kate turned an amazed face toward her husband.

"How can they do this thing?"

"Well, it's the commissioner law. Also says we have to take our gold to their bank and get paper for it."

"Worthless trash," Clarkson Ludlow growled. "If only we could get it down to McQuestan."

"Now you're repeating yourself," J.T. snipped. "Went over all of that in our own cabin."

"Can we not take it to Ramsey bankman?" Kate asked.

"I wish it was that simple," George said. "They're going to check on us each week."

"Then we let them see only what we want them to see," she said simply. "Like first year. We take right to Dawson and hide under their noses."

"Sounds fine, Kate," Ludlow said, "but they'll be checking every pack mule on the trail."

Kate giggled. "I'd like to see them check under my skirts, or Graphie Gracie's skirts as we walk or paddle down to the post. Seems your baggy pants could hide a pouch or two each time."

J.T. frowned. Then his face cleared.

"It's a good idea, but we have to add to it. Ramsey can keep some for us without breaking it down, but everyone knows we all got good claims. We've got to do some business with Walsh's banks to keep it all looking good."

"And what about the rest?" Ludlow demanded.

"Many things are for sale in Dawson that folks don't want to take that phoney money for. Among the old-timers we just have to spread the word quietly to purchase that way to protect ourselves from these robbers."

"Can we get away with it?" Ludlow asked, a little puzzled.

"Don't know till we try."

The first thing the next morning J.T. took a canoe to Dawson. The moment he landed he had a McBridge man right at his side for the walk to the Bank of Canada, where he had already established an account for the Monte Carlo. He was greeted cordially, as the two bags he carried looked heavy. But J.T. did not waste time or mince words.

"I want this weighed, your damn tax taken out, and that leering Mounty ass out of my sight!" he announced.

The banker blinked at him. J.T. gave him no chance to reply.

"And," he added, "I'll take no paper money for it. Keep it on deposit as gold."

"How much is it?" the banker stammered.

"Weigh it," J.T. said firmly. "I figure about $200,000." Fat chance you have of finding out about the real nuggets I have strapped to my legs, he thought.

"It seems hefty," the banker muttered. "I've been hearing good things about your claim."

J.T. leaned forward confidentially. "You're new. People boast a lot. But your inspector can tell you that I was sick some last week. This is just three days work."

A gleam stole into the banker's eyes.

"You . . . ah . . . know the forty percent rule?" he gulped.

"Know it," J.T. said curtly. "Now just give me a piece of paper showing my deposit for the rest. I'm thirsty as hell."

The banker was quick to accommodate such a customer. It was the first time he had taken in $80,000 in tax money from a single person and it shattered his mind.

At about the same time George Carmack was doing near the same at the Bank of Ottawa, after having left Kate and his daughter at Mizner Mercantile.

Kate and her daughter spent several minutes feeling and touching everything new that was in sight.

Edgar didn't recognize Kate and took her to be just another Indian squaw.

"Don't touch that stuff unless you can show me you have money to buy!" he screamed.

"Husband bring money."

"Then you go get money from him or wait outside!"

Kate flustered and waddled out. She looked about for the McBridge man who had followed them into town. As they had hoped, he had followed George to the other bank.

She nodded quickly at her daughter, and the two of them walked down the street to the Dawson Commercial Bank and Trust Company.

Because the law forbade Calvin to have Crow as a hired clerk, the pale young man behind the wire cage gave Kate a moment of fright.

"I see Mr. Ramsey?" she muttered.

Although she was the only customer he had seen all day, he acted overly busy. "He is in his office. What do you wish?"

"Shopping money. He arrange. I be Carmack George's wife."

His jaw actually dropped as he looked at the squaw and her child. Next to Alex McDonald's, the Carmack account was their largest. He had only been in town two weeks, but had quickly given up on the idea of making a fortune in gold. He had been a bank clerk in San Francisco and was grateful to Harriet Henderson for recommending him to Mr. Ramsey. But he had no idea that white men actually married Indian women—or that they could produce such plain looking daughters.

"Tell me how much and I will speak with Mr. Ramsey."

"See him in private," Kate insisted.

"All right," he said slyly, thinking he could leave them in the waiting room while he went to warn Mr. Ramsey. But Calvin was just coming out of his office as they entered.

"Ah, Ramsey Calvin, hello!" Kate brightened. "I see you private where you keep my money, maybe?"

Calvin was a bit taken aback, but waved Milton Brancher back to his cage.

"Where is your husband?"

"He at other bank making deposit. We come to shop and meet new buyer of house, maybe. I come for shopping money."

"This way," Calvin said sadly. He knew his customers would have to deal with the other banks. He was being forced to the wall by all the rules and regulations, without a single way to fight back.

He was also in deep trouble. If they kept taking out, he wouldn't be able to cover all of their money he had loaned. On paper, the bank was worth close to two million. In the individual crates, because he could not smelter any more, was only a quarter of that amount.

"How much do you need, Kate?" he asked, after they were in the "new" sanctuary.

Kate chuckled. "Turn back. We leave more in our box than we take out."

"I don't understand."

Kate explained as she took moosehide pouches from between her legs and those of her daughter.

When he turned, he looked at Kate with real admiration in his eyes. It turned to gratitude when he took the pouches and weighed them.

"Do you know what these are worth?" he asked softly.

"Most aware!" she said. "More sit with son at canoe. You give me their kind of money to purchase goods. I go to Mizner and back to canoe. I come back and go to McQuestan and buy goods. George and son come looking for us and bring the last. We do it weekly, no?"

Calvin nodded happily. Now, if he could just get a few others to do the same.

Lolly walked out of the Monte Carlo and blinked against the sun. It was nearly ninety degrees, but she felt as cold as death. She pushed blindly through the mass of men. At the corner, a man was milking the first cow to arrive and selling the milk for twenty dollars a gallon. But she didn't see it.

Men streamed by, flinging open their mackinaw blanket coats, sweating in the June heat. They made comments in her direction, as though she were one of the saloon girls in a satin dress and plumed hair. She didn't hear or retort.

Before the walk bridge a man was selling eggs for fourteen dollars a dozen. Harriet had told her to keep her ears open on the street for the first arrival of eggs so that she could bake a cake.

But Lolly didn't see the man or notice that he was selling eggs. Nor did she hear the blast of the whistle to announce the arrival of a sleek new steamer. She dropped off the bridge and began to weave through the hurly-burly of Lousetown. It was worse than Dawson, with thousands of restless men wandering about, unable to find anything to do. The steamboat whistle didn't thrill them. It only meant the arrival of more men just like them, who would fight for claims that weren't there and too few jobs.

Lolly turned into the Row. It was now bedlam day and night. Because every boat now carried any number of girls who would sing and dance and push drinks for just what they could con out of the customers, the "winter girls", as they were now called, stayed in their shacks and plied only one trade. The number of unlit lanterns above the door announced their specialty in the trade and price.

"Hey! This one is for me! How much little lady?"

Lolly shuddered and was freshly chilled. Her head whirled; she had to clutch at some of the waiting men to keep from falling. Everything rocked and swayed. Then she had to push them away because they took her meaning wrong.

"Keep your grubby hands off her. I saw her first!"

"Yah! Well, she chose me."

"Like hell! I saw you drag her away from him!"

As happened a hundred times a day, a light scuffle turned quickly into a brawl.

"Knew it had to be you!" Gertie bellowed, sticking her head out of her shack door. "Get the hell in here, 'fore they tear you limb from limb."

She caught Lolly by the hand and pulled her into her shack with pretended concern. Inside Lolly stopped short, white and trembling. "I–I can see you're busy–I can make it to my shack."

Gertie turned and glowered at the grinning man. "Shag off, buster. You've had your few dollars' worth. I have others to see to."

He looked from one to the other. "Piss! If you take on women, too, that's the last you'll see of me."

Gertie laughed. "With what you've got between your legs, I haven't seen the first of you! Now git!"

Lolly sank into a chair, even before he was out the door. All she really wanted to do was get to her own bed, but not through that street fight.

"Baby starting to give you problems?" Gertie asked, with false solicitude. "I told you how to get rid of it."

"It's not that. Bailey fired me. Hired some young boy off the street for a meal a day and a place to sleep."

"And I bet I know which bed he'll be sleeping in. That's the way he hires his bartenders, too."

"But I did my work good," Lolly whispered, about ready to cry. "I've got to have that job."

Gertie sat down, trying not to burst into laughter. She thought Lolly stupid to have stayed there as long as she had, what with the abuse Bailey handed out. In her opinion, Bailey had turned it into a low-class dive and J.T. didn't give a shit.

"You got Alex paid off?"

"Yes."

"Then get rid of the kid while you can and use your shack to make some money."

"I'm scared to death to do it," Lolly shuddered.

"So was I the first time." She bit her lip with assumed contrition. "But after I popped my first kid I said I'd never be put out of commission for that long again. You go think on it. I got a guy waiting, but we'll talk again later."

"But it's still murder," Lolly stammered.

Gertie shrugged. "Then there must be twenty thousand or so murders done a night in Dawson by the guys who take it in hand or we gals who flush ourselves out."

Lolly didn't want to think about any of it. She was doubly scared—scared to abort herself and scared she couldn't take one of these men for pay after she had done it.

Gertie growled the men back so Lolly could make it to her shack door. Entering, she knew that Gertie was right *and* wrong, but which was best for her?

"Thought I had missed you."

All at once Lolly experienced a spasm of overwhelming joy.

"Murton! I thought you had left!"

"Left the Monte Carlo," he said dryly, "but hardly town. Been busy interviewing these wags as they have come off the boats."

She smiled feebly. "Interviewing for what?"

"Men with talent and instruments among their trappings for the opera house. Ladies who have a bit more talent than the taking off of flimsy clothing. I am, in a word, to stage the shows and conduct my own orchestra."

"But you never mentioned it to me!"

"Ah, my dear," he chuckled, his eyes sparkling. "I learned a million years ago that a boast turns a dream to ashes and a secret helps bring it about. I kept my secret and the man who is bringing it about kept his."

"Addison Mizner?"

"On that score, let us just say that Addison is also getting his secret wish, to the chagrin of Edgar. Brother Wilson, it would seem, arrived with a boat load of the most remarkable things for the opera house, and nary a scrap for the mercantile store. But you will see all. And the sooner the better, now that I don't have to fight you away from Bailey."

"What are you talking about?"

"My dear, you are being offered a job, because you are loyal, trustworthy and a very good friend. I promise there will be no glasses to carry, no saw-dust to sweep and no drunks to fight off."

She almost laughed in sudden delight. But instead she remained quite sober. He was too good a friend to lie to.

"Thank you for thinking of me, Murton, but I can't work for long. I'm going to have a baby."

"A fact, Lolly, that I have known for some time. For what I have in mind, we can arrange your work schedule accordingly."

"You called me Lolly."

"Just another little secret I made sure that I learned. Chickee! Bah! Made me want to puke every time I had to say it."

"Oh, I don't care about that silly name!" she cried, her eyes glowing with excitement. "When can I start work?"

"How soon can you get fully packed?"

"Packed?"

"I refuse to have anyone associated with the opera house who has any association with this place whatsoever. You are to have a room of your own there. It is right down the hall from my own."

It gave her a pang of uneasiness. "Murton . . . I . . . my shack here is not . . . I don't—"

He held up a hand to silence her and forced himself to smile. "I am a little hurt that you took the meaning wrong. I am most aware of you and your conditions. It was a joke with the girls, but I did not laugh. I am not a man who allows human entanglements to break his heart. They can raise too much hell. But you are special. You give friendship without asking for reward. On that basis, do you want the job and room?"

"I'll pack!" she exclaimed, and now tears rushed into her eyes, tears of happiness. "Right away!"

"And what shall you do with this . . . ah, shack, as you call it?"

She stopped short. "Well, that's something to think about. For the first time in my life I have something to sell, for a change."

Murton smiled to himself. He thought she had a great deal to sell, if the right person just brought her along slowly and convinced her of her worth.

LeRoy Napoleon McQuestan was greatly impressed with the worth of the woman and what she carried aboard the *Brisbane II*. It had seemed to float upon the river after picking him up at Circle City. It could have carried hundreds, but it carried only the woman, her twenty unseen guests, servants, cargo and the daughter of the ship owner.

Dawson, after a first astonished stare, made way for the off loading of a handsome landau carriage. A moment later a tall old Negro, thin and stiff with age, came down the gangway. He was very black, very distinguished-looking, with crisp features and a haughty gaze. He was dressed like a rich gentleman in black broadcloth, with a diamond pin in his tie. His hair was a white fringe around a glistening dome. The top hat he used as a signal to have the two pure white horses hoisted from the deck to the wharf. Two more blacks, liveried in scarlet, scrambled down the gangway to harness the horses to the carriage.

When everything was to his satisfaction, Bother Munson put the top hat on his head at a jaunty angle and waited.

McQuestan had never been so honored to escort a woman down a gangway in his life.

Clara Bennett was regal and elegant in white lace over

creamy silk, an outfit that showed that she was a woman of exquisite form. The ostrich plume picture hat was slanted so that no one would miss her handsome features. The wharf was her stage and she would command it with a single entrance. But Clara was performing for a single pair of eyes. McQuestan had warned her about the import tax and she had quietly stated she would discuss the matter with no one but Judson Walsh.

She had purposely turned him into an impatient man. Making him wait an hour on the wharf, and refusing him permission to board the vessel.

He now stood in silence at the foot of the gangway, fuming that no one had informed him that LeRoy McQuestan was aboard the vessel.

"What trick is this, McQuestan? You know the import tax rules."

McQuestan's Scots gorge rose, but he held his temper. "Commissioner Walsh, may I present Miss Clara Bennett."

"I received her engraved card and arrogant summons. That explains nothing. What is her business here?"

McQuestan had to bite his tongue. "She is here to purchase the home of my business partner, George Carmack."

"That does not explain her business here," Walsh declared snidely.

His meaning was very obvious. Clara gently squeezed McQuestan's arm, as though to signal that she would handle the matter from that point.

"Bo, the letter, if you please." Her voice was mellifluous and tinged with a slight English accent. "I think the man questions my right to enter my own country."

"Your country?"

"I was born in Leitrim, just out of Ottawa."

"I see," said Walsh, who did not. He was becoming irritated at it all. "That still answers nothing."

"The letter answers all." Clara's hauteur increased. "I

was promised courtesy and cooperation. I shall hate to report that I have found neither."

Walsh's face held instant disdain. "Report as you will, Miss Bennett. The law is the law."

Bo rudely shoved the letter right under the man's nose. Walsh read hurriedly, his face turning scarlet. He suddenly lost his temper, his eyes bright with anger.

"I still demand to know your business here."

Clara looked at him with concealed amusement. "Gold, Mr. Walsh. Isn't that why everyone is here? Come, Mr. McQuestan, I desire to see my house."

McQuestan whispered as he helped her up into the carriage. "You're the first person who has been bold enough to back him down since his arrival. Must have been a powerful letter."

"Actually," Clara laughed, her enormous gazelle's eyes bright with mischief, "it was a most simple letter, asking for nothing more than courtesy and cooperation."

"Then it must have been signed by the Queen herself," he jested.

"Nearly as good," Clara said seriously. "The Earl of Minto, Governor General of Canada."

McQuestan turned in his seat, his face filled with amazement. "Gilbert Elliott Murray-Kynynmond? You know him?"

Clara smiled sweetly. "In my profession, Mr. McQuestan, it is not exactly who you know, but who your friends might know on up the ladder. The Canadian chargé d'affaires in Seattle is a most dear friend—and debtor. He was most concerned about my coming here, because of the despicable conditions. It would seem his government has a vastly different picture than actual fact. Light poles? Hardly the back woods as described."

Suddenly McQuestan wanted to laugh, but without mirth and only bitterness. "They are a Walsh addition, Miss Bennett. Something to make the people happy—until they get their bill. It's costing some as much as $5,000 just to be wired and hooked up. I don't think they have started wiring the Carmack house as yet, but after today Walsh will make sure that your bill is staggering."

Clara was silent. These days, costs everywhere were staggering, she thought. Seattle was still going crazy getting men ready to leave for the gold fields. But what she saw here was unbelievable. Dawson was already larger than Seattle. For the first time in her life she had made a real fortune and now she was putting that money to work to make more money.

It was now called the Duboise-Monroe house. Their bench claim was on the hillside some fifty steps from the back door. It had produced enough "color" to keep the inspectors and Bank of Canada happy—without them having to reveal the secret of what lay beneath the house. For the time being, both men were happy. The bench claim had produced almost sixty thousand dollars before taxes, and Matt was kept busy each day.

"Tired, Matt?" Henry asked as they came down the hillside together.

"A little," Matt admitted with a sigh.

Henry chortled. "You just want to get under the house. You've got to have patience."

"More so now. They say that Walsh wants to raise the tax to fifty percent."

"And get priests out of their hair." At the back door he put his hand affectionately on Matt's arm. "I cannot stop speaking out against his evil, Matt. Nor will I be able to keep silent about Clara, if she turns that house into what I think she will turn it into. If I held silent on that, I would have to hold silent on Crow and Peter. How did they take my message?"

"Astringently—as usual."

Henry nodded. "They do it to keep from breaking the law of Walsh, and thus they break the Law of God. I cannot understand my son allowing Crow to sleep with his younger wife, even if Walsh does say a man cannot have more than one wife."

"Perhaps it is only sleeping. Your . . . Kilria is in the same village."

"Well," Henry said, ignoring that point, "I have to get ready for hospital duty if Laura Lee is to get away." He sighed. "So many ill with the scurvy. After a winter without any fresh fruit or vegetables they thought it would be like being down home. It is costing me a dollar an orange. Poor Laura Lee. She works until she is nearly dragging."

"I'm surprised she accepted Clara's invitation to see the house."

"I think it was due in great part to Mickey and Phoebe."

"Phoebe—here? Clara said nothing, and I didn't see her when I went to visit the *Brisbane II.*"

"I don't think she wanted to see you," Henry said dryly.

"Poor fat sow," Matt laughed. "She will never forgive me for leading her on. This will be some dinner party. Phoebe and Laura Lee not talking with me, and I dread having to face Lolly."

"You won't have to worry about that," Henry said gently. "She has been on again, off again, sick with the child."

"What child?" he demanded.

"It would seem Nolan left her with a child."

"I must do something! I feel so responsible."

"That is the very reason I hesitated to mention anything about it to you. She does not want pity, even now. When you're my age, you start to see people for the first time. People wear so many different masks, I wonder how God knows which face to let into heaven."

"Well, right now I'm wearing an angry one. You might at least let me know where she is and what she's doing."

"No harm in that. Murton has her at Jackson Turner's

opera house. Oh, that was a slip of the priestly tongue. No one, and especially Walsh, should know that J.T. bought it lock, stock and barrel with gold. J.T. purposely had her fired from the Monte Carlo when he found out that Bailey was turning her into a slave. Oh, by the look on your face I see I've left something out. Yes, she worked at the Monte Carlo—but it wasn't the kind of work you're thinking of. And, you will have to forgive me the lie of saying that you were not welcome there because of the shooting."

"She must really hate me," Matt said sadly.

"At the moment she doesn't have time for such an emotion. Murton keeps her busy with wardrobe and helping to train the chorus. They are planning quite a showy Fourth of July opening. I have a box, if you would care to attend. The evening will be loaded with surprises, if you do not mind sitting with Laura Lee and Mickey."

"Let me first see how I fare with her this evening," he grinned.

14

Only Clara would have dared to invite the survivors of the *Brisbane I.* Surprisingly, they all attended except Henry, Lolly and Harlan Henderson.

It was hardly the same house. Clara had paid dearly for her seven day miracle. Her greatest struggle was getting them to install the electricity. A few future promises to the workmen soon had them stringing up electric chandeliers and overlooking Walsh's edict to leave the woman in the dark.

Amalida saw it and fumed. The bank building and her apartment were still lit by kerosene lamps.

A cute little maid of some seventeen years opened the door. She wore a black dress and a frilled white apron and cap and had the innocent face of one not knowing the eventual use of the house. Calvin smiled at her, but Amalida rustled past with a haughty uplifted face as if the girl was not human.

Calvin had worried over the invitation. He had even considered coming alone, to keep Amalida from making a scene over the Seattle incident. But Harriet, who was the only customer he allowed to make her payment in the upstairs apartment, had gushed out the news. Then, because it was some place to go, Amalida had insisted upon attending.

That night Calvin Ramsey would not have cared if Amalida made a horrible scene. His heart was singing after a day of near disaster.

No sooner had Milton Brancher opened the door that morning than Judson Walsh, four of McBridge's mounties, two auditors and a stranger barged right in and made him relock the door.

Calvin had nearly fainted upon seeing Jethro Calhoun again. This time Jethro had a stack of legal papers so impressive that Judson could not ignore them. Of course, Judson was ignorant of the fact that every one of the papers had been forged no farther away than Skagway by one of Soapy Smith's men.

Throughout the morning, as the auditors went over the books, Judson was kind enough to let Calvin tell his side of the story. Even though he wanted to put the man out of business, he was the law in Dawson and resented having a judge in New Orleans telling him how to run his affairs with a lot of legal clap-trap that was endorsed by the Canadian consulate in Chicago.

The story fascinated him in more ways than one. It was the first he knew of a link between Father Henry and Ramsey—two men he wanted out of his hair. But oddly, it made him believe Calvin's side of the border story more than Calhoun's. If nothing more, he knew Father Henry to be a man of God—and the main reason for getting him out of Dawson. Which he felt would be accomplished no later than that day.

As the afternoon began to wear on, Judson had to side even further with Calvin. The books proved, beyond a shadow of a doubt, that Calvin had built his banking business up from scratch and with the help of handling "lay" claims and loans for Alexander McDonald. Nor were Calvin's personal accounts impressive. Money had been poured right back into the bank for the building and expansion. Calvin had himself on salary and the $50,000 seemed lost forever in the maze of his clever accounting.

Judson M. Walsh found himself in a quandry. He had made a great error. The bankers he had brought in were proving to be far too conservative with him and far too liberal in seeing that the government tax money *stayed* government tax money. What Calvin had done with his bank was impressive and could grow more impressive if he took off some of the restrictions against the man. Suddenly he wanted him as an ally and not as an enemy.

Walsh's decision in Calvin's favor so riled Jethro that he grew abusive toward Judson and made a fatal error. He threatened to take the matter to a personal friend who would not fear getting to the truth of the matter—Soapy Smith.

Judson had only smiled and had the Mounties escort Jethro from the bank. Then he had a most cordial "businesslike" chat with Calvin Ramsey.

Yes, Calvin was sitting on top of his little world. With a new friend like J.M. Walsh, he would never fear Jethro Calhoun again.

"Hello there!" Calvin called out.

The Dunn brothers stood in the hall, smiling sheepishly, in near matching dark gray suits excellently tailored in the back room of McQuestan's Dry Goods Store. They were the first store-bought suits Jerome and Cornell had ever owned, and they really felt as elegant and handsome as they looked.

"The maid was about ready to show us in when you rang."

"Then we shall go in together," Calvin laughed. "Although I should not speak to either of you. Good friends should do business with each other."

"It's because of the restrictions they have against you," Cornell said, without hesitation.

"Then talk with me on Monday. There are to be some changes made."

Amalida looked at him in surprise. It was the first she had heard of it. But then, she had not seen him until the carriage had arrived to pick them up. She had refused to allow him to enter as she dressed, so she would have a chance to nip at her whiskey bottle.

She stopped short as she entered. This was hardly the ill-furnished living room in which she had lived.

"Amalida!" Harriet cried out, as if it had been years since they had seen each other. "Didn't I tell that Mrs. Adams was a marvel? She has made that dress enchanting on you!"

"Why, thank you, Harriet," she said, in a bewildered voice. A half hour before she had hardly been able to see herself in the mirror. She had had to gargle with scented water to hide her drunkenness from Calvin. The ride in the carriage had begun to clear her head. She had felt quite grand riding behind Bo and the liveried coachman. She could see the miners gawking and staring, and it had made her feel like at last she was someone in Dawson.

And now the compliment. Her face was transformed; it became so radiant with happiness that she was almost pretty. That night, Amalida thought, she wouldn't need drink; she wanted to be a part of everything.

While Calvin and the Dunn brothers exchanged casual conversation, she let Harriet lead her into the room.

Crow greeted her, smiling, in a heavily beaded Tlingit costume. She gave him her hand. He led it for a long moment, and her heart lurched. Crow had been the first man to make her wonder what it would be like to have someone other than Calvin, and she still wondered.

"Come to the fireplace, for the biggest surprise of all," he chuckled, taking each woman by the elbow.

Amalida paid little attention to the knot of people ahead. The walnut furniture was gone. Now it was all delicate French, upholstered in pastel needlepoint, the lamps of crystal or subdued gilt, the rugs Aubussons, the draperies rich velvet. Everywhere were crystal vases of lupines, bluebells and shooting stars. The fireplace had been resurfaced in marble. An exceptionally fine portrait of Clara hung above the mantel, on which stood an ormolu clock.

In a lady chair to one side of the fire sat a young woman, beautiful in a blue velvet gown embroidered in gold. She looked like a child perched there; her masses of gleaming chestnut hair knotted in a classical fashion, but tendrils had escaped to frame her perfect face, giving her an aspect of innocence and defenselessness. But there was nothing defenseless in the large dark blue eyes. As Clara had predicted she would, Phoebe Hall was having the time of her life shocking the hell out of people.

"What an exquisite dress, Mrs. Ramsey," Phoebe said in a soft and fluting voice, as she rose and offered Amalida a little white hand.

"I don't believe I know . . ." Amalida started and stopped as everyone began to chuckle.

Each of them had been similarly fooled. Laura Lee had known because Phoebe had come and looked her up at the hospital, and she had told Mickey of the incredible change. Matt had stood transfixed and Crow had embarrassed her with the slavish adoration in his eyes.

"I am Phoebe," she chuckled merrily.

"But the fat?" Amalida gasped. She regretted the statement immediately, after the second compliment on her gown.

Phoebe made an eloquent gesture of what she once was, because nothing from the past could disturb her.

"Melted away. It started after I learned we had left you in the wrong place. I found myself having to be engineer and fireman to the Chinese—thus leaving the other one in the galley. He nearly starved us on the way to Seattle. When we got there, I first noticed how much weight I had lost on the trip. Clara talked me into keeping it off. But they have all heard this already."

"We haven't heard," Calvin said, coming up with the Dunn brothers. "My dear, dear Phoebe. You are breathtaking."

"My heavens," Cornell beamed. "It's enough to make a man wish he wasn't already married, doesn't it, Jerome?"

"It doesn't make any difference, to some men," Calvin said with a chuckle.

Too late he realized in what bad taste was his comment. A sudden silence filled the room. Laura Lee paled and Matt shot her a worried look. Mickey dared not look at her. It was a subject he carefully avoided around her. Harriet pursed her lips, because she was torn in her feelings about Laura Lee. She really couldn't blame her, and felt somewhat responsible for having thrown Laura Lee and Nolan together in the canoe. But she couldn't pity the girl either, because of what she had done to Lolly. Amalida decided she would have a drink after all.

They were all saved any further thought by the quick arrival of Clara Bennett. She was obviously annoyed about something.

"I'm sorry to keep you all waiting," she said, her voice edgy. "I had to take care of some business." She flushed over how that sounded. "I didn't mean customer business in the sense . . ." Her voice trailed off as her confusion and anger grew.

Matt looked at her wonderingly. Never had he seen her so perplexed.

"No, dammit!" she said suddenly. "We all know each other and my business is well known to each of you. I have never hidden that fact under a bushel basket before and see no use in doing it now. Bo, get Simone in here with drinks. After my introduction to Dawson's seamier side, I need a stiff one."

She glided forward, giving her dress a molded look on

her frame. On purpose she had worn something simple, with no jewelry. She still looked elegant.

"I am sorry," she kept saying, as she greeted everyone, "but I have never seen a man turn from southern gentleman to lecher so quickly in my life. Have any of you, perchance, run into a Mr. Randolph Smith? He calls himself Soapy."

No one made a sound and Calvin was especially quiet, hearing the name for the second time that day.

Bo offered the tray of wine glasses around, moving with his usual foxlike grace. Even the Dunn brothers took a glass.

"The man has a very high opinion of himself, probably deserved." Clara paused. "But that doesn't give him license to demand a percentage of my business, either, and I made that plain. Then he grew nasty. Purely evil. Claims to have the law on his side."

"Which he has," Calvin said smugly. "The dancehall girls' shacks are only allowed over in Lousetown. You should have checked your facts before you bought here.

There was a subtle charge in the air. Clara rarely discussed her business with others and that comment riled her. Now she assumed a cold, threatening appearance, and even Amalida was impressed.

"This hillside property was registered as a claim and never as a Dawson city lot. I am just as far away from Dawson as that hovel across the river."

"That is immaterial," Calvin said, trying to show off his acuteness and intelligence. "It is all now within territorial boundary under Commissioner Walsh. Perhaps I could speak to him on your behalf."

"Oh, no!" cried Amalida, giving her husband an accusing look. "We have enough trouble with that man."

"Don't we all," Harriet chimed in. "Ten percent room tax and now a ten percent food tax because I offer a supper!"

"Add it on to the bill," Calvin suggested, "just like everyone else does."

Harriet frowned. "Doesn't seem proper. Just like your one percent a day interest doesn't seem proper, Calvin. Nothing seems proper up here. We fought so hard to get here, and fought so many to get here. Seems we should have a voice, but we ain't. We ain't 'insiders' or 'outsiders', we are just the 'inbetween'."

"Poppycock!" Calvin snorted. "Walsh is trying to give us some stability and order."

Matt chortled. "Is that why you had to get Crow out of your bank? For stability and order? Bullcrap! The man is a dictator and Soapy Smith is just one of his henchmen. Ask any dealer in any saloon. They have to give a rake off to Smith's men. Jerome, do you give a fair count to the inspector and the bank, or salt some away to sneak out of here?"

Jerome laughed, his endearing laugh. "Luckily, we 'lay' from Big Alex. Time was everything went through Calvin. The forty-tax made it rough. We had to take through the Bank of Canada or Ottawa. But like many up the creeks, we felt it was better to leave it lie fallow than work for the bankers."

"You are not working for the bankers," Calvin fumed. "They do not get to keep that tax money for themselves."

"You're being charitable," Crow said, grinning. "We only took out ten percent when I worked for you. New banks come on the scene and it's suddenly forty. They have to be making a hefty amount out of that."

"That's beside the point," Calvin insisted.

"No," Mickey said, "it *is* the point. The point of everything. Look, I haven't been here as long as the rest of you, but I wasn't a school teacher for nothing. I can't go dig for gold, so I thought about going back to teaching. Did anyone ever stop to think that some brought children here, yet there is no school? I did, and you know what I was told by the great commissioner's office? There are no funds available for it, and if I wanted to start a private school I would have to pay a $5,000 license fee. You can't sneeze without Walsh figuring out a way to put a tax on it or license it."

"Or damn the Indians," Amalida said with loftiness. She was feeling her wine on top of the liquor. Bo came to refill the glasses and Calvin gave her a warning glance. She purposely ignored him. This reminded her of when everyone had their say on the trail. She was determined to have her say on this matter.

"Men are easily fooled," she went on, taking a sip of the wine. "We women are prime examples of that. I was nearly twenty-five years old before I learned that women dressed for other women and not for men. But in this god-forsaken town, except for Clara's invitation tonight, when have we had a chance to be women? Harriet slaves over a bakery turned boarding house. Laura Lee slaves over patients who probably tried to keep her from getting here. I slave over sheer boredom. Fight them, Clara Bennett! Fight them with every female trick in your bag!"

Calvin was disgusted with her. He longed for her to be once again the simple and unknowing Ann Forbes. This ungainly, drunken woman was embarrassing and irritating, and he said something that he knew would hurt her womanly vanity. "You are the last to know about female tricks, my dear. No, no more wine for her, Bo."

"But of course I'll have more wine," she said, taking no offense and speaking quite clearly. Suddenly, the talk and participation had sobered her. "I didn't mean that to sound brash, I just wanted to make a point. Yes, we are aware of your business, Clara. From my own father I had to learn that such was a part of this world. His explanation of his mistress now strikes me as most amusing and fitting to the present situation. He denied up one street and down the other paying for her—"

"Enough!" Calvin gasped. He looked at her incredulously.

"Calvin," she said, almost fawning, "he was *my* father. If I do not feel the least bit vaguely ashamed in discussing his plebeian romance, then I don't see why you should be discomfited by it."

The room was held in silence. Everyone, right down to the Dunn brothers and Harriet were totally fascinated. Amalida was stellar.

"My point," she went right on, before Calvin could protest further, "is that he did not pay. He left her little gift envelopes to pay for the drinks that he shared with her."

Clara began to chuckle and then roared with delightful mirth. "Oh, Amalida, I think your story priceless. I cannot help but admire your father, even though it must have given you pain at the time. He did the gentlemanly thing. I shall ask my gentlemen to do the same. Oh, Simone is nodding. I took the liberty to have Phoebe ask Laura Lee what you may not have had up here that would be different. They agreed on corned beef and cabbage. And boiled potatoes. Shall we go in?"

It was a remarkable choice of a simple homey fare, but it was served superbly, and everyone talked pleasantly and laughed. Laura Lee allowed herself to be half-way nice to Matt, but gave most of her attention to Mickey and Phoebe—when she could get Phoebe away from Crow. He was smitten, and smitten bad by her new beauty and she played with him like an eagle with a cornered rattlesnake.

But Calvin felt danger in the atmosphere, as if Amalida was growing too smart. She seemed to be handling the wine as though it was mere water.

The bank talk caught Matt's attention. "Just how does one bank with you like Turner, Ludlow, Carmack and McDonald, Calvin?"

Calvin looked politely surprised. "No different than other customers," he said, smiling his charming and seductive banker's smile. "Deposits. Managing their lay claims. Investing in loans."

"In gold?" Matt's smile was dour.

"Well, as you know I have not been allowed to smelt since I moved from here."

"Oh," Clara chimed in, "so that's what is behind the kitchen. I thought it was some ugly furnace for heating the whole house in winter."

"Now wait just a minute," Crow chuckled. "I have paid you back on my loan, so I won't have you talking about my pride and joy that way."

He shut up quickly before Calvin could think to ask where he had gotten the money to pay back the loan.

Calvin didn't have a chance to think about it, because Matt was pounding on the table again.

"That has nothing to do with it, Calvin. People are still using gold for barter. Clara should do the same, I would suggest. How does she go about it without Walsh putting his nose in?"

Calvin said nothing to that, and his stare became piercing.

"Well," Clara broke the little silence, "let us all adjourn to the living room. We have plenty of time to discuss business."

She was soon to learn that things moved very quickly in this town that never slept.

Henry clenched his fists. On a chair in the little surgical room sat Jethro Calhoun. He had been badly beaten and one arm hung limp at an unnatural angle. His craggy face was almost unrecognizable.

"McBridge's men," he said grimly. "I was lucky to get away."

Somebody snickered. Henry spun around, looking for the author of the sound. Three of McBridge's men crowded into the room.

"Get out of here at once–"

He never finished the sentence. One henchman shoved him roughly out of the way. Henry staggered back against a table of instruments. Another went for Jethro. Suddenly there was a knife at Jethro's throat. Jethro pushed the arm aside angrily but the man seized his shoulder.

"You're coming with us, buster!"

"He's not going anywhere," Henry said curtly.

The henchman spat contemptuously at Henry's feet. Without giving him a chance to protest again, he pulled his gun and slammed it against the side of Henry's head. The priest fell heavily. He was half stunned. He tried to get to his feet but before he could do more than get to one knee the man was upon him. He hit him across the face with the gun butt. Blood spurted from his nose and Henry blacked out.

"Get the other one out of here!"

"Why? Let's solve all of our problems at once. They ain't got electricity."

The man wet his lips in anticipation. "Snyder, go bar the back door . . . good!"

"Sick people back there, Sarge!"

"They ain't going to question what you do in a Mounty uniform. Git! Murphy, our friend!"

He turned and picked up an oil lamp from the instrument table. By the time he had turned back the other had plunged the knife in and out of Jethro's chest so quickly he had not even had time to cry out. He fell forward off the chair as the man quickly stepped away and into the hall. The Sergeant paused at the door, threw the oil lamp to the floor with a crash, and quickly closed the door to the room. The shattered glass and kerosene splattered over Jethro's back and was instantly aflame.

A hall lamp was smashed on the steps leading to the attic ward and another at the entrance before the door was closed. Then, calmly, the three men rounded the corner and entered the church. The door they had barred into the hospital was barred again from the other side and the church set to flame.

By the time the twelve patients were aroused by the smoke they found themselves within a raging inferno, with no way to save themselves. Inside the surgical room it was just a ball of white-hot heat and exploding alcohol and medication bottles.

By the time they were down from the mansion, the bucket brigade had given up hope for the building and were throwing their water on the nearby buildings to save them. It was the logical order issued by the Mounties in charge. No one would have thought to question that they were turning all evidence to ash.

Laura Lee put her fist to her mouth and set her teeth against the knuckles. Mickey watched her bite down till the blood flowed.

"Get her the hell away from here!" Matt barked.

"Where to?" Mickey asked, in his own state of shock.

"To the house! I'll find out what I can here."

"Find out," Laura Lee muttered grimly. "This can't be. We were so careful. He . . . he was so careful."

Sergeant Lothrop walked up scowling. "Look, Miss Boise, you may not be in a mood to talk but there are some things I need to know. First of all, who was inside that fire-trap? Second—"

"Just a minute," Matt snarled. "Are you forgetting that her father was in there?"

A look of surprise replaced the bewilderment on Laura Lee's face. She put a hand on Matt's arm to still him.

"It's all right." Her tone was heavy. "The families have to be considered over my own feelings. I—I . . ." She tried to clear her head and think. "Oh, Mickey, the children with Belinda."

Mickey thought it time to direct the conversation. "Sergeant, she speaks of Belinda Mulroney. Two families had both mother and father down ill. Mrs. Mulroney has been seeing to their children over at the Fairview Hotel. Could we please go discuss it over there, instead of here?"

Lathrop hadn't expected that. He was taken aback. He had thought that the patients would be only worthless stampeders.

"After you tell the kids, leave a list of the others with Belinda. I've got a room at the Fairview."

They watched him depart, and Mickey put an arm around Laura Lee's shoulders to reassure her. He couldn't believe the man was leaving it to Laura Lee to tell the orphans. Matt was also stunned.

"I'll go," he said, "if you give me the names."

Laura Lee glowered at him. "I know them. They came daily to the hospital. I will do what my father would have done. Come, Mickey!"

There was a silence. Matt and Mickey looked quickly at each other. They had thought she was in shock, but maybe it was best to let her handle it.

Laura Lee looked rueful. "Matt, my father had many friends among the common men. Find out what you can, will you?"

He nodded, but didn't think it would do much good. He just wanted to cry bitter tears.

The next day, miners stood in little knots about the cold ashes, their faces turning now and then toward another little knot of people. When word spread up to the diggings that Father Henry had died in the fire, J.T. took matters into his own hands. The "insiders" put aside their shovels and came to town. Those who had wintered in Dawson closed their saloons and stores and cafes. J.T. asked the other three ministers to say a prayer at the only grave site for the thirteen souls—unaware that there were fourteen.

Everyone had a little something to say to Laura Lee or to Matt.

Judson Walsh, as usual, had the wrong thing to say.

"I have already started making plans to build a proper hospital."

Matt looked at him, his face silent and still. All morning long the miners had been coming to him, he had not had to go to them. He was still having trouble putting together the odd bits of news and gossip they brought him.

Peter was there, his heart a hot ball, blocking his throat. Of such a man am I born, he thought, unconsciously beating in his mind the rhythms the nobles would chant when the canoe he had dispatched would reach the Lake LaBerge village.

"My sister," he whispered, so only Laura Lee could hear, "our mother sits alone in her lodge with only pleasant thoughts."

Laura Lee touched his arm and they looked in one another's eyes. She understood his meaning fully and he smiled at her understanding. The part of him that was of his father had made him come to do honor, now he would return to his own lodge and honor him in the Tlingit manner.

It was, to Matt, astonishingly curious that he could be around Laura Lee without his usual trepidation and hope for a word of forgiveness. The hope, he realized now, was clouded by two other issues. He could not understand his feeling of relief upon returning to the house to have Laura Lee ask for privacy from them all for awhile. Crow understood and refused to stay even when Matt tried to insist.

"I wanted the three of us to talk," Matt said, hours later, "just like in the old days. Crow always comes up with good thoughts and I am totally bewildered, Mickey. Last night Windy Nelson had Henry take a splinter out of his finger. He sent a pail of beer over from the saloon in thanks. The kid said Henry thanked him but was busy helping a battered man into the hospital. The kid said it was the same man who had had words in the saloon earlier with one of Soapy Smith's dealers. I've found out that the man was Jethro Calhoun."

"Calhoun!" Mickey croaked.

"Quiet," Matt whispered. "I don't want her hearing. Windy finished his drink and went back to see if he could help Henry. He saw three of McBridge's Mounties entering and went back to the saloon quick. You know Windy, he is not about to let Walsh know when he is in town, out of town, or where he has his diggings. Next thing he knew someone was running into the saloon and yelling about the fire."

"Next thing?" Mickey insisted. "How much time? You know he's an old drunk."

"He claims it was no more than ten or fifteen minutes later. He has two other sourdoughs who back up his claim. But they're scared to make any noise about it, even though it was common knowledge that Walsh wanted to shut Henry up."

"Good God!" Mickey exploded. "Damn right we have to keep this from Laura Lee."

"Laura Lee has already heard," she said softly from the doorway. Quickly she entered and went to gaze out the window. "Thank you for finding out for certain what I already believed to be the truth."

"We didn't want you to know," Mickey whispered.

"I'm all right, Mickey," she said clearly, surprised at the strength of her own voice. "I am remembering only the good. The twenty years of love and kindness given in his own special way. Not love as I have come to know it—or wrongly know it. A million little things that you might call fatherly. There is no use crying over what I have done of late. I would just be crying for myself and not for him. It would dishonor him."

"What are we to do?" Mickey asked. He was suddenly, horribly afraid for her. If Walsh would do that to get rid of Henry and his church, what would he do to Laura Lee?

"We are to do nothing!" Laura Lee said.

"But," Mickey objected, "we can't go on just like nothing has happened!"

"Let her state her reasons," Matt said, looking at her fondly, his hazel eyes bright and proud.

"Thank you, Matt," she said stoutly. She was far less confident than she sounded, though she somehow knew that Peter would agree with her had he been there. "That was love and friendship we saw today. They came because they wanted to come. If I ran out of fear ot Walsh I would turn that into a mockery. But we cannot openly accuse, because we wouldn't have Walsh. It would also put them in danger. For the moment I think they would fully understand our silence as we rebuild."

"Just to have him burn it down again," Mickey said. "The bastard made it well known that he would build his own hospital."

Laura Lee lifted her hand with authority and, startled again, Mickey subsided. Matt smiled to himself. He had seen Henry use that same hand gesture perhaps a hundred times.

"Let him build it. Every man there offered to rebuild ours. J.T. even offered all of the profits from the grand opening of the opera house. I told him to give it to the orphans and widows. Then I had a different thought as I was in my room. That is what I was coming to tell you when I overheard you. It now even makes more sense, for all of us. There is no damn way that Walsh can stop us from building an orphanage for them and you teaching them in your own school rooms."

"You could do that on your own," Matt said. "You and Peter will now have a share in the mine."

"It would hardly pay for Ladue's lumber charges," Mickey said.

A strange look came over her face. "I know what Matt is talking about. Father's mine," she said, and the words were a caress, something that Mickey missed, though he was aware of the sudden quiet in her voice. "No, Matt, he said the time was not right for it. Besides, Peter and I will have trouble claiming it, as we are part Tlingit. He said he trusted you as a gentleman to protect us fairly."

"Henry said that?" His voice was soft and trembling.

"At the time, I thought he said it to hurt me because of what . . ." She paused. "Let's bury that ghost, Matt. I accused him of tricking you into killing Nolan. I thought he would do any mischievous thing to break us apart. But my father never lied to me about anything important. He was too much a priest for that. But he also gave me my stubborn French blood. I can't put him to rest without making amends."

"With *everyone*?"

"Yes. Lolly sent a message by Harriet this morning. I was not aware of the child, although that has nothing to do with what I am saying. She was doing honor to my father with her message, even after what I did to her."

Laura Lee's eyes filled with tears. The softness of her expression, her faint smile, made her extremely beautiful. The protected, spoiled childlike quality was gone. She had been a part of, but never fully a member of the breed that had been hammered on the anvil glacier. Her schooling and her father had always made her feel a little apart from the rest. Even with Nolan she had felt she could do what she wished because she was above the crowd. Many in that Yukon breed may not have been as intelligent as she, but she now saw them as far more acute. The death of her father made her realize she wished to be the same.

Mickey was puzzled. He had never expected a reaction like this out of her. She seemed to be not only sad but also strangely happy.

"I don't understand."

"Some day soon I shall explain," she murmured. "Now, I have a favor to ask. Will you escort me to the opening of the opera house?"

"Of course," Mickey said, still puzzled.

Laura Lee walked from the room. She was deep in

reflection. Her father had only tried to protect her; her love for Nolan had been as fleeting as he had predicted. Only to herself would she admit that he never behaved like the romantic heroes she had read about in the novels. And his face was now foggy in her memory. Her lips trembled with emotion. Her small breasts rose and fell rapidly. She never expected Lolly to forgive her. She could never fully forgive herself. But the purge was helpful. She was torn by being sorrowful and unbearably happy.

When Jackson Turner made his intentions known, tickets for the opening night became auction items. It was to be a gala affair, with champagne on the house. When the bidding war got to $500 a ticket, J.T. would only sell them in pairs.

"Why's that?" Clarkson Ludlow mumbled.

"Hell! I want everybody in this town that owns a pair of tits there to give it some class."

"Where we gonna find such?"

"Well," he drawled, "had me a little talk with that Clara Bennett. Talked her into putting her new fillies on the auction block, after you and me get first pick. We gotta have something mighty nice on our arms, pard'ner."

A Greek named Alexander Pantages bid the highest to escort one of Clara's girls. While others sought riches from the ground, he collected it at a dollar a head in a log cabin he called the Orpheum Theater grinding out jerky silent films. His opposition in that enterprise, Sid Grauman, with his Chinese Theatre, bid second highest.

The other girls, as yet unseen in Dawson, went to the likes of Wilson and Addison Mizner—even though Wilson had schemed to do a ragtime number in the show—and millionaire miners like Big Alex McDonald.

Clara made it pointedly known that she expected Matt to escort her. Phoebe, who had stalled the departure of the *Brisbane II* because of the fire, had no trouble getting Crow to ask her.

Calvin smarted paying a thousand dollars just to take his own wife to the theater. As though it were a wicked thing to do, Amalida stayed away from her whiskey bottle the whole day. It was just as well, with the popping of champagne corks as frequent as the popping of firecrackers.

Only Judson Walsh and Edgar Mizner felt ill at ease. They sat in the Commissioner's box unattended, staring at the dazzling array that J.T. had assembled. The dance hall girls, who always dreamed of such a life, were less nervous than their escorts. Champagne and the first act soon put them at ease.

Murton made sure he opened the show with dazzle, sparkling music and beautiful women in daring costumes.

At first Judson had felt a little intimidated. The auditorium was overwhelming in the splendor of gilded chairs, velvet curtains and crystal chandeliers set in bronze scroll work—and the opposite box draped heavily in black.

A simple man, he thought wryly that Clara Bennett looked overdressed with Matt as her escort, paid little attention to Laura Lee and Mickey, but thought Harriet a dowdy addition to the group.

Calvin, in the next box, he recognized. With the lights up for the first intermission, he was amazed that a man like Calvin Ramsey possessed such a wife. Phoebe Hall and Calvin he could have pictured together. He didn't want to give Lonsworth Crowley a single thought. He was fuming enough that the Carmack box was filled with Indians.

But the second act made his jaw drop. Then, despite himself, he began to laugh. Here was excellent theater and fine comedians. Even the puns thrown at him as the commissioner he took in good grace.

Edgar Mizner took none of it in good grace. All he could see was the money that had slipped through his fingers because Addison had sold the opera house so quickly. The thought gave him such heartburn that he left before the start of the third act.

The houselights dimmed to blackness. A light came up on the callboard easel and a new card was placed. It meant nothing to anyone, but was a curiosity to a few.

Murton built the ten man orchestra to a rousing fanfare and then brought it down to a single violin.

"Ladies and gentlemen," a voice boomed out of the darkness, "the Dawson Opera House is proud to present 'A Tribute,' as sung by Miss Lolly Lollaine."

A murmur of confusion rippled through the audience again as the orchestra swelled again, the footlights began to glow, and the heavy velvet curtains slowly parted. The stage was almost bare, but at the back was a three-tiered platform upon which sat a high-backed cushioned chair, with its back turned three-quarters to the audience. A spotlight came up on it, bathing it in soft light. A woman stepped up to it and posed casually. The back of the chair covered all but her chest and head. The gown was cut low to her shapely breasts, giving the illusion of a long, haughty neckline. The dark brown hair flowed over her white shoulders, which seemed extended when she placed an arm on the top of the chair and seemed to let the handful of waxed roses droop and become a part of the needlepoint. The music swelled around her as she raised her head.

Lolly's eyes never left Murton's face. He had sprung this surprise in his quiet voice, but very firmly. She knew the music; only the words were changed. She had not been able to answer. He had rehearsed her over and over, until she was near numb. As Murton had said, this was just another rehearsal.

Her eyes widened on him. She was flushing like a startled young girl. The music hardly sounded the same.

"I sing of the legend of a man," she started. Her voice was unsteady, her mouth uncertain of the next words. Unseen stagehands began to push the platform forward.

She hesitated. She plucked a rosebud from her bunch of blossoms and bent and laid it gently on the chair seat. "I loved him, too," she sang. She looked down at Murton, and he smiled with confidence. "I loved him, true."

The music rose again and she looked up. Lolly felt a hard jolt in her chest. There was a sea of faces beyond Murton's nodding white head. She had to quickly look down to the chair seat and flower.

("Why do you think I ask you to do this?" Murton had cried. "To make the man with the backward collar live forever!")

She took out another rose and put it down as she began the legend of the man. Her voice rose and soared as she sang. She was singing what was in her heart. She could now lift her eyes and fill the opera house with her voice. Plaintive and then rousing. Joyous and then sad. Murton's words and music, her rendition, made very few not see him.

Matt could only watch and admire her striking figure clad in a black linen dress, simple and unadorned. Suddenly he was aware of no one else, not even those in the box. He felt a mixture of immeasurable joy for her, and pain and longing and desire. His mouth had become dry, with a metallic taste.

He was unaware of the stomping and pounding and wild applause. They called out her name until they were hoarse. They continued even after Murton had the curtain brought down and tried to start the number for the next act. The cheering would not subside.

A hand touched Matt's shoulder. He glanced up and saw Clara clearly, as he had never seen her before. This was not the worried look she normally had as though he were a child, leaving him reduced to laughter because she was just another woman for him to use. Clara was looking at him seriously, and the stage lights lit up her curls, and made her suddenly the innocent. Then he saw her pallor. The lights giving color only to her dress and her hair and her eyes. She looked desperately frightened.

He stood and put his hand on her partly bare arm. No one noticed when they left and went out into the corridor. Everyone was still demanding more of Lolly Lollaine.

Clara tried to speak, but it was some moments before she could. Even then it was hardly more than a whisper.

"How long have you loved her?"

"It doesn't matter. I killed her husband."

"In self-defense, as I hear it."

"I still killed him."

"Because of her?"

"Clara, she doesn't even know I'm alive."

She could look at him now; her eyes great with human understanding, and he did not know it was for him.

"Then she should know. I have never seen such a change in a person. She is worth a fortune."

"Is that all you can see?" he suddenly flared. "Is she just a piece of horse flesh?"

"That was an old 'Clara the Cow' trick, Matt," Clara said, unperturbed. "The tinkling bell to see who was alert and listening. You have it bad, my boy, real bad. You had best grab onto that brass ring quickly or this merry-go-round is going to spin away from you. I am going to have Bo take me home now. Everyone is coming to the house after the performance, you know."

She felt his warm hand on her flesh. She wanted to put her hand over his, to press it close and never let him go. But she knew she could not have him. His love for Lolly was not common desire. This was something deeper.

God help me, she thought, as she walked away. I'm giving him up without a fight! There was some sadness in the thought; one does not relinquish love that easily, unless one was in a profession whereby they never should have loved in the first place.

It seemed that everyone in Dawson passed in and out

through Clara's doors that night—except Mickey and Laura Lee.

They had walked back to the house hand in hand. She had not wanted to be with anyone. The evening had been too touching and personal.

"The only thing I worry about, Mickey, is that perhaps she might have made him more of a hero than he actually was."

He made an incredulous sound, and laughed. "That's what legends are all about!"

She sighed happily and squeezed his hand. He took heart and then grew tongue-tied. He had never had trouble expressing himself with a woman before. His handsome mouth literally watered for her, but he could think of nothing to say that was not chiché.

They were almost to the house when Matt came pounding up behind them, in a fit of rage.

"What's happened?" they asked, almost in unison.

"I went backstage," Matt growled. "I wanted to congratulate her and see if she was going up to Clara's. I could hardly get to her because of the pack of people around her. I thought Harriet and Amalida would never stop gushing."

"I see," Laura Lee said thoughtfully. "Go on!"

"Sure," he said, like a pouting little boy, "and have you two laugh at me. It was just horrible. I finally got up next to her and all of the millions of things I had thought to say went right out of my mind. And do you know what she did then?"

"No," they said as a duo.

"She was polite," he wailed. "She was so damn polite I couldn't stand it. I just had to leave."

Then they did laugh. Laughed until tears ran down their cheeks. Matt grew furious, banged into the house and crashed into the room he shared with Mickey.

When their laughter began to subside, Mickey bent and quickly kissed Laura Lee fully on the mouth.

"I–I . . ." she stammered in surprise. "Goodnight, Mickey."

She fled as quickly as Matt. Now Mickey was furious with Matt and himself. Had Matt not returned he knew that he would have been able to prolong that kiss and bring the words in his heart up to his lips.

Matt was on his bed fully clothed, face to the wall. Mickey had already decided not to say a single word to the man—maybe never again. He removed his clothing and put on a dressing robe that Calvin had loaned him. It reminded him of the man. He looked at himself in the mirror and tried to take a stance like Calvin. It wasn't ego that told him that he was far better looking than Calvin, it was honest fact.

He waited half an hour, impatiently. Finally Matt began to snore softly. Mickey hesitated. Then he opened the door and crept out, closing it after him. Again he hesitated, trying to formulate an excuse in his mind.

He walked lightly down the hall, and the excuses became reasonable, but he did not hurry. He tapped on Laura Lee's door. It opened at once.

Laura Lee, without a question on her pretty face, stood before him, clad in a nightgown as thin as diaphanous moonlight. Wordlessly, she put her arms about his neck and offered up her face. They kissed long and with rising passion.

"Oh, my God," Mickey whispered against her mouth, and kissed her again. "You're Catholic. Who is going to marry us?"

Laura Lee laughed softly. "I guess we will just have to do it the Tlingit way."

He carried her to the bed and lay down with her. He blew out the lamp and took her in his arms.

"I now belong to no other," she whispered, "or can be cast out with stones."

Mickey pulled her closer. He thought his heart would burst with joy.

15

As THE July days grew warmer so did the news of the Spanish-American War. The fastest way home, if one could afford it, was the riverboat to St. Michaels. For reasons of her own, Phoebe only plied the Yukon for the summer with the *Brisbane II.*

The exodus had begun.

Peter's canoe again brought more passengers down to Whitehorse than he carried cargo back. Front Street began to pile as high with miners' gear as had been the case the year before on Seattle streets. Everything was for sale to gain passage home—jewelry and furs, gold scales, picks and pans, boots and hats, satin dance hall dresses and staples. The price of flour dropped so rapidly that it went for less than the original price in Seattle. Daily, Harriet Henderson could be seen going from group to group, in a battered fedora hat and home-spun gray dress and shawl. Behind her one of her young boarders, dressed just as poorly, followed with a push cart. As though she were nothing more than a snaggle toothed haggler, she bartered for flour, sugar, salt, spices and live chickens. Most of her boarders were now clerks, woodcutters or carpenters, but even they, she knew, would not last forever. By the end of August she would have half of her loan paid back, and she was making sure she would have supplies to reopen the bakery to see her through the winter.

What had risen to nearly 35,000 began to dwindle daily.

The kingdom of J.M. Walsh was beginning to show cracks.

Four days after the Fourth of July, Jefferson Randolph Smith was shot in Skagway. The town went wild to rid itself of the rest of the henchmen of the "uncrowned King of Skagway." Sam Steele was elevated to superintendent of the North-West Mounted Police, with orders to clean up the whole territory.

When news of Soapy Smith's death reached Dawson the "insiders" decided to hold a secret meeting, and sent word to Steele of the questionable activities of McBridge. Over three hundred crammed into the opera house and the meeting was not secret for long. Judson, feeling he was Steele's superior, sent down his own report to Skagway and flatly denied Steele permission to come for an inspection tour.

Sam Steele came into town in one of Peter's canoes, dressed like a prospector. His face was too well known to McBridge's men. By morning McBridge didn't have any men—and the Bank of Ottawa was mysteriously short $300,000.

Faith in that bank failed. Calvin's business boomed. Just to get out before the lynch mob the bank officials were more than happy to sell out to Calvin—which Walsh heartily agreed upon. According to his estimation over $16 million in gold had been taken out of the diggings by that date. Calvin's estimate, which was far more accurate, put it quietly at $22 million. But even with access to a smelter again, Calvin could not get Crow to come back to work for him. Milton Brancher was made manager of the Bank of Ottawa.

There was one crack Walsh did not try to mend. Everyone in town wanted to help in the building of the orphanage and school. Addison Mizner had ordered a whole cargo load of bricks to build a replica of the Mizner home in San Francisco. When the bricks sold for a dollar apiece and were donated brick by brick for the construction, even Edgar had to rub his hands in glee.

The hospital fire had created thirteen orphans. The growing exodus created twenty-two more, some because families felt it cheaper to leave a child at the orphanage until they could secure passage money home for them. Others were the children of dance hall girls, who had made their summer fortune and didn't want to be bothered dragging their brats around any longer.

The mellow days of summer waned. The nights grew nippy. Shorter and shorter became the daylight hours. The new Mounties came. It only took four to replace McBridge's dozen. McBridge was not sorry to leave. His "take" from Soapy Smith's operation had made him a tidy fortune. Gambling and prostitution returned to pre-Soapy days.

Amazingly, J. M. Walsh remained on as commissioner. The government was very happy that he had been able to collect their "thirty percent" mineral tax without protest. Because he now feared the needle-nose of Sam Steele, he grandly announced that the government had "lowered" the tax to thirty percent. There was now a rush to all three banks—legal and otherwise. Men wanted their gold in the banks before the snow flew.

Matt, Laura Lee and Peter decided it was time to move the dirt piles from beneath the house and make them look like they came from the bench claim. Even they could not believe their total in each bank.

"But we've only scratched the surface," Matt assured them.

"By next summer, Big Alex tells me, there's going to be a lot of dumping of claims. Too many don't have the knowledge or equipment to get down to the rest of the gold. The big companies will come in and gobble everything up."

Matt looked at Mickey in amazement. "When did you get so friendly with Alex McDonald?"

"Building the orphanage. He also wants to put his kid in the school and his wife is the chairman of the parents who want to get all the kids in school."

"Kid? Wife? When did they arrive?"

Laura Lee giggled. "Matt, they have been here all along, but it isn't his child. He proposed the night the opera house opened and they were married the next day. But don't you go making a slip now. She goes by Mrs. Gertrude McDonald."

"Diamond Toothed Gertie!" he gasped.

"I told you not to make a slip," she laughed. "Mrs. McDonald now goes in for philanthropy and social causes. She spearheaded the drive, with Belinda and Harriet, to get Walsh to reduce the room and board tax. And she is no dummy. From those who are leaving, she's been buying every kerosene lamp and candle for the orphanage and school."

"Why? I thought Addison had designed that for the latest in electrical wiring and fixtures?"

"He did," Mickey said, "but Gertrude remembered what winter electricity was like in the Montana camps. The generators are run by waterwheels, just like here. Where do we get our electricity when the Klondike freezes solid?"

"I never would have believed it of her."

"Many think of winter now," Peter mused. "The wandering caribou are not to be found. Moose are becoming scarce. The great black and brown bears are hibernating early. Wolves already howl in the hills. Each trip I make for Mizner, I make one for the village. Winter will come soon and stay long. If you stay, prepare well." He looked at Laura Lee and Mickey. He was very pleased with their marriage. Here was a man who was taming her into a good wife.

"My brother and sister," he continued. "You have many young mouths to think about. Think of what they will eat next May and not this September."

"Next May," Matt mused. "Big Alex is right. Even J.T. feels there is a good $300 million yet uncovered. This may sound crazy, but I wonder if I shouldn't go back to the states for the knowledge and equipment that we are going to need next summer."

"You're crazy, all right—crazy like a red fox," Peter said with a grin. "Such a fox has three to four dens, each stocked as if it is the only one for a whole winter. He can move from one to the other, hunting in between, hardly touching his supplies. You make a winter den to learn more about this one."

"But that would leave no one on this property," Matt frowned.

"What about Crow? Closer here for him to work for Miss Clara than the village."

This was almost as much a surprise to Matt as the McDonald marriage.

"When did he go to work for her? What is he doing?"

"If you got off this property once in awhile, Matthew Monroe," Laura Lee chided, "you would know what is going on in the world. He's been converting the old bank area and smelter into a real furnace to heat that huge barn. Clara is going to stable her fillies comfortably for the winter. Don't you ever see her? Don't you ever see *anyone*?"

Matt knew exactly what Laura Lee meant by "anyone." Like a sulking boy he had avoided the opera house or anywhere else he thought he might run into Lolly. And he was now too embarrassed even to see Clara.

"Yes," he said, but not in answer to her question. "I think it would be wise for me to go and learn. I can take the *New Racket* the next time it goes to St. Michaels."

Laura Lee smiled to herself. "The *Brisbane II* leaves tomorrow for Seattle. Phoebe came to say goodbye. She wants to get one more shipment back up here before winter."

Matt nodded. Tomorrow would not be soon enough for him. He suddenly wanted to get back to where he could look at a woman as a woman, and forget the ache in his heart.

Peter was right, the first snows came before August had a chance to turn into September.

The Carmacks returned to their Tagfish village, with Skookum Jim and Tagfish Charlie taking Henry on to San Francisco. Mickey had advised an education for the young man so that the Carmack millions could be wisely handled. No one would dare try to jump Carmack's four claims—they were too well established.

Now a new form of money making came into being—"claim sitting." For those who weren't interested in running off to the war, and thought they could winter it out in a claim shack, they were supplied with food, ammunition and $500 a month. That was still more than a family of four needed to live on for a whole year in the lower states.

Jackson Turner and Clarkson Ludlow had so enjoyed their opera house evening that they thought they would make a winter of being "young again" in San Francisco.

Dawson's population began to dwindle, but would level off at about 15,000 winter residents.

There was elbow room once again at the Monte Carlo, which was now owned by Ned Bailey. Bill McPhee's Pioneer Saloon began to offer free lunches. The opera house closed so that Murton could write and direct a whole new show.

The night of the first freeze Harlan Henderson died quietly in his sleep. His room was redone for Lolly and Kimberly Sue. Harriet had a room on the first floor for herself. She was down to twenty boarders for the winter and began to train her push cart boarder as a baker. She would still do the cooking for her "boys."

By October, Dawson was snowbound.

Lolly heard the sleighbells coming down the street and smiled to herself. Only Clara would have thought to have a sleigh brought up from Seattle for her on Phoebe's last trip. There were no large bells, but hundreds of tiny ones that tinkled much like those about her neck.

Lolly grunted and straightened in the chair. She knew the baby would have to be a boy. It weighed a ton and wore her out. Still, never had she felt such ebullience. For the first time she really wanted the child, because she knew she could take care of it.

The tinkle of the bells came down the hall, almost drowned out by laughter. The door flew open and Clara sailed in.

"That woman," she roared with laughter, "is exactly what people call her—a character. I'm glad I am not in competition with her. She gets away saying things to her boarders that I would be slapped for."

She threw back the hood of the sealskin parka, her golden head braided into coils over each ear. Even in mukluks and sealskin trousers like the Indian women it did not distract from her beauty and feminine grace.

"Clara, thank you for coming. I didn't mean for you to run here the moment I whistled."

"Nonsense," she said, slipping out of the parka. Beneath it she wore a sweater of soft white wool. "I had to come down today to see Edgar Mizner. That skinflint sold me kerosene barrels that were only three-quarters full."

"I didn't know you did business with the Mizners."

"Lolly," she laughed, pulling up a chair, "with what Wilson spends at my place, I thought it only fair to put a mite back into their family coffers. Now tell me—how are you?"

"Fine, except for my legs. They are so filled with water that I can hardly stand."

"I told you to give up the show when I saw you in September. I told you that you would have trouble with your legs."

"Oh, Clara," she laughed. "It was only a couple of songs a night and I leaned on the chair most of the time. Besides, what made you such an authority on the subject?"

Clara roared with delight. "About two to three hundred girls passing in and out of my life. Honestly, Lolly, I want you staying off your feet. How soon now?"

"I figure a couple of weeks," she sighed. "Oh, the reason I sent for you was that Lola Ferguson paid me the rest of what she owed me on my shack." She drew a linen napkin out from under the afghan across her lap. "You will find two thousand dollars in each of the two knotted ends. That was the loan and now we have to figure out a new percentage. Nolan never went into the lumber business, you know."

Clara was taken aback. "How did you gather up so much?"

Because it was Clara, Lolly didn't figure it was a rude question. "Well, I told you I was selling my shack, and I was making a hundred a night at the opera house. But when Murton announced that it was the last week to see Lolly Lollaine, the men started throwing nuggets and coins onto the stage each night. Maybe you should be getting a percentage of that."

"Maybe I should," Clara chuckled. "But tell me, who came up with such a stagey name like 'Lolly Lollaine'?"

Lolly looked a little hurt. "What do you mean, stagey? Why, Clara—that's my own name. Lollaine Fedderson—only my folks pronounced it as Loll-ann. Murton rolls it out as Low-lane. Mr. Pantages said it sounds like one of the actresses in his moving pictures. Do you know I still haven't seen one. I wonder what it would be like to see yourself in one?"

"Lolly, if they ever figure out a way to put sound with the picture, you *would* see yourself. You have such a beautiful voice."

"Go on. I only sang that tribute song because Murton needed me, and then a fill-in number because Myrtle McCoy got sick. Why, Murton isn't even using me in the new show. It's back to wardrobe after I have the baby."

Clara stared at her in amazement. She really doesn't know her God-given talents, she thought. Everyone in town, but her, knows that Murton was writing his holiday opening show with her as the star.

"Well," Clara snickered, "I hope you enjoy the costumes."

Lolly got thoughtful again. "Which brings me back to the percentage, Clara. I don't know if they will pay me the same for wardrobe, but what will I still owe you?"

"Child, you have already paid me back in full. Neither of us could help what happened to Nolan. No one is doing up here what they set out to do—except maybe Matt. Crow works for me and Mickey is teaching school. Because of circumstances I have held them to the full bargain. Because of the—the way Nolan left you, I consider your debt fully paid."

"Nolan didn't leave me pregnant," Lolly said frankly. Her breath made a loud rustle in the room. Because it involved the money she felt she had to be perfectly honest with Clara. "Nolan hardly ever touched me after he started going around with Laura Lee. It was another."

"Matt?" Clara asked, in dread.

"Matt!" Lolly was incredulous. "Whatever made you think of him? Why, he's just about the best friend I ever did have."

It was Clara's turn to be stunned. "You can say that, even though he killed your husband?"

Lolly paled. "It took a long time, Clara, for Father Henry to make me see what really happened that night.

My husband was a bully. I cannot hate Matt for what happened."

"Do you love him?"

Lolly blinked and giggled. "Oh, Clara, be reasonable. I am about the last person in the world that Matt Monroe would fall in love with, so it would be foolish for me to even think about it."

Clara held her silence. It wasn't her place to disclose Matt's feelings. Nor did it have anything to do with her own personal feelings toward Matt. She simply felt that Matt would have to speak for himself.

"And the father?" she finally asked.

"Unimportant," Lolly said cryptically.

"He doesn't know?"

"Certainly not," Lolly laughed. "After he tried that one time, for a loan payment, he was too scared to come back, I guess. Oh, I didn't mean it that way. I didn't want him to come back."

Clara quickly changed the subject. One clue had told her more than she wanted to know. She had come to like Amalida and to detest Calvin. But she was successful partly because she could hide her real feelings about people when necessary.

Clara hefted the napkin. "That's a good honest weight, Lolly."

"Better be," Lolly laughed. "I never could get the pinch method down right and finally had to buy a pair of scales. Funny the things you have to learn to live here that you never had to know before."

Winter had reduced the Mounty force to two. The banks again would give only paper money in exchange for gold, and Calvin Ramsey had become the greatest enforcer of the rule. The people did not like the paper money. They liked even less the fact that they had no electricity after the steep prices paid. Mainly, they didn't like Judson Walsh. With only two Mounties about he became quite dictatorial again, pegging the paper value of the money at a different rate for friend or foe. As Calvin was slowly becoming his only friend, they were both reaping huge profits on the paper exchange.

Smoke billowed from the tall chimneys of the mansion as Bo charged the horses back up the hill. Gone were the days when the smoke would have brought O'Toole on the run to check on the smelter. Everyone knew of the vast new heating system and the tons of coal that had been brought in for it on the *Brisbane II.*

Bo took the sleigh around to the old bank-sanctuary entrance. The waiting room, offices and general area had been redone as Clara's private office and retreat. It was a far cry from the rooms above. Here were dark wooded walls, heavy walnut furniture, chintz and copper and a colonial feeling. It was warmth and comfort.

Beyond the old general bank area partition, which was now brick, little had changed. A wood plank walkway still stretched to the kitchen door. The wood stacks were now coal bins, and duct arms jutted from the boiler like an octopus, sending a constant supply of steam and hot water up to the radiators. The furnace now sat in a brick wall, but the smelter was gone.

Clara stopped in her own sanctuary only long enough to rid herself of the parka and mukluks. In furry slippers she entered the furnace room, but did not stay on the wood-plank walk. She went right up to the blank brick wall and pushed in a loose brick. A section no larger than a door swung open and she stepped through, closing it behind her.

Beyond the brick wall was the rear of the furnace, the smelter, equipment and work tables of old.

"Hello, genius."

"Hello, sweetheart!"

"Don't be fresh," Clara chuckled.

Crow grinned. "I have to be fresh with someone. I was sure hoping that Phoebe would get frozen in here for the winter."

Clara pulled a high stool up to the worktable. "Just be thankful she got you all of your supplies on the last run. Besides, she needs the winter to get ready for a spring wedding."

Crow slowly broke the lead mold in two. "That scares me. Why couldn't we have just been married like Laura Lee and Mickey?"

"Because Laura Lee had all the advantages of being a lady for all of her life. Give Phoebe the fun and excitement of being a bride."

"How would you know being a bride was fun and exciting?" he kidded, dusting the talc from the object he took from the mold.

"Don't be a smart ass. Every girl knows that feeling in her dreams. It's not as if I've never been in love, you know. As a matter of fact I am in love right now."

Crow stopped his work. "I thought you said you had gotten Matt out of your system."

"I am not speaking of Matt," Clara smiled.

"Who then?"

Clara sighed. "It's not a 'who,' Crow. It's a 'what.' I always looked at an area and a house for what I could get out of it. I'd make my profit and move on. This monster of a house I love. From my bedroom window I can see mountains and rivers and sky. I know the gold won't last forever—it never does in places like this. One morning someone will come into town hollering about another strike and everyone will move on. They will abandon their cabins and this might well become a ghost town. Moss will grow on the logs of the cabins and in the summer the aging, sagging sod roofs will become gardens of wild flowers. Man will be gone, but the mountains will still stand and the Yukon will keep flowing. . . ." Her voice trailed off, and then, as though embarrassed to be caught in a sentimental mood, she laughed as if it had been a joke.

"What new surprise have you for me, Crow?" she asked after a pause.

"This," he beamed, handing her the object from the mold.

"Why, it's just a doorknob," she said, obviously not impressed.

Crow laughed heartily. "A solid gold doorknob worth about $800. I have counted, and you will need eighty-four of them for your little monster house."

"The clients will steal them!"

Crow leaned forward, a serious expression on his face now. "No more than they will steal the gold statues that I covered in plaster of paris. The doorknobs will be dipped in white enamel, Clara. Except for working capital, every bit of gold you get from your clients has to be put into something that you can move out without suspicion."

Clara smiled. "Your work is beautiful, Crow, but isn't it a shame we have to stoop to their level of trickery?"

Crow's eyes were narrow slits as he studied the molds on the table. "It was good that I learned what I did from Calvin—and that I left him thinking I was just a dumb Indian. After all, he's smelting down the gold deposits from summer and fall."

"But he calls his operation a bank."

Crow smiled. "Speaking of which, I had Peter talk to the smelter foreman at each bank. They were more than delighted to let his men come with baskets and carry off the slag and ash. It certainly keeps our furnace room clean, too."

Clara was gloomy. "How long will it take Calvin to sniff the little ruse out?"

"Spring," Crow laughed. "Wait until he learns that the Tlingit have been making bricks all winter out of the residue."

"And that we have also been making bricks of a different nature for Matt?" she asked.

"That he will never learn, unless he recalls Kate Carmack's old trick. I only bring so much each day hidden under my parka and strapped to my legs. I return with nothing at night. And don't forget that Matt said you will get a percentage of it because of your loan to him and Mickey."

That was a bright side. Still, she hated the conspiracy.

On November 8, 1898, Matthew and Mark Fedderson were born. They were not identical twins. Matthew was a pretty baby, Mark was moon-faced and husky.

Two weeks later the first mail for that winter came in by dog sled from Whitehorse.

Walsh came to Calvin's office, his face white and still.

"It's Laurier," he groaned. "Damn that French-speaking liberal. Damn the Canadian provinces for electing a parliament that made him Prime Minister."

"Would you please sit down and explain what you are mumbling about."

"Sir Wilfrid Laurier," he whispered, as though the man was in the next room, "is going to ruin us by bringing the provinces together in union. The banks are being nationalized, Calvin. Because of our location it will not be until spring, but we are ordered to curtail all unnecessary operations until then. No new money is to be printed, because only Ottawa will print the standard money after the first of the year."

"I see," Calvin said slowly. "Well, we shall just have to learn to live with that problem—come spring."

Walsh's face cleared, but only momentarily.

"Spring will bring the worst. The Minister of the Interior is naming new commissioners—Commissioners of Mining. They want the big companies in and are going to give them tax breaks for getting the minerals out faster. Not just gold, but copper, zinc and everything else."

"Again, I say, let us wait for spring. And let's be sure that no one knows of this but you and I."

After he was gone, Calvin sat back, grinning. The news would be kept from the Bank of Canada and the two Mounties. He would keep on printing money through the Bank of Ottawa, although it would be worthless after January. As a matter of fact, he saw no reason not to flood Dawson with the money throughout the winter. His private assets were in gold, locked in boxes hidden in the upstairs apartment. Then his thoughts turned to spring—and departure. His books would prove that he turned the bank over to the government as an honest operation. Walsh would just have to swim against his own current.

The next day Amalida came to Calvin's office. She was deeply troubled.

"I—I went to see Lolly and the babies today, Calvin. I hope no one else can see what I see. Your mother, I am sure, would marvel at the sight of little Matthew."

"All babies look alike," Calvin said heavily.

"Hardly true, Calvin. They are your children, without a doubt."

"That is hardly possible," he replied, with a haughty shrug.

Amalida laughed bitterly. "Oh, Calvin, I have been as naive as Lolly about certain things. For years I thought our inability to have children was due to your wasting yourself on whores. Oh, yes, I told you that I didn't believe father's stories . . . but, when a woman goes loveless and barren she'll eventually believe anything. Lolly knows the truth about it, and so do I—now."

He stormed up from his desk, his face black with wrath. "She discussed it with you?"

Amalida remained calm. "You might say I discussed it with her, after viewing Matthew."

"Damn bitch!" he growled. "Why didn't she get rid of it like all other whores do?"

"Mainly," Amalida said simply, "because she is not a whore."

"What is she then?" he demanded.

"More than I am," she said, rising. "But not more than I intend to become."

"What in the hell do you mean by that?"

"Laura Lee has a little orphan boy who is below school age. I have the time and the room to see to him upstairs."

"What!" he snorted. "I don't think I like the idea."

"I don't care what you think. I'm not doing it for you, Calvin. I'm doing it for myself."

"Do you think you can stay sober long enough to care for him?" he sneered.

"Quite," she said curtly, "because I shall not be lonesome, and I'll have no need to drink."

She blew him a mocking kiss and walked out. Calvin was reminded once more how much of life was not under his control.

Amalida Ramsey was not the only one to see the resemblance. Clara saw it, but she had already had a hint of forewarning. Harriet saw it, clamped her lips tight, and cornered Clara on her way out.

"I have good steady boarders for the winter and the bakery is doing well again, but I need money."

"Why?"

Harriet raised her eyes to the ceiling, as though looking right through to Lolly's room. "Because of that I want to pay Calvin Ramsey off in full."

It was the first Clara knew of the loan. "How much do you owe him?"

"I've reduced the $60,000 down to $28,000 and still kept right up with the one percent a day interest," she boasted proudly.

Clara was both impressed and chagrined. She had been so busy with her own business affairs she was not aware of the Dawson interest rates. Unlike the old days, these clients didn't have to come to her from time to time for a loan. Perhaps, she thought, Harriet was opening a long unused door—and one that could quietly punish Calvin Ramsey. She didn't mind making interest on her money, but she liked to sleep at night. Then she had a sudden inspiration.

"Harriet, how do you normally pay Calvin?"

Harriet didn't fully understand. "Just when I get enough profit ahead each month."

"I mean do you pay in paper money or gold?"

"Oh, I see. He loaned me gold coins and expects gold in return."

Clara giggled devilishly. "But even his own banks insist that we deal only in paper money. Even I have to accept it from some clients, if I want to keep them as clients."

She was thinking mainly of Calvin himself, but even though she detested the man, she had a standing rule never to discuss her clients with outsiders.

"It's good, isn't it?"

Before Clara could answer, two boarders came in to go to their rooms. They had to go through the bakery, which served as the dining room for their evening meal, to get to the stairs. One of them, a man named Milton Brancher, looked at Clara as though she were a loathsome thing. It was not because of her profession, but because she refused to have an account in the Bank of Ottawa.

"The babies are delightful," she said cheerily. "Put a shawl over your head and see me out, Harriet."

Harriet did so, a little bit confused.

The snow was falling, but they paid no attention to it. Here only Bo's ears could hear.

"LeRoy McQuestan quietly got word down from Circle City to his manager here. After the first of the year he is not to accept any of the local paper money for goods. I can easily loan you the $28,000 in paper now, if you can make Calvin accept it."

"I think I can convince him to accept it," Harriet said.

"I've heard him say it's legal tender." Then she frowned. "Lots of folks going to be hurt if that paper money all goes sour in the new year, if you heard right."

"I heard right, Harriet. If the American side had heard that the government is issuing new money, it stands to reason that the Canadian side has heard and is purposely keeping quiet. Just protect yourself."

"Myself," Harriet said, a mite strangely. "This is your first winter, Clara. Your house is warm with that furnace, your cupboards brimming with food, and servants to fix it and shovel away the snow. Don't take me wrong, but it wasn't like last winter. We were the 'outsiders' and had to fight to become the 'insiders.' Some helped us in that fight. Belinda . . . McPhipps . . . others. I can't just protect myself—there are others who will need help."

Clara understood, and kissed her lightly on the cheek. It reminded her of one more reason why she was in love. It was the people. As the Earl of Minto had said in his introductory letter: it would be "the industry of few, for the future of many."

The holiday season brought a return of the opera house and Lolly Lollaine. Candlelight, kerosene footlights and spruce garlands added to the Christmas flavor of Murton's music, and Lolly's beauty. The whole town turned out for her opening performance, and it seemed that all of Dawson was in high spirits.

But on February 30th of that year a pall was cast over every man, woman and child in Dawson.

The majority of the people took LeRoy McQuestan's refusal to accept paper money as an insult, and brought their business to the Mizners. Edgar gloated, taking in the paper money by the handful.

To the delight of the bartenders, Ned Bailey and Bill McPhee brought back the gold dust pinch for a drink by the first of February. To keep their business, the Aurora Saloon had to follow suit.

The roomers at the Fairview Hotel had to start paying Belinda in gold, as did Harriet Henderson's boarders. Milton Brancher had no problem. He just quietly exchanged his paper payroll wages for gold out of the Bank of Ottawa vault. He had feared something like this would happen ever since Calvin gave the order for the mass printing of money.

By March the second, what had been known to just a few was realized by the many. The paper money was worthless. Confidence in it melted like a snowflake on a dog's tongue. The three banks were besieged by men and women demanding gold for the value of the paper money to buy the necessities. Even Edgar Mizner now refused the paper money and groaned over the stacks he had accumulated.

Those with deposits began demanding full withdrawals—in gold, of course.

On the twentieth, Calvin finally persuaded Walsh to announce the nationalization of the banks, and close the doors for thirty days for audit purposes.

Those who had been forewarned did not suffer. Those who had not been roamed from saloon to saloon, and threatened to form a vigilante squad.

16

"MURTON," LOLLY said in a low voice, "I don't think the song is right for me."

"Just sit for a moment and let me tinker with it."

Lolly had learned early on that self-control was important in dealing with Murton. He could go for hours on end without food or rest. She still tired quite easily since the birth of the twins, and right now her self-control was nearly exhausted.

"Why? It is only the twentieth of April. If the temperature stays at forty-five below we have many weeks before opening."

"I want to tell you something, Lolly," Murton said. "I think you are very special, very talented. I think you have a vocation."

Beneath the blue wool of her dress, she clenched her hands together. She would not hurt Murton for anything on earth, but each time she stepped on the stage she died a million deaths.

"But it is nearly two o'clock in the morning, Murton."

The pianist gave her a somber glance. "When you have music in your soul, Lolly, there are no hands on the clock."

She was not deluded by him; she knew his faults, though she loved him deeply. "Tomorrow, please."

"But I will have this in a moment."

"Tomorrow, please . . . please."

He looked at her beautiful profile, the lips set firmly, the haunted expression, the long lashes shading the oval eyes, the soft hair falling onto her shoulders. Oh, what a great star he could make of her if she'd only give him the chance.

"All right! All right!" he said gruffly. "Tomorrow it is, then. Bundle up warmly—it's cold out tonight."

Lolly obeyed, thankful for the chance to go home. She raced out of the windowless rehearsal room, down the back stairs to the opera house stage and up through the dark auditorium. It was pitch black, but she knew the way well. Once outside she stopped dead, the cold hitting her like a hammer blow. She tucked her mouth and nose into the folds of the parka and hurried down the street and around the corner.

The tinkle of a piano filtered out from the Pioneer Saloon, but no sound of customers. The next few shops were dark and forlorn. She turned the corner, heading toward the bakery, warmth and sleep.

She dodged hastily along the jagged pathway that had been cut through the eight-foot snowbanks. Tunnels led to the silent Aurora Saloon, Calvin's bank and the Yukon Hotel.

There was a rosy glow on the snowbank in front of the hotel that lit her way. She had only a half a block to go and she would be . . .

She stopped short, and looked at the growing light that wavered on the snow. When she turned back her worst fears were realized. The whole top floor of the hotel was ablaze.

"Fire! Fire!" she screamed and rolled down into the street. The street was two worn frozen ruts that she fell in and out of, the jagged ice was as sharp as broken glass. Even as she raced for the log cabin which served as the fire house, the glow in the sky grew.

The second burst of flame came from the second floor of the Aurora Saloon—the private apartment of Judson Walsh.

The first fire had been started with careful timing. Judson had let Freda Winslow slumber after bringing her up from the saloon. She had been very drunk. Making an exit by her window, he set the lamp right next to the gauzy curtains and made his way across the bank roof to his own apartment. When he saw that Freda's room was aflame, he set his own apartment on fire. He was determined to burn out the traitor Calvin Ramsey between the two buildings. His kingdom was in a shambles and he was determined to make Calvin pay for helping to bring it about. Nothing else mattered to him.

Lolly found the fire house dark. She pounded and screamed at the door. Then, to her amazement, she found the door slightly ajar and pulled it open. The unused new fire engine sat just inside with the fires out, and the steam pumpers cold and empty.

"Is anybody here?" she yelled.

A few heads popped up from the cots.

"What in the hell do you want?" someone demanded.

"Want?" she spat. "The Yukon Hotel is on fire!"

"Go tell Walsh," someone yawned. "He paid us with that paper money we can't buy anything with, so we're on strike."

For once, Lolly was thankful Nolan had left her something that was useful—lumberjack jargon.

"Listen, you donkey ends, the people of this town paid for that equipment. Now, drop that warm thing you're holding and get out here and man a real hose!"

By the time they were in action, with some still trying to light a fire in the steam pumper, the whole of the hotel was on fire, and from the saloon flames were shooting straight up into the sky and back onto the Front Street buildings.

The dim streets were now filled with dogs, howling and yapping, men shouting and yelling, and women screaming and crying.

Lolly made her way to the bakery, where the noise had awakened everyone and brought them out into the freezing weather in their nightclothes.

"Get the children out of here," Lolly screamed at Harriet. "Take them up to Clara's."

"Piffle," said Harriet, who wanted to use a stronger word. Then she paused, as she saw that the flames were whipping quickly along toward the bakery. "Oh, shit!"

Lolly didn't stop to hear more. Her immediate concern was to warn Murton.

People now blocked her from getting back quickly. The buildings in peril were being evacuated of what could be saved. She scurried past Amalida carrying out a canary cage from the bank building. As she was rounding the corner she saw Bill McPhee dart from his blazing saloon, an enormous moosehead wrapped tenderly in his huge arms.

Front Street was a madhouse. The firemen had stretched their hoses to the riverfront wharf and built fires to melt through the ice. Others came with axes to chop at the ice, but quickly found that the metal shattered on impact.

"Dynamite it!" a fireman shrieked.

Judson Walsh, his scheme grown out of hand, was still quick to protest.

"I forbid its use by the miners a long time ago—and I still forbid it!"

"I know where it's stored," said Starnes of the Mounted Police, his face grim. "Come on, men!"

Walsh dared not stop him. He had set out to ruin Calvin Ramsey and was ruining all. He went to where he had a dog sled hidden, his fortune safely tucked aboard, and left Dawson blazing behind him.

A pack of several hundred sled dogs, crazed by the uproar, also fled the town. They howled down the frozen river, answering wolf calls from the hills.

Judson's dogs also answered and became uncontrollable. The pack snarled and raced past the sled and dogs. Judson's lead dog would not be outdistanced. He raced on after the pack and Judson screamed, but was unable to stop him and his charges. They left the river and charged up into the timbered hillsides, battering man and sled between the trees until their harnesses broke, and they were free to join the ancient wolf pack and never return.

Only when someone assured her that they had seen Murton come out of the opera house would Lolly stop screaming about getting inside.

The dynamite had still not arrived, but holes had been made through the ice and the hand pumps were manned. The water began to fill the hoses, which quickly froze and became useless.

"Jesus!" a fireman screamed, as the leather seams burst with a crackling pop. "The whole town is going to go!"

Starnes and his men came running up at that moment with the wooden dynamite crates. "We've got to blow up the buildings around the fire to stop it from spreading. Do it, now!"

"No!" came an anguished cry. "My bank vault!"

"Stuff it, Ramsey," Starnes bellowed, waving to the men to start setting up the charges.

Calvin stumbled back. A fog made by the heart of the fire hitting the cold air above was settling down, obscuring his view.

He retraced his steps, unbelieving. He had been able to get his personal boxes out of the apartment and onto the street, but the bank vault contained . . . for the first time ever figures would not stay in his brain. He grew confused. The smoke and fog impeded his vision. The snow was melting around him, becoming slush under his feet as he ran. Then he saw a familiar archway.

The door was open, because he hadn't closed it when he had brought out the boxes. He had left the boxes with Amalida when he had gone to the fire house for help.

But Amalida was of no help to him, and now he would have to save the contents of the vault by himself.

As he stepped through the archway a tremendous blast shook the earth, and seemed to awake the ancient gods in the mountains and make them quiver. Calvin turned at the wrong archway, and as he realized it he turned back. Suddenly, the Aurora collapsed in a pile of rubble upon him.

The explosions continued on both sides of the block. The Monte Carlo went. The Bank of Ottawa went. The Henderson bakery and rooming house went.

But the fire was kept from spreading to the Fairview Hotel and the Mizner store.

Then an explosion burst the vault Calvin had tried to save. Even though they were held back by the intense heat, the milling crowd could plainly see the stacks of paper money crinkle to ash, the mass of nuggets, gold dust and coins melt into a solid lump in the soggy snow.

But it was not important now. Stumbling and exhausted, they had to work through the whole next day before the fire was finally extinguished.

No one paid much attention to Amalida as she huddled on the wooden crates, with the child she had been taking care of clutched to her breast, until Milton Brancher came along.

The drunken, foolish bitch! thought Milton vindictively. He had never liked Amalida at the best of times. Now, with Calvin dead and both banks in ashes, he saw her as a burden.

"What shall I do with you?" he said curtly.

"See to the boxes," she said, as though they had just

that moment been delivered to the street. "Have them taken up to Clara Bennett."

"Mrs. Ramsey," he said rudely, "how can you think of boxes when your husband lies dead under that rubble?"

Amalida looked at him oddly. "You've got to live for yourself the second time, if you make it off the glacier the first time."

He thought her totally mad and quickly got her, the child and the boxes off the street and up the hill to Clara Bennett.

Now Lolly knew grief. Murton had died in the fire. Lolly and others would cry for him, but there were few tears shed for Calvin and Walsh.

Even as the intense cold held the town tightly in its grip, they began to clear away the rubble. A million dollars worth of property was gone, with most of the major buildings gutted.

The Bank of Canada, unsure what to do with Walsh dead, did nothing. It was left for the "insiders" to see to themselves. Clara, Big Alex and McQuestan found themselves in the loan business. After Crow talked with Laura Lee and Peter, Matt's gold was put out on loan. Edgar Mizner was quite willing to loan, but no one wanted his paper money.

As May brought the first thaw, miners came straggling into Dawson from their cabins on creeks and in gulches. They saw a more permanent Dawson rising with Peter's bricks and Ladue's lumber.

That year the Yukon broke up with a whimper and not a roar. But the thousands who came down the river behind the ice cakes were a different breed from those who had arrived the spring before. They were engineers with new kinds of mining equipment: hydraulic hoses to wash down the hillsides, and big dredges to work through the mud of the creek bottoms.

At first they had a problem getting a toehold. The new Commissioner of Mining was sympathetic to their desire, but he had many Walsh problems to straighten out first. The Bank of Canada was in a similar mess, trying to nationalize and handle the affairs of the other two banks with all of their records destroyed. Milton Brancher tried to go by memory as to the size of each account that was to share in the melted gold. Amazingly, he was quite accurate in almost all cases.

The *Brisbane II* brought Matt back with his equipment. It also brought Phoebe Hall, who was quite ready for the largest formal wedding Dawson had ever seen.

Everyone was family on that day. After giving away his daughter, Foster Hall gave the *Brisbane II* as his wedding gift to Crow and Phoebe.

The Yukon breed were splitting up. Crow and Phoebe would honeymoon on the ship and then run it. Amalida would return on the *Brisbane II* with the locked boxes. She did not have to know the contents. She figured it was about triple what she and Calvin had arrived with and ample to make her comfortable for the rest of her life.

Belinda Mulroney, who had become part of the breed through friendship, would return on the ship with Pierre Carbonneau. Rather than rebuild the bakery, Harriet had bought the Fairview Hotel from her with another loan from Clara. Belinda and Pierre combined their fortunes and their lives as the Count and Countess de Carbonneau of Paris.

Other insiders decided to leave on the ship. The George Carmacks hungered for their son. The four claims were sold to the Montreal Mining Corporation for $100,000 each.

Jackson Turner and Clarkson Ludlow, who had come up on the spring run of the *Brisbane II*, were devastated over the loss of the opera house and Murton. And even J.T. couldn't answer the question most often asked since the fire. Even he had forgotten if Murton had more of a name than just Murton. They sold their claims to the Treadwell Mines for an undisclosed amount.

Another undisclosed amount was what the Dunn brothers would take back to Mormon Utah with them, after releasing their "lay" claim back to Big Alex McDonald.

The winter had been too much for four of Clara's girls and they, too, would return.

Lolly knew she would never sing again, except to her children, even though Alexander Pantages wanted to take her back to the United States as his protegee. She had made a little over $6,000 on the holiday show and had become quite a seamstress in the wardrobe department. She figured her stake was ample enough to establish a small dress shop in Seattle or Portland.

There was one good-bye she felt had not been properly said at the wedding reception.

Matt stood very still, remembering what the property had been like when Henry Boise was alive. Where the house had stood was a mine shaft building. From a shed came the pounding of the steam engine that ran the hydraulic hoses and jack-hammers eating down into the earth. He couldn't know it then, but he stood above a vein of ore that would eventually produce as much as everything so far taken out of Dawson by hand. Up the hill was a bunk house for the ten miners he had brought from Seattle. Men well versed in this type of mining. Farther up the hill the dynamite was stored that would soon rip up the hill even more.

"Just what you didn't want happening to the land, Henry," he said to himself.

He turned away from it. He gazed at the rest of the land about him, the untouched beauty, and felt sick at heart. He knew that a scar similar to the one he was inflicting on the land here was being made at both Bonanza and Eldorado creeks. He had pleaded with the new commissioner to establish a special tax for reclamation of the land after the companies were finished with a claim. Because of all the left-over Walsh problems the plea had fallen on deaf ears. The man, in this way, was even worse than Walsh. He was only interested in letting them get the minerals out of the ground; tomorrow could take care of itself, was his attitude.

A movement caught his eye. It was Lolly on the path alone. As the wind moved her dark hair off her face, he could see her profile, strong and clear and pensive. He felt like crying. He could hear his heart beat in his ears, and feel it throbbing in his temples. Lolly. Her name was a note of ecstasy to him, of longing mingled with despair. How was he ever going to say goodbye to her?

He stood in silence until she came closer and sensed his presence. She looked up and brushed the hair from her eyes.

"Matt," she said, as if she had expected him to be right at that spot.

He said her name slowly as he went toward her. She looked at him gravely. He wore miners' clothes, but as usual he was hatless, his blond curls catching the sunlight. His face was eloquent, though he did not know it, his hazel eyes shone and his mouth trembled at the corners.

"Matt," Lolly said again, and her voice was a husky whisper. "I've come to say good-bye."

"I don't want you to go," he said, taking her hand.

"There is nothing to keep me and the children here."

"Why did you name him Matthew?" he asked quickly, holding her hand tighter.

"Because you were always such a dear, good friend to me," she said, her voice soft and comforting.

They were silent. She moved her hand in his as if she would take it away. He held it tighter. A shadow ran over her profile, and she was reminded of Clara's words—words that had haunted her all winter and made her wonder. The minute she had seen the first twin born she had known he had to be a Matthew. She had vowed at that moment to raise both her sons to be like Matthew and not like Nolan or Calvin. She wanted them to be men, but still sensitive and loving.

He bent his head. "Would you reconsider?"

She did not ask why. She said nothing.

"I love you, Lolly. I've loved you since the first day I saw you on the ship."

She smiled, her face still in profile. "That seems many lifetimes ago."

"And you have many lifetimes yet to live, Lolly."

She took her hand from his, her face becoming stern. "I can no longer think only of myself. I must go. It is too much for Harriet to run the hotel and mind the children, too. Good-bye, Matt."

He felt despair and a frantic need to keep her there. He caught her arm. "Don't leave me, Lolly, for God's sake. I still have nightmares about Nolan and what I did to you. I would have come to you then, but I couldn't stand the thought of seeing hatred in your eyes. One part of me was so glad that you were free of him, but the other part knew that I had lost you forever because of it. And since then . . . you with child and all."

She was struck by his anguished expression, by the dread in his voice. She took it wrong. Thinking he had stayed away the second time because he knew about Calvin.

"What about the children, Matt?"

"What do you mean, what about them? You know I've always loved Kimberly, and the boys are beautiful. But all three need a father."

She smiled somewhat mournfully but did not look at him. "I think you have the right to know that the boys are not Nolan's. Calvin Ramsey forced himself on me one day in the shack."

She half-expected him to take back his words of love. He turned toward the mining operation. "I think I knew that. I think I knew it all along." He turned back to her. "Will you marry me, Lolly?"

She took his face in her hands and kissed him on the mouth. "I don't know, Matt," she said, her voice full of compassion. "I'm not sure of my own feelings. I don't know if I really love you, although I've thought about you a great deal this winter. Please, may I have a little time to sort this all out and be sure?"

His shining face from the kiss dimmed. "Where in the hell am I to find you for the answer?"

She put her hand on his mouth. "Why don't you try calling on me at the Fairview Hotel. I was never really courted, you know. They say that courtship can help a man to win a girl's heart."

She took her hand from his mouth and sprang off swiftly down the path. Matt watched her go and felt very strange. He had never actually courted a girl before. Yet, he was not unwilling to try. At the very least, she would not be gone from his life or Dawson. He felt so coltish. It was as if he had just learned the meaning of love.

By July of 1899, Dawson had not only risen from its ashes, but the new buildings had running water and sanitation. The town looked forward to a promising future, and Matt and Lolly to an August wedding. A new brick Georgian house was rising on the site of the old bakery, which Matt had bought from Harriet.

Daily, new company boats arrived. The various companies were fighting each other, trying to get the miners to sell their claims. They were not the manner of businessmen who wished "lay" claims. Most were just managers taking orders from men in New York, Denver, Montreal, Ottawa and San Francisco. They wanted the full claim so they could have all of the mineral rights. Their smelters would take as much worth out of the slag, in copper, iron and zinc, as in gold bullion.

Then, a week before the wedding, Dr. Loyal Wirt came up the river by boat from Lake Bennett on his way to St. Michaels and a place on the Bering Sea called Nome. He was not a prospector, but had been appointed by the governor of Alaska to oversee the gold strike in that area so it wouldn't be a madhouse like the Klondike.

It was the first anyone in Dawson had heard of this new gold strike. It was like sounding a fire alarm. Claims were auctioned off right on Front Street so the miner could scramble to his boat and be off up the Yukon. The mining companies could now pick up ten to twelve claims at bargain prices. The commissioner closed his mind to the old rule of one claim per man.

There were only about 4,000 good claims in the area, but by the end of the week they were owned by about three dozen companies—some of them very hastily organized. The Clara B, Tlingit and Monroe II among them.

On the day of the wedding, Dawson had a total population of 127 "insiders." As yet they were not ready to start counting the company miners as anything but newcomers.

McQuestan had sold out the trading post, and it became a company store for Montreal Mining. The Mizner brothers were ready to do the same with Treadwell, when the "insiders" suddenly realized that having all company stores in town would be worse than putting up with Edgar Mizner and his prices. Through Addison and Wilson, Peter Duboise made Edgar an offer he couldn't refuse.

Most of the old faces were gone. Big Alex McDonald and Gertrude were off to lay claims on the Bering Sea beaches. Two of Clara's girls pooled their money and bought the Monte Carlo from Ned Bailey. Bill McPhee took his moosehead to Nome, leaving the New Pioneer Saloon locked up.

The bells rang for the wedding. Matt raised his eyes and looked up the aisle. Lolly was radiant in Phoebe's wedding dress. They were surrounded by friends, family and love—people who had endured much with them, and would endure more.

They would now be the minority among the company

people who would swarm in and keep the population at close to 10,000 for the next few years. Come what may, they would fight to keep it their town, and some day return the hills to their natural beauty.

No longer did it mean just the gold dust and nuggets they could take from the ground and pan from the creeks. This was home.